Dear Romance Reader:

This year Avon Books is celebrating the sixth anniversary of "The Avon Romance"—six years of historical romances of the highest quality by both new and established writers. Thanks to our terrific authors, our "ribbon books" are stronger and more exciting than ever before. And thanks to you, our loyal readers, our books continue to be a spectacular success!

"The Avon Romances" are just some of the fabulous novels in Avon Books' dazzling *Year of Romance*, bringing you month after month of top-notch romantic entertainment. How wonderful it is to escape for a few hours with romances by your favorite "leading ladies"—Shirlee Busbee, Karen Robards, and Johanna Lindsey. And how satisfying it is to discover in a new writer the talent that will make her a rising star.

Every month in 1988, Avon Books' *Year of Romance*, will be special because Avon Books believes that romance—the readers, the writers, and the books—deserves it!

Sweet Reading,

Susanne Jaffe
Editor-in-Chief

Ellen Edwards
Senior Editor

Other Books in
THE AVON ROMANCE Series

Coming Soon

PASSION STAR

MALLORY BURGESS

AVON BOOKS ◢ NEW YORK

AVON BOOKS
A division of
The Hearst Corporation
105 Madison Avenue
New York, New York 10016

Copyright © 1988 by Mary Sandra Hingston
Published by arrangement with the author
Library of Congress Catalog Card Number: 88-91498
ISBN: 0-380-75383-9

First Avon Books Printing: August 1988

AVON TRADEMARK REG. U.S. PAT. OFF. AND IN OTHER COUNTRIES, MARCA REGISTRADA, HECHO EN U.S.A.

Printed in the U.S.A.

K–R   10   9   8   7   6   5   4   3   2   1

**For Jan,
because she shines**

The heaven, even the heavens, are the Lord's:
But the earth hath he given to the children of men.

—Psalms 115:16

Prologue

"Humphrey, will you ask the blessing?"

Laura Darby, peeking out from beneath her lashes, saw her half brother wince at the polite request. Hastily she stared back down at her empty trencher and asked a silent blessing of her own: that there would not be another row between Humphrey and her father on this night. There was a moment of silence. Charles Darby waited patiently at the head of the long oak table. The moment stretched.

Laura looked up again, saw Humphrey's wife, Blanche, open her mouth, and hurried to forestall her. "I'll ask it if you like, Papa."

Charles smiled at her. "Very well, Laura love."

Hands clasped in her lap, Laura recited the Lord's Prayer; surely no one could object to that. "Forever and ever, amen," she concluded, to stony silence from Humphrey and Blanche. She reached for the roast she'd made. Her father cleared his throat.

"We would be remiss, Laura, if we did not put in a prayer for Archbishop Cranmer on this, the anniversary of his martyrdom to the faith."

"You do," Humphrey rumbled, "and we'll leave the bloody table."

Laura glanced pleadingly at her father. "We can pray for him in the chapel after supper, Papa. For now, let's eat, shall we?" Again she reached for the roast.

This time Humphrey stopped her. "It is one thing, *sir,*" he told Charles, inflecting the honorific with a sneer, "for you to persist in adhering to an outlawed religion. It is quite another for you to risk Laura's future by encouraging her to do the same."

1

"Papa doesn't encourage me," Laura protested. "I am old enough to know for myself what I believe."

"You are also old enough," Blanche said in her haughty, nasal voice, "to think about marriage. And who in the world would consider marrying a heretic?"

"Another heretic?" Laura ventured with a smile.

"Laugh if you like, young lady." Humphrey scowled, pointing his knife at her. "You think you're safe, both of you, living here like hermits. But I've news for you. No one is safe anymore, not anywhere. Queen Mary has paid spies and informers all over the kingdom looking for people like you. One loose tongue wagging, and you'll end up tied to a stake on Smithfield Plain, just like Thomas Cranmer. And believe you me, you won't be laughing then."

"There are worse calamities in this world than to die for what one believes in, Humphrey," Charles Darby said mildly.

"Such as what?"

"Not believing in anything."

"Oh, honestly." Blanche blinked her pale eyes. "A few words' difference in the Mass hardly seems worth quibbling about—much less dying for."

"I'm afraid," said Charles, "the Reformed religion involves a bit more than that."

"Don't patronize my wife," Humphrey snapped. "She's a damned sight smarter than you are when it comes to religion. At least she's not putting all of our lives at risk."

"I put no one at risk but myself," Charles objected in the same pacific tone. "All I ask—"

"All I ask," Humphrey broke in, mocking his stepfather's gentle voice, "is the freedom to worship God as I see fit. I know, I know—I've heard your speeches before. And I tell you, they won't wash, not in this day and age. It isn't Blanche or myself that I worry about. It's Laura."

"Well, don't," Laura told him firmly, starting to carve the roast. "And there's no need to be rude to Papa."

"He's your papa, not mine."

"Humphrey!" Laura cried, shocked.

Charles calmly passed his plate down the table. "I'll take a bit of that crispy outside there, Laura love. Is that garlic I smell? Heavenly!"

Laura glowered at Humphrey, then forked neat, thin slices of mutton onto Charles's trencher, added mashed turnips and some carrots, and ladled rich brown gravy over the lot. Blanche watched as she cut her father's meat into manageable pieces and heaved a sigh. "The servants would do that, Laura, you know."

"I *like* cutting Papa's meat," Laura said from between clenched teeth.

"I mean all of it." Blanche wrapped a silvery curl around her beringed finger. "The carving, and the saucing, and the passing around. That's how 'tis done in the finer houses."

"Howarth Manor is a fine house, I think. Don't you?" Laura handed her father his plate.

Blanche peered down her nose at the sparse, tidy banqueting hall. "If you ask me, it needs improvement rather desperately. Some nice Flemish hangings, a good carpet—Persian, of course—and some decent plate and silver would make all the difference in the world."

"Dorrity furbished this hall." Charles smiled, contemplating the room.

"Well, for God's sake, that doesn't mean it has to stay like this forever. The woman's been dead for more than five years. Don't you think it *might* be time for a change?"

Humphrey, the bald spot atop his head flushing slightly, said, "All right, Blanche."

"I just don't see why we all have to treat this house like some sort of mausoleum," his wife said crossly. "Your mother may have been a saint, Humphrey, but when it came to style—" She made a disparaging face.

"Well, one man's meat is another's poison," Charles said pleasantly.

"Are you calling my wife's taste poisonous?" Humphrey demanded.

"Oh, Humphrey, of course he's not." Laura giggled. "Would you please pour Papa some ale?" Humphrey did so, less than graciously, and set the cup on Charles's left side. Laura frowned at her brother and went to move it.

"I can reach it," Charles assured her, stretching for the cup.

"You know better than that," Laura chided Humphrey.

"I forgot," he said.

"Forgot?" Laura echoed. "How could you forget?"

"Well, dear," Blanche purred, "your father is so strongwilled that sometimes it is hard to remember he isn't a whole man."

Laura turned to her, unable to believe she'd said that. Charles Darby set down his ale. "Laura," he said, "Blanche is waiting for her meal." Then he picked up his fork in his right—his only—hand, and began to eat.

Laura filled Blanche's plate silently, stabbing at the mutton and wishing it were her sister-in-law's heart. She and Humphrey have no right to treat Papa this way, she thought angrily, with all he's done for them.

Blanche accepted her trencher with a small, tight smile, then sniffed the sauce suspiciously. "Is there rosemary in here?"

"Aye," said Laura.

"I *hate* rosemary," said Blanche.

"I forgot," said Laura, a dangerous edge to her tone. Her father caught her eye in warning, shaking his head.

Turn the other cheek. That was what the Bible said, Laura reflected as she served Blanche a new plate, sans sauce this time. But Humphrey and Blanche surely did make it hard.

Her half brother hadn't always been this way, not when they were children. But a few years past he'd started drinking too much, and since he'd married Blanche he'd gotten worse and worse. She looked at him now, gauging from the redness of his face how much he'd had before he came to dinner. At least six cups of wine. He'd inherited his love for liquor from his own father, and apparently the mean streak drinking brought out in him too.

As different as she and Humphrey might be in drinking habits, Laura thought, anyone seeing them together could have told they were related. Despite Humphrey's beefy jowls, his balding head, the complexion he'd ruined with ale and wine, he and she shared one unmistakable feature: their mother's striking eyes, large, wide-set, a remarkable pale brown flecked with hazel that in sunlight or candlelight shone pure gold.

Laura had been surprised when Humphrey found a beauty like Blanche Tippett to wed him: Blanche with her pale, cool skin, her silver-blond hair, her eyes the color of periwinkles. Of course, from what Laura had overheard the maids, Becky and Lucy, saying, the Tippetts had fallen on hard times of late. And Humphrey would be very wealthy someday.

"Best mashed turnips I ever ate," Charles said heartily, rubbing his stomach.

Humphrey grunted. "Laura will never catch a husband by mashing turnips."

"Who wants to catch a husband?" Laura asked blithely. "I shall want him to catch me."

"Humphrey's right," Blanche put in. "It isn't fitting for a girl of your station to do servant's work. Cooking, cleaning, sewing—why, you'll ruin your looks in no time."

"What is wrong with work?" Laura asked, and took a bite of juicy lamb. "I'd go mad if I just sat about all day."

Blanche's straight back stiffened. "If by that you're insinuating—"

"Oh, Blanche, of course I'm not!" Laura said quickly. "I know how much you do every day. Why, there's—" She paused, trying to think of something, but the only examples that came to mind were her sister-in-law's scolding the help and sitting still to have her hair curled, and neither seemed particularly apt. "There's loads of work you do," she finished lamely. "Could you pass the butter, please?"

"'In all labor there is profit.' Proverbs fourteen, verse twenty-three," Charles quoted, coming to Laura's rescue. "Even scullery work has its rewards."

"Damned if I can think of any but chapped hands and broken nails," Blanche said bitingly. Laura saw her father frown at the swearword and quickly stepped in with what she hoped was an amusing story of how she'd just discovered she had mislabeled all ten dozen jars of jam she'd put up the summer before. Humphrey, stone-faced, let her finish and then took up his theme again.

"Men today aren't looking for a woman who can make jam," he said with disdain.

"What are they looking for?" Laura asked.

"Wives who will help further their careers at court."

Laura laughed outright. "Heaven knows I won't be able to do that, not so long as Queen Mary reigns!"

"That's precisely my point," Humphrey said in a voice like ice, and glared at Charles. "If you really loved Laura, you wouldn't let her ruin her future over this damned religious nonsense."

"Humphrey, you are not being fair to Papa!" Laura cried indignantly.

"And he's not being fair to you, though you're too bloody stupid to know it. No one of consequence is ever going to wed you, Laura Darby, until you give up the Reformed religion."

"What is this fixation with my getting married this evening?" Laura asked, trying to tease him out of his temper.

"Do you know something I don't, Humphrey? Have you been negotiating with someone behind my back?"

"There wouldn't be much sense in that, would there, so long as you're determined to flout this nation's laws!" Humphrey threw down his napkin, shoved back his chair, and stalked out of the banqueting hall.

"Humphrey, I was only jesting!" Laura called after him. "Come and finish your meal!"

"Why? The meat is dreadfully undercooked." Blanche sniffed and followed her husband from the room.

Laura watched helplessly as her elegant sister-in-law slammed the doors. "I *was* only jesting," she said again, and looked at her father.

He patted her hand. "Never mind, then. Say a prayer for poor Humphrey; he's a desperately unhappy soul."

"Do you think this lamb is underdone?" He smiled and shook his head. "I don't, either. And what do you mean, Humphrey is unhappy? What has he got to be unhappy about?"

Charles Darby sighed. "He's married to an ambitious woman, he hasn't got any money, and he drinks too much."

"It is not your fault, or mine either, that his father ran through all of Mama's money before he died. And anyway, Humphrey will have plenty of money someday. Though I dearly hope not for a very long time," Laura said.

Her father's weather-beaten face bore a peculiar expression. "What do you mean?"

Laura speared a carrot medallion. "Well, when you die, I mean. He'll inherit Howarth Manor and all."

Her father was still eyeing her strangely. "Laura, Humphrey can't inherit Howarth Manor. He's no blood kin to me. I can't devolve the estate to him."

"Devolve—what a silly word!" Laura laughed, raising her fork to her mouth. "Who will it go to, then?"

"To you, Laura."

She choked on the bite of carrot. "Oh, Papa, be serious!" she said when she'd recovered.

"I am serious. I thought you knew. You're the last of the Darby line."

Laura's golden eyes had grown very wide. "But I don't want it," she said somewhat wildly. "I mean—what would I do with it? Oh, Lord, give it to anyone else but me!"

"That reaction's surely a first," Charles Darby said wryly,

"from someone who's just learned she's to inherit an income of forty thousand pounds a year."

"Forty thousand—" Laura could not conceive of such an amount of money. "And Humphrey gets nothing?"

"That's what was left of your mother's fortune when Walter got through with it. I wish I had said something to you sooner." Charles's smile was rueful. "But I always assumed you knew about the inheritance laws."

Laura rolled her eyes. Her father was always assuming she knew things she didn't; that was one drawback of their close relationship. He seemed to think she could absorb knowledge merely by being around him, like a sponge. Just a month earlier he'd been shocked to discover she did not know geometry. "But *I* know it," he'd told her, nonplussed.

Still, there was no sense in reminding him of that now. "I'll be rich, won't I?" she asked instead. "Does forty thousand pounds a year mean I am rich?"

"Quite rich."

"But it is bad to be rich!"

Charles squeezed her hand. "That's not true. It's the love of money is the root of evil, Scripture says, not the gold itself."

"I still wish you would just give it all to Humphrey," Laura said worriedly.

"And I tell you, even if I wanted to, I can't. Laura love, you'll have a chance to do good with the money. You can use it to make England a better place."

"I hate England," said Laura. "And I hate Queen Mary."

Charles put a finger to his daughter's full, red mouth. "Hush. That's the sort of talk *will* land you on Smithfield Plain. Mary's a wretched and misguided creature, but she's still our ruler."

"I don't understand you, Papa. Queen Mary has burned more than two hundred and fifty men and women who believe as we do. How can you defend her?"

"It is God's place to judge her, Laura, not mine. The martyrs' fires are candles in the darkness. They are lighting the way."

"The way to what?"

"To a better England, of course. To what this nation could be."

Laura looked at his empty doublet sleeve that she'd pinned up neatly that morning. "The queen would never hurt you, Papa, would she? Not when you lost your arm fighting the French for good King Harry."

"I've loved my God and my country as best I could all my days," Charles said quietly. "And I trust in God's plans for England and for me."

Laura remembered the horrible anguish she'd felt when her mother died. Five years past now, but it seemed like only yesterday... "Papa, I don't want you to die," she said fiercely. "I couldn't bear it if you did."

He chucked her chin. "Then I won't, I promise. Now, is there any more of that rhubarb pie you made?"

"I'll go and fetch it." She started toward the door to the kitchens, then heard her father call her and turned back. "Yes?"

"Look on the bright side," he told her with a cheery grin. "For forty thousand a year, you're sure to find someone to marry you, even if you are a heretic!"

Charles ate two big helpings of pie with clotted cream, while Laura picked at her own piece, fretting over the news that she was an heiress. Her mother, Dorrity, had inherited a fortune from her father, but she'd always said the money only brought her unhappiness. She never talked much about Walter, her first husband and Humphrey's father, but she had told Laura he married her for her wealth, which he'd promptly spent drinking himself to death.

Dorrity had despaired of ever finding happiness once he died. Who would want a penniless widow with another man's son? And then, by chance, she'd met Charles Darby, Baron of Howarth, while she was visiting her Hertfordshire cousins. She'd been out picking strawberries—Laura smiled, remembering how her mother's golden eyes had lit up whenever she told the tale. He'd ridden past her on a big black horse, then circled back around and sat staring down at her. "We were both so shy," Dorrity would recall. "I think it must have been hours before he got up the courage to say hello!"

Dorrity swore she never noticed that the man on the horse had but one arm, or that he was twenty years older than she. "I just looked in his eyes," she'd say, her own gaze soft and dreamy, "and I knew from that moment I was in love with him, and would be 'til the end of time."

Charles Darby had shared her conviction. They'd been wed less than a month later, with seven-year-old Humphrey in attendance, and a year after that Laura had been born.

Her parents' love for each other was the foundation of

Laura's world, nourishing and sheltering her through her childhood. She'd scarcely been aware of the political turmoil that gripped the nation in 1547 with the death of King Henry the Eighth, who'd broken England's ties to the Church of Rome over a love of his own. Henry's only son, Edward, who supported the Reformed religion his father had founded, died at the age of sixteen, after fewer than seven years as king. His untimely death brought his much older half sister Mary—"Bloody Mary," some called her now—to the throne four years ago.

Mary, Henry the Eighth's daughter by his indomitable first wife, the Spanish Catherine of Aragon, had assumed the crown with one goal: to restore errant England to the true Catholic religion, reconciling her people to the papacy her brother and father had repudiated. No one doubted Mary's sincerity: it was her methods that were terrifying. If the English would not be reasoned into submission, then they would be harried and tortured and burned into it. Her network of spies extended everywhere, eyes and ears peeled for the taint of heresy. Sometimes Laura was glad her gentle mother had died before witnessing the awful carnage that had earned the queen her savage nickname.

Laura shuddered, seeing the red rhubarb juice stark against the white cream on her plate. She pushed the sweet away, and her father glanced over. "What's the matter, pet?"

"Nothing," she said quickly. "I'm stuffed, that's all."

"You don't eat enough," Charles said, frowning. "That's why you're such a tiny thing. Don't you want to grow up big and strong?"

"Papa"—Laura sighed—"I am sixteen years old. I could eat from now until doomsday and I wouldn't get any bigger. I am meant to be short, just like Humphrey."

Her father blinked. "Sixteen? Really? Lord, where does time go? I could have sworn you were only fourteen. Humphrey is right; we must start thinking of a husband for you."

"Anxious to be rid of me?" Laura teased.

"Of course not." He reached for the pie she'd abandoned and finished that, too. "I shall miss your cooking desperately. But marriage is a wonderful institution. I can only hope you'll be as blessed in your choice of husband as your mother was."

"You vain thing." Laura stuck out her tongue at him and got up to clear the plates.

Her father rose, too, with a satisfied groan. "Just this once, leave that for Becky and Lucy; they could use the blessings of labor. Come along to the chapel with me."

Laura tucked herself under his arm, hugging his waist, her head barely reaching his chest. It was remarkable how much he could eat and still stay so fit. She glanced back at Humphrey's unfinished supper. 'Twould do him no harm to miss a meal, or Blanche either—though more than likely they'd be pestering Becky and Lucy for trays in their rooms before the night was out.

Why, she wondered, had Humphrey been so edgy of late? He took offense at the slightest provocation, and sometimes for no reason at all. Perhaps he was just worried about money. Blanche must have spent a fortune in the scant three months since they'd been wed. That was another new gown she'd worn tonight, peacock-blue taffeta trimmed with Brussels lace. Laura didn't know what Humphrey had paid the dressmaker out of the allowance her father gave him, but she'd signed the bill for the fabric herself and knew what Charles had paid for that—thirty pounds a yard.

She ran a hand over her own serviceable gray fustian, which she'd made herself. It was severely plain, high-necked, with long pegged sleeves and not a trace of trimming. Her clothes alone would have told a visitor she was Protestant. But there were very few visitors to Howarth Manor these days; her father's natural reclusiveness had been compounded by his wife's death, and he and Laura relied on each other for company.

Laura reached up to straighten the white hood that covered her hair. With her housework and cooking, she found simple clothing most practical. Still, she wondered sometimes as she watched Blanche how it must feel to have soft silk swirling around one's legs instead of plain serge and fustian and worsted, to wear dainty slippers all the time and not just for dancing lessons.

Still hugging her father, Laura entered the family chapel. Once, long ago, the hushed, high-ceilinged room had been lavishly adorned with statues of Christ and the saints, and a huge crucifix of solid gold had hung above the altar. That had been before Laura's time, when the house of Darby was still Roman Catholic. She only knew the chapel as it now stood, spare and plain, the icons gone, the crucifix melted down and its precious metal distributed to the poor. She could not imagine the room any different from this, quiet and holy, smelling of beeswax and the lemon oil she used to polish the wood.

Charles lit the candles on the altar and knelt beside Laura in the first pew, bowing his head. "Dear Lord," he said softly, "on this, the anniversary of your servant Thomas Cranmer's death, we ask that your merciful forgiveness descend upon his persecutors, cleansing them of hatred and misunderstanding."

"Amen," said Laura, even as she marveled at her father's ability to live by Christ's injunction that one love one's enemies. She tried, but it was impossible for her to forgive Queen Mary and her ministers for their wicked hounding of the Protestants.

Charles Darby went on to pray for the queen's younger half sister, Elizabeth Tudor. Laura frowned down at her knees. For her, Elizabeth was the worst sort of Christian, one who changed her faith as readily as Blanche changed clothes. She'd been a proponent of the Reformation during King Edward's brief rule, but now, with Mary on the throne, it was said she willingly attended the Roman Mass.

Sensing his daughter's displeasure, Charles glanced down at her, eyes twinkling. "Is something troubling you, pet?"

"I don't see why we have to pray for her," Laura muttered.

Charles chuckled. "Best cover your ears; I'm about to ask the Lord's blessing on King Philip."

"Papa, how *can* you?" Laura wailed. Mary's belated marriage, at age thirty-seven, to King Philip of Spain was enormously unpopular among Catholics and Protestants alike. The nation grumbled that the match had lost England her independence, making her but another of Philip's vast dominions that stretched from the Netherlands to Milan to Africa and the New World. The people blamed Philip's harsh Spanish temperament for the bloody persecutions of the reign—forgetting that Mary was half Spanish herself and prided herself more on that than on her father Henry's English blood.

Charles touched his daughter's cheek. "Don't let religion make a bigot of you, Laura, as it has so many. Reasonable men ought to be able to differ on matters of religion without hating and killing one another."

"The Papists aren't reasonable. And besides, we are right and they're wrong."

Her father laughed. "Would it were so simple as that! But

there are good, holy Catholics, just as there are wicked Protestants. The most important commandment is the one Christ gave us: 'Love one another as I have loved you.'"

"There are people," said Laura, "whom it is very hard to love."

"Sometimes the people whom it is hardest to love need our love the most."

For some reason that made Laura think of her half brother. "Do you love Humphrey?" she asked.

"Aye, with all my heart."

"And Blanche?"

"Aye, I love Blanche too."

"But not the way you loved Mama. Or the way you love me," Laura said hopefully.

"Oh, pet. Love's not something you dole out like strawberries, arguing over who should get the biggest share. Love's just something you do." He saw the uncertainty on her small face and smiled. "Don't you believe your wise old papa?"

"I don't know..."

"Well, let's pray for King Philip anyway." Reluctantly Laura bowed her head. "Lord," Charles Darby continued, "we ask that you bestow peace and happiness upon Queen Mary and King Philip, that you bless their marriage and make it fruitful." He means God should give them children, Laura thought, remembering the mysterious conversation between Becky and Lucy that she'd overheard a few years past, when the palace had announced the impending arrival of an heir to the throne, expected in June 1555.

"Queen's too old for bearin'," Becky had said crisply, arresting Laura's attention as she passed by unseen in the hall.

"Is that so?" Laura peeked around the door to see Lucy ask the question, hands on hips. "And will ye tell me then why everythin's been made ready for this baby, even the birth announcements printed up?"

Becky had tapped her forehead meaningfully. "Because Queen Mary's bats."

"Bats? Hell's bells," Lucy scoffed, "even she ain't crazy enough to tell the whole world she's pregnant when she ain't!"

"Mind, now," said Becky, "that ain't to say she don't think she is. It happens with women that age."

"Well, ye'd know," Lucy said slyly.

Becky snapped a towel at her. "Go on, laugh if ye like,

but I'll bet ye next week's wages there ain't no more inside Queen Mary than a load of air."

Laura hadn't understood all they were saying, especially about the air, but she waited eagerly to see what the result of their wager would be. Weeks went by, and then months. The court doctors, Lucy informed Becky, said they'd miscalculated the date. Another was set. That, too, went by without result, until finally the matter of the expected heir faded away into nothingness, and Lucy paid Becky ten shillings, begrudgingly.

Shortly afterward, King Philip left England and his wife to go to the Continent and wage war on the French. The war was fought by soldiers from his other kingdoms, not by the English: Parliament, upset by Mary's choice of husband, had inserted into the marriage contract a clause prohibiting Philip from dragging England into the internecine combats of his Holy Roman Empire. The king stayed away a year, then returned briefly to raise English money for his campaigns before leaving again. Laura could not imagine the sort of marriage he and the queen must have. She did not think her mother and father had spent a single night away from each other in the dozen years they had been wed.

His prayers concluded, Charles Darby went to the altar and fetched the English Bible lying open there. He came back to the pew, resting the heavy book on his knees, and asked, "Ready to point out a verse?"

Laura's gaze slanted toward him. "That's a children's game, Papa. I've learned the Bible by now."

"Learning and understanding are two different matters, pet."

"Oh, I understand it," Laura said confidently.

"Well, then," said Charles Darby, with a hint of a smile, "just to humor your old papa?"

"Oh, all right." She closed her eyes and waited, hand poised above the stiff vellum pages, while her father leafed through the book. "Stop," she said after a bit, and ran her finger down the right-hand side.

"The twenty-second chapter of Luke." Charles peered at the page. "Verse thirty-six."

Laura searched her memory. Christ in the garden of Gethsemane? No, the Last Supper. The verse popped into her head. "'Then he said unto them, But now, he that hath a purse, let him take it, and likewise his money, and he that hath no sword, let him sell his garments and buy one.'" She opened her eyes, grinning in triumph.

"Perfect," Charles pronounced. "Let's read the rest of the chapter together."

"Oh, pick another, Papa. That part is so sad. First Judas betrays the Lord, and then Peter denies he knows him—"

"It is sad," Charles agreed. "But it is also appropriate for the anniversary of Archbishop Cranmer's death. After all, he denied the Lord, too, when he recanted under torture. But in the end, just like St. Peter, he followed his conscience and died for his faith."

"Still, it's so gloomy. Let me choose another."

Laura expected her father to argue, but instead he closed the book to leaf through the pages again. "Very well, but if you think that's gloomy, mind you don't pick the Book of Job!"

Laura smiled, eyes clenched, hand hovering above the vellum. "Stop," she said, and pointed.

"Luke again," said her father. "Chapter twenty-three, verse thirty-four. Oh, dear."

"What's the matter, Papa?" When he didn't answer she opened her eyes. "Papa?" He had turned in the pew and was staring back at the chapel doors. Laura turned as well and saw half a dozen armor-clad men in the entranceway.

"Charles Alexander Darby, Baron of Howarth?"

The loud query reverberated through the chapel. Laura's father set the Bible gently on the pew beside him and stood. "Aye," he said. "I am he."

The soldier who had spoken stepped forward. "In the name of Mary, by the grace of God Queen of England, Ireland, and Wales, and His Eminence Bishop Edmund Bonner of London, I arrest you and charge you with the crime of heresy."

Laura screamed.

Her father's hand sought hers, squeezing it in reassurance. "Hush, pet," he murmured, as the man stalked toward him with a set of heavy iron shackles.

"Don't you dare touch him!" Laura cried, clinging to her father.

Charles pried himself free of her grasp and walked into the aisle to meet the men. "There's no need for those," he said, nodding to the irons.

"Bishop Bonner's orders," the soldier snapped, and then colored faintly at the sight of his prisoner's empty doublet sleeve. "I mean—sorry, sir." For a moment he tried to figure some way to use the cuffs on a man with only one arm; then he passed them to a companion instead. "Have I your word you'll come with us peacefully?"

"What the devil's going on here?" That was Humphrey, his face redder than ever from running down the stairs. Blanche was close at his heels. When they saw the soldiers they stopped dead. "Oh, my God," Humphrey said.

Blanche's blue eyes were narrowed. "I just knew this would happen sooner or later!"

"Humphrey, do something!" Laura scrambled out of the pew. "You can't let them take Papa!"

Looking dazed, Humphrey put his fist on the hilt of his dagger. Charles's voice rang out: "Son. No. They are only doing their duty."

"Duty?" Laura sprang at their leader, pommeling him with her fists. "Leave him alone, I said!"

Her father pulled her back. "Laura." She was sobbing now, tears streaming down her face, and he brushed them away with his thumb. "Look at me, Laura."

"Don't let them take you away! Don't go with them, Papa!"

"God is watching over us, Laura. Don't you trust in him?"

"They will burn you to death!"

"Pet, do you remember what Bishop Latimer said to Bishop Ridley as they stood in the flames? 'We shall this day light such a candle in England as shall never be put out.'" He kissed her forehead. "I love you, Laura." Then he pushed her gently toward Humphrey. "Look after her. Please."

"Y-yes, sir," Humphrey said uncertainly. The soldiers surrounded her father and led him out of the chapel toward the doors to the yards.

Laura followed, yanking at the leader's mail-clad back. "Take me too, then," she told him, golden eyes flashing. "I'm a heretic too. I don't believe in the pope's authority. I don't believe the Host becomes the body of Jesus. I don't believe in the seven sacraments! I don't—"

"Laura, for God's sake!" Blanche blurted, aghast.

"Shut up, Laura." Humphrey clamped his hand over her mouth, looking at the soldiers apologetically. "She's only a child. She doesn't know what she's saying."

Laura squirmed in his grasp. "I do too know! Take me with you! I'm a heretic, I tell you, I am, I am! Take me..."

Her voice trailed away in a wail of despair as Humphrey jerked her against his chest, nearly smothering her. She kicked at him frantically, hearing the heavy doors swing open, hinges creaking, and then clank shut.

"Laura," Humphrey said urgently, "there's nothing we can do."

"He brought this on himself," Blanche put in. "We tried to warn him—"

Laura broke free of her brother at last, delivering a violent kick to his shin. "How could you let them take him?" she screamed. "How could you just stand there?"

"He told me to! Laura, stop. Laura, where do you think you're—"

She was running after her father, through the manor and out the doors.

The moon was a ball of pale fire shining down on the wintry yards. The wind tore at her skirts as she plunged through the open gates. The soldiers were already far ahead on the road to London; she could see the moonlight glitter on their silvery mail.

"Papa!" she called, and heard the wind carry the word away. "Papa, I'm coming with you!"

"Laura!" Humphrey bellowed from the gate. "Get back here! You'll catch your death out there!"

Laura kept on running. At her back Humphrey cursed and shouted for a stableboy to fetch his horse.

Her boots pounded against the stony road in a steady rhythm. As she ran, Laura realized she was repeating the same phrase over and over to herself: "Luke twenty-three, verse thirty-four. Luke twenty-three, verse thirty-four." The passage she'd pointed to just as the soldiers arrived. She couldn't remember the passage, only the numbers; they were like a little song she sang as Queen Mary's men lengthened their distance from Howarth Manor. Why couldn't she remember it? Luke twenty-three, verse thirty-four.

Far ahead on the road, the soldiers spurred their mounts toward Latham Hill. Behind her, the hooves of Humphrey's horse were drawing near. Laura's lungs ached from the cold night wind, knotting her chest in pain. Her legs were still moving, pumping, but she didn't seem to be getting anywhere.

The soldiers rounded the crest of the hill and thundered on, their silvery helmets vanishing from view. Luke twenty-three, verse thirty-four, Laura thought, and stumbled as

Humphrey wheeled his horse in front of her, sending her sprawling facedown on the chilly stones.

He dropped from the saddle and knelt beside her. "You damned little fool," he muttered, rolling her over. "Come along home. He'll be all right. You'll see."

But Laura knew he was wrong—dead wrong. As she lay in the dirt she'd remembered the passage at last. Luke twenty-three, verse thirty-four. Jesus on the cross at Calvary.

Father, forgive them, for they know not what they do.

Part I

Chapter 1

"For heaven's sake, Laura, what are you doing sitting in the dark?" Blanche swept across the bedchamber and lit the candles on the mantel. Laura looked away as the wicks flared into flame. Blanche noticed, mouth curving downward as she came to sit beside Laura on the settee beneath the window. "You can't go on mourning forever, you know," she said briskly. "What's done is done. You've got to look to the future now."

"It hasn't even been a month," Laura told her. "I would hardly call that forever."

"Well, of course not, dear, but you know what I mean. Your father wouldn't have wanted you to mope about this way. He would want you to get straight back to enjoying life again, don't you agree?"

"I don't know what Papa would have wanted." Laura's red-rimmed eyes filled again with tears. "I might have—if Humphrey had let me go to see him before . . . before . . ."

"Laura, dear, we've been over this and *over* this! Humphrey was looking out for your best interests, just as he always does. Imagine how upsetting it would have been for you to see your father in jail!"

"Imagine how upsetting it was not even to be able to bid him goodbye!" Laura burst out, and bit down hard on her lip to ward off her tears.

Blanche sighed, getting up from the settee and smoothing down her silken skirts. "I know better than to try to talk to you when you're in one of these *moods*," she declared. "I do wish you would show just the *tiniest* bit of concern for the feelings of others, though. Humphrey has done nothing but work on your dreary legal problems ever since your father's death. I hardly think 'tis too much to ask that you express some appreciation."

"I am very grateful to Humphrey for all he has done." Of course, Laura thought wearily, she'd be even more grateful if

21

he'd take the time to explain what it was he was doing, instead of just dashing back and forth to London and Hertford and wherever else he went.

Blanche smiled down at her. "Then why not show him," she coaxed, "by putting off that long face of yours and coming downstairs for supper tonight?"

"Very well," Laura conceded, too listless to argue.

"Wonderful!" Blanche kissed her cheek. "I'm quite sure you'll feel ever so much better once you start taking an interest in life again." She breezed out of the room with a cheery wave.

Against her will, Laura's gaze was drawn to the flickering candles. The long gold flames danced higher in the fresh spring breeze from the window. She shuddered and looked away.

Such a horrible way to die. The flames starting at your feet, inching upward, licking higher and higher. The smell of your own flesh charring. Blood boiling in your veins, bubbling 'til they burst. How long had it taken? What had it been like, tied there, helpless, waiting to die? Hungry flames devouring you bit by bit, searing hair and bone, crackling and roaring—

She stood up abruptly and snuffed the candles out.

Through the open window she heard hoofbeats on the road from Hertford. Humphrey coming home. I really must make him tell me what he is doing, Laura thought. What legal problems could there be? Something to do with the money, she supposed.

She tightened the ties of her hood and dried her eyes on her sleeve, prepared to honor her promise to come down to supper. Blanche meant well, she supposed, encouraging her to put her father's death behind her. But it was so hard to forget! If only they could have had one last meeting together. But Humphrey had forbidden that, on the ground he did not intend to have Charles blame him if Laura tried again to turn herself in as a heretic. Cardinal Reginald Pole and Bishop Bonner were in a frenzy of heretic-hunting at the moment; since Charles Darby's death, five more men had burned at the stakes set up on Smithfield Plain.

The bell rang for supper. Laura headed down the stairs.

Humphrey was already in the banqueting hall, sitting in Charles Darby's chair at the head of the table, with Blanche at his right. Laura forced a smile when she saw him. "Hello. Been to town again?"

He nodded, tearing a thick chunk of bread from the loaf Becky laid in front of him. "At a hearing of the Court of Wards. Damned thing went on forever. But I've got it all settled at last."

"Oh?" Laura watched as Becky gingerly handed round the soup. It hadn't taken Blanche long to change the way meals were served to suit her liking, or to buy her Flemish hangings for the manor walls. "What's settled?"

"I've got it all worked out." Humphrey dunked the bread into his soup and gnawed it hungrily. "All in your best interests."

Becky set Laura's soup on the edge of her plate, sending a wave cascading over the rim of the bowl. "Damn you, Becky," Blanche snapped, "be careful!"

"Sorry, mum."

Laura gave the maid a surreptitious, sympathetic smile, then turned to Humphrey again. "What have you got all worked out?"

"Well, first off, I got control of your wardship, though it wasn't easy. Had to grease palms right up to fat old Francis Englefield, Master of the Court of Wards himself. An estate this size, there's always plenty of bidders. Where's the damned bloody ale?"

"I'll bring it right away, sir!" Becky scurried off to the kitchens.

"What does that mean," Laura asked, "that you got my wardship?"

He swallowed a huge bite of bread. "You're under age. By law, when your father died you became a ward of the queen. And I bought your wardship back from her."

Laura considered the new hangings, the recently bought silver plate that her soup had been served on. "Where did you get the money?"

"I borrowed it. Anyway, as I say, I got hold of your wardship with a great deal of trouble and expense. And then I was lucky enough to find an excellent buyer for it."

"I don't understand," said Laura. "You bought it, and then you sold it again?"

"Well, I deserve something for all my time and trouble, don't I?" he asked reasonably.

"What *did* you get?" Blanche demanded.

Her husband grinned, chest puffed with pride. "Eight thousand a year plus a tenth of the income from the lands.

And use of the manor for an annual rent of a hundred pounds."

"Oh, Humphrey, that's splendid!" Blanche declared. "Only a hundred a year for the house?"

Humphrey nodded. "Guilford put up a devil of a fight over that, but I just said to him, Look, you've already got that big bloody house of yours to live in; what do you need two houses for? And of course he couldn't argue with that. Besides, he has charge of the dowry, and you can bet there'll be even higher stakes when that time comes round."

"Excuse me," Laura interjected, "but who is Guilford?"

"Thomas Guilford," Humphrey explained. "That's the man I sold your wardship to. He's coming for you tomorrow morning, by the way; you'll have to hurry to get packed."

"Coming for me? Where am I going?"

"To Guilford Hall. Don't worry; it's not far away." Humphrey slurped up soup. "He's a neighbor, in fact. His lands adjoin ours out by the river Beame. That's one reason I got such a good bargain. He's had his eye on our north pastures for years, but your fool father wouldn't sell them to him. So now he'll get that, and everybody will be happy."

"Just a minute," said Laura. "If he's a neighbor, why don't I know him?"

"Laura, dearest," said Blanche, "your father was hardly the outgoing sort. Thomas Guilford may be a stranger to you, but his family is quite well known in court circles. *Quite* well known," she repeated, with odd, not entirely pleasant emphasis. "Surely you've heard of—"

"Blanche," said Humphrey, his eyes meeting hers in a quick glance. "It's a very old family, Laura. One of the best."

"I won't go," said Laura.

"You haven't any choice," said Humphrey, sopping bread.

"Of course I have a choice!" Laura found she'd risen to her feet. "You can't make me go!"

"It's all according to the law, Laura. It's all in your best interests."

"I cannot believe this!" Laura leaned on the table for support. It was some kind of jest, she thought dazedly. It had to be. This was England, after all; people didn't go about selling one another like the heathen Moors! She looked at Humphrey pleadingly. "You don't mean it, do you? You're teasing."

"That's exactly the sort of ingratitude I spoke to you

about earlier, young lady," Blanche broke in. "Humphrey had to work very, very hard to find you a suitable guardian."

"I don't *need* a guardian!"

"Of course you do," Humphrey said. "You need someone to look after your lands and money and choose whom you're going to marry."

"Who I'm going to— I intend to choose for myself, thank you very much!"

Humphrey shook his head. "That right goes with the wardship. It's all in Thomas Guilford's hands."

Laura stared at him, struck speechless. She was certain it was all a bad dream, that at any moment she'd awake. She pinched herself just to make sure and winced at the pain.

"Do sit down and finish your soup, Laura, and stop gawking," said Blanche, ringing for the next course.

Laura stayed on her feet, though her knees had begun to feel weak. "Do you mean to tell me," she said, finding her tongue at last, "that without so much as consulting me you have handed my future—my *life*—over to a man I've never met? For eight thousand pounds?"

"Plus the rent of the manor. And the tenth income from the lands," Humphrey confirmed. "I don't see why you should be so upset. That's the way it's done."

"You sold off your own flesh and blood to a stranger like some sort of *chattel?*" Laura demanded, voice creeping upward.

"Oh, really, Laura, there's no need for hysterics," Blanche told her. "You're ruining supper." As Laura began to laugh, she added, "I fail to see what is so amusing."

"Of course," Laura gasped. "I am ruining supper. Supper!" She doubled over in another laughing fit.

"Get a grip on yourself," Humphrey warned, "or else leave the table. After all I've done for you, I sure as hell don't need this."

Laura thrust back her chair, eyes flashing golden fire. "I'll be ready when this Thomas Guilford comes for me tomorrow," she cried, "and I'll go with him gladly! Because I would sooner go off with the devil himself than stay here with the two of you!" She ran from the hall and up to her rooms, slamming doors behind her as loudly as she could.

In her bedchamber she realized she was shaking all over; she had to lean against the wall to stand. She felt so alone, so lost and betrayed! So she meant no more to Humphrey than eight thousand pounds a year, and the chance for him to go on living here, pretending he was Baron of Howarth. How could he have done such a despicable thing?

Knowing Humphrey, she thought in fury, he'll run through all the money in six months, not be able to pay Thomas Guilford the rent, and wind up penniless, living in a hut somewhere with his horrible wife. Blanche wouldn't look so fancy without Becky and Lucy to wait on her hand and foot. All her fine gowns would be in tatters, and she and Humphrey would come begging to her, Laura, for help! And she knew just what she'd tell them: "I bet you wish you'd treated me better now, don't you?" She'd make them crawl on their hands and knees and then turn them down anyway.

That is just what I'll do, Laura decided, throwing open the doors to her wardrobe, yanking out her clothes. She would make them wish they'd never been born! She threw boots and stockings and nightgowns and shifts and dresses onto the bed, emptying the wardrobe, then stuffed the whole lot into her mother's old traveling trunk, not even bothering to fold the clothes. Her throat grew tight; tears swam in her eyes.

It just wasn't fair! First Papa and now this—why, it was as though the whole world had turned against her. She hadn't done anything to deserve such awful misery!

She stood by the window, sniffing back her tears, staring down at the moonlit yards. Tomorrow at this time she'd be living in the house of a stranger, looking out from another window. What would he be like, this Thomas Guilford? How old would he be? Would he be kind? What might his house be like?

She'd never lived any place other than Howarth Manor, had scarcely spent a night away from here. For sixteen years she'd looked out from this window before going to bed. Oh, God, she didn't want to leave the only home she had ever known!

And it was all the fault of greedy awful Humphrey and his greedy awful wife. Laura turned away from the window, searching the room for anything she might have left behind. On the table by the bed lay her father's Bible. She picked it up and added the book to the trunk, thinking of the last verse she had pointed out before the queen's men took Charles Darby away. *Father, forgive them* . . .

One thing was certain: She would never forgive Humphrey for doing this, not so long as she lived.

She slammed the trunk lid shut, snapped the latches, and

sat down atop it, hands folded in her lap, waiting for the morning—and Thomas Guilford—to come.

The sound of carriage wheels woke her, rattling through the gates and up the drive. Still crumpled in a heap atop the trunk, Laura rubbed her eyes with her fists and yawned, trying to stretch a kink out of her back. Why wasn't she sleeping in her bed? Then she remembered what was to happen that day and ran to the window to glimpse the man who had come to take her away.

The carriage was a handsome one, painted yellow and crimson, with a coat of arms engraved on the door in gold and a fine set of bays hitched to the staves. The driver was climbing down from his box to open the coach door, while Blanche and Humphrey were waiting on the portico stairs. Laura held her breath, watching as the occupant of the coach emerged.

How tall he is! she thought, as he unfolded his long limbs to step down from the coach. He had black hair shot through at the temples with white, though he did not look old enough to be turning gray. He wore a rich purple doublet trimmed in gold, wide puffed breeches, and purple hose. Catholic clothes, Laura observed, but they were handsome. He bowed to Blanche, and he and Humphrey shook hands. It seemed to Laura that her brother was a bit in awe of this elegant man who towered over him. She could not get a clear view of his face, but she liked the way he carried himself as Blanche ushered him into the manor.

If he was a neighbor, why hadn't Papa ever mentioned him? Of course, what Blanche had said was true, Laura reflected: her father was reclusive, especially since her mother had died. He was shy about going out, because strangers always made comments about his missing arm. And the need to keep his religion secret had made him even more hermit-like.

What had Humphrey said? That Papa wouldn't sell the north pastures to this man. I wonder why not, thought Laura, trying to smooth out her rumpled black skirts. She'd even slept in her hood; the white linen pleats were all crushed to one side. She straightened them absently in the looking-glass, then washed her face and squared her shoulders. Then she marched down to the receiving room to see what this Thomas Guilford looked like at close hand.

Humphrey caught sight of her as she came through the

doorway. His red face turned blotchy with anger. "Good God," he rumbled, "you look like something the cat dragged in."

Blanche was serving the guest a glass of sherry; she, too, turned and eyed Laura in dismay. "Get back up those stairs, young lady," she threatened, "and put on a decent gown, or I'll whip your—"

"Please." The man had risen from his chair. "Please. It doesn't matter. One should never wear one's best clothes for traveling, anyway." He gave Laura a charming bow, then straightened with a smile. "How do you do? I am Thomas Guilford."

"Laura Darby," Laura said shyly, dropping in a curtsy. She looked up into the man's clear, pale gray eyes. He is handsome, she thought with surprise. His forehead was wide, his brows very dark and straight, and he had a black beard that covered his chin. His mouth was full-lipped and red as a cherry, so very red that it almost did not look real.

"I am very pleased to meet you at last, Laura Darby," he told her, still smiling. He had a lovely smile. "I trust your brother has explained our arrangement to you?"

Laura nodded, noting that Humphrey and Blanche were watching her nervously. "More or less," she said. "Humphrey sold me to you." She turned to her brother. "My trunk is packed and ready in my rooms. Would you have it brought down?" Her voice, she decided with satisfaction, was perfectly cool and calm. Humphrey disappeared to find the porter. Blanche poured herself a very full tumbler of sherry and gulped it down.

Thomas Guilford laughed, settling back into a chair, the movement fluid and graceful. "It is not quite so mercenary as that," he told Laura. "I don't own you. I'm merely to serve as your guardian until you come of age."

"Well, it really doesn't make any difference now, does it?" Laura asked tartly. "It's all finished and done."

"Laura, darling," said Blanche, darting a glance at the visitor, "you might show a bit of gratitude. This gentleman's generosity has helped us all out of a very difficult situation."

"Helped you and Humphrey, you mean. I don't see that it has done anything for me."

"Laura, please!"

Humphrey reappeared, mopping his forehead with a

handkerchief; he was sweating profusely. "Trunk's all packed in the carriage," he announced.

"Then we'd best be on our way, hadn't we?" Laura started toward the door.

"Oh, but Lord Guilford," Blanche said hastily, "we had hoped you would stay to dinner. We thought you might like to look over the grounds and the house. We have some fine new Flemish hangings—"

"Some other time, I think," said Thomas Guilford, setting down his sherry glass and going to Laura's side. "Right now I suspect this young lady is anxious to see her new home. Shall we?" He offered Laura his arm. She took it, grateful for his sympathetic support; her knees were feeling weak again.

Humphrey and Blanche followed them out to the carriage. "Well," Humphrey said heartily, and then cleared his throat. "Well, Laura. We will certainly miss you very much, but it is good to know we are putting you in such capable hands. I trust you'll make us proud of you." He leaned down to kiss her. Laura wrenched away. Thomas Guilford stared at her for a moment with his clear eyes the color of doves' wings. Then he helped her up into the carriage, bowed to Humphrey and Blanche, and climbed in beside her. Humphrey folded up the carriage steps and shut the door.

"Take care, Laura darling," Blanche called, waving her kerchief.

Laura stared fixedly out the window on the other side of the coach.

"Well," Humphrey said again. "Well."

Thomas Guilford whistled to the driver, and the carriage started off. Laura did not once glance back at the house as they pulled away. Instead she sat, hands folded in her lap, and looked at the green fields that rolled past the window, and the bright blue sky, and the low dappled hills in the distance, and a flock of partridges that the clatter of the coach threw up against the sun.

That was that. The past was behind her. She bit down hard on her bottom lip, clenching and unclenching her fingers, waiting for the stranger beside her to scold her for having been so unspeakably rude to her brother and his wife.

But he did not say anything for a long time, just sat quietly as the carriage wheels swallowed up mile after mile. At first, still fuming at Humphrey and Blanche, Laura welcomed his silence, but as it dragged on she could not resist sneaking a glance at him to see what he might be doing.

To her embarrassment, he was looking at her. Hastily she turned back to the window and heard him say quietly, "I take it you don't think much of my arrangement with Humphrey."

"Since neither of you saw fit to consult me beforehand," she replied coldly, "I don't see how it matters what I think."

"I beg your pardon." His deep voice was bewildered. "Humphrey said you'd agreed the arrangement was in your best interest."

She faced him then, on the verge of tears. "In my best interest? How could it possibly be in my interest to be auctioned off to you?"

"There are good reasons for the wardship laws, you know." He handed her his kerchief.

"Aye—such as making you and Humphrey wealthy at my expense!"

"Neither Humphrey nor I gets a penny of your money. Except for a monthly stipend for your needs, it will all be kept in trust for you until you wed."

"Then why did you buy me?" Laura demanded.

Thomas Guilford winced. "I wish you'd stop using that term. And you might make use of that kerchief. Your eyes are much too lovely to be filled with tears."

"You didn't answer my question."

"Let me explain it this way. The wardship laws were established to keep minors like yourself from being exploited."

"You mean to take us away from our families," Laura said spitefully.

"Sometimes it's the family that does the exploiting," he told her. "From what I know of your brother—"

"Half brother," Laura interrupted.

"—Half brother— I wasn't at all sure he could be trusted to keep your estate intact until you came of age. There doesn't seem to be any love lost between you."

"I hate him," said Laura. "And I utterly *detest* Blanche." Guilford laughed at her fierceness, and she blushed but insisted, "I mean it! And Humphrey lied if he told you I knew what he was up to. I didn't hear anything about you or being a ward or any of it until last night!"

Guilford took the kerchief from her clenched fist and wiped her cheeks. "I should have known better than to trust him. Believe me, had I any notion you were being kept in the dark, I would have remedied it. But what's done is done. We will just have to make the best of the situation, I suppose. I hope you don't hate me as well. I want very much for us to be friends."

"How can I hate you? I don't even know you."

"That we *can* remedy." He folded up the kerchief and tucked it into his handsome velvet doublet. "What would you like to know?"

Laura thought for a moment. "How old are you?" she asked.

"I'll be twenty-seven this summer."

"Really? Well, happy birthday. Mine is not far off either."

"Yes, I know."

"I suppose you do know about me, if you've gone to the trouble of making me your ward. Did you know my father?"

"I met him. My own father knew him, I believe, many years ago."

"Fancy that." Laura pondered what else she might like to find out about him. "Blanche said you were well known at court. Is that so?"

"Your sister-in-law is easily impressed. My business does not take me to London very often."

"What work do you do?"

"Oh, this and that. A little of everything. I'm a typical country gentleman."

Laura searched his long, handsome face. "Do you know the queen?" she asked, unable to keep the loathing from her voice. The carriage jostled suddenly, passing over a wooden bridge. Guilford slipped his arm around her shoulders to steady her. Laura felt warmed by the gentle pressure of his hand on her cloak. Then the coach bounced back onto the road, and he withdrew his arm.

"Laura," he said, his gray eyes dark with shadows, "what is past is past. One of the reasons I sought your wardship was so that you could make a new beginning, start afresh away from your home and your memories. Do you understand me? Are you willing to try?"

"I—I think so," Laura replied, blushing a bit beneath his intense gaze.

He smiled his beautiful smile. "That's my good girl. Now, have you any more questions for me?"

"Only one. What am I to call you?"

"My name is Thomas. I reckon you should call me that."

"Thomas." She tried it and nodded with satisfaction. "That's a good name. Thomas."

The carriage rumbled out of the deep Hertfordshire forest and up a steep hill. Thomas Guilford leaned across Laura to point out the window.

"Look. We're home," he said.

Chapter 2

Laura's first impression of Guilford Hall on that sun-drenched spring afternoon was that the roof was on fire. The man beside her seemed to notice nothing amiss, though, so she blinked and looked again. Between the twin stone towers on either end rose a glistening dome that reflected the sun's rays and sent them shooting back toward the sky. "What is that up there?" she asked.

"One of the additions my father built. I keep meaning to have it removed."

"It certainly is distinctive," Laura said politely, shielding her eyes from its glare as the carriage climbed the steep drive to the gates. "The whole house is—distinctive." She could think of no other word to describe the strange conglomeration of architecture that made up Guilford Hall. There must have been ten different types of stone and brick just in the facade; the roofs dipped and pitched and swooped in all directions; windows seemed stuck haphazardly all over the place. There were battlements and parapets, wings jutting out here and there, pointed gables and mysterious piping, and, of course, the dome.

A stableboy ran to open the tall iron gates in the wall surrounding the yard, and the carriage rolled to a stop on the brick paving. The boy let down the steps, and Thomas disembarked, turning for Laura. Hands on her waist, he swung her from the coach and stood for a moment, looking down at her. "I hope you'll be happy here, Laura Darby," he told her. Laura had a sudden premonition that she would.

The carriage driver and the boy were hauling her trunk down from the boot. Thomas gave Laura his arm. "I'll send the coach back right away for the rest of your things."

"Oh, I haven't got anything more," she told him.

"One trunkload? You must be a most efficient packer."

Laura colored faintly, thinking of how she had crammed her clothing into the trunk the evening before. But she was spared from making any rejoinder when the carved doors to the house swung open in front of them. "Time to meet the household staff," said Thomas. A wiry man of medium height entered the yard. He had long, straight hair the color of muddy wheat, a long, thin nose, and very green eyes. "My secretary and majordomo, Theodore Innes. Theo, this is Mistress Laura Darby."

Laura smiled at the man. He was about Humphrey's age, she supposed, or a little younger. "How do you do?"

He bowed stiffly from the waist, narrow chin touching the ruffles of his shirt, then straightened slowly and looked Laura over from head to toe. Those green eyes took in her sturdy black boots, the black gown that showed beneath her black cloak, the white hood that covered her hair. His thin upper lip curled slightly.

"A bit small, isn't she?" he asked, addressing Thomas.

His master laughed, though not, Laura noted, before flashing the man a hard glance. "You must forgive Theo, Laura; he tends to outspokenness. But he is quite indispensable to me.'"

"Used to be indispensable," Theo corrected him. He had a thin voice too, reedy and whistling.

"Theo," Thomas suggested, "why don't you help the boys with Mistress Laura's trunk?"

The secretary's grass-green gaze glinted. Then he turned abruptly and stalked away.

Laura watched as, his back ramrod straight, he crossed the yard to lend a hand with the trunk. "He is not terribly social, is he?" she whispered to Thomas.

He laughed. "Theo takes a bit of getting used to, that's all. He is shy, but you'll discover he is truly a genius. He speaks any number of languages fluently. And he has exquisite handwriting. But you know how difficult talented people can be to get along with."

"Of course," said Laura, though she hadn't the faintest notion what he meant. Theodore Innes might be talented, but she'd gotten the distinct impression he didn't like her one whit.

"Ah, here's our Polly!" Thomas cried gaily, as a face peered out from the doorway. "Polly, come and meet Mistress Laura." Hesitantly the woman came into the yard. She was in her late twenties, Laura guessed, rather tall, quite slim. She wore a stained white apron over a checked gingham smock, and had brown eyes and two long braids of a remarkable butter yellow hanging down from her kitchen cap. Laura had never seen hair that color before. "Polly Vaughan, my cook and housekeeper. Polly, Mistress Laura."

"Pleased to meet ye, missy," Polly whispered, bobbing nervously.

"And I to meet you." Laura smiled. "I am looking forward to helping you in the kitchens, Polly."

"Oh, missy." The woman's brown eyes widened. "That wouldn't hardly be fittin'."

"I don't see why not. I'm sure your master won't object."

"Let's discuss that later," said Thomas. "Right now I want to get you settled into your rooms. Polly can help you unpack."

"Oh!" Laura remembered the mess in her trunk. "I'll just do it myself, thank you very much."

"'Tain't no trouble, missy—"

"No, really, thank you."

Polly looked uncertainly at Thomas. "Well—should I get back to supper, then?"

"Dinner," said Thomas, wincing.

"Aye, dinner," Polly corrected herself. "Eight o'clock sharp, ain't that right, Master Thomas?"

"Isn't. Not ain't. For God's sake, Polly."

"Isn't," the cook mumbled. "Isn't." She bobbed her head, yellow braids swinging, and scurried back inside.

Thomas rolled his eyes, watching her go. "One does try, but really, sometimes one wonders is it worth the effort?" He shrugged his broad shoulders. "Let's go in." He led Laura over the threshold into Guilford Hall.

"Oh, my gracious!" Laura stared in wonder at the entranceway in which she stood. The floor was paved in pale green marble, polished bright as a penny. The walls were paneled in rich, dark wood and hung with grand tapestries of hunting scenes, and the high ceiling was covered with what looked like shiny hammered gold.

Thomas nodded to their right. "Through those doors are my study and the chapel. This way—" He pulled her to the left. "This is the receiving chamber."

Laura's mouth dropped open at the sight of the cavernous room. From ceiling to floor, one wall was lined with mirrors that reflected the gleaming flames of dozens of candles set in brass wall sconces. "Are you expecting guests?" she asked, seeing all those tapers lit in midafternoon.

"No. Why do you ask?"

"You ought not to waste beeswax," she exclaimed. "It's frightfully expensive!"

"I don't care for gloom," said Thomas, with a small frown. "Do you like the room?"

Laura turned in a circle, trying to take it all in. The tall windows were lined with heavy green velvet drapes pulled back with golden ties. Delicate little tables and chairs were strewn between dark wood pilasters carved with shapes of pine cones and flowers, and arching over it all was a ceiling painted with nymphs dancing in a wood. "I have never seen anything like it," she answered truthfully. She tiptoed across the echoing floor to inspect a huge stone vase brimming with daffodils. "Have you a garden?"

"Five or six of them, I think. Theo looks after them for me."

"He certainly grows lovely daffodils."

"So he does. The banqueting room is through those doors, and the kitchens beyond that. And your rooms are this way."

He led Laura back into the hallway and up the wide, curving staircase at its far end. From there they progressed through a bewildering array of corridors, with Thomas stopping now and again to point out the library or the music room, or to explain which of his relatives was the subject of one or another of the big, dark paintings, all in gold-leaf frames, that lined the wainscoted walls. Laura had never seen such splendid furnishings; everywhere one turned there was some new treasure. The thought occurred to her, as she surveyed an exquisite hallway table inlaid with mosaic glass, that Thomas Guilford was very rich; little wonder he'd rented Howarth Manor to Humphrey for only a hundred pounds a year.

"Up this flight, and then just one more," he said, opening a door leading to a stairway. "I've put you in the west tower, so that you'll have the best view of the grounds." She followed him to the top of the stairs, through another door, down a long hallway, around a corner, down another hallway, and up yet another flight of stairs.

"It is such an enormous house!" Laura marveled, letting out a giggle. "I do hope I won't get lost in it."

"You'll be used to it in no time. Howarth Manor is quite large, isn't it?"

"Aye, but we only used one wing of that, really. And to think of the trouble I had keeping that much clean!"

He stopped, turning to look at her. "You don't mean to say you did the housecleaning yourself."

"Most of it," she told him cheerfully. "And all of the cooking. Polly seems very nice indeed; I am looking forward to working with her."

"My dear girl." Thomas smiled. "I'm afraid you will find our Polly rather set in her ways. She is used to being the queen of her kitchens."

"Oh." Laura's face clouded over. "You think she would resent my help. Well, perhaps I can work in the gardens, then."

"The gardens are Theo's domain."

"Dear me. I shall have to find something to help with, or I'll go quite mad."

"I'm sure you will find plenty to keep you busy here at Guilford Hall," Thomas reassured her, and opened another door. "Here are your rooms."

Laura entered the bedchamber. Her mother's old trunk was already in the middle of the floor, its worn leather straps and wood staves standing out in awkward contrast to the rest of the furnishings. "My," said Laura, and she could barely manage that much, for the room took her breath away.

"I think you'll be quite comfortable here." Thomas went about opening doors, explaining what they led to. "Wardrobe, sitting room, lavatory. This one is for the servants' back stairs."

Laura was still gazing, awestruck, at the huge testered bed in the center of the room, draped with rich red hangings. It seemed big enough to sleep an army! There were three soft chairs upholstered in patterned velvet, an enormous armoire, and big ballooning curtains of white lawn speckled with crimson roses at the windows that lined the far wall. Here, too, there were mirrors everywhere; the carved paneling shone with polish, and the ceiling above was painted robin's-egg blue.

"If there is anything you need," Thomas went on, "here is the bellpull. I'll leave you to unpack and rest. Dinner is at eight, as Polly mentioned. Oh, and I always dress for the evening meal; you'll want to put on more suitable clothes. I hate to see women in black; it reminds me of funerals."

Laura glanced down at her gown and then up at him. "I'm in mourning for my father," she explained.

He arched a black brow. "It is hardly customary to mourn for a heretic."

Laura nibbled her lip. "If you know all about me, then you must know that I believe as my father did. That I am a—a heretic too."

"My dear child." He smiled indulgently. "You are hardly old enough to form opinions on matters of religion."

Laura stood up very straight. "I may be young," she told him, "but I know exactly what I believe."

The muscles in Thomas Guilford's forehead tightened, and Laura saw a thin blue vein pulse at his temple. The way his gray eyes turned opaque, almost milky white, made her want to flinch. But in another moment his angry expression softened; he shrugged his wide shoulders. "Your religion is of no consequence to me, so long as you keep your beliefs to yourself. These are dangerous times we live in, as you must be aware. Eight o'clock." He headed for the door.

"Thomas."

He stopped, turning back. "Yes?"

"I—" Why did she feel an urge to apologize to him? Then she realized—because he had saved her from Humphrey and Blanche. "Thank you very much. For everything," she said haltingly.

"You are very welcome, my dear."

Left alone in the splendid room, Laura pulled off her boots and padded to the windows in her stockinged feet. The gardens lay spread out before her, four storeys below, with neat rows of spring flowers already in bloom and rich, dark earth waiting to be planted. There was a hedge enclosing a small rose garden closest to the house, the leaves of the bushes and neatly trained climbers showing fresh and green.

It was a lovely house, thought Laura, even though Papa would not have approved of such ostentation. She ran her fingers over the drapes, warm with sunshine, and could almost hear Charles Darby say, "One could feed a family for ten years on what these must have cost." She had always liked the stark simplicity with which Howarth Manor was furnished, but it seemed rather shabby to her now. She felt her cheeks blush the color of the roses in the linen, imagining what Thomas Guilford must have thought of Howarth's receiving room.

A bit of movement in the garden below caught her attention. She saw Theodore Innes's dirty blond head as he emerged from the house, a long pick slung over his shoulder. He moved across the brick path between the rosebushes, reached its end, and swung the pick right at the roots of the tallest specimen. The thin branches shuddered beneath the force of his blows; he went on hacking until the plant toppled over, thorns and leaves lunging back at him as they fell.

Laura started as she saw Thomas come running out of the house. He must have shouted something, for his secretary whirled around, still clutching the pick, and brandished it as if he would strike Thomas next. Laura covered her hand with her mouth, horrified. Thomas kept on running, straight up to the blond man, and wrenched the tool from his hands.

Thomas's back was to Laura's window, but she could see Theodore's face, tight and angry, as he argued with his employer. He made a fierce gesture, then looked right up at Laura. She realized that the two men might think she was spying on them, and hastily moved out of sight.

When she peeked down a few minutes later, both had disappeared from her view, though the mutilated branches of the rosebush still littered the walk. She shrugged, then went to the door she thought was the lavatory, found herself in the dressing room, and tried two more doors before she found the right one. The lavatory had a white marble basin with a metal tap, like the sort one might find on an ale keg, sunk into its top. Curiously Laura depressed the metal, and jumped as a clear liquid came gushing out. She bent down to smell it, then to taste it. Water—how remarkable! Water whenever one wanted it, without going to a pump!

There was a brass tub in one corner of the room, and in the other a big wicker chair with a hole in the seat—just where one would sit, Laura thought, going over to stare at it. What she really needed right now was a chamber pot, but that she could not find. There was a metal ball hanging from a chain at the back of the chair. Another bellpull to summon the servants, she supposed, and gave it a yank. She heard the sound of rushing water and peered into the seat of the chair with alarm. A trapdoor in the bottom had opened, and a flood of water was coursing around and around the white bowl inside.

As I live and breathe, thought Laura. This must be some sort of fancy chamber pot. She hiked up her skirts, feeling utterly silly, and perched tentatively on the edge of the seat. When she had relieved herself she hopped down again and pulled the chain. Sure enough, the little door in the bottom of the bowl opened, and another cascade of water washed the waste away.

Laura was enthralled. She tried the strange mechanism a

few more times, just to see if it would keep on working. It did. Imagine, she thought, never having to empty a chamber pot again! This house was paradise! What other wonders might it have in store?

She washed her face and hands in the other basin, the one with the tap, and dried herself on thick, fluffy white towels that smelled of lavender. Somewhat reluctantly she left the miraculous lavatory and went to have a look at the bed. The mattress must have been made of feathers, for when she sat on it she sank deep into the crisp linen covers. The sensation was heavenly to someone who'd spent the night before crumpled in a heap atop that hard wood trunk.

Laura tested the pillows and found them exceedingly comfortable. Crawling into the middle of the bed, she closed her eyes and fell fast asleep.

When she woke, the room was draped in shadows. She sat up, seized by near-panic at finding herself in this unfamiliar room. The mirrored walls reflected her frightened image against the sky outside the windows, bright now with the flames of a fiery sunset, streaked with bloodred and gold.

"Goose," she told herself firmly, realizing at last where she was. She leaped out of bed, wondering what time it might be; she did not want to be late for dinner on her first night at Guilford Hall.

She opened her trunk and pawed through its contents, grimacing at the rumpled condition of the clothes within. Well, she could press them tomorrow. For now she could only select the least mussed, a dark serge with tight-cuffed sleeves. She dressed hurriedly, struggling to reach the long row of buttons running down her back.

Then she yanked off her twice-slept-in hood and searched the bottom of the trunk for the tortoiseshell brush that had been her mother's. Thousands of times Laura had sat in Dorrity Darby's bedroom chamber and watched her mother brush out her magnificent hair with long, steady strokes. She had always found it fascinating that her mother's hair was the same colors as the tortoiseshell: beautiful rich, deep brown streaked with red.

Dorrity would count off each stroke as she brushed, all the way to two hundred, and Laura would count along, watching wide-eyed as that great rippling mass of curls gleamed brighter and brighter. During the day all that beauty was carefully kept tucked beneath a starched hood, but at night, when she went to sleep, Dorrity left it free and loose, hanging past her knees.

When Charles Darby presented the brush to Laura after her mother died, she'd protested. It seemed sacrilegious to use that magical implement on her own head. Timidly she'd explained her hesitation to her father. He'd laughed and led her to a looking-glass, tugging off the hood she wore. "Laura," he'd said, "you have your mother's hair."

Laura stared, and wondrously, miraculously, her own brown braids, which she'd always thought of as lank and dull, had taken on a red glow. "Oh, Papa," she'd whispered, "how did that happen?"

"Sometimes when we look too hard at another's good fortune," her father told her, "we fail to see our own."

Now Laura wound her long, thick plaits round and round her head and carefully pulled on a fresh hood, making certain no stray curls peeked out. Back at Howarth Manor, she'd overheard Becky and Lucy, very grave for once, discussing a girl they knew who had lost what they called her "maidenhead." From what Laura, crouched beneath the stairwell, could gather, the girl had gotten into trouble because she was running about with her curls uncovered—for hadn't Lucy said, "Aye, the silly soul went and let down her hair"? Laura, pondering the matter, had decided that must mean a girl's husband had to be the first man—other than her own family, of course—to see her hair loose; otherwise the girl lost her maidenhead and became, as Becky sniffed, "used goods," or somehow impure. Ever since then, Laura had gone to great pains to make certain not a single wisp escaped her hood in public. She tied the band that ran across her forehead and around to the nape of her neck, checking in one of the mirrors. All covered now, every bit of it. She was ready to go down to supper—to *dinner*—at last.

She found the door to the hallway and started along the corridor, turned to the left beneath a portrait of a grim-looking bearded man that she remembered, and opened what ought to have been the door to the stairs. It was a linen closet. Laura retraced her steps to the portrait, turned right instead of left, followed that corridor to a door, and found behind it yet another hallway. She shrugged and started down that. Good—there was the table with the glass mosaic top. But which way did she go now? She searched for clues. Had she passed that chest with the clawed feet before? What about the painting of the woman on a horse? It was impossible to remember; the journey upstairs with Thomas was all a blur in her mind.

I really am lost, she thought, and giggled. Well, there was nothing for it but to begin opening doors. She moved along the passageway, locating a pair of bedchambers, another closet, two vacant rooms, and a lavatory. Finally there was only one door left, a great huge one of figured iron. That *has* to be the stairway, she decided with relief, even as she thought she ought to have remembered that door. She grasped the brass handle and pushed. The iron portal swung open with a faint creak of hinges.

Laura caught her breath.

She'd stumbled into the chamber she'd seen from the carriage, the one with the roof made of glass. The evening sky was spread out above and around her, deep azure studded with stars. She moved cautiously inside, staring up at the heavens. To the right a tiny slice of pale pink moon hung like a glistening jewel.

In the center of the room was a big round platform, its floor painted into four divisions, like a pie waiting to be cut. Circling the edge of the platform was a sort of table, a high one, reaching to Laura's chest. The floor around the platform was tiled in an intricate design made of intercoiled circles and half circles and the six-pointed stars called Solomon's seals.

Laura suddenly felt a twinge of apprehension. Though her father had brought her up not to believe in witchcraft and superstition, she knew from Becky and Lucy that Solomon's seals were a sign of the devil. And the platform, with its polished stone and mysterious markings, looked to her like nothing so much as an ancient altar, the sort on which sacrifices might be made to pagan gods.

She turned in a slow circle. The perimeter of the room was lined with bookcases, and on the shelves were hundreds of huge, heavy volumes bound in leather; their dead, musty scent filled the air. Atop the shelves lay strange metal instruments, so oddly shaped that she could not imagine what they might be for. She remembered the ghostly things that Becky and Lucy used to whisper of beside the kitchen hearth on cold winter nights: tales of necromancy, the dark arts, ghosts and demons and spirits of the dead . . .

"Who's there?"

Laura nearly leaped out of her skin as the deep voice sounded from the doorway. She whirled around and sighed in relief at the sight of the tall, dark figure silhouetted there. "Thomas, what a start you gave me! I got lost trying to find the stairs and ended up in here. What on earth *is* this place?"

She heard the scratch of steel against flint and saw a candle flicker into flame. "Why—you've shaved," she said in surprise, as the pale yellow glow suffused his face.

"Who's there?" he demanded again, anger in his voice as he took a step toward her.

Laura took a step back.

The man who stood glowering at her in the candlelight did look like Thomas, at first glance. He was just as tall and broad-shouldered; his hair was black, but without Thomas's traces of gray. His clean-shaven face was all hard angles where Thomas's was gentle: hard hawklike nose, squared chin, a wide white forehead punctuated by two heavy black brows. His mouth was full, the upper lip curling back on itself in a way that made Laura think of a wolf baring its teeth. There was something of a wolf in his eyes as well: beneath heavy lids and coal-black lashes, the irises were pale and cold as a winter sky, ringed with blue.

"I—I beg your pardon," she stammered as he came closer still, moving with feral silence despite his great height. Within the plain black doublet and breeches he wore, his muscles seemed coiled to spring at her while that curled lip snarled. Laura felt the hairs on the back of her neck tingle and rise, and fought off a sudden, violent urge to flee, to run. Never in all her life had she encountered such a threatening figure as this huge, angry man; just looking into those frigid, black-rimmed eyes filled her mind with strange thoughts of dark nights, of wild, nameless beasts stalking innocent prey, of danger lurking unheard, unseen, in a shadowy wood. She fought off the ominous sensation. It was only that he had startled her, here in this eerie room. "I thought you were Thomas," she went on quickly. "My name is Laura. Laura Darby."

His hooded eyes glinted. "The heretic's daughter."

Ire replaced Laura's fear. "My father was a good man," she said angrily.

"Your father was a fool. He got caught," he told her, and laughed.

Laura drew herself up tall as she could. "You'll burn in hell for that."

One of his heavy black brows slanted upward. "When I burn in hell, it will be for more substantial matters." And

Laura, looking at him, was certain it would. "Still, you are fiesty for just fourteen."

"Fourteen? I shall be seventeen in May," she told him hotly.

"Really?" He seemed to find this intriguing. "That's not what Thomas told me."

"Then he must have been mistaken."

He laughed again, though she did not see what he could have found amusing. "You had better not let him hear you say that." He glanced up at the dark sky above the dome. "It is nearly eight. My brother is more punctilious about his meals than about his conscience. Shouldn't you be in the banqueting hall?"

For some reason Laura hated to admit to this haughty man that she was lost. "I was just on my way there," she told him coolly.

Again his black brow arched. "You've chosen a round-about route."

Despite herself Laura blushed, knowing he had seen through her. Beneath their heavy lids his smoky eyes were so keen they might have seen through stone. She edged past him toward the door. "Excuse me. I must be going."

"I'll walk you down." It was not an offer, but a statement of fact, and it pricked Laura's temper again.

"I can walk myself, thank you," she said stiffly, starting off along the corridor, boldly turning right at its end.

From behind his hand closed on her arm, pulling her to the left instead. "This way," he said.

Laura felt the raw, surging force in his grip and let him lead her.

He did not speak another word as they wended their way through the twisting hallways, down the lengths of stairs. Laura said nothing either; she was puzzling over why Thomas had not mentioned this brother to her. At last she began to recognize some of the furnishings they passed; then the man stalked down the long, curving front stairway, still clasping Laura's elbow, and pointed toward the receiving chamber just as a clock in the hall began to chime the hour. "In there," he said shortly, and turned to go.

"You're not dining with us?" Laura asked, and realized how relieved she sounded.

"I've no appetite in my brother's company." He looked her up and down. "Still, on the occasion of this, your first meal together, I might raise a toast."

"Don't trouble yourself on my account," Laura told him, and saw his eyes—they were blue, not gray like Thomas's—darken with inner laughter. She spun on her heel, hurrying through the receiving chamber to the banquet room doors, entering just as the bell tolled the last of eight strokes.

Thomas was seated at the far end of a great long table laid with sparkling silver cutlery and plate. He shook out his napkin as Laura came in and spread it on his lap. "Good evening, my dear. I hope you don't intend to make a habit of cutting the clock so close. I like my meals on time."

"I am sorry." Contritely Laura slipped into the place which had been set for her, all the way at the opposite end of the table from him. "I—I lost my way. Your brother showed me down."

Thomas Guilford looked up, dove-gray eyes narrowed. "My brother?"

"Good evening, Thomas." The man walked from behind Laura's chair over to a sideboard, seizing a goblet and a pitcher of wine. "Next time send Polly up to fetch her. It won't do to have her wandering about any place she likes."

"My name is Laura," Laura told him, angry again. "I'm not 'she' or 'her.' I don't care to be spoken of as though I wasn't here."

He ignored her, filling the cup at Thomas's elbow, slopping red wine onto the snowy linen cloth. He didn't even try to mop it up, just circled around until he reached Laura's place. He poured her goblet to brimming and then the one he held. Then he said, "I can't imagine how you intend to pull it off, Thomas. Fourteen indeed."

"I think you'd better leave," Thomas told him evenly.

"I wanted to propose a toast." He touched his cup to Laura's, spilling still more wine, watching her through his black lashes. Wolf, she thought again, as the candlelight made his eyes flash like sunlit ice. "To the latest ward at Guilford Hall. Though I can't help noticing, brother, that this one is different."

"I apologize for this primitive behavior, Laura," Thomas said shortly. "My brother is drunk."

"Not yet I'm not." Laura glanced at the man who stood towering over her. His knuckles were stark white as he gripped the handle of the pitcher. He noticed her watching and set it down. "I will be, though. We all have our vices. Little Laura's seems to be popping up where she isn't invited. I'd be wary of that, brother mine."

"If you mean the room where you found me," Laura told him, bristling, "let me assure you, I'll never set foot in it again."

He drained his wine cup and refilled it. "As a matter of fact, that's not the room I meant. Is it, Thomas?"

Thomas picked up a bell from the table and rang it, glaring at his brother. "If you're quite finished, we'll begin our meal."

Polly trotted in from the kitchens. When she saw the man standing beside Laura's chair, her dark eyes grew enormously wide. "Ah, pretty Polly!" he cried gaily, raising his cup to her.

"Master John." She gulped. "Will you be havin' supper?"

"He will not," Thomas said firmly. "And I have told you a million times, Polly, the proper term for the evening meal is 'dinner'—which I despair of ever getting at this rate. Get out before I throw you out, John."

John Guilford swayed on his feet, finishing off the wine in his cup, then setting it down on the tabletop so close to Laura's that the rims kissed. "Fourteen," he said again, and shook his head. Then, grabbing up the pitcher, he laughed and staggered out the door.

"First course, Polly," Thomas said sharply. It was plain to see the encounter with his brother had upset him. Laura leaned across the enormous table.

"I'm sorry, Thomas, truly, but the house is so big—"

"You were in his room." His voice was harsh, accusing. Laura blushed guiltily. "Listen to me, Laura. You must never, ever go into that room again. Keep to your own side of the house. I don't want you to risk running into him."

Laura's hands grew cold as she thought of the gloomy domed chamber. "What does he do up there?"

Thomas stared at her down the length of the table. "He's a sorcerer."

"There's no such thing as sorcery," she whispered. "Is there?"

Polly backed through the kitchen doors with two haphazardly arranged green salads on a tray. Thomas waited until she had served them and departed again before he spoke, voice lowered. "No, of course not. But my brother believes there is. You see, he is mad."

A madman! Of course, Laura realized—that was why he'd unsettled her so. She thought of his icy blue eyes, the power she'd sensed in his long, taut muscles, and shivered. "I suppose it is very kind of you to let him stay here, instead of sending him to a Bedlam," she said tentatively, even as she wished Thomas would.

Thomas was frowning. "I would send him away if I could find someplace that would take him. But he's far too dangerous."

"I see." Laura tasted her salad and found the leaves crunchy with sand. "Why do you suppose he thought I was fourteen?"

Thomas had taken a bite of his salad as well; as she watched in astonishment he spat it back onto his plate and roared, "Polly!"

The cook peeked timidly through the door. "What've I done now, Master Thomas?"

Thomas stood, took his salad plate, and dumped its contents onto the floor. "Inedible," he pronounced, kicking the lettuce toward her.

"I'm sorry, Master Thomas." Polly crept in and gathered the mess in her apron.

"It is beyond my comprehension how you can manage to ruin a salad!" Thomas fumed. "A salad, for God's sake!"

"Well, ye knows me, Master Thomas; I'm all thumbs, just as ye say." Skirting him nervously, Polly snatched Laura's plate from the table and darted away. "Shall I wash it now, then, or bring in the fish?"

"The fish," he told her, shaking his head, taking his seat.

"Yes, Master Thomas," the woman mumbled, backing out again.

"Hopeless," Thomas muttered at her retreating figure, then looked at Laura. "What did you ask?"

Laura hadn't realized just how much he'd been disturbed by his brother's behavior, to take his anger out on poor Polly that way. She hesitated to mention John Guilford again, but he was waiting expectantly. "I only wondered—why your brother thought I was fourteen."

"I told you. Because he is mad. You must promise me, Laura, that you'll stay clear of him," he said sternly. "Not that you'll have to worry about encountering him during the day."

"What do you mean?"

"He sleeps during daylight. He is only awake at night."

The matter-of-fact way he stated this sent another chill running up Laura's spine. "Awake all night long?" she whispered.

Thomas nodded, meeting her frightened gaze. "You'll want to lock your door when you go to sleep. It was wrong of me not to tell you about him before. But I was hoping the two of you would never meet." He shrugged, smiling at her. "Shall we talk of something more pleasant? I've engaged a dressmaker for you. She'll be here on the morrow."

"That's very kind of you, Thomas," she said, "but I sew my own clothes." Noticing his frown, she blushed, glancing down at her rumpled gown. "This doesn't look like much now, but I packed rather hurriedly, and I haven't had a chance to press it. But it's perfectly serviceable."

"Laura, my dear. Clothing should be more than serviceable! Clothing should set one off, like the setting of a precious jewel. You're a remarkably lovely girl, but who would ever notice it in that outfit you've got on?"

Laura's cheeks burned more brightly. "That's very kind. But my father always said clothes don't make the man, or the woman either. It is the beauty in one's heart one must let shine through."

"If that's so, what difference does it make what you wear?" Thomas shook his head, bemused. "Protestants are the most illogical bunch."

"That's not so!" Laura objected, just as Polly came in with a mop for the floor. "Why—" She started to say more, then stopped abruptly as she saw the muscles in his temples tightening, that vein pulsing above his eye. She thought suddenly of what John Guilford had told her when she said Thomas had been mistaken: *You had better not let him hear you say that.*

Polly had seen the expression on her master's face too, and hurriedly withdrew. "I would appreciate it," Thomas said in a low, controlled voice, "if you would refrain from contradicting me in front of servants. Such behavior can only encourage them to do the same." He dabbed at his mouth with his napkin. Laura stared as the linen came away red as blood. But he wasn't bleeding—though his carmine mouth seemed a touch less bright.

He saw her staring at the napkin and bundled it up. "Rouge," he said shortly. "A frivolous custom, but quite *de rigueur* at court."

"Whatever is it for?" Laura asked curiously.

"To accentuate one's features. In just the same way a fine gown should. I'll give you some to try."

Laura recalled he'd told her he spent little time at court,

but before she could mention that, Polly reappeared with a platter of *something* blanketed in a lumpy white sauce. If Laura hadn't been expecting fish, she never would have guessed that was what it was. The cook set the platter down before Thomas, who scowled and stuck his knife into the sauce. It hung from the blade in a clump. "What," he demanded, "is this?"

"S-sauce, sir," Polly whispered.

"It looks more like paste."

"Now, Thomas." Laura smiled, feeling sorry for Polly's misfortune. "I know myself how tricky white sauce can—" She froze as Thomas's chin shot up.

"I beg your pardon," he said from between clenched teeth. "Did you say something, Laura?"

She shook her head mutely, inwardly damning John Guilford for ruining the first meal she and Thomas had ever shared.

Chapter 3

Laura did not sleep well that night, though whether because of the nap she'd had that afternoon or because she imagined she could hear John Guilford prowling through the house she could not tell. She got up from her bed twice just to make certain she'd locked the doors, then drifted in and out of consciousness just as she drifted in that sea of a bed, mulling over what John might be doing in that eerie domed chamber, with its sorcerer's books and mysterious altar. Each possibility she imagined grew more horrible, until at last she got up, washed her face, and lay back down, telling herself not to be a fool.

When she did fall asleep at last, near dawn, her slumber was deep and dreamless. For the first time since her father's burning she had no nightmares, and she awoke thinking that must be a good sign. She would be happy here. There would be adjustments, of course. She must be careful to respect Thomas's wishes; after all, it was his house.

She made a quick toilette and took the back stairs down to the first storey, reasoning that they ought to lead right to the kitchens. They did, and Polly gave a gasp of fright when she turned from the hearth and saw she had company in the big bricked room. "I didn't mean to startle you," Laura said quickly. "It's just that I'm having an awful time finding my way about. I've never seen a house that was built like this one."

The cook smiled tentatively. "That's Old Master's doin'. He bought the place when he got married and then found out there was somewhat wrong with the foundations. Kept shiftin' on him, it did, so he was always putterin' about addin' somethin' on, tryin' to shore it up."

"Do you mean Thomas's father?" Polly nodded. Laura pressed her foot against the brick floor and laughed. "Well, it surely feels solid to me!"

Polly smiled again. "Go and sit in the eatin' hall, missy, and I'll fetch yer breakfast."

"Is Thomas in there?"

"Land sakes, no. Master Thomas, he's an early riser. Been up and gone since daybreak, he has."

"Then why don't I just sit in here with you and eat?"

"That wouldn't be regular, missy," said Polly, with a worried frown.

"Nonsense, Polly. I have to get to know you and the rest of the staff, don't I?" Laura plunked herself down on a bench at the cook's worktable.

"Rest of the staff?" Polly looked bewildered. "'Tain't nobody else 'cept Theodore and me."

"Just the two of you for this enormous house?" Laura asked in amazement.

"Aye, missy, there's nobody else. I can make ye porridge or eggs fer yer breakfast, but that's all the mornin' foods I know."

Laura sniffed the warm kitchen air. "Do I smell cinnamon?"

"Cinammon? Oh, my, missy, no!"

"But I'm sure I do!" Laura got up from the table and went to one of the ovens, certain that was where the mouthwatering aroma was coming from. "What's in here?"

"Oh, missy—" Polly tried to ward her off, but Laura opened the oven door and saw a pan of golden-crusted sweet rolls. "Why, what's this?"

"Oh, Lord, missy," Polly whispered, backing away, "I'm sorry, truly I is—"

"Sorry? For making sweet rolls? Why?" Laura plucked the pan from the oven. "I think these are done."

"Ye'll burn yourself, missy!" Polly cried.

Laura laughed, carrying the pan to the table. "Not hardly. My father used to say my hands had turned to stone from all the cooking I did. Did you make these for yourself, Polly?"

"Fer myself? Oh, no, missy, I never would presume!"

"Then for whom?" Laura asked the quaking woman. "And what on earth are you acting so peculiar about?"

"Ye've found me out, missy, that ye have." Polly wrung her hands in her apron. "Them there rolls, them's fer Master John. But please don't tell Master Thomas; he don't want me doin' nothin' special fer that brother o' his."

"Don't be silly; I'm sure Thomas wouldn't care. Can I have one, please?" Polly nodded nervously, yellow braids bobbing, and Laura pried one of the buns from the pan and bit into it. After the leaden meal she'd been served the night before she did not expect much, but to her astonishment the pastry was rich and crumbly, baked to a turn.

"Why, Polly," she said, hoping she did not sound as surprised as she was, "this is wonderful!"

Polly blushed becomingly. "Well, that's the only thing as I knows how to make proper, missy—breads and dough and such. That's all I was trained fer, ye see."

"Mm. Thomas ought to hire someone to do everything else and let you bake these all day," Laura declared, reaching for another roll.

"Well, 'tain't easy, missy, ye know, findin' folk what will work here at Guilford Hall."

"Why is that?" Laura asked, brushing cinnamon sugar from her fingers.

"Why, missy, because—" Polly stopped and regarded her with wide brown eyes. "Why," she went on after a moment, "because of the house bein' so far out of the way and all."

"That's a silly reason. Howarth Manor is much farther from London than we are here." Laura waited, but Polly wore that fearful expression again, so she changed the subject. "Is it true that Master John sleeps all day and is awake all night?"

"Aye," Polly said warily. "What of it?"

"I just wondered why you make sweet rolls for him in the morning, then."

"I told ye—'cause Master Thomas is away now, and he don't like me doin' fer Master John. But my mum, she always made a pan of rolls fresh fer Old Master and took 'em to him every evenin' when he woke up."

Laura choked on her roll, having sudden visions of a long line of Guilford madmen. "Don't tell me the Old Master used to stay up all night."

"Aye, missy, he did."

Laura heard her own voice rising in disbelief as she asked, "Was he a sorcerer too?"

"Oh, aye, missy! 'Twas he made the water run into the sink whenever I pushes this tap. And he built them privies upstairs too, with the water that flows in 'em. Ye want some milk with yer rolls?"

"Please. Have you worked at Guilford Hall long, Polly?"

"Grew up right on the grounds. My mum was lady's maid to Mistress Estelle, and wet-nursed the twins."

"What twins?"

"Why, Master Thomas and Master John."

"Thomas and John are *twins?*"

"Don't see why ye should be surprised, missy; they looks like enough as two peas in a pod."

"They act so different, though." Laura pondered this surprising news. "Mistress Estelle and the Old Master—are they still alive?"

There was a moment's hesitation before Polly answered, "Oh, no, missy. They's dead. Long dead." She turned back to the hearth. "By the by, Master Thomas said to tell ye, dressmaker's comin' at noon."

Laura sighed. "I told him I didn't need a dressmaker. I'd rather just make my own clothes."

"Land sakes," Polly said wistfully, "if I'd the chance to do less work, then I would!"

Laura leaned forward on the bench. "I meant what I said yesterday, Polly. I'd love to help you. I can cook and clean and launder and mend—"

"Hush yer tongue, missy! Why, ye can't be workin' and scrubbin' like common folk!"

"But I've got to find something to do, or I'll go out of my mind!"

"Then I reckon," said Polly, "ye'd best find somethin' to do. But not here in my kitchens, oh, no, missy. Now if ye're finished with yer breakfast, ye'd best move along."

"If you should change your mind, Polly—"

"It won't be changin'. Now shoo. And don't forget 'bout the dressmaker."

With nothing else to do, Laura wandered through the open kitchen doors to the yards. There was a pretty little herb garden laid out there, with bushes of mint and thyme and comfrey that she recognized and many more plants she'd never seen before. Each was labeled on a little wooden plaque, in a gorgeous, elaborate handwriting she presumed to be Theodore's. She read the signs as she passed: paeonia, alkanet, anemone, mala insana, mandragora, lobelia, scammonie. This last was a weedy thing, vining and twining against the wall, but with lovely white flowers. She twisted one off and sniffed it. As she did, she had the distinct impression of being watched.

"I do the garden work around here." Theodore Innes, his thin face stamped with anger, stalked toward her and snatched the blossom from her hand.

"I only picked one little flower!"

"Anything needs doing in these gardens, I do it. That's the way the master wants it."

"Really?" Laura said coolly, vexed by his attitude. "Master Thomas didn't seem too pleased about that rosebush you chopped down yesterday."

"It had canker. Eating it away bit by tiny bit, from the heart out." His green eyes gleamed. "Rot doesn't always show on the outside—not with plants or people. You can't look at a person and tell what's in his heart. Whether he is a murderer, or a thief—or a heretic."

"Of course one can't," Laura said quickly—too quickly.

"There are always clues, though," Theodore purred, raking her with those green eyes. "In the bark. The blossoms. The foliage." He stared at her plain black gown, the hood that covered her hair.

Laura took a deep breath. "Theodore, it is plain we have gotten off on the wrong foot together, you and I. If I've done something to offend you besides pick a tiny little flower—"

"You came here. That's what you've done."

"So I have. And now that I'm here, hadn't we better make the best of it?"

"There's no best of it to be made."

Laura was nonplussed by his unreasonable enmity, but determined to be pleasant. "I am sorry you feel that way," she said quietly. "But you really haven't given me much of a chance."

"Keep your bloody hands off my plants," he snarled in answer, and walked away.

He went to the far side of the garden and knelt by a hedge of lavender, fussing at the base. Just to show him she wasn't cowed, Laura went on strolling through the lines of herbs while honeybees buzzed around her. She didn't touch, but she looked her fill.

She stayed there until Polly came to the kitchen doors and shouted, "Missy! Dressmaker's here! She's waitin' in yer room!" As she went inside, Laura could feel Theodore's eyes, green as a grass snake, boring into her back.

She started up the servants' stair and heard Polly cluck her tongue and mumble, "Ye shouldn't ought to be usin' those steps, missy, that ye should not."

What a peculiar household, Laura thought crossly. Except for Thomas, the lot of them were nuttier than a walnut pie.

The dressmaker, at least, appeared normal. An elderly

woman, white-haired and faintly stooped, she was busily laying out samples of fabric on Laura's bed. "Hello, ma'moiselle," she greeted Laura, looking up from her work with a toothless smile. "I am Charlotte. If you will please take off your clothes?"

Laura perched on one of the fat stuffed chairs to pull off her boots. "I ought to warn you, Charlotte, that I have never really had a dressmaker before. My mother made my clothes when I was young, and then I made my own. But I fear Master Thomas does not think me much of a seamstress."

The dressmaker appraised Laura's black gown with a professional eye. "There is naught wrong with what you wear, ma'moiselle. But the color does not suit you. A young girl should never wear black. It deadens the skin."

"I'm in mourning for my father," Laura explained.

"Master Thomas does not like to see his wards in black."

"So I gather. Have you made gowns for his wards before?"

Charlotte tittered. "The others were all young men, ma'moiselle."

"Oh." Laura pulled off first her hood and then her dress. The seamstress reached out to touch her long, shining curls.

"You have very beautiful hair, ma'moiselle." She produced a tape and chalk from her valise. "Now I take your measurements."

She worked quickly, mumbling to herself as she wound the tape around Laura's waist and bosom and hips and noted down the results in a little book. Then she stood Laura against a wall, marking where the top of her head reached and measuring it off. "So small! Are you still growing, ma'moiselle?"

"Not even a smidgen in the past three years," Laura admitted cheerfully.

"Short." Charlotte shrugged. "But very nicely formed. Good proportions. The right gown will make you look taller." She searched through the samples on the bed and chose a swatch of crimson silk as red as cherries. "Do you like this?"

"I cannot wear that color!"

"And why not?" The dressmaker's dark eyes were shrewd.

Laura bit her lip. First Theo and now this woman . . . She remembered what Humphrey had said the night her father was taken away: *Queen Mary has paid spies and informers all*

over the kingdom... "I already told you," she said. "I am
mourning my father. I don't want to dishonor his memory."

"I see," said Charlotte, and Laura wondered how much
she did see with that sharp gaze. "But no more black." She
searched again through the samples. "This?"

Laura examined the flat-weave gray satin, the color of
doves' wings, of Thomas Guilford's eyes. But she knew she
ought not to wear satin. "It's beautiful," she said. "Have you
got a color like this in linen or wool?"

"Master Thomas prefers silk."

"Oh." Laura looked over the swatches. The flat-weave
satin was the plainest of the lot, and she hated to offend
Thomas when he'd been so kind to her. "Then the gray will
be fine," she told Charlotte, adding quickly, guiltily, "It must
have long sleeves, of course, and a good high neck."

"But ma'moiselle has such a lovely throat, such exquisite
shoulders!"

"I'm sorry. On that I really must be firm."

"As ma'moiselle wishes." Charlotte fixed Laura again
with her cunning dark stare. "I will return for your fitting on
Thursday." She gathered up her fabrics and notebook and
bundled them into her valise. "Farewell, ma'moiselle."

Laura hastily shut the door behind the dressmaker, her
heart beating fast. Had she given herself away? Had Charlotte guessed she was a Protestant? Was the woman an in-
former, and would the queen's men come to take her away?

How strange, she thought. When the soldiers came for
Papa, I begged them to take me, too. And now I am terrified
that they might do just that! Of course, that had been before
she knew there were wondrous places like Guilford Hall in
the world, or men like Thomas Guilford, so strong and
handsome and wise. Papa had been an old man. Who knows
how much longer he might have lived? Whereas ever since
she'd come to this house, Laura felt she'd embarked on a
whole new life.

A new life... with Thomas Guilford. Lord Thomas Guilford. Laura, Lady Guilford. Mistess of Guilford Hall...

Oh, Laura, you are a goose, she told herself sternly. As
rich and handsome as Thomas is, he could have any woman
he pleased. He feels sorry for you, that is all. And she went
to draw herself a bath.

She washed with unhurried leisure, unbraiding her hair
and rubbing the long curls with sweet-scented soap, enjoying
the rich, creamy feel of the lather against her skin. To have

so much free time seemed unspeakably decadent, but what else was she to do when both Polly and Theo had spurned her help?

When her fingers and toes began to turn wrinkled, Laura climbed out of the tub, toweled off her hair, and put on a robe. Then she sat well back from the window in the slanting rays of the late-day sun, wondering what she ought to do next. Surely there were books somewhere in the house—besides, of course, the moldy sorcerer's volumes in John Guilford's domed room. For now, she could read her Bible. She fetched it from her trunk and opened it at random, near the middle.

"The Song of Songs, which is Solomon's. Let him kiss me with the kisses of his mouth: for thy love is better than wine," she read, just as she had a hundred times before. Her father had taught her that this section of the Bible was a parable, that the bridegroom was Jesus and his bride the church on earth. She sat with the warm sun pouring over her loose hair, the breeze fluttering her robe, and read on. "I have compared thee, O my love, to a company of horses in Pharaoh's chariots. Thy cheeks are comely with rows of jewels, thy neck with chains of gold."

Thomas had said she was lovely. Charlotte told her she had exquisite shoulders and beautiful hair...

"A bundle of myrrh is my well-beloved unto me; he shall lie all night betwixt my breasts."

Hesitantly she opened her robe and looked down at her own breasts. They were pale as the linen bedclothes, lined with blue veins, tipped by rosy nipples. What would it feel like, she wondered, to have someone touch her there? To have Thomas lie with his black head against her and kiss her with his red, red mouth?

A knock sounded at the door. Blushing at her thoughts, she yanked the robe shut just as Thomas called to her, "Laura?" There was an angry edge to his tone.

She looked about for something with which to cover her hair, found the towel, and wrapped it hurriedly around her head. Thomas pounded on the door again. "Laura, let me in!"

"I'm not dressed!" she cried.

"Open the door."

"But—"

"Do as I say!"

She ran and flung it open. He did not even seem to notice

what she was wearing as he pushed past her and turned, hands on his hips. "I spoke to Charlotte," he said, glaring at her. "She showed me the fabric you chose for your gown."

Laura nodded, clasping her robe at the throat. "I hope it met with your approval."

"Gray." There was that vein on his forehead. "All the samples, all the colors she had, and you chose gray!"

"I thought you would be pleased! It was the color of—" She stopped. His eyes were no longer dove gray; they were narrowed and milky pale.

"I told you I dislike seeing women in dull clothing!"

"All you said was black," Laura protested. "I didn't choose black. I'm sorry; I didn't mean to make you angry. Please don't be cross with me!"

Abruptly his manner changed. "You are right, Laura. I did say black. Forgive me." He passed a hand over his forehead, grimacing wearily. "I had a wretched day in the city. I did not mean to take my troubles out on you."

Laura's bewildered fright vanished. He looked so terribly unhappy! She hesitated, then put her hand on his sleeve. "Is there anything I can do?"

Thomas smiled, shaking his head. "Sweet Laura. No, thank you. It is only a mood; 'twill pass." He patted her hand. "Wait—you can let me explain why I am so concerned about this new gown. On Saturday evening I am having some friends to call. They are very important people, and their goodwill is vital to me."

"And I am to be there?"

"I had hoped you would do me the honor of serving as my hostess."

Laura's heart fluttered. "Me?"

"I would consider it a very great favor."

"I would be delighted," she said softly, "to help you in any way I can."

"You would?" His long, handsome face creased in a grateful smile. "Oh, Laura, thank you. You don't know how much that means to me." Suddenly he noticed the robe she was wearing. "Good Lord, you're not dressed! Forgive me for bursting in on you this way!" He averted his gaze and hurried to the door.

"That's all right, Thomas," she told him. "I shall see you at dinner. Eight o'clock sharp!" She closed the door and leaned against it, nearly swooning. Sweet Laura, he'd called

her! Remembering how he'd smiled at her made her shiver
with happiness.

And he wanted her—needed her—to serve as his hostess.

Laura felt like dancing. "Oh, Thomas," she whispered
fervently, "I intend to make you very proud of me come Saturday night!"

Chapter 4

Clearly the guests who were expected were *very* important, for Polly was up to her ears in work for the next three days. Laura offered her assistance more than once, but each time the cook refused. "My sisters-in-law will be over to help with the servin'," she said, "and fer the rest, well, 'twill get done somehow." Laura could only look on impotently while the woman rushed about in the kitchens, scalding sauces, dropping eggs, breaking crockery, and generally making every task she attempted twice as hard as it ought to be.

"*Please* let me help," Laura begged, wincing as she watched the woman mangle the beautiful huge salmon she was deboning.

"Best thing ye can do for me, missy," Polly said darkly, "is stay out from underfoot. Ouch!" She had sliced her finger with the boning knife.

A note came from Charlotte on Thursday morning, explaining that she'd been taken ill and would not make the appointment for the fitting, so Laura didn't even have that to relieve her restlessness. Laura worried that perhaps her gown would not be finished on time, but Thomas assured her that Charlotte would not let them down.

Her guardian left Guilford Hall each morning before Laura rose, and some days got home not much before dinner. His hectic schedule reminded Laura of the way Humphrey had dashed about in the weeks after her father died. Left to her own devices, she took long walks about the grounds after breakfast and spent the afternoons reading her Bible or trying to play the virginal in the music room, though it was dreadfully out of tune. She had asked Thomas one night if there were any books in the house, and when he said no, asked tentatively if he might buy her some in London with the money from her estate. He promised he would, but then he kept forgetting, and Laura did not like to remind him when he was so terribly busy all the time.

When Laura came down to the kitchens for her breakfast on Saturday morning, she found every hearth in the big room blazing and Polly collapsed at the table in tears. "Whatever is the matter?" Laura cried, rushing to her side.

"I can't do it!" the cook wailed, wringing her hands. "Try as I might, things just won't get done, and here's fifty people comin', and Master Thomas sayin' he'll bite off my head if it all ain't just right—"

"Fifty people?" Laura echoed in dismay.

Polly nodded miserably. "And Susie and Tillie won't be here 'til noon, and that Theo, he don't give a damn. All this I've got to do, and he's off arrangin' flowers!"

"Hush, Polly." Laura put an arm around her shoulders. "You know I've been offering to help for days. Now just tell me, what should I do?"

"I can't take yer help, missy, thank ye kindly."

"But it's not right that you should work so hard while I sit about doing nothing!"

"That's what Mistress Estelle used to do." Polly sniffed into her apron. "Jest set about lookin' pretty, never dirtyin' her hands—"

"Well, I'm not Mistress Estelle. I'm Laura, and I'm going to help whether you want me to or not."

"Master Thomas—he'll be angry with me!"

"Oh, Master Thomas can just go jump off the roof!" Laura said cheerily.

Polly stared at her in shock. "Missy," she whispered, "ye mustn't say such a thing!"

"Oh, why not? Now, give me a task." Polly was still goggling at her, and Laura sighed. "Polly. I *order* you to give me a task."

"Well—" The cook glanced around the chaotic kitchen uncertainly. "I need five quarts of strawberries fer the cakes I'm makin'. And they ought to be picked afore the sun hits 'em and bleeds 'em out; 'tis a dreadful hot day."

"Oh, dear." Laura nibbled her lip. "Aren't the gardens Theodore's domain?"

"I don't know what that there 'domain' means, missy, but like I tells ye, he's busy with his dad-blamed flowers in the receivin' room."

Laura thought about it. The berry patch was a good quarter mile down the hill from the house, by the stream. Even if Theodore was looking, he wouldn't be able to see her from the windows in the receiving room. "All right,

Polly. Have you got a couple of good big baskets I can use?"

A few minutes later she was on her way to the berry patch, a vine basket over each arm. Though it was not yet eight o'clock, the morning air was already leaden and hot. The sun poured down like melting butter, raising beads of sweat beneath the band of her hood. When she reached the sprawling spread of berries, Laura pulled off her boots and stockings and rolled back the sleeves of her gown.

The earth beneath her bare toes was dark and loamy, cool beneath its shading of green leaves, but the heat overhead was merciless. Now and again she paused in her picking and searched the blue sky hopefully for clouds. Her hood kept slipping down over her eyes, and the strawberry runners clung to her skirts, tangling round her ankles. When at long last she'd filled one basket, Laura left the patch and went to the stream for a drink.

The water was heavenly cool. She cupped her hands, drinking thirstily from juice-stained fingers, then splashed her hot, sticky face. Her braids were coming loose beneath the tight hood she wore; she darted a cautious glance back toward the manor and then pulled the headpiece off. Dangling her bare toes in the stream, she tugged out the plaits and began to braid up the left side.

"Oak leaves in autumn," said a deep male voice at her shoulder. Laura started and nearly fell into the stream. A huge arm caught her round the waist, pulling her back. She scrambled about on the bank, searching for her hood, and found a large booted foot set squarely atop it. She tugged at it desperately, not looking up, letting out a fearful cry.

The hand moved to her chin, tilting her face to the sky, and against a flood of warm sun she saw John Guilford's hard wolf's face. "Give me my hood!" she pleaded, desperately trying to hide her loose curls.

"You ought never to cover such hair as that," he told her, prying her hands away.

"But I have to! I must!" She began to cry. "It's my maidenhead, and now you have seen it, and I'm ruined!"

He released her hands. "What did you say?"

"You've taken my maidenhead!" she sobbed, tears streaming down her cheeks. "What will become of me?"

He stared at her, his eyes a deeper blue, almost indigo. Then he laughed. "I see. Innocent little Laura. Does my brother pretend to be taken in?"

She clawed at his sneering face. "Give me back my hood. Haven't you done enough damage already?"

Abruptly he moved his boot. "Don't worry. I won't give away your game. I won't tell Thomas I found you lolling about out here like the loose-heeled trollop you are."

She pulled the hood over her hair, struggling to tuck in the ends. "What did you call me?" she demanded.

"I called you what you are. A trollop."

She gathered up her skirts and got to her feet. "I don't know what that means, but I don't like the way it sounds."

He wagged his head at her. "Really, little Laura. The charade's for my brother, not for me. Why play the prim Protestant when we are alone together? There are so many more interesting games we could play." And with that he unbuttoned his black doublet and pulled off both it and his shirt.

Laura felt her mouth drop open. Her heart stopped beating. She had never seen a man with so few clothes on, had never imagined one could look so completely different from the way she did. His chest was broad as a church door, covered with curling black hair that trailed down in a vee at the top of his low-slung breeches. His bare arms were thick as young tree trunks, their muscles threatening to burst out of his taut white skin.

He took a step toward her. "Oh, you're good, you are," he said admiringly. "Very good indeed. But it's your turn now." He reached for her bodice, his blue eyes smoldering.

Laura screamed. Forgetting strawberries and boots and stockings, she ran for her life back to Guilford Hall.

She ran right past poor, startled Polly and up the stairs to her room, slamming the door and locked it behind her. How could he have been so brazen as to strip nearly naked in front of her? Trembling, she threw herself down on her bed, burying her face in the pillows, trying to block out the image that seemed branded in her memory: skin white as the moon against curling midnight hair, muscles wound like ropes in his shoulders and chest. His eyes as he'd groped for her, smoky blue beneath lashes black as pitch . . .

She would have to tell Thomas what he had done, of course. At the thought Laura felt her cheeks burn bright red. How would she ever work up the courage to tell her guardian that his own brother had taken her maidenhead? No doubt Thomas would send her away, back to Humphrey and Blanche. She began to tremble. Lord, she couldn't bear it if he did!

She sat up on the bed, trying to think how she could explain the incident to Thomas so that he would not be angry with her. There had to be some way. After all, it hadn't been her fault; she hadn't done anything wrong—

Someone rapped at her bedchamber door. Laura crept backward on the bed, thanking God she'd locked it. "Who's there?" she called fearfully. There wasn't any answer. "Who's there?" she cried again, heart pounding faster. Then she heard a crinkling sound as a bit of paper was slipped beneath the door.

She waited, but nothing else happened. At last, her fright fading to curiosity, she pushed up from the bed and tiptoed toward the scrap of paper, staring down at it.

"Your hair is not your maidenhead," read the message in a bold, square hand. "Ask Polly if you want to know what is."

Startled, Laura flung open the door. The hall outside was empty except for her stockings and boots—and two big baskets brimming full with ripe, red strawberries.

She blinked at the second basket of berries. He had to be a sorcerer to have picked them that quickly. She caught up the note, crumpling it in her hand. Then she put on her shoes, took the baskets, and crept down the stairs.

"There ye are!" Polly said gratefully. "I thought ye'd forgotten about pickin' those berries!"

Laura set the baskets down on the table. "No. No, I didn't forget. Here they are."

The cook was stamping out shortcakes. "Way ye rushed in here, missy, I thought maybe ye'd seen a ghost!"

"There's no such thing as ghosts," Laura said absently, still wondering how John Guilford had picked those berries so fast.

A kettle on the fireback suddenly boiled over, sending a cascade of liquid sputtering onto the flames. "Damnation," Polly muttered, up to her elbows in flour.

"I'll get it." Coming to her senses, Laura grabbed a stick and swung the pothook back from the flames.

"Bless ye, missy." Polly hesitated a moment, then said diffidently, "While ye're at it, ye might have a taste of it, then, to see what ye thinks."

Laura took a ladle, dipped it into the pot, blew on the steaming liquid, and sipped. She tasted nothing. She tried again. "Polly," she said slowly, "what is this?"

"Why, broth to sauce the quails."

Laura stirred the pot's contents. The liquid was perfectly clear. "Are you sure? It looks like plain water to me."

Polly's brown eyes bulged. "Land sakes," she whispered, "I've forgot to put anythin' in. Master Thomas'll kill me!" And she burst into tears.

"Don't cry, please!" Laura pleaded. "You can always make a demiglace; that takes no time at all."

"I don't know how to make no demi-nothin'!" the cook sobbed. "I only knows one sauce, and now I've ruined that!"

"I'll make it, then. All I'll need is some shallots and wine—"

"Master Thomas'll kill me if he finds ye've been cookin'!"

"Polly," Laura said briskly, "if he's going to kill you one way and the other, I may as well make the sauce!"

"I don't dare cross Master Thomas, missy," the woman whispered fearfully.

"Well, I'll cross him, then," Laura declared, impatient with her timidity. "Where are the shallots?"

"Oh, missy—"

"*Where* are the shallots?"

The cook nodded toward the cooler. "In there."

Laura patted her quaking shoulder. "Don't worry, Polly. Thomas will understand." She settled at the table with a paring knife and began to work.

Polly watched her nervously for a moment. "'Tis right handy with that knife ye are," she said at last, admiringly.

"I did all the cooking for my family after my mother died." Laura looked up at her. "Thomas told me you wouldn't want my help in the kitchens."

"He what?" she asked, plainly startled.

"He said you preferred working by yourself."

"I ain't never said that, missy! 'Tis Master Thomas don't want ye helpin'!"

"I wonder why not?" Laura mused. "I shall have to talk to him about it again." She glanced sidelong at the cook. "It's odd, you know, but I thought I saw Master John while I was picking those berries. I thought he always slept during the day."

"Aye, that he does, 'cept when he's over to Hertford to visit the whorehouse. He's a terrible one for the strumpets," said Polly, "is Master John. Every Tuesday and Friday night, regular as rain."

"Oh." Laura had read about whores in the Bible, though she wasn't sure exactly what they did. She knew they were

wicked, though. It made sense that a madman like John
Guilford would visit their house. She took a carrot and
scraped it with the blade of her knife. "Polly, what's a trollop?"

The cook let out a nervous giggle. "Just that, missy. A
whore." She went to the fireplace to test the lamb that was
roasting there.

Laura's cheeks flushed red. She'd been right, then. She
was ruined! Still, the note had said she should ask...
"Polly," she said as casually as she could, "what's a maidenhead?"

The cook nearly stuck herself with the skewer she'd
pulled from the lamb. "Land sakes, child, didn't yer mama
tell ye of such things?" Laura shook her head. "Hmph," said
Polly. "Well. D'ye know anythin' 'bout what goes on between women and men?"

"I know about love."

Polly snorted. "That ain't got nothin' to do with it; ask
Master John! Well, now, let me see. A maidenhead's a thing
what's inside a woman, down in here." She pointed to her
belly. "It gets broke the first time she has relations with a
man."

"What do you mean—relations?"

"Ye know. Intercourse, they calls it. Some says, makin'
love." At Laura's blank expression she scratched her nose.
"Land sakes. Let me see. Did ye ever see a couple of cows or
horses out in a field, one on top of the other, and the one on
top kind of pushin' and shovin'?" Laura nodded hesitantly.
She had seen such a thing once, with two horses. The one on
the bottom had been in awful pain; it was whinnying and
screaming to get away. "Well, that's what a man does to a
woman when they has relations."

"No!" Laura blurted in horror.

Polly laughed. "Oh, 'tain't exactly the same. But 'tis close
enough."

"And the man is the horse on top?" Laura demanded
incredulously.

"Aye, most often. Though I has heard—" Polly broke off
as Theo came in from the hallway with a big bundle wrapped
in brown paper. "Your gown," he announced to Laura, and
dumped the package on the floor.

"Theodore!" Polly scolded, hurrying to scoop up the bundle.

"Go to hell," he told her, and went out again.

While Polly shook her head at his back, Laura reached for the package to untie the twine. "Not here, missy," Polly cautioned. "Not with all this to-do! Take it up to yer room. And ye'd best try it on case it needs some adjustments."

"I'll be back as soon as I do," Laura promised, and skipped off upstairs.

Once in her rooms, she sat by the window, the bundle in her lap, and tugged off the twine and brown paper. Inside was a nest of tissue; she pawed through it eagerly. Then she stared down in dismay at the garment she held.

There had been some awful mistake. The gown was red.

Puzzled, Laura shook out the dress and held it up by the shoulders. The bright crimson silk was not the only mistake. Where she'd specified a high neck and long sleeves, this was cut low across the bosom. And the sleeves were slashed nearly to the shoulder, hanging down in long points trimmed with cloth-of-gold.

How could such a thing have happened? She'd distinctly told Charlotte she wanted the gray. The seamstress must have gotten her package confused. Clutching the gown, Laura hurried down to the receiving room to send Theo after Charlotte before she got too far away.

To her relief, Thomas was with Theo, both of them standing contemplating a huge vase of foxgloves and larkspur set on the mantel. "Too much blue," Thomas was saying gravely as Laura rushed in.

"Thomas, thank heavens!" she cried. "You have to do something. Charlotte has delivered the wrong gown!"

The two men turned to face her. "Doesn't it fit?" Thomas asked, pulling at his beard.

"I haven't tried it! 'Tis the wrong color, you see; you know I ordered gray."

"And I changed your order. I told Charlotte to make it red."

Laura's eyes widened. "You did?"

"Aye. I thought 'twould suit you better."

"But, Thomas, you know I can't wear this! It's against my—" She broke off as he grasped her elbow and yanked her out of the room with an angry scowl. As he pulled her into the hall she saw Theodore watching them, a tight smile on his thin face.

Thomas kicked the doors shut behind them, grabbed Laura by her elbows, and shook her. "What did I tell you about keeping your religion secret?" he demanded.

"Thomas, you are hurting—"

"What did I tell you?" he roared.

She recoiled from his terrible rage. "That I was free to practice my beliefs as long as I kept them to myself."

"Precisely," he snapped, releasing her at last. "And how long do you think they will stay a secret if you show up this evening in gray, with one of those damned hoods over your hair?"

"I'm in mourning for my father!" Laura cried.

"Charles Darby was a heretic, a criminal!"

"He was my father, and I loved him!"

Thomas made a visible attempt to control his temper, taking a deep, long breath. "Of course you did," he said more quietly. "Forgive me, Laura, my dear child. Sometimes I forget what a very sheltered life you have led. Try to understand. Some of the guests coming here tonight know who your father was. If I was angry with you, it was only because of my fear someone might discover that you too are a heretic, that what happened to your father might happen to you. I've grown very fond of you, Laura, and I could not bear to see your life wasted that way. That's why I had Charlotte make you the gown in red. For your own protection."

Laura was silent for a moment. "That explains the color," she said finally. "But what about this low neckline and the sleeves?"

He flashed his enchanting smile. "I must plead guilty to responsibility for that too. I fancy myself a bit of a designer, you see. I made Charlotte a sketch of a gown I thought would look lovely on you. She never mentioned that you had asked for something else."

Laura looked down at the gown in her hands. "You designed this yourself? For me?"

He nodded. "Do you think it hideous?"

"Oh, no, Thomas! It is beautiful. It is just that I've never worn anything like this before."

"But you'll wear it tonight? For me?" His voice was boyish and eager. Laura was touched by the trouble he'd gone to for her, and by what he'd said—*I've grown very fond of you* . . .

"Of course I will wear it, then."

"And no hood?"

She laughed. "If you like. But on one condition."

"And what might that be?"

"That you let me help poor Polly in the kitchens. You give her entirely too much to do, Thomas, really. I came down to breakfast this morning and found her in tears!"

One corner of his red mouth tightened. "I don't appreciate your interfering with the way I run my household, Laura. And I don't want you spending time with Polly; she has an idle mind and a busy tongue."

"I don't mean to interfere," she said stubbornly. "I only want to help. Please? It would make me so very happy."

She heard a rude snigger from beyond Thomas's shoulder. "Please," Theodore mimicked her voice from the doorway, "please. It would make me so very happy."

"Get out, Theo," Thomas said sharply, not turning around.

"That is what you care about, isn't it, *master?*" Theo asked with sneering emphasis. "Making little Mistress Laura happy—"

"I said get out!" Thomas whirled, his fist clenched, and clipped his secretary on the jaw.

"Thomas, stop!" Laura cried in fright.

Theodore rubbed his chin, his green eyes narrowed and catlike. Then, as Laura watched in astonishment, he strode back into the receiving room, pulled the vase of foxgloves from the mantel, and hurled it to the floor. It shattered in a hail of water, pottery shards, and flower petals. Polly came running from the kitchens at the thunderous crash, her sisters-in-law at her heels. "What in the name of Christ—"

"Get out of here, all of you!" Thomas bellowed. "Laura, you too."

She took one last glance at Theodore's twisted, wrathful face and meekly followed Polly away.

At eight that evening, with the food and drink for the dinner party prepared and garnished, Laura went to her room to dress. Reasoning that Thomas was too preoccupied to notice, she'd helped Polly and her sisters-in-law despite his orders to the contrary. The women had been nervous and subdued, though, and there was no more talk of maidenheads and relations, only much hard work.

Laura bathed and put on the new red gown, blushing to see how low the bodice fell, trying unsuccessfully to tug it up so the tops of her breasts would not show. In the midst of her efforts Thomas rapped at the bedchamber door.

"Come in," she said faintly, giving up as the red silk refused to budge. He pushed the door open and stood on the threshold in silence. Then, "Sweet Laura," he said. "What a vision you are."

Laura felt the blush spread down to the top of the bodice. "I feel very immodest," she confessed, glancing down uncertainly.

"Well, you look absolutely radiant. I never dreamed you had such exquisite hair." He circled her slowly, nodding, then pulled a box out from behind his back. "A present for you. From London."

"My books?" she asked eagerly.

"Books? Good God, no. Go on and open it."

Swallowing her disappointment, Laura raised the lid of the box. Inside was a cunning little pair of red silk slippers, the toes twinkling with golden embroidery.

"I didn't think you ought to be clumping about in those boots of yours tonight," he told her, smiling. "Do you like them?"

"They're exquisite." Laura turned them over by habit, examining the soles. "But they don't seem to be very sturdy."

"Silly child, when they wear out I'll buy you ten pairs more. Sit down and I'll put them on you." Laura dutifully gathered her full skirts together and perched on the edge of a chair. Thomas knelt in front of her and slipped the shoes on over her stockings. She felt a little shiver of excitement as his big hands cupped her heels and eased them into the silk.

"There," he said with satisfaction, drawing her to her feet. "Almost perfect." He pulled something from his purse. "You lack only this—the finishing touch."

Curiously Laura unwrapped the velvet bundle he gave her, then drew in her breath. Gleaming against the rich black fabric were two golden combs set with bloodred jewels.

"They belonged to my mother," Thomas went on. "I know, I know—such ornaments are against your religion. But it will give me such pleasure to see you in them, just for tonight. Here." He took one from her, brushed a thick brown-red plait back from her brow, and secured it. Laura could not help trembling as his fingertips grazed her bared shoulder. He fastened the remaining comb, then stood back and stared at her as if she were some precious jewel herself. "These rooms were Mother's, too," he said softly.

"I didn't know that." Laura gazed at the long mirrors, the luxe drapes, the huge testered bed, flattered that he'd seen fit to install her there. "What was your mother like?"

"She was the most remarkable woman I have ever known." His eyes were soft as doves' wings. "She was the life of every party. Everyone loved her. I miss her terribly."

Laura's heart melted at this tender confession. At times like this, she felt so close to him. "I shall make a poor substitute for her tonight as hostess," she said softly, "but I will do my best."

"You don't know how much that means to me, Laura." His smile blazed out at her, and he offered his arm. "Shall we go downstairs?"

The first carriage was already drawing up to the doors as they entered the front hall. Laura darted a glance into the receiving room. No trace of the mess Theodore had made remained; another vase of flowers occupied the mantel. As for Theodore, he looked quite dashing in a tight-fitting purple livery and was on duty to open the doors and take wraps.

The next hour was a blur of names and faces for Laura. As the guests arrived, Thomas introduced her to each one. She curtsied to the women, and all of the men bowed and kissed her hand. She was hard put to keep everyone straight, but a few of the callers stood out in her mind.

There was a very tall, buxom, blond-haired woman, the Marchioness of Salister, who made a great to-do over Laura's gown. There were two men who came in together, whom Thomas called Richard and Tony, who were dressed exactly alike in royal blue doublets and yellow hose, with yellow roses in their girdles; one was very tall, and the other no bigger than she.

She remembered Lady Cecily, the Duchess of Strathearn, because she had never met a duchess before. There were tons of other titles as well, viscounts and earls and Lords This and Ladies That. All were dressed very grandly, and the masses of jewels they wore made Laura feel much less guilty about her own two relatively simple combs.

The most elaborate gown was worn by a beautiful black-haired woman whom Theodore announced as Mademoiselle la Comtesse de Talboir. As she came forward swathed in magnificent cloth-of-silver, with red ostrich plumes in her hair, Thomas greeted her in French, telling her how lovely she looked and kissing both her cheeks. Laura followed their conversation perfectly; when Thomas presented her to the woman she curtsied and said, *"Je suis enchantée de faire votre connaissance, Mademoiselle la Comtesse."* She heard a rude snigger from Theodore in the doorway; the woman was

staring at her in disbelief. What had she done? Laura wondered, and then found out as, with a little sniff, the woman
swept on.

"Where in God's name," Thomas muttered angrily, "did
you learn your French?"

"My father taught me," Laura answered, nonplussed.
"Why?"

"Because your bloody accent sounds as if you were chewing glass between your teeth. For Christ's sake, speak English; you're adequate in that." Stung, Laura looked up at him
with wide, hurt eyes. "I'm sorry," he said shortly. "I've much
on my mind."

One other guest in particular made an impression on
Laura. Thomas introduced him as Sir Francis Englefield and
told Laura that he was Master of the Court of Wards; she
remembered Humphrey having mentioned him. He was
about forty, jowly and stout, with poor teeth and a face
marked with pox scars. His voice was very loud and pomp-
ous, and when Thomas turned away from presenting them to
greet a new arrival, he winked at Laura and pinched her
side. Flustered, she moved closer to Thomas and vowed to
avoid Englefield for the rest of the night.

A troupe of musicians had magically appeared in the gallery of the receiving chamber, playing merry tunes on the
viol and tambor and pipes. In a lull between guests Thomas
pulled a list from the breast of his doublet and consulted it,
frowning. "What is wrong?" Laura whispered.

"The Duke of Norfolk hasn't shown up, damn his black
soul. And neither has Throckmorton or Cecil—think they're
too good, do they?" His scowl turned abruptly to a welcoming smile warm as sunshine; Theodore was announcing the
arrival of Lord and Lady Dacre. "Hello, darlings!" Thomas
cried, kissing the glamorous blond woman, shaking the gentleman's hand. "So glad you could come to my little gathering."

"And this must be Laura." The woman raked her with
sharp blue eyes. "My God, what a tiny thing. Don't you feed
her, Thomas?"

"Oh, milady," Laura protested, "he is wonderfully good
to me."

"I imagine he is," the woman said, with a dry humor
Laura could not fathom. "Where in hell is the wine,
Thomas? I am utterly parched." She marched off into the
receiving chamber, her frail, quiet husband trailing behind.

"She was making a jest," Thomas said when they were out of earshot, sounding pained. "You ought to have laughed."

"Oh." Laura pondered this. "Still, it was not very amusing, was it, for her to jest that you would mistreat me?"

"When someone as rich as Matilda Dacre makes a jest, everybody laughs." He looked again at the guest list. "Norfolk and Cecil and Throckmorton won't show. To hell with them. Let's go in."

The hall had been enchantingly transformed by the elegant crowd. The women shone like birds in fantastic plumage, their jeweled heads, hands, and throats reflecting the sparkling candlelight. The men stood in knots and talked in grave tones of mysterious matters such as foreign trade and the balance of power, or else sat at the little tables set around the edges of the room, playing at cards. Laura blinked when she saw the vast sums of gold they wagered on each deal.

Of course she did not know how to gamble, but one end of the room had been set aside for dancing, and she loved to dance. Unfortunately Thomas showed no interest in that diversion, preferring to circulate among his guests. He knows everything about everyone, Laura thought, listening as he discussed King Philip's war against France with a grim-looking lord, then moved smoothly into a debate on the merits of pruning boxhedge with the Comtesse de Talboir, conducted entirely in French. He was by far the most elegant man there, she decided, and felt a thrill of pleasure that despite the presence of all these beautiful women, she was the one at his side.

The man called Tony asked Thomas if he might dance with Laura, and to her delight Thomas said yes. They took their places in line for a faine-I-would.

Laura knew all the steps from her dancing lessons and clapped along as the first pair of partners skipped between the rows of men on one side and women on the other, arm in arm. But where she had been taught that one curtsied to one's partner at the end of the line, the man and woman kissed—and not quickly, either, but for a full four beats, mouth to mouth. She tried to remember from the introductions if they were married and decided they were. But when the next couple moved down the line, they kissed too, open-mouthed and clinging, and she knew perfectly well they were not wed, for the lady was the marchioness of Salister, and she'd come alone.

As Laura and Tony moved closer and closer to the head of the line, Laura grew quite frantic. She could hardly kiss her partner—after all, he was a virtual stranger! Yet she could not figure any gracious way to leave the dance now. Her heart pounded wildly as together they skipped between the rows of gay, clapping guests. Fortunately, at the vital moment Tony was very considerate, and merely held her hands and pretended to kiss her, his face a good six inches from hers. The rest of the dancers jeered at her partner, but Laura smiled at him thankfully.

When the song was finished, Tony asked her to dance with him again, but some of the kisses she'd witnessed had been quite scandalous, and she begged off, pleading the excuse of new shoes. He escorted her back to Thomas's side with a compliment on her performance, and she decided she liked this soft-spoken young man very much indeed.

Laura was hoping for a moment alone with Thomas so she could ask him about that kissing, but he was embroiled in a conversation with Lord and Lady Dacre about excise taxes. With Lady Dacre, rather, for her husband had very little to say. Neither did Laura, but it didn't much matter, since even Thomas had trouble getting a word in edgewise once the woman got started. Laura stood off to one side with Lord Dacre, listening as his wife railed about how far the price of wool had fallen and highway robbery by the Exchequer, until at last he asked Laura rather abruptly if she would like a glass of punch. She nodded, and he led her to a crystal bowl in a corner and ladled them each out a cup.

"It really is astonishing, isn't it," Laura whispered as they stood gazing out over the crowd, "how many titles there are in this one room."

The sad-faced man smiled. "Aye—and how few of them old and noble."

"Yours is, of course," Laura said politely.

She thought he sighed as he glanced at his loud, angry wife. "It used to be."

Supper wasn't served until nearly eleven, by which time Laura was famished. She also had a trace of a headache from the level of noise in the receiving room. It really was a most peculiar sort of gathering, she thought, as Thomas escorted her into the banqueting hall. The doors to the garden had been left open, and now and again she had seen one of the dancing couples glance furtively about and then slip outside. If they wanted a breath of air, she didn't know why they should look so suspicious. She would have enjoyed a stroll among the roses herself, but Thomas had been too busy with his guests, and she had not quite the courage to venture out alone.

Two extra tables had been set up in the banqueting hall to accommodate everyone. The room looked most elegant, Laura decided, with gold-trimmed cloths, sparkling crystal for the wine, and Thomas's silver plate. Candles gleamed in the wall sconces and down the lengths of the tables, and at each plate was a tiny nosegay of violets and celandine.

Thomas sat at the head of the center table, with Laura at his right. To her right, she noted with dismay, was Sir Francis Englefield, who'd pinched her in the entranceway. Across from them were the Duchess of Strathearn and Lord and Lady Dacre. Polly and her sisters-in-law each had one table to serve, and Theodore was in charge of the wine. As the maids finished handing round the gorgeous asparagus tarts Laura had labored over, she waited for Thomas to lead the blessing. Evidently there wasn't going to be any, for everyone started eating right away.

Lady Dacre crunched her tart between her long teeth, looked up, and said, "Have you got a new cook, Thomas? This filling is extraordinary."

"I had better not have," Thomas said in an ominous tone that made Laura spill a bit of wine. Blushing, she reached for the napkin on her lap and encountered Sir Francis Englefield's hand creeping toward her knee. She pushed him away inconspicuously and sopped up the spill with her napkin edge.

When she went to put the napkin back, there were Englefield's thick, stubby fingers again, crawling over her skirts. She thrust his hand away once more, a bit more forcefully, and glared at him for good measure. He smiled, polishing off his tart, then let out a hearty belch.

The rest of that course passed without incident, but when Polly cleared the tart plates and brought out the quail, Laura felt a pressure on her thigh, looked down, and saw Englefield reaching between her buttocks and the chair. Disgusted, she pinched his wrist as hard as she could and glanced at Thomas, hoping to bring her predicament to his attention. He was engrossed in conversation with Lady Dacre, however, and even when she cleared her throat quite loudly, he did not turn to her.

Laura squirmed in her seat and moved to its very edge

with as much casualness as she could muster. How could a
man with such a responsible position as Master of the Court
of Wards, she wondered, be such a dreadful boor? She
picked at her quail, unable to enjoy the crisp bird or silken
sauce for fear he would touch her again. She did not want to
cause a scene, but neither could she bear to have him pawing
her that way.

She had just lifted her wineglass for a sip when, like some
persistent spider, the man's fingers came inching onto her lap
again. Vexed beyond endurance, Laura turned and looked
him right in the eye.

"Sir," she said, quietly but distinctly, "my brother told me
he had to grease your palms to gain my wardship. I cannot
understand that, for I find your hands slippery enough as is."

There followed a moment of utter silence. Then Lord
Dacre threw back his head and laughed until it seemed he
would burst. Englefield's jowly face turned as crimson as
Laura's gown.

"My, my, my, Thomas," said Lady Dacre, her elegant
eyebrows arched, "your betrothed has a sharp tongue on her,
hasn't she, for one so young?"

Laura blinked. Thomas's betrothed? She waited for him
to correct the woman, to explain she was only his ward, but
he said not a word.

Laura felt her stomach turn an abrupt flip-flop. She
pushed back her chair. "Would you all excuse me, please?"
She managed to walk as far as the doors to the receiving
room, then she began to run.

She rushed out to the gardens, feeling a desperate need
for air, then stood in the rose-scented moonlight, trying to
catch her breath. Thomas's *betrothed?* He'd said nothing to
her of marriage. What had the woman meant?

"Laura!" She turned and saw him coming toward her
from the house, tall and solemn in the shimmering moonlight. "Laura, I am sorry. I never meant for you to find out
this way."

"I don't understand. We are not betrothed."

"Laura, my sweet, we are. Your father and I arranged it
while he was in prison in London, before he died."

"That can't be! Humphrey would have told me."

"That's my fault, I'm afraid. I pleaded with him not to.
You see, I had the foolish notion that if you got to know me
first, you might—well, you might become fond of me." He
hung his head, rushing on. "And so we arranged for me to

purchase your wardship, and for you to come and live here. I was hoping that, given time, you might find it in your heart to care for me."

"Oh, Thomas." He looked so forlorn, almost shy, standing there, quite unlike the debonair man of the world he had been with his guests. She started to say more, but he forestalled her, reaching for her hand.

"I know this must seem very sudden to you, Laura. And I know I am not—that I cannot be—the man of your dreams. I am so much older than you, for one thing. And I've a dreadful temper sometimes—well, you have seen that. But I am trying very hard to overcome it. Because I—I've fallen in love with you, Laura. It is as simple as that."

Laura caught her breath at this declaration. He smiled at her and went on. "I never would force you to marry me against your will. Your happiness means far too much to me. All I would ask is that you consider the matter. After all, it was your father's wish that you and I be wed. I have a contract signed and sealed by him, setting out the terms."

Laura nibbled her lip. "May I—could I see the contract?"

He laughed. "My cautious little Laura, don't you trust me? But of course. I'll show it to you first thing in the morning, shall I?" Laura nodded. "And do I dare go on hoping, my dear, dear Laura, that you might someday care for me?"

"I—I am fond of you, Thomas. You have been very kind to me."

His sad face lit up. "With those words, Laura, you have made me the happiest man in the world. May I—would you permit me to kiss you?"

Though taken aback, Laura nodded again.

He moved a step closer, his arm slipping around her waist, drawing her to him. Laura looked up into his pale eyes. He bent his head, lowering it to hers. His stiff beard tickled her chin, and she could smell his lavender perfume. Then his red, red lips touched hers.

The kiss lasted no longer than a heartbeat, but it made Laura tingle from her head to her toes. Then he drew away from her with a sigh. "Thank you, Laura darling. Thank you for giving meaning to my life." He smiled sweetly, gently. "I'm sure there is much you would like to think over. If you want to go to your rooms and not return to our guests, I will understand." And then, suddenly overcome with emotion, he turned and hurried back inside.

Laura stood in the moonlight, trembling. Her very first

kiss—and how wondrous it had been! She put her finger to her mouth, dreamily rubbing the spot where his lips had touched hers. She could still feel a trace of his waxy red rouge on her fingertip.

Out of the shadows came the sound of someone applauding very slowly. She whirled around and saw John Guilford coming toward her through the arching arbor, his hard, angular face twisted in a sneer.

"My God, what a touching scene," he said, and swayed on his feet. "My brother has missed his true calling; he ought to seek out a post with the queen's players, don't you agree?"

Laura's cheeks flamed crimson. "How—how long have you been hiding there?" she stammered.

"Long enough to have heard my brother's quaint declaration." He dropped to one knee on the stones. "Oh, Laura, darling, thank you. Thank you for giving meaning to my life—"

"How dare you mock him? I think it is perfectly horrid of you to—to spy on us and to ruin my very first kiss!" She reached out and slapped his leering face.

He reeled back, sprawling across the stones, and she caught the distinct scent of ale above the sweet aroma of roses. So he was drunk! Still, she hadn't hit him hard enough to send him falling that way. Laura stared down at him in the moonlight, worrying that she had hurt him. He had the most peculiar expression on his lean, taut wolf's face as he lay on the path, looking up at her.

He pushed himself up slowly, his heavy hooded eyes fixed on her. "My God, Laura Darby," he said softly, "are you real? Where did you come from?"

"I'm sure I don't know what you mean."

"And you don't, do you?" He laughed, almost in disbelief. "Your first kiss. What, did you spring full-grown from the sea, like Venus, or fall from the stars?"

He was making no sense to her, but the spark of moonlit fire in his sleepy eyes was most alarming. His white shirt was open to the waist, and she could see the vee of curling black hair that stretched from his chest to the band of his breeches, just as she'd seen it that morning by the strawberry patch. "Let me give you a kiss too, little Laura," he coaxed. "To welcome you into the family."

She took a step backward toward the house, remembering

what Polly had told her about this brother and his wicked strumpets. "Stay away from me."

"But we're to be brother and sister, you and I, Laura." His voice was low and throaty. "One small, chaste kiss for my brother's small, chaste wife." His hand snaked out to grasp her wrist.

"Leave me alone!" Laura cried, genuinely frightened by the barely restrained force she sensed simmering beneath his cool, taunting words.

Instead he yanked her toward him, pulling her right off her feet and into the air. One of his powerful arms encircled her waist; the other caught in her hair, tugging at her braids. Laura tried to scream as he forced her head back, but before she could catch her breath, he covered her mouth with his, smothering the protest.

She could feel his heart pounding against her throat, could hear his breathing, ragged and shallow. He did not smell of perfume, but of ale and salt-sweat and something more, something like the rich black loam in which the strawberries grew. His body was hard and unyielding as he crushed her against him, and his mouth was hard, too, bruising hers with such strength that tears swam in her tightly clenched eyes.

Then, suddenly, the pressure of his mouth softened; his tongue, feathery and warm, pushed at her lips, parting them, slipping inside. He had moved his hand, bringing it up from her waist, his long fingers reaching until they stroked her breast—God, he was touching her breast! He cupped it in his hand, rubbing the nipple while his tongue plunged into her mouth, savoring, exploring. Laura's eyes flew open, staring into his, and she shuddered at the strange sensation, like a dart of light, that spread from his touch. Her flesh was warming, tightening beneath his caresses; her own breath came short and fast.

He moved his hand to her shoulder, pushing the sleeve of her gown down in one smooth, swift motion. His mouth left hers, grazing the smooth white flesh of her throat and moving lower still. Laura's face was buried in his silky black hair; his tongue glided over her breastbone, tracing its curve with slow, lingering pleasure. "Christ," he murmured, "Christ, sweet. So sweet . . ."

He ducked his head, and Laura felt his bared teeth at her breast. Horror coursed through her as she realized that, lost in a flood of fascinated sensation, she had given up fighting him off. "No!" she cried, pushing him away, hands flying to cover her bodice. To her surprise he released her, then stood looking down at her in the moonlight, his chest heaving, a sheen of sweat glistening on his skin.

"Remember that, Laura Darby," he said quietly, "in the long nights to come."

Laura was shaking with shame and anger—at him, at herself. "I intend to inform Thomas of this outrage!" she spat, straightening her skewed gown.

"I doubt you will."

"Oh? Why wouldn't I?" she demanded.

The moonlight had shaded his wolf's eyes to silver. "Because you enjoyed it too much."

Fuming, she turned on her heel. "If you grow lonely," he called, "you know where to find me. I am up in my dome, every night."

Laura fled through the garden toward the kitchen doors.

Halfway there she stopped, trying to compose herself, taking deep breaths, pinning her braids again where he'd pulled them loose. He was right, she realized in dismay; she would never be able to confess to Thomas what his brother had done. But she hadn't enjoyed it. She'd hated it, hated the way she felt now: guilty and all unsettled. Thomas's kiss hadn't made her feel like that.

She shivered, standing on the lawn in her fluttering red silk dress, with jewels in her hair. She stared up at the house, at the dark towers, the crazy pitching roofs and black spires, and for a moment she had the bizarre sensation that they were tilting toward her, shifting on their foundations. Then she saw a flash of light in a window high above the rose garden. Theodore, she realized, recognizing his thin, pale face. How long had he been there? How much had he seen?

From now on, she swore, I am going to stay far, far away from John Guilford. Catching up her skirts, she ran to the kitchen doors as fast as she could and slipped up the back stairs to her room.

Chapter 5

Laura rose early on the morning after the party, anxious to see the contract with her father that Thomas had promised to show her. When she could not find him in his study, she went to the kitchens to ask Polly where he might be.

"Gone," said the cook, busily polishing silver. "Gone to London for business. He left with the last of the guests."

"He didn't say anything to me about going to London!"

Polly shrugged. "Something must've come up sudden. Master Thomas, he's always off somewheres at the drop of a hat."

"Did he leave something for me with you, Polly? A note? A paper?" The cook shook her head. "Well, did he say when he would be back?"

"In a week or so."

"A *week?* What am I to do all by myself for a week?"

Polly laid down her finishing cloth. "Well, missy," she said shyly, "that there party last night's the first one in ten years I ain't ended up after with my ears boxed. And I was wonderin'—oh, I knows as I'm hopeless and all, God knows Master Thomas tells me often enough. But do ye suppose ye might try and—try and teach me some o' them things ye knows about cookin'?"

"Oh, Polly, of course I will! And you mustn't say you're hopeless; nothing's ever hopeless. Especially not you." Something the cook had said stuck in her mind. "Thomas doesn't really hit you, Polly, does he?"

"Only when I deserves it, missy. Though that's often enough, Lord knows."

"No one deserves to be struck by his master," Laura said in shock. "I shall have to talk to Thomas about that the minute he comes back!"

"Please, missy, don't," Polly begged. "He'd only hit me again. Best thing ye can do to help me is to teach me how to cook right and proper, so's I don't deserve it so often."

81

"Well." Laura decided she would, nonetheless, talk to Thomas. "We'll get right to your cooking lessons, then—as soon as we have this house cleaned up a bit!"

So she spent the morning polishing silver and washing crystal, scrubbing wine stains from the table linens, sweeping and waxing the floor in the banqueting hall. At noon she and Polly sat down in the kitchen for a meal of leftover tarts and strawberry cake. The cook rubbed her back with a sigh as she eased onto the bench, then looked at the beaming, fresh-faced girl across from her. "Ye truly do like workin', don't ye, missy?"

"I should rather be busy than not. Wouldn't you?"

Polly eyed a huge stack of plates that still wanted washing. "Not all the time I wouldn't."

Laura laughed. "You know what the Bible says, Polly. 'In all labor there is profit.' Proverbs fourteen, verse twenty-three."

"What profit was there in your labor last night in the gardens, Mistress Laura?"

Laura looked up at the sound of the sneering male voice. Theodore stood in the doorway.

"What does ye want, Theo?" Polly asked curtly.

"Food."

She thrust a platter at him. "Take it and be gone."

He picked up the platter and flashed his thin, sly smile. "You know your Bible well, do you, Mistress Laura? Do you know the verse about serving two masters?" Then he disappeared as quietly as he had come.

Polly stuck out her tongue at his back. "Gives me the shivers, that one does, always sneakin' about. What was he sayin' about the gardens?"

"I can't imagine," Laura said faintly, slicing off a piece of strawberry cake. She glanced at the doorway to make certain Theo was gone, then leaned across the table. "Can you keep a secret?"

"Been known to. Ye got one?"

Laura nodded. "Master Thomas wants to marry me."

"Well, now. Well, how about that?"

"You don't sound very excited for me," Laura said, disappointed at this reception of her great news.

The cook pushed herself up from the table and went to fetch a pitcher of milk. "Master Thomas ain't no easy man."

"I know that, Polly. He knows it too. But he is going to change for me."

"Leopard can't change his spots, can he?" Polly asked, her back to Laura. "They tell me that's in the Bible too, though I couldn't say where."

"Jeremiah thirteen, verse twenty-three," Laura said absently, then laughed. "Anyway, Thomas isn't a leopard. And people change. They do it all the time."

"If ye says so, missy." Polly set the pitcher on the table with a clink. "Ye plannin' on marryin' him, then?"

Laura licked icing from her fingertips. "I haven't said yes, but I haven't said no." The sugar reminded her of the sweet, waxy taste of Thomas's rouge—and that made her think of the earthier taste of his brother's mouth. "Tell me, Polly," she said offhandedly, "have Thomas and John always been so different from each other?"

"Oh, aye. My mum told me that Master Thomas, he came shootin' out into this world just like one o' them rockets ye see in the fireworks—and that he was laughin', if ye can believe it. But Master John, he didn't want to come out fer nothin', not love nor money. Mum said 'twas just as if he knew he wouldn't be happy here." The cook shook her head, staring into space.

Came shooting out of where? Laura wondered, but before she could ask, Polly was going on. "'Twas a wretched birth, was Master John's. And Mistress Estelle, she held it against the poor child." She laughed. "Guess she never could forgive him fer makin' her work so hard! Master Thomas, that was her favorite. Oh, my, ye couldn't wedge a pin between 'em. 'Course, he and she, they always liked the same things. Fancy clothes, jewels, parties 'n' suchlike. John, he got left to Old Master—'n' what did he know about raisin' a child?"

"What was Thomas's father like, Polly?"

"John's just like him. Kept to himself, he did, always putterin' about up in that glass room or tryin' to do some such crazy thing as make a candle that wouldn't burn down."

"Some of what he tried worked, though, didn't it? Like the chamber pots."

"Oh, aye, there's some did, but lots more did not. Ye take them there machines he was always buildin' to try to fly."

"Machines that flew?" Laura echoed, wide-eyed.

"Oh, none of 'em ever did, mind ye. But every year or so, there he'd be draggin' one up to the roof, with Master John down below in the rose gardens, stringing up blankets and packin' straw so's his father wouldn't break his neck when he

landed. Used to drive Mistress Estelle plumb out of her
mind, seein' them roses crushed all to kingdom come."

"My Lord! The Old Master must have been a terrible trial
to live with," said Laura, polishing off her cake.

Polly made a face. "I reckon 'tis true what ye said about
people changin' after all, fer God knows he did."

Laura was thinking again of Thomas's brother. "What do
you suppose John does up in that room all night, Polly?"

The woman crossed herself. "Alch'my," she whispered.
"Raisin' up spirits by the black arts. That's what Master
Thomas says."

Laura got up to clear the plates. "I'll tell you one thing. If
I do marry Thomas, his brother is going to have to leave this
house."

"If'n ye marries Master Thomas," Polly muttered, "ye'll
have more to worry about than poor Master John."

"What's that, Polly?"

"I didn't say nothin', missy. I didn't say nothin' at all."

Polly proved an apt student in the kitchens, once Laura
got her to stop denigrating herself at every task she tried. In
three days she had mastered white sauce and demiglace and
strawberry preserves. She only seemed fumble-fingered
when Theodore sneaked up on them, or when Laura mentioned Thomas. Eventually she almost stopped cowering
when she did something wrong.

Despite their lessons, the week passed slowly for Laura.
She took walks, read her Bible, washed and ironed all her
clothes, but still time seemed to hang on her hands. She decided that must be a positive sign. She missed Thomas, so
surely she must be a little in love with him.

But that made her only slightly less restless. By Thursday
afternoon she was so stir-crazy that she proposed to Polly
they clean out all the kitchen cupboards and wash them
down. Reluctantly the cook allowed as how the job, awful as
it was, really ought to be done.

The task took them straight through to suppertime. They
were restocking the last of the cabinets, Polly perched on a
stool because she was taller, Laura handing up canisters of
sugar and oats and dried beans, when a tiny gray mouse
popped out of the cupboard, ran right down Polly's arm and
leg, and scampered out to the garden. "Ai-yee!" Polly
screamed, losing her footing and tumbling down from the
stool. Laura tried to catch her, but it all seemed to happen so

quickly that the next thing she knew Polly lay in a heap on the floor, clutching her ankle and moaning under her breath.

"Is it broken?" Laura cried in dismay, kneeling beside her.

"Oh, no, missy," Polly said bravely, belying her tears. "Just twisted, that's all."

"You cannot be sure," said Laura, helping her up from the floor. "I'd best fetch a doctor."

"A doctor? What, 'n' have him chargin' Master Thomas fer the visit? No thank ye, miss!"

"But if you are hurt—"

"I don't need no doctor," Polly said, leaning against the table. "Best thing's just to rest it a bit." One of the house-bells jangled, and she started toward the cooler.

"What are you doing?" Laura cried. "Sit down; I'll get the bell. What is it, Theo wanting his supper?"

Polly shook her head. "Master John. And 'tis breakfast he wants."

"Oh." Laura hesitated. "He is up in that room. Thomas said I was never to go there."

"Well, then, I'll go." Polly hobbled across the kitchen. Laura chewed her lip.

"You'll never make it up four flights of stairs on that ankle, Polly."

"But if Master Thomas told ye—"

"Never mind Thomas. You sit down. I'll just knock on the door and leave the tray there, so I needn't go in."

"Well," said Polly, "if ye're sure—there's his plate of sweet rolls and an orange. And he always get a good, tall mug of milk."

"Milk?" said Laura. It did not seem the drink for a madman.

"'Case he's been drinkin'," said Polly. "It settles the bowels."

A few moments later Laura stood before the heavy iron door to the domed room, balancing the tray in one hand, knocking with the other. "Bring it in, Polly," came Thomas's brother's deep voice. "I can't stop right now."

Filled with dread, Laura opened the door a crack. "It isn't Polly. It's me. Laura," she said.

He was standing at the table on the platform, supporting a big brass disk with one hand while he scribbled a quill across a sheet of parchment. He glanced toward her briefly, lip curling. "Ah. Come for another kiss?"

Laura's temper flared. "Hardly," she said as coolly as she could. "Polly fell from a stool and twisted her ankle."

"My God." He dropped the brass disk with a crash. "I'll go and fetch a doctor."

His clear, honest concern for the cook took Laura by surprise. "She says she doesn't want one," she told him. "That she only needs to rest it a bit."

His forehead was still creased with worry. "You're sure it isn't broken?"

Laura nodded. "She can walk on it."

He frowned. "A twisted ankle is very painful. I know. I got one once. My father landed on top of me in a flying machine. But then I suppose Thomas has already told you all about Apollo."

"Apollo?" she echoed.

She imagined he flushed slightly. "His real name was Paul. I only called him Apollo."

"Why?"

"I suppose because once upon a time I thought he could do anything. Just like a god." His hard, cool voice had softened; he seemed to catch himself and scowled at her again. "Are you going to stand there all night? Bring me my bloody breakfast and get out of here."

Laura circled the platform warily to hand him the tray. As she did, she darted a glance at the disk he'd been holding. It was the most mysterious thing she had ever seen. Engraved on the shiny brass surface was a circle superimposed on a circle, both marked with waving lines and crosshatches. Fixed to a knob in the center was a brass rod, pointed at each end, carved with eerie symbols. It was so plainly an instrument of sorcery that she gasped aloud: "What *is* that thing?"

"This?" He lifted it up in his big hands. "An astrolabe. 'Astro,' star. 'Labos,' to take. Star-taker."

"What are you doing with it?" Laura whispered.

"Waiting for Venus," John Guilford said. He raised the disk so its edge was against his cheek, fiddling with the rod, sighting along it through the glass dome. "And there she is."

Nonplussed, Laura turned to look. Low on the horizon, above the treetops in the valley below, she saw a spark of white fire. "You were waiting for a star?" she asked in confusion.

He shook his head absently, making a notation on the parchment. "Actually, a planet."

"What is a planet?"

"Any of seven celestial bodies characterized by motion relative to the fixed stars," he told her, scribbling away. "Sun, moon, Mercury, Mars, Jupiter, Saturn, Venus. Orbiting the earth in circles, only of course they don't move in circles at all, which was Ptolemy's problem. A Polishman named Kopernik came up with the notion they all go around the sun instead. He was right. They do." He looked up from his note-taking and grimaced fiercely. "Why are you hanging about? Get out of here."

Laura tilted her head at him. "Are you really a sorcerer?"

"Do you believe in sorcery?"

She shook her head tentatively. "No."

"Good for you. Neither do I. Get out."

"But if you're not a sorcerer, what are you?"

"I study the stars."

"Oh. You mean you tell fortunes and such." Laura's voice showed her contempt. "I don't put any stock in that nonsense."

"I'm not an astrologer," he told her impatiently. "I'm an astronomer."

"What is the difference?"

"Astrology deals with people. I don't like people. Astronomy only deals with what is out there." He nodded toward the dome. "Have you finished with pestering me?"

"I'm sorry," she murmured, starting toward the door. "I was only curious."

"Wait." She turned back to him. He smiled down at her in the twilight. "Curiosity is too precious a thing to be stifled. What are you curious about?"

"It doesn't matter," she mumbled, inching away.

"No, really. Come up here. I'll give you a lesson in astronomy." She hesitated. "I don't bite," he went on. "At least, not when I haven't been drinking."

Laura flushed at this reference to what had happened between them in the rose garden. Still, he had been drunk then. And there was something wonderfully alive, vital about him as he looked down at her. His eyes were deep blue, like the sky above them; his mouth had lost its angry sneer.

"I don't know anything about the stars," she protested.

"'A journey of a thousand miles must begin with a single step.'"

"Is that from the Bible?" Laura asked suspiciously.

"No. From the works of a Chinaman named Lao-tzu. If you don't like that, how about Plato? 'Astronomy compels the soul to look upwards and leads us from this world to another.'"

"My father loved Plato," she said with an involuntary smile.

"Then I take back what I called him once. He was no fool. I've got a Latin translation of the *Dialogues* here somewhere; would you—but then I don't suppose you read Latin."

"I read it rather well," she said stiffly. "And French. And Greek."

"Really? I'll wager you and Elizabeth would get on well."

"Elizabeth who?"

"Elizabeth Tudor. I go every Tuesday and Friday night to Hatfield House to instruct her in astronomy."

"Polly told me you go to a whorehouse in Hertford," Laura said without thinking.

John Guilford arched a black brow. "I generally do stop there on my way back."

Laura's color deepened, but what he had said about Elizabeth Tudor intrigued her. "Do you mean the Princess Elizabeth?" He nodded. "What is she like?"

"Quick," he said approvingly. "Curious. She watches and listens, and she does both well."

"Is she interested in the stars?"

"She is interested in everything. That's why I like her."

"Is she pretty?"

He considered the question, brow furrowed. "I never thought about it. She is tall and very pale with black, black eyes. She has her father's hair, red as fire. And she has extraordinary hands. Long, thin, elegant hands." Laura glanced at her own hands, which seemed rather short and stumpy. "She asked me about you," he added, to Laura's shock.

"About me? Why?"

"That jest you made about Sir Francis Englefield's greasy palms is making the rounds of the kingdom. Elizabeth herself told it to me at Hatfield House. She has a wonderful gift for mimicry; you should hear her do Englefield. Cecil nearly fell off his chair when he heard it, he was laughing so hard."

Laura stared at her toes. "I ought never to have said it. I must have embarrassed Thomas dreadfully."

"Thomas doesn't need your help for that." He saw her chin rise. "Never mind. Come up here for your lesson."

Laura knew she ought not to stay, but it seemed such a long time since she'd learned anything new. She missed her father, the lessons they used to share, the books he'd given her to read. She sidled toward the platform. John Guilford patted the high stool beside him, and she climbed up on it gingerly. Her feet dangled in the air, and she giggled nervously, steadying herself on the edge of the table. He brought another stool and sat beside her, picking up his quill.

"Do you know anything about the constellations?" he asked.

Laura wrinkled her nose. "I know some people believe the stars influence your life by their positions at your birth. But that's a wicked belief. It denies the power of God."

"'And God said, let there be lights in the firmament of the heaven to divide the day from the night, and let them be for signs, and for seasons, and for days and years,'" the man beside her quoted.

Genesis too? Laura thought, irked at the way he showed off his knowledge. "What has that got to do with it?"

"Who do you think put the stars up there? But that is astrology, the study of how the stars influence people. This is an astronomy lesson. Astronomy helps us organize the skies."

Laura looked out at the masses of twinkling stars that surrounded them. "How could you ever begin to organize all that?"

"I'll show you. Here." He took a clean sheet of parchment and made seven dots with his quill, connecting them with lines. "This is Ursa Major. The Great Bear."

"It doesn't look a bit like a bear."

"It helps if you squint a bit. Now look out there." He pointed to the sky. "Can you see the same shape in those seven stars, with the four bright ones making a box?" She nodded. "Good." He drew a curving line downward from the bear's head, or what Laura thought would be the head if it looked like a bear. "Follow this same line in the sky and you come to Arcturus."

"Arcturus? Why, that's in the Bible!"

"Job thirty-eight, verse thirty-two. 'Canst thou bring forth Mazzaroth in his season'—"

"'Or canst thou guide Arcturus with his sons?'" Laura finished with him.

"It's the same star that Job saw," he told her.

"Fancy that." Laura stared up in wonder. "The very same star!"

"The stars in Ursa Major are Alkaid, Mizar, Alioth, Megrez, Phad, Merak, and Dubhe." He wrote the names on the sketch next to the dots he'd made, and Laura struggled to repeat them. "They're Arabic," he went on. "The Arabs were the first astronomers. Now if we draw a line from Merak to Dubhe and extend it, we come to Polaris, which is in Ursa Minor. The Little Bear." He drew that as well, then pointed to show her where to find it in the sky.

"It is just the same shape as the big one," she said in surprise. "Only upside-down."

He nodded. "Polaris is also called the North Star, or Pole Star. It is always in the northern sky. Wait, I'll show you something." He reached into his girdle and pulled out a needle, then reached for the cup of milk she'd brought him. "Here," he said, offering her the needle. "Drop it in."

Puzzled, Laura let the needle fall onto the surface of the liquid. It floated for a moment, quivered, then turned of its own accord until the tip pointed away from her, out through the dome. "North," he said over her shoulder. "Try it again."

She plucked it from the milk and dropped it once more, this time deliberately placing it crosswise. It corrected itself with a tiny shudder and pointed in the same direction as before.

Laura looked at him, wide-eyed. "What makes it do that?"

"No one is certain. Not any needle will do it. You have to touch it to a kind of rock called a lodestone first. But once you do, it will always point to Polaris, the Pole Star."

"Why is it called the Pole Star?"

He grabbed the orange from the tray she'd brought and poked it through with his quill. "Say this orange is the earth."

"But it's round," she objected.

"The earth is round," he said impatiently. "Even the ancients knew that much. Look at what Virgil wrote: 'We sail out of the harbor, and the countries and cities recede.'"

Laura looked at the huge books that lined the far wall. "Is that what you've got up here? Virgil and Plato and such?"

"What did you think they were, sorcerers' manuals?" Fortunately he did not notice her blushing again. "Now, the earth turns on an axis, like this." He twirled the quill, holding it by its two ends, and the orange spun around. "These two points on the top and bottom, where the quill is, stay in the same place while it turns. The one on top is the North Pole, and this one is the South Pole."

"Is there really a thing like a quill stuck through it?" Laura asked dubiously.

"There may be. Who knows?"

She contemplated the spinning fruit. "If the world is going round and round like that, why don't I feel it?"

"Because the earth is so big. Huge. But it does go around, once every day. And at the same time, it is spinning around the sun."

"The sun goes around the earth." Laura was quite certain of that. "You can see it does so. It's perfectly clear."

"That's what Ptolemy thought too. Here, look." He was sketching again. "Earth at the center of the universe, and then the sun and the moon, and all of the planets. But when you watch the way the stars behave, you see it can't be that way. It doesn't make sense." He crumpled up the page, tossing it aside, and began a new drawing. "But this—now look at this! Sun in the center. Then Mercury, then Venus. Then earth, with the moon turning around us, while we turn. The moon goes around the earth, but everything else goes around the sun."

Laura shrugged, already lost. "Well, it's not as though it makes any difference."

He stared at her. "It makes all the difference in the universe. It puts us in a different place."

"It certainly does not," she declared. "It puts us right here."

"No, no, no!" He pounded his fist on the table. Laura blinked. She had never seen anyone get so agitated over such an irrelevant question. "Don't you see, it's all a matter of what's at the center. It's—it's an entirely new way of looking at the earth and man—" He saw her total bewilderment and sighed. "It takes a long time to explain it all. But believe me, it matters. If you want to learn more, you could come with me to Hatfield House when I give Elizabeth her lessons. It isn't far. Just five miles due north, right under Polaris."

"I don't think Thomas would like that."

At her mention of his brother, a veil seemed to drop over his blue eyes. "I don't suppose he would. Well. When is your birthday, Laura Darby?"

"Just two weeks hence. The twenty-fifth of May."

"I'll be damned. You were born under the sign of Gemini,

the twins. There, you can see them up in the sky together, in a line out from Megrez and Merak. Castor and Pollux, the twins."

"I told you, I don't put any stock in that stuff," Laura said primly, then paused. "What would it mean if I did?"

"I don't know. I told you, I'm not an astrologer." He was staring at her. "I've never in my life seen anyone with eyes the color of yours. They're gold, aren't they? Autumn gold, to go with your oak-leaf hair."

"I have to go." Discomfited by his sudden intense scrutiny, Laura hopped down from the stool. The toe of her boot caught on the bottom rung, and she nearly landed on her nose. Just in time John Guilford reached out and caught her, one hand clutching her shoulder, the other brushing her breast.

He drew her to her feet. Laura's skin was tingling. She was quite steady now, but still he had not moved his hands. They stood motionless, the velvet sky arching above them, and for an instant Laura imagined she could feel the earth spinning, very slowly, beneath her feet.

John Guilford lowered his head, bending down, his mouth coming closer and closer to hers.

Laura wrenched free of his grasp, leaping down from the platform and out the door.

Polly looked up from the kitchen table as her mistress rushed headlong down the servants' stair. "That took ye long enough, missy," she said curiously.

"Yes," said Laura, and blushed at the breathless way the word came out. "Yes, it did."

Chapter 6

Thomas returned to Guilford Hall the following evening. Laura had been watching for his carriage from her window in the west tower, anxious and fidgety. An old adage—"Out of sight, out of mind"—had been running through her head all day, along with the memory of how John Guilford had stared at her up in his observatory. She was sure it was only Thomas's long absence, and her loneliness, that made her think of John. When at long last she glimpsed the carriage, she hurried down to meet Thomas in the front hall.

Theodore had taken his master's hat and was brushing the dust of the road from Thomas's traveling clothes. "Finish that in the yards, Theo," Thomas said brusquely, shrugging the cloak off as Laura came toward them. He held out his arms. "How unspeakably delightful to be welcomed home by you, my dear." Laura slipped her hands into his, and he kissed her forehead. "Did you miss me?"

"If I did, I shouldn't tell you," she said pertly, eyes sparkling. "It was very naughty of you to run off without bidding me *adieu.*"

He chuckled. "I see I must be more careful whom I invite to my *soirées;* you've become as flirtatious as the Marchioness of Salister. An urgent bit of business came up. Forgive me, please." He rubbed her hands in his and suddenly frowned. "Your fingers are chapped."

"I've had to help Polly," Laura explained. "Poor thing, she fell off a stool in the kitchens and turned her ankle."

"Help her with what?" he asked angrily.

"Why, with the cooking and cleaning."

"Dammit, Laura, I expressly told you—"

"Thomas, she is hurt!"

"She's a shirker, and she always has been."

"That's not so! I was right beside her when she fell; she's been in awful pain. I wanted to fetch the doctor, but she wouldn't let me."

"I should hope not. A fine waste of gold that would be."

Laura sighed. This homecoming was not going at all as she'd imagined. "Don't let's quarrel, Thomas, please. I don't mean to interfere with the way you run the house, honestly I don't—"

"Then don't," he snapped, ignoring her pleading gaze and marching off to the east wing. "It had better not happen again!" he shouted over his shoulder.

Drat, thought Laura, now he is in a temper. He must have had a troublesome trip. It was lucky she hadn't mentioned her visit to the domed room; he likely would have bitten off her head.

Well, there was nothing she could do about it now. Except—she looked down at her plain black dress. She could put on the red gown he'd given her to try and cheer him. He didn't like to see women in black . . .

For an instant, thinking of the fancy garment, she felt like a traitor to her father's beliefs. Then she remembered that Charles Darby had arranged for her to marry Thomas. He would not mind the red dress if he knew she only wore it to make Thomas happy.

She went upstairs to change.

Precisely at eight Polly hobbled out of the kitchens carrying the gold-crusted oyster pie she had prepared that afternoon under Laura's direction. She withdrew nervously, leaving Laura to watch as Thomas parted the crust with two forks. A cloud of fragrant steam poured out. He took a bite.

"You've been teaching Polly to cook," he said, swallowing.

Laura nodded timidly. "She's not hopeless or dim-witted, Thomas, you know. You just have to give her a kind word, a compliment now and then. And—" She was about to mention his hitting the cook, but he'd laid down his knife and fork and was glaring at her, gray eyes turned milky white.

"I like my household run according to certain rules, Laura. Rules which you seem determined to flout."

"I don't mean to displease you," she whispered, tears stinging her eyes. He hadn't even mentioned the gown she'd put on.

Her misery must have made him relent, for he smiled down the length of the table. "Dear Laura. There's no need for us to quarrel, so long as you do things my way." His cold eyes softened. "How lovely you look tonight. You make me very glad indeed of the news I have for you."

How quickly his moods could change! Laura smiled through her tears. "What news is that, Thomas?"

"I have set the date for our wedding. It is all arranged for the twenty-third of May."

Laura stared.

"The invitations have already gone out," he went on, "and I've ordered the food and wine, and Charlotte will be here tomorrow to help me choose your gown. Is something wrong?"

"I thought you said I would have time to consider your offer of marriage," Laura said, bewildered. "Time to get to know you better—"

"You said you were fond of me. I took you at your word." Laura still could not find her tongue. "You let me kiss you," he said accusingly.

She'd let his brother kiss her too, Laura wanted to tell him, but that hardly meant she was ready to marry *him* in a fortnight either! She sat back in her chair, feeling dazed, dizzy; her world was an orange stuck through with a quill, spinning out of control . . .

"Christ." He pushed his food away. "Christ, now I have made you unhappy. And that is the last thing on earth I would ever want to do."

Laura looked up at him. His gray eyes were clouded with concern. "I don't—it is not that I am unhappy," she faltered. "It is only that I thought I would have more time."

"And I thought I could give you more time, Laura. But now I find I can't."

"Why not?"

"The truth is—this is not something I am proud of." He frowned, not meeting her eyes. "The truth is that I cannot trust myself to go on living with you in this house, day after day, unless we are married. I am so much in love with you. And a man . . . a man has certain urges, Laura, strong ones. I know you cannot understand exactly what I am saying. But I am terribly afraid that unless we are wed, and soon, I will lose control." He hunched over the table, face buried in his hands. "God, Laura, if that happened—I could never forgive myself."

"Oh, Thomas." Laura was awed by this demonstration of the power she held over him, and by the strength of his love for her, that had brought them to this pass. Lose control— why, he meant kiss her the way John had, she supposed. Put his hands on her breasts. She was filled with pity for him as he sat there sobbing, and with something more—a warm inner glow she had not experienced since her father's death. *He needed her.* That warmth, that glow, that was love, wasn't it? It had to be.

He raised his head, dabbing at his eyes with his napkin. "I'm sorry, Laura," he said hoarsely, "I hate for you to see me this way."

"Please don't say you are sorry. You must never be ashamed to show your true emotions."

He smiled wanly. "How wise you are for one so young! But I am spoiling our meal. I'll withdraw to my rooms."

"No, Thomas." She stood up quickly. "I'll go to mine. You need to eat; I can tell you have had a wretched week. We can talk more about this tomorrow, when you are rested."

His dove-gray eyes shone with tears. "What a perfect wife you will make me, Laura."

"I hope so, Thomas. Good night."

"Good night, my heart." He blew her a kiss from his fingertips.

Laura hugged herself tightly all the way up to her bedchamber. What a marvelous feeling it was, this being in love. Who would ever believe it could happen so quickly? She unwound the braids she'd pinned at the nape of her neck and brushed out the long, thick waves with her mother's brush. She *would* marry him in two weeks, she decided, her heart aglow. Two weeks and she would be Lady Guilford... Thomas's wife.

Guilford Hall would not be his house then; it would be their house. She could make changes in the way it was run; she'd hire Polly more help for the housework, let her bake bread and do the rest of the cooking herself. Thomas couldn't object once they were married; they'd be partners then.

Someone rapped at the door. Thomas, she thought, smiling, come to apologize again. She ran to throw open the door to him, her unbound hair hanging to her knees—

John Guilford stood on the threshold. His expression as the door flew open was quite extraordinary; his eyes were more wolflike than ever, only not fierce but lean and hungry and wild.

"Oh," said Laura, and hoped her disappointment was not too palpable. "I expected your brother." He said nothing, just looked at her with those hungry eyes until she thought that if she'd been a bone, she would have been devoured. The notion made her laugh. "Was there something you wanted?"

He shook himself, just like a wolf. "I—I was on my way to Hatfield House—"

"Yes?"

"I—" He reached under his cloak. "Plato." He thrust the book at her. "I said I would bring it."

"Well, thank you very much." Laura took the heavy book in both hands and went to kick the door closed. He didn't move. "Is something amiss?"

"You—are shining. Like a star."

"Am I?" Laura laughed, unable to resist sharing her news with him. "I am very happy. Thomas has set a date for our wedding. The twenty-third of May."

"The twenty-third of—" He glanced back into the corridor and then, to her astonishment, pushed past her into her room and shut the door. "This is my fault," he said with a muttered curse.

"Your fault? Your *fault?*" Laura echoed, dumbfounded.

"Aye. Englefield must have told him that Cecil was filing a motion to reopen the inquiry."

"I'm sure I haven't the foggiest notion what you are talking about," said Laura, trying to move around him to the door. The hungry-wolf look was gone from his eyes; he was angry instead.

"Did my brother happen to mention why he wants to wed you so soon?" John demanded.

She blushed and nodded. "Because he is so much in love with me. Because he cannot trust himself with me until we are—"

"That son of a bitch!"

Laura recoiled from the wrath in his voice. "You've no right to call him names!"

"By God, I do. Listen to me, Laura Darby, and listen well. I had a friend of mine, Sir William Cecil, look up the record of the inquiry into your wardship. According to the papers filed in the Court of Wards, you are fourteen years old."

"Everyone is always getting my age confused," Laura told him crossly. "I suppose because I am so short—"

He caught her wrists and shook her. "I said listen! You aren't fourteen, you're sixteen. And on May twenty-fifth, you'll be seventeen years old. At seventeen you pass out of wardship. Once you turn seventeen, you're free to choose your husband for yourself. Thomas can't make you marry him."

"He isn't *making* me marry him," Laura said indignantly.

"No? Then explain to me the coincidence of the date—and why he is rushing you into this three days after I had Cecil file that motion asking for a new court of inquiry to be held concerning your age!"

Laura yanked herself free of his hands, her gold eyes blazing. "I'd like to know what gives you the right to go about having motions filed, whatever that means, on the matter of my age or anything else concerning me!"

"The fact that I know my brother," John Guilford said grimly.

"Not very well you don't! For your information, this marriage was all arranged a long time ago between Thomas and my father!"

"Good God!" His face had gone stark white. "He told you that?"

"It is true! He has an agreement signed by my father!"

"Have you seen it?" Laura opened her mouth to say yes, then stopped. "Have you seen that agreement, Laura Darby?" he repeated harshly.

"No . . . but that is only because Thomas had to go away. And because he wanted to wait for me to fall in love with him of my own accord!"

"For Christ's sake, girl, don't be such a bloody fool! Do you honestly believe your father would have betrothed you to a man like Thomas?"

"If you mean because he is Catholic—"

"Catholic?" Those chilly wolf's eyes raked her in disbelief. Then he laughed. "Ask to see that agreement," he told her. "If he has such a thing, then go on and marry him—and I'll do a jig for the guests, stark naked, on your wedding day."

John Guilford was insane.

Laura was more certain of that than ever as she watched him stalk out, slamming the door so hard that the sturdy oak quivered. He was a liar and a madman; she had proof of it now. And she intended to march straight to Thomas and tell him: if he wanted to marry her, his brother was not to be readmitted into this house, not ever again! Not even stopping to put down the book of Plato, she hurried down to the banqueting hall.

The big room was deserted, the candles extinguished. She peeked into the kitchen, but saw no sign of Polly. She checked for Thomas in his study and in the receiving room, but they were empty too.

He must have gone to his bedchamber. Ordinarily Laura would not have gone up into the east tower to look for him; he had told her not to wander about. But this was no ordinary situation, as she was sure Thomas would understand once he learned what his brother had done. Laura ran up the front staircase and turned right instead of left, passing through the big oak door there.

The furnishings here were even more sumptuous than in the west wing. The corridors were covered with thick Persian carpets; on the walls hung tapestries depicting characters from Greek myths. A pall of silence hung in the air as she hurried along, peeking into the rooms she passed. Those on the first storey were vacant; she found a stairway and rushed up to check the second, the lush carpets swallowing the sound of her footsteps. At the top she paused for a moment, catching her breath.

From behind a door at the end of the hallway she heard a sudden loud, long groan of pain. "Thomas?" she called, frightened by the noise. The only answer was a fearful scream. "Thomas? Who's there?" She ran to the door and threw it open in terror, then stopped on the threshold, staring at the scene within.

In the center of the room was a bed. Through its gauzy hangings Laura could see Theodore facing her, crouching naked on his hands and knees. Behind him knelt Thomas, also naked, his hands on Theodore's waist, his hips pushing at Theo's raised buttocks again and again. Theodore was the one screaming; his fists were clutching at the bedclothes. Thomas was silent, eyes clenched, mouth set in a tight smile.

Horses. It was just like the two horses Laura had seen in the field, with the one on the bottom screaming to get away. But that was what a man did to a woman, Polly had told her, not a man to another man. She thought of a verse from Leviticus that she had read dozens of times but never understood: *Thou shalt not lie with mankind as with womankind . . .*

The bed was rocking wildly with the force of Thomas's thrusts. Teeth bared, Theo screamed again, throwing back his head—

Thomas must have felt Theodore's start of surprise, for he looked up too. His gaze, narrowed and dove gray, met Laura's, and for a moment he froze. The bed slowly ceased rocking. Theodore reached up and rubbed a bit of spittle from the corner of his mouth with the back of his hand.

At last Thomas reached for the linen sheet and wound it around his waist. Then he got up from the bed, pushing through the hangings, and very calmly said, "Laura, my dear. Was there something you wanted?"

"What are you doing?" she whispered.

"Wrestling, of course. Wrestling like the ancient Greeks. I always like a bit of exercise before I retire."

From Theodore, on the bed, came a high, reedy laugh. "Why don't you tell her the truth, Thomas?"

"But that is the truth. Isn't it, Theodore?" Thomas's voice had an edge like steel.

"Damn you to hell." Laura didn't know whether Theo meant this for her or for Thomas. Not even bothering to cover his naked body, he got up from the bed, shoved Laura aside, and stalked out of the room.

"Did he hurt you, my dear?" Thomas took a step toward her, warm and solicitous. Laura backed away, clutching Plato to her chest.

"Where is the agreement you made with my father?" she asked, voice trembling.

"I haven't got it here," he said smoothly. "It's in London. Part of the official record of your wardship, filed with the court." Laura watched him with eyes that seemed newly opened. Why had she never noticed the little twist to his mouth when he spoke? He looked like one of the satyrs from the hallway tapestries, wrapped in the sheet. She felt cold suddenly, cold and frightened, and she did not believe him any more now than she had when he'd told her he and Theo were wrestling.

"If the agreement is in London," she whispered, "then why doesn't John know about it? His friend Cecil looked at the court records."

His body went rigid. Laura saw his nostrils flare, and a thin blue vein pulsed at his temple as his eyes changed from dove gray to milk white. "John," he said, and the name was a snarl. "I might have known. So he put you up to this."

"He says there isn't any such agreement with my father," Laura said bravely, then screamed as his heavy fist came flying straight at her head. She raised up the book, warding off the blow, but its force still sent her reeling back against the wall.

"I told you to stay away from him." He was advancing on her.

"He's right, isn't he?" Laura said with sudden conviction. "You lied to me. And I am not going to marry you, not in two weeks or ever." She crept toward the door.

"Where are you going, Laura?" he asked, his voice a silken purr.

"Home. Home to Howarth Manor. Humphrey never would have sold you my wardship if he knew the sort of man you are."

He laughed. "You pathetic innocent. I haven't got any agreement signed by your father. I have got one signed by Humphrey, though. We worked all this out between us months ago, when he first came to me and told me your father was a heretic." Laura stopped moving, the blood draining from her face. "That's right, Laura," he told her, smiling. "I turned your father in to the queen and Bishop Bonner. And you will marry me on the twenty-third. Because if you don't, you'll spend the day tied to a stake on Smithfield Plain."

"You devil," Laura whispered.

Thomas Guilford shrugged, taking another step toward her. "Those are your only choices, my dear. Marry me—or burn."

He was wrong; she had one more choice. Laura dove for the door and ran.

Down the stairs she flew, through the empty corridors, while he came after her, cursing the sheet he wore as it slowed him down. Laura wanted to retch, to scream as the horror of what he had told her sunk in. But she dared not stop; he was narrowing the gap between them. She could hear his loud, ragged breaths as she slipped through the oak door to the staircase in the front entranceway.

He followed, bellowing for Theo. Laura glanced down and saw the heavy book John had given her, which she still held tight to her breasts. She reached the foot of the stairs, whirled around, and hurled the heavy volume as hard as she could, straight at Thomas's face. He let out a startled oath, grabbed for the railing, and then, as he missed a step, tumbled headfirst toward her through the air.

Laura did not stop to see him land. She dashed across the

marble floor, yanked open the front doors, and escaped into the night.

Panting, she fled across the courtyard, boots ringing on the bricks, and slipped sideways between the bars of the iron gates. At the foot of the hill was the road back to Howarth Manor. She thought of Humphrey and shuddered. Oh, God, Thomas was right; she could not go there.

Beyond the road lay the forest, dark and foreboding. She stopped running abruptly. She had nowhere to go, she realized. There was not a single soul in the world she could trust. The night sky stretched out above her like a thick black cloak of despair...

But not quite black. As she looked up she saw the sparkling outline of Ursa Major, the Great Bear, and recognizing the constellation, she felt as though she was greeting some long-lost friend. Of course! John Guilford had warned her about Thomas. He had helped her; she could trust him. And he was at Hatfield House tonight. *It isn't far,* he'd said. *Just five miles due north, right under Polaris...*

The Pole Star glittered, beckoning the way to safety.

It was her only hope.

Laura caught up her skirts and ran.

Chapter 7

Laura had only the vaguest notion of how far five miles might be. She knew it was a fifth of the distance from Howarth Manor to London, and so by division figured one could travel that far in a carriage in about an hour. But she had never walked five miles that she could recall. And she surely hadn't walked that far alone, at night, through the Hertfordshire woods.

Robbers roamed this forest, she knew—desperate men without mercy or honor. And there were bears and wolves—what else might there be? Wild boar that could run you through with their tusks. Snakes. Toads and spiders. At the edge of the trees she paused, nearly losing her courage. But the memory of the choice Thomas had offered forced her on.

So Humphrey had told Thomas about her father. And Thomas had delivered Charles Darby to his death, to gain hold of her inheritance. Who would ever have thought Humphrey could do anything so evil? And oh, God, how had she been so blind as to believe she was in love with her guardian?

Something soft and black brushed her cheek, and she thrust it away in terror. A pine branch, nothing more. When her heart stopped pounding she moved on, trying to forget the strange scene she had stumbled upon in the bedchamber. Thomas and Theodore... how horrible they had looked, panting, sweating, screaming. If that is what intercourse is like, she thought, then I want no part of it, ever, not with anyone.

Two men making love to each other. That must be what John had meant when he said her father would never have betrothed her to a man like his brother. And that was why Theo hated her so much: he was in love with Thomas; he'd been jealous of her.

Wind moaned through the trees, rustling the leaves with a sound like raindrops. She blundered into a fallen log and stumbled, losing her breath. How much movement there was in the woods, under cover of darkness! Her heart pounded as she heard a crash in the distance. A bear? Or Thomas coming after her? Surely he would not pursue her all this way; surely marrying her could not be so important to him. Then she remembered—he'd thought it worth turning her father in to be killed. Clutching up her skirts, she pressed on.

That night seemed to last forever. The five miles might have been fifty, so slowly did she progress, picking her way through the tangled trees and undergrowth, terrified that at any moment she would hear Thomas at her heels. Only the comforting sight of the Pole Star gave her strength to keep moving; it sparkled high above her, a distant jewel.

At long last, the dawn came. Whole hosts of thrushes and sparrows burst into song around her, driving away the shadowy gloom. The western sky glimmered gold and red through the leafy branches; Laura had never in all her life been so glad to see the sun. A brook burbled across her path, and she knelt and drank; the water was cool and sweet, more bracing than wine.

The trees parted up ahead, and she glimpsed a wide swath of lush green meadow, a high stone wall, and beyond that a long, low-slung gray building. Hatfield House, she thought, sighing in relief. It has to be! Forgetting her weariness, she caught up her mud-splashed skirts and ran for refuge. She could see smoke curling up from the brick chimneys, and from the side of the gatehouse, still draped in shadow, she heard the high whinny of a horse. "Hello!" she cried, heading toward the sound. "Good morning! Can you let me inside?"

"I'm afraid that's impossible, Laura, my dear," said Thomas Guilford, not smiling, sitting tall atop a big bay horse.

Laura skidded to a stop in the dew-slick grass, staring in disbelief. "How—"

"How did I know you would be coming here? You mentioned my brother. And Theo tells me you and John are friendlier with one another than I had imagined. As demonstrated by the kiss John gave you in the rose garden."

"What are you going to do?" Laura whispered.

"Take you home, my dear." He dug his knees into the bay's flanks, fingers curling around the handle of his crop. "Shall we go?"

"No," said Laura, and then screamed it as he spurred

toward her. "No! I won't come with you! Murderer! No!"
Again she turned and ran, back across the meadow, the
sound of hooves thundering in her head. She heard a crackling hiss and cried out as the whip licked her shoulder like a
tongue of flame. She stumbled and saw Thomas's face as she
fell; he was smiling now, the crop raised above his head.

"I can hound you all the way there if you like." The whip
lashed out again.

"No—" Laura rolled herself into a tight ball on the grass,
hands over her face. "I won't go with you!"

He leaned down from the saddle, grasping her arm and
wrenching her into the air. She screamed with all her might
as he slung her over the saddle in front of him; his grip was
hard as stone. He clapped a gloved hand over her face.
Laura could not move, could not breathe; below, she saw the
meadow grass whirling in front of her eyes, the lush green
going black—

And then she dreamed she heard a cool, imperious female voice call out, "Let her go!"

But she could not have dreamed the voice, for Thomas
answered it, growling, "Go to hell."

"I order you to release her," the voice said again.

Thomas laughed, ready to spur the horse away.

"I wouldn't." Now there was a tiny hint of pique in the
woman's tone. "Not if you value your life. Look up there."

Laura heard Thomas's indrawn breath, felt the sudden
slackening of his grasp, and raised her head. The top of the
wall surrounding Hatfield House was lined with archers,
their crossbows trained straight at Thomas's cloak. "One signal from me," the woman went on, "and you, Thomas Guilford, are a dead man."

"I'm the girl's legal guardian," Thomas barked. "I can do
with her what I will."

"If you intend to argue law, Guilford," another voice, this
one male, called, "I should be careful. She's rather good."

"Cecil," Thomas spat. "You son of a bitch. You've no
grounds to interfere."

"I beg your pardon, I do. There's reason to believe you
perpetrated a fraud in gaining the wardship. Some question
as to her age—"

"Prove it," Thomas challenged.

"Your brother is in London," the woman said crisply, "at-
tempting to do so now. Master Guilford, I am finding this
conversation increasingly tiresome. My ennui will likely re-

sult in an arrow in your back. Now let the girl go."

Laura gasped as she was shoved abruptly to the ground. She landed in a heap of loose hair and red silk, and looked up to see Thomas glaring at her venomously. "I'll be back," he swore, and she knew from the rage in his voice that he meant it. He gouged his spurs into the horse with vicious force and galloped away.

Slowly Laura turned to see her saviors. Standing not five feet from her was a middle-aged man, tall and dapper, with a pointed gray beard and dark eyes circled with weary rings. Beside him was a woman, also tall but very thin, in her mid-twenties, with red hair coiled round her head, a determined mouth, and luminous black eyes.

The woman smiled. "How do you do?"

The man next to her snorted. "There's a silly question, Bess; 'tis plain the poor thing's frightened to death." He stepped forward and helped Laura gently to her feet. "You can stop shaking, Mistress Darby. No one will hurt you now."

"How do you know who I am?" Laura whispered.

"From John," said the woman. "I've learned more about you in the past few weeks than I have of astronomy."

Laura looked again at the woman's bright red hair, those coal-black eyes. "Are you—the Princess Elizabeth?"

"Sometimes," she said with a laugh. "At the moment, though, I am only a lady. My sister is in the process of trying to prove yet again that I'm not my father's daughter."

"Which anyone who looks at her," the man put in, "can see is absurd."

"Thank you, sweet William," said the princess. "Mistress Darby, Sir William Cecil."

Laura dropped in a curtsy. So it had been the Princess Elizabeth who saved her from Thomas—the same woman she'd chided her father for praying for! "I'm most grateful, milady," she stammered.

Elizabeth Tudor cocked her head. "Are you? Well, I am rather hungry. Shall we go in? It must be nearly time for Mass."

Laura was trembling as Sir William Cecil and the Lady Elizabeth led her into Hatfield House. Clearly John Guilford hadn't told her rescuers everything about her, not if they were taking her to hear the Mass. Out of the frying pan and into the fire, she thought—and then recoiled at the unfortunate choice of metaphor. If she did not participate in the service, they would know she was a heretic!

They passed through a reception hall that was even more scantily furnished than Howarth Manor, then up a flight of stairs. In a doorway on the second storey stood two figures, one a stout older man in the queen's white-and-green livery, the other, no older than Elizabeth, in the robes of a priest. "You're late, milady," the priest called when he saw them.

"We were saving a soul," she told him gravely. "Father Burton, Sir Nicholas Throckmorton, this is Mistress Laura Darby, that John Guilford was telling us of."

"Charmed, I'm sure," said the knight.

"My pleasure," said the priest.

"How do you do?" Laura whispered. There was only one solution. She would have to pretend to faint.

"Let's go in, shall we?" said Cecil. Heart pounding, Laura followed Elizabeth through the chapel door. If she grew any more nervous, she would not have to pretend.

"Here we are!" Elizabeth announced. Laura took one quick glance around before holding her breath and, hoping she looked convincing, swaying on her feet.

It wasn't a chapel at all, she saw, so surprised that she stood upright again. It was a bedchamber of a good size, as simply furnished as the rest of the house they'd passed through. One entire wall was taken up by a huge fireplace, with a motto carved above the mantel in bold script: *Video et tacit.* I watch and am silent, Laura translated.

"Mine," said Elizabeth, seeing where her guest was staring. "Kate Ashley says I chose it when I was five, though I can't remember. It's proven singularly appropriate." She crossed the room in long strides, and Laura saw that a table in one corner of the room had been set for a meal. Elizabeth plopped down into a chair Cecil held for her; Sir Nicholas Throckmorton held another out for Laura, and she sat, nervously. Elizabeth uncovered a platter as the two men joined them. "Oh, goody, rashers and eggs. Bless you, Sir William, for bringing bacon. Go on, Father Burton; we'll save some for you." She scooped a hearty helping onto her plate. Father Burton pulled a prayer book out of the sleeve of his cassock and began to recite in Latin:

"In the name of the Father, and of the Son, and of the Holy Ghost—"

Elizabeth passed the eggs to Laura and began to eat.

Laura stared at her hostess in shock. The priest went on reading the Mass. "Toast, Mistress Darby?" William Cecil asked.

"Here, you must try some of this berry jam," Elizabeth suggested, and noticed Laura's scandalized expression. "Oh, dear, I ought to have explained. By order of the queen my sister, I'm to hear a Mass every six hours. Loyal subject that I am, that's exactly what I do. Hear it, I mean. Father Burton is most obliging." The priest acknowledged the compliment with a smile and read on.

"Isn't that—" Laura set down the jam jar she was handed. "Isn't that dishonest?"

"How so?" Nicholas Throckmorton swallowed a mouthful of bacon. "She is carrying out the queen's decree to the letter."

"The letter, aye, but not the spirit!"

Elizabeth Tudor sighed. "There are times in this life when one must resort to stratagem. Sir William suggested this compromise. When Mary asks Father Burton has he said Mass, he can say yes. When she asks me have I heard it, I can say yes too. And neither of us has to wind up in the Tower of London." She frowned at her breakfast. "She sent me there once, you know, when Tom Wyatt rebelled. Three months I spent, in the same room my mother lived in before my father had her beheaded. I would prefer anything—*anything*—to going back there."

Laura remembered then that the princess, like her, had lost a parent to a horrible death: Anne Boleyn, her mother, had been executed by Henry the Eighth for adultery. Still, if the princess was a Protestant, she ought to have the courage of her convictions! "My father thought his faith worth dying for," she said stiffly.

"And I think my country worth living for," was Elizabeth's reply. "If I live long enough, I may yet be queen."

Laura could think of nothing to say to that. The food Cecil had heaped on her plate smelled tantalizing. She cast a last anxious glance at Father Burton and began to eat.

The meal and the Mass concluded at nearly the same time. The priest closed his missal and pulled a chair up to the table. Cecil poured himself another tankard of ale. "We must make some plans, Laura Darby," he said then. "Plans for your future."

"I haven't got much of a future at the moment, I'm afraid."

"Don't give up yet," said Nicholas Throckmorton. "John may well be successful at getting your wardship inquiry opened up again."

"Though I'd feel better about his chances," Elizabeth put in, "if he didn't have to apply to Francis Englefield. From what I hear, Mistress Darby, you made yourself a powerful enemy at Thomas Guilford's last entertainment."

Laura shuddered, remembering her encounter with the Master of the Court of Wards. "Thomas is my legal guardian," she said miserably. "I am in his power completely until I am seventeen."

"But that's only a fortnight away," Cecil pointed out.

Laura stared at her plate. "He said if I didn't wed him, he'd see me burned at the stake. He knows I'm a heretic." Her eyes filled with tears. "'Twas he that informed on my father. Oh, God, I cannot marry him!"

Sir William Cecil was rubbing his beard. "Well, there are two sides to that, you know. It's as much against the law to marry a heretic as to be one. If you were to confess—"

"Excuse me, Sir William." The princess's voice was gravely bemused. "That might take care of Thomas Guilford, but Laura would still wind up burned."

"Ah. Quite right. So that won't do. Well, any other ideas?"

There was a moment's silence. Father Burton chewed bread sopped in egg yolk and swallowed. "Stall," he suggested. "Keep her here until she turns seventeen."

"Perfect!" cried Elizabeth.

"So it is." Cecil looked at Laura. "My dear, what do you say?"

To Laura's intense embarrassment, she let out an enormous yawn. She clapped her hand over her mouth in horror. Elizabeth laughed. "How thoughtless of us to keep you sitting here after all you've been through! We can discuss all this later, when you are rested. Come along, I'll show you to your bed."

Laura had never felt so exhausted in her entire life. She thanked Cecil and Throckmorton and the priest between more flurried yawns, then started to follow Elizabeth out of the room. As she passed the bedchamber window she paused, arrested by a blaze of bright sunlight glinting on a distant hilltop. "What is that?" she asked.

"Why, Guilford Hall," the princess said. "I can see it from here whenever 'tis sunny, or when the moon shines, because of the dome. I like to think of John in there working, looking at his stars."

Laura shivered. Suddenly the hilltop did not seem so distant. Thomas was there now, plotting and scheming to get her back again...

Elizabeth took her arm and steered her gently into the corridor. "Don't worry," she said gently. "Hatfield House has been my safe haven for years now; I reckon it can stand you in good stead for a mere fortnight."

"Milady," Laura said around another yawn, as they entered a bedchamber.

"Call me Elizabeth," said the princess, helping her off with her boots, turning down the covers on the bed.

"Milady Elizabeth," Laura mumbled sleepily. "Why are you going to so much trouble for me?"

Elizabeth eased her out of her red gown and into the bed. "Because John Guilford would want me to."

Because John Guilford would want her to. Laura thought of his slow, hot kiss in the gardens, the touch of his hand at her breast, and smiled as she fell asleep.

In the days that followed, Laura learned what life was like in the household of a princess—a dishonored princess, that is, for Queen Mary was only too aware of her half sister's potential to serve as a catalyst for subjects dissatisfied with Mary's reign. In the scant years since Mary had assumed the crown there had been half a dozen attempts to depose her in favor of Elizabeth. The most widespread had been organized by Tom Wyatt, son of the poet who had been Elizabeth's mother's lifelong friend; when it failed, Wyatt had ended up beheaded, and Elizabeth in the Tower of London.

Neither Mary nor her two closest advisors, Cardinal Archbishop Reginald Pole and Bishop Edmund Bonner of London, had ever been able to prove any direct complicity by Elizabeth in the uprisings—the sole reason, Elizabeth told Laura ruefully, that she still bore her head. They had their suspicions, though, and if the force of public opinion prevented the queen from keeping her sister in prison, that opinion could not prevent the myriad meannesses Mary used to try to break Elizabeth's spirit. By her order Hatfield House was run on a budget so meager that it bordered on poverty. Elizabeth had only a handful of attendants of her own choosing; she preferred that to accepting the servants Mary sent her, whom she suspected of being spies.

Few of Mary's subjects were willing to risk provoking the queen by showing favor to Elizabeth publicly, but a small, steady stream of anonymous gifts—game birds, fruit, butts of wine—appearing at the gates of the manor gave proof Elizabeth was not forgotten in England. Sir William Cecil was daring—or foolhardy—enough to visit the princess openly; Sir Nicholas Throckmorton came only when the queen sent him with messages.

For companionship Elizabeth relied on her governess, Kate Ashley, a Devonshire woman who had served her for fifteen years, since the princess was ten. And there were always the tutors her sister employed, whom she bullied and cowed with her impressive knowledge of Latin and Greek, Italian, French, Spanish and German. Years of watching and listening had sharpened the princess's ear for mimicry as well as for languages; she tormented the grim doctor Mary assigned to teach her mathematics by repeating everything he said in a perfect reproduction of his slight lisp.

Like the tutors, Laura might have been intimidated by Elizabeth's diamond-sharp intellect, but the princess was no bookworm. She had her father's enormous zest for the pleasures of life. She competed so well at chess and cards that she defeated Cecil with a regularity the knight found infuriating. She played the lute and virginal beautifully, adored hunting, relished good food and wine. But most of all, as Laura was delighted to discover, Elizabeth Tudor loved to dance.

She made a grumbling Sir William bring her minute descriptions of all the latest steps he saw performed at the court; Cecil, who thought dancing a frivolous pastime, was only too glad to relinquish his place as Elizabeth's practicing partner to Laura. They danced together for hours on end in the evenings, while Father Burton plucked out tunes on the princess's virginal, and Cecil, studying the notes he'd brought from London, shouted out, "Now lead with the left foot—now circle—now jump—no, wait, now skip—" Between Father Burton's less than sterling playing and Cecil's garbled instructions, more often than not they all ended up collapsing in laughter before they were done.

Elizabeth was also enamored of fashion, and within the constraints of the miserly allowance sent by her sister she was as vain about her appearance as she could afford to be. "Do you think Protestants ought to dress plainly?" Laura asked her one afternoon, as the princess modeled for her a new gown of Venice lace and green satin.

Elizabeth frowned. "I don't know. There is not much about it in the Scriptures, is there? I mean, if just one of the apostles had been a woman, she certainly would have put a

few words into the Gospel about what Jesus wore." Laura
giggled; sometimes the princess said the strangest things!
"However," she went on, with a sly wink, "I am fortunate
enough to be masquerading as a Roman Catholic. So what
do you think of this gown?"

She had a small chest of jewels that she treasured—"Not
so much for themselves," she told Laura, showing her that
cache, "as because if I ever should have to flee the country
they shall be easier to take with me than the same worth in
gold. Oh, except for this—I should never sell this." She held
up a locket on a golden chain: a "B" pavéed in diamonds,
surrounded by Scottish pearls. "B for Boleyn. It was my
mother's. A gift to her from my father the king."

"Do you remember her?" Laura asked, admiring the
milky pearls.

"A little. I was three when she was beheaded. I
remember . . . how beautiful she was. Beautiful and gay."

Laura watched the handsome locket twist slowly on its
chain, wondering how the fairy-tale marriage of Henry the
Eighth and Anne Boleyn could have turned so quickly to
tragedy. Elizabeth gathered the jewel in her hand and
slipped it back into its velvet pouch. "It is my fault my
mother died," she said matter-of-factly. "Had I been born a
boy, the son my father wanted, he wouldn't have had her
killed."

"That you were born female was the will of God," Laura
pointed out.

"God's punishment, rather, the Catholics say. On my father, for having divorced Mary's mother. 'The Little Bastard,' that's what they used to call me. Cecil says poor Mary
still does." She smiled, seeing Laura's moue of distaste at this
mention of the queen. "You've never met Mary, have you?
Believe me, if you ever do you will pity her too. She is like
a—a sheep, doing whatever Cardinal Pole and Bishop Bonner and King Philip tell her. She doesn't think for herself.
She has no backbone. I feel sorry for her, honestly I do."

"I could never pity her," Laura said fiercely. "Not after
what she did to my father. I shall hate her as long as I live."

"My father had my mother killed," Elizabeth observed.
"Does that mean I ought to have hated him?"

"Didn't you?"

"Good God, no! I loved him with all my soul. Now *there*
was a king!" Her black eyes sparkled with intensity. "Look at
all he did for England, Laura. He broke the pope's hold on

the English people. He played the French off against the Empire, the Empire against the French—he understood power, the power of kingship. He remade the entire world according to his will!" She waved a long, elegant hand. "And now Mary has presented all that to Philip on a platter. You should see how she dotes on that vicious little husband of hers; it would turn your stomach." She closed her jewel box with a snap. "England deserves a better ruler than Mary."

"England," said Laura, unconvinced, "deserves what it gets."

Laura sat in on the princess's lessons each day, though she could make little sense of them; they were too advanced. Elizabeth did notice her new friend listening avidly to her French tutor as he lectured. "Do you speak French?" she asked Laura.

"It is the most peculiar thing," Laura said shyly. "I can understand it when others speak it, and read it perfectly. But when I try to speak it myself, well—" She explained what had happened at Thomas's party with the comtesse de Talboir.

"Oh, your accent cannot be so bad as all that," Elizabeth scoffed, and handed her a book of the *ballades* of Charles d'Orleans. "Read some of this to me."

"'*Je meurs de soif en cousté la fontaine,*'" Laura dutifully read out, and looked up to find the princess biting down on her hand, black eyes sparkling.

"Dear me," she gasped out between giggles, "I am sorry. But it does need work!"

Laura was astonished to find that Elizabeth worked hard at her studies of Catholic theology. "But why, if you don't believe in it?" she asked curiously.

The princess shrugged. "People fear what they don't understand. I intend not to be afraid of anything."

Laura disagreed. She thought she understood Thomas, but she still felt a pang of fear whenever she saw the dome of Guilford Hall from Elizabeth's bedchamber window. And she never got over her discomfort at hearing Father Burton run through the Mass while Elizabeth ate or sewed or went on with whatever she was doing. After a few days she summoned up the courage to ask the priest if he didn't feel he was betraying his faith.

"Faith in what?" he asked.

She cocked her head at the young priest. "In the doctrines

of the Catholic church, of course. According to them, the princess is a heretic."

"Let me ask you a few questions, Laura Darby. Did God create man in his own image?"

"Of course he did."

"And did God create man with a conscience through which to know right and wrong, through which God speaks to him?"

"That is certainly so."

"Well, then," said the priest, "if Elizabeth, listening to her conscience, which is the voice of God, decides she cannot celebrate the Mass, and I, listening to mine, decide I must, which of us hears God truly?"

"It has to be one or the other," Laura told him crossly. "God cannot be saying something totally different to each of you."

Father Burton wagged a finger. "That is where you and I differ in our theology, Laura. Why couldn't he? What right have I to limit God?" He saw her bewildered expression and laid a hand on her shoulder. "My child. Your father gave up his life for his religion because his conscience would not let him do otherwise. In the England I dream of someday seeing, no man or woman would have to choose whether to heed conscience or to die. Queen Mary has shown she is incapable of forging such a nation. I believe that Elizabeth Tudor could. And that is why I am here celebrating the Mass."

John Guilford did not appear at Hatfield House for the princess's Tuesday astronomy lesson. Elizabeth was disappointed. "I look forward to his visits so much!" she told Laura. "He is marvelous company."

"How did you ever come to take lessons from him?" Laura asked, glad Elizabeth had raised him as a topic of conversation. She felt too shy to bring him up herself, though there was much she longed to know about him.

"I kept seeing that big dome shining out my window and could not imagine what it might be. Finally, about three years ago, I sent Kate there with a note. Thomas didn't respond, of course; he was too busy playing up to my sister Mary. But a few nights later John appeared on my doorstep. I invited him in, and we started to talk, and the next thing I knew he was coming two times a week. I want to visit his observatory some day and see his library. From what he tells me, it must be one of the finest in all of England." She looked at Laura. "Do you find him attractive?"

"Certainly not!"

"Really?" said the princess. "I think he is one of the handsomest men I have ever seen."

"I think he looks like a wolf."

Elizabeth laughed. "He is a bit fierce, perhaps."

"And he is so—so strange," Laura went on. "The way that he lives—awake at night, asleep during the day. Why, I don't think he ever sets foot out of that dome except to come here."

"Well, he has to be careful—especially with his brother turning in heretics."

"What on earth do you mean?"

"Didn't you know? He's a heretic too." At Laura's surprised expression the princess laughed. "Oh, not about God; I don't know what he thinks about God. But what he believes about the sun being the center of the universe instead of the earth—that's completely contrary to what the Catholic church teaches. Men have been burned for believing that."

"How can that be? John said it was perfectly obvious to anyone who looked!"

Elizabeth Tudor frowned, searching for words to explain. "It's got to do with what's at the center. According to the Catholic church, the whole universe was created by God, *for* man, so that man could be redeemed and saved. That's why it's so vital to them that the earth is at the center. If they let people wonder what it might mean that the earth isn't at the center, heaven only knows what else they might start to think!" Laura blinked. The princess sighed. "John is much better at explaining it than I am. He says it's a whole different way of looking at man's relationship to the universe. You can ask him about it when he comes for my lesson on Friday."

But John did not appear at Hatfield House for his Friday lesson either. Cecil and Throckmorton were visiting, and Elizabeth wanted to organize a reading of a play by Sophocles, but Laura did not feel up to struggling with Greek, and so she excused herself and went up to her room to read.

But she could not concentrate on the book of poetry Elizabeth had lent her. She put on her borrowed nightdress and curled up in the window seat of her bedchamber. The moon outside the casement was at its half mark; she could see its pale reflection glinting off the glass dome of Guilford Hall above the dark trees on the hill. From the receiving chamber

below came the strains of a lute; she heard Elizabeth and
Cecil singing a duet, the princess's high, clear voice soaring
over the knight's gruff tones.

How lucky I am to have found this refuge and such splendid new friends, she thought, leaning her cheek against the
chilly window glass. Only another week and she would turn
seventeen; Thomas Guilford would have no more claim on
her then. She would be free to marry whomever she
pleased...

The moon drifted in the sky. Laura drifted to sleep right
there in the window seat, thinking of the kiss John Guilford
had given her in the gardens, and she dreamed of his blue
wolf's eyes.

She was shaken awake hours later by Elizabeth, clad in
slippers and a nightgown. "Laura," the princess whispered,
"John has come back, and just in time for the Eta
Aquarids!"

"The what?" Laura mumbled sleepily.

"The Eta Aquarids. Meteors. You know, shooting stars.
They're all over the southern sky; come outside and see!"

Laura stumbled to her feet. "I shall have to dress."

"Don't be silly," said the princess, "we are all in our
nightclothes. Now hurry, or Sir William will beat me out for
the prize!"

Too dazed to protest, Laura dutifully followed Elizabeth
downstairs and out to the lawn. In the silvery light of the
high half moon she could see a scattering of figures seated on
the grass: Cecil in a white shirt and long nightcap; Father
Burton without his clerical collar; the princess's Greek tutor,
Roger Ascham; Kate Ashley; Nicholas Throckmorton.
Standing before the assembly in a long black cloak was John
Guilford, gesturing toward the heavens with the point of his
sword.

"Plot the track of each meteor you see with your quill,"
he instructed the company, "and note it on your chart, with
duration of appearance, duration of tail, and brightness. You
can use any of the named stars in Aquarius for comparison.
Any questions?"

"Aye," William Cecil grumbled, "how long does this
bloody show last?"

"With any luck, 'til dawn."

Cecil groaned and muttered, "Pray for rain!"

Elizabeth sat on the dew-soaked grass and picked up her
quill and a notebook. Laura sat beside her, torn between

looking at John Guilford and the sky. "There!" Roger Ascham shouted, waving his quill. Laura looked in the direction he'd pointed and caught the merest glimpse of a streak of white light. Elizabeth licked her quill and made a line in her notebook.

"What are you doing?" Laura whispered.

"Plotting the radiant point. The paths of all the meteors converge in one place."

"Oh," said Laura. Another burst of white light flew by overhead. Elizabeth made a second line in her notebook. Cecil cursed; he'd been blowing his nose and had missed that one.

What a peculiar pastime, Laura thought, considering the heavens as the night wind blew back her hair, listening to the excited shouts of the men and women around her as the shooting stars streaked through the sky. "How do you get the prize?" she whispered to Elizabeth.

"By coming closest to the true radiant, of course. My Lord, will you look at that!" A whole flurry of streaks lit up the night; she was sketching furiously.

"They're going too fast," Cecil moaned, throwing down his quill.

"You are just not paying proper attention," Elizabeth chided him, and slid across the lawn to his side, leaving Laura alone.

Sheathing his sword, John Guilford strolled around the circle of figures, bending now and again to offer a word of advice. Laura felt her heartbeat quicken as he drew near her. He looked impossibly tall and handsome in the faint moonlight, his black hair shadowing his face. When he'd come within a few feet he quickened his pace, moving past her. Thinking he must not have recognized her, Laura called to him, "John?"

Slowly he turned back. "Aye?"

"It is I, John. Laura."

"I know."

Why was he being so unfriendly? "I haven't had a chance to thank you yet."

"For what?"

"Why, for warning me about your brother. If not for you, I'd be marrying him."

"You may be still. Francis Englefield hasn't yet heard the petition to open the inquiry."

"Oh, but surely he will, when he hears what Thomas has

done to me. And anyway, in a week I will be of age and free to choose my own husband."

"I wish you luck." His voice was cool and remote as a star.

Laura studied his hard wolf's profile in the faint silver moonlight and felt a longing to tell him of the heat that had surged in her when he kissed her. "John," she whispered, "you have been so very kind to me—"

To her horror he laughed. "Laura Darby, what a vain little thing you are."

"I'm sure I don't know what you mean," she said, stung by his coldness.

"You think you're the center of the cosmos, don't you? All else revolves around you."

"I certainly do not!" she cried indignantly.

He gestured toward one of the brilliant stars that streaked low across the horizon, then faded abruptly into nothingness. "That's the space of a life in this universe, Laura. Less even than the blink of an eye. And whom you marry or don't marry has as much consequence in the scheme of the world as a meteor."

Laura's lower lip was trembling. "If you believe that," she cried, then lowered her voice as their fellow stargazers turned to stare? "If you believe that, then why have you gone to so much trouble for my sake? Why did you file that petition with the Court of Wards? Why bother helping me?"

"Did it ever occur to you, Laura, that my objective might not be helping you?"

"Why—" In truth, it hadn't. "What else could it be?"

"Hurting my brother," said John Guilford, eyes narrowed and dark as the midnight sky. As Laura stared up at him, chagrined, he turned and walked away.

Chapter 8

The Princess Elizabeth's household slept late on the morning after the spectacle of the Eta Aquarids. Elizabeth had won the prize for calculating the radiant point—a little pendant of a silver star—and she was in high spirits as she and Laura shared dinner, or rather breakfast, at noon.

Laura had no appetite for her plate of cheese and fruit and bread; she was too angry with John Guilford to eat. He had no right to call her vain and selfish, she thought furiously. She might have her faults, but she wouldn't claim those! It was only natural for her to think he cared for her; after all, he had kissed her and told her she looked like a star!

"How fiercely you are glaring at your gooseberries," Elizabeth said with a giggle. "Is something amiss?"

Laura set her spoon on the edge of her plate. "Your astronomy instructor was unconscionably rude to me last night when I tried to thank him for helping me."

Elizabeth sighed. "Poor John. He is a fish out of water when it comes to the social graces. But what else could you expect, really, with his family background?"

"You mean his father," said Laura, remembering Polly's tales of the Old Master and his weird inventions.

"His father? I mean his mother. By all accounts Paul Guilford was a living saint to put up with it as long as he did."

"Put up with what?" Laura asked curiously.

The princess blinked at her. "Honestly, Laura, sometimes I think you must come from another planet. Don't you know about Estelle Guilford?"

"What should I know?"

"It was only the biggest scandal in England in a hundred years—barring my beloved father's escapades, of course. Let's see, where shall I begin? Her affair with the Earl of

Driscoll, or the one with Lord Beverley? Or perhaps the one with the Duke of Suffolk—"

"I take it she was unfaithful," Laura broke in, blushing.

"Unfaithful? She was notorious. A slut."

"You ought not to malign the poor woman when she is dead," Laura protested, shocked.

"I'm not maligning her," Elizabeth said, spooning up gooseberries. "That is what the jury at the inquest found."

"What jury? At what inquest?"

"Oh, dear, you really don't know anything about it, do you?" Elizabeth seemed distressed. "John's father murdered his mother. He stabbed her to death in her bed at Guilford Hall."

"God in heaven," Laura whispered. "Oh, dear God!"

"It was all the buzz of the kingdom when it happened," the princess went on. "It must have been, oh, ten years ago. As I said, the jury found the murder justified, though of course by then it didn't matter."

"What do you mean, it didn't matter?"

"Why, that same night Paul Guilford jumped off the roof of his house. He killed himself too."

Laura was reeling with shock at this story the princess related so matter-of-factly. Lord, was it any wonder John and Thomas were such strange men? She thought of them wandering through their huge grand house and shuddered. Thomas had told her the bedchamber he gave her had been his mother's—that meant Paul Guilford had murdered his wife in the very bed she had slept in! Just thinking of it made her shiver uncontrollably.

The door to the room where they supped swung open. "Good afternoon, ladies," John Guilford said.

He looked rumpled after his night of stargazing, black hair tousled, a thick shadow of beard darkening his face. His heavy-lidded eyes seemed sleepier than ever, and his doublet and shirt were open at the throat. Laura took all that in in the instant before she stared studiously down at her plate.

"Good morrow, John," Elizabeth said cheerily, gesturing him to a seat beside her. She picked up the bell at her elbow and rang it, mimicking the Yorkshire-born cook's thick, guttural voice. "Wot'll it be, then, Marster G'ford, some nice 'ot porridge, er pancakes?"

The cook bustled in. "Wot'll it be, then, Marster G'ford —some porridge, er pancakes?"

Elizabeth crowed in delight, but John merely smiled,

shaking his head. "Thank you, Josephine, but I'm not very hungry. Fruit and cheese will be fine."

"You are just like Laura," Elizabeth said fondly, looking from one to the other. "Neither of you eats enough to keep a bird alive. You ought to be starved; we were up all night."

"I've got to get to London. Englefield is scheduled to hear our petition to reopen the inquiry Monday." John picked up a knife and began to peel the rind from an orange with quick, sure strokes. Laura could not keep from staring at his long-fingered hands as the knife wound round and around, slitting the skin from the fruit. He pierced the pulp with a quick, hard stab that sent up a spray of juice.

"I'll go tell Sir William; he wanted to ride with you," Elizabeth offered.

"No!" Laura did not want to be left alone with John Guilford even for a moment. "I'll go." She rose from her chair.

"Don't be silly, Laura. You must have a million questions to ask John about the hearing. Sit down." Elizabeth skipped out, closing the doors.

"Well," said John Guilford, his voice low and cool. "Have you a million questions?"

Laura shook her head, turning away from the table to the sideboard, pouring a cup of perry as slowly as she could.

"While you're up, I'll have some of that, if you would."

She circled around the table behind him with the ewer, filled his cup with the pear juice, and circled back to the sideboard again, not meeting his eyes.

"I see Elizabeth has been filling you in on my family history," he observed in that same offhand tone. "I wouldn't have believed there was anyone in England who didn't know the story; trust Thomas to find the one girl who didn't. Did he choose you for that, I wonder, more than for your gold?"

Laura knew she really must say something, anything, but her tongue seemed coiled in knots. She took her seat again, hands in her lap, and stared at her cutlery.

"God in heaven," John Guilford said quietly, "I almost don't blame him. I know how sweet it was to meet you and not see that look in your eyes."

"What look?" Laura whispered.

"Oh, you know. It is partly fear and partly curiosity. But always, mostly, fear. You're the first soul I've met in ten years who didn't wear that look when you heard my name." Suddenly he laughed. "I'll wager you're wearing it now."

"I am—sorry for your troubles," said Laura, not glancing up, knowing he was right.

"Well, it doesn't matter, really, does it, in the scheme of the cosmos and all?" He was pulling the segments of his orange apart with those long, strong fingers. "Do you know what I thought the first time I saw you, Laura Darby? I thought, there is a rock."

"A what?" Laura asked, taken aback.

"A rock. A good, solid one." He sucked at a slice of orange. "The sort of rock a man might build a fine house on, someday."

Laura did not care at all for being thought of as a rock.

"The house of Guilford, now," John went on idly, "that's doomed to extinction. It's built on all the wrong sorts of things, you see."

"Do you mean Guilford Hall?"

He laughed again. "I wonder sometimes, was I ever as innocent as you? If I was, I can't remember it."

Laura thought of her warm, loving father and mother and shivered. "It must have been awful for you, growing up that way. With your father hating your mother so terribly, I mean."

"Hating her?" he echoed, plainly startled. "He didn't hate her. She was the center of his universe. He loved her more than he loved God."

Laura's spine tingled. Oh, Lord, she thought, these people don't understand what love is!

"Morning, Laura. Morning, John. Ready to be off?" William Cecil asked from the doorway.

John pushed back his chair, setting down the mutilated orange. "Aye," he said shortly. Laura looked up to bid him farewell, but he was already gone.

The following evening, just at sunset, Elizabeth Tudor was in her chambers, in the process of beating Kate Ashley at chess. Laura sat by the window, pleating and unpleating the red silk skirts of the gown Thomas had given her, staring out at the glittering dome of Guilford Hall. The terrible, sad story Elizabeth had told her about Paul and Estelle Guilford kept running through her mind; she was so lost in thought that she jumped when the captain of the household guard appeared at the door. "Milady," he announced, "there's a rider coming up the London Road. Thee asked to be told."

"So I did, Guerrin. Thank you." Elizabeth smiled at

Laura reassuringly. "John's a far better horseman than my poor, sweet William; he must have outpaced him with the good news from the hearing. Let's go down to the yards."

But the man who came pounding through the gates a few minutes later, long cape whipping at the flanks of a great bay steed, was not John Guilford. Laura, standing between Elizabeth and Father Burton, gasped as she saw his pointed black beard and gray eyes.

The princess recognized Thomas as well. "Guards!" she called sharply as he reined in before them. "Put him out again at once!" Her soldiers stepped forward.

"I wouldn't," said Thomas, "unless you're prepared to defy the queen. I've a writ with me this time, signed by Sir Francis Englefield *and* Her Majesty Queen Mary, confirming my guardian rights to the body and goods of Laura Darby."

"But—the hearing," said Elizabeth. "Your brother and Sir William—"

"Your friends, alas, never had a chance to testify." Thomas shrugged, pulling off his black leather gloves finger by slow finger. "Queen Mary decided the matter herself." He tossed a parchment at Elizabeth's feet. She snatched it up and unrolled it, tilting it to catch the dying rays of the sun, scanning it hurriedly. Thomas Guilford whistled a little tune, smiling tautly beneath the brim of his fine plumed hat.

Elizabeth finished reading the writ and looked up at him, eyes flashing. "What did you have to pay for this?"

"English justice is not for sale, milady," he said with exaggerated shock. "I merely made a small contribution to King Philip's war against the French."

"Oh, Mary, Mary, that greedy husband of yours." Elizabeth hesitated, then ripped the parchment in half and tossed it to the stones. "She's not coming with you." She threw an arm around Laura's quaking shoulders. "I won't let her go."

To Laura's amazement, her guardian did not lose his temper, only nodded thoughtfully. "As you wish, milady. But might I have a word with Laura in privacy?"

"What are you up to now?" Elizabeth demanded, brow furrowed in suspicion.

"I'm not up to anything. I paid four thousand pounds for that piece of parchment. Surely you'll agree that is worth two minutes of Laura's time."

Elizabeth studied him in the waning light. "It's a trick, Bess," Father Burton warned.

Thomas's mouth curled; he pulled at his beard. "I don't intend to snatch her away."

"Milady," Laura said softly. The princess turned to her. "I'll speak with him."

"But—"

Laura shrugged. "It is not as though there is anything he could say that would make me leave with him!"

The princess hesitated a moment longer. Then, "Close the gates," she ordered the guards, taking no chances. "And have your crossbows at the ready." She gestured to a tall oak tree nearby on the lawn. "You may speak over there."

Thomas dismounted and offered Laura his arm. She ignored it, walking to the tree alone. He followed close behind. "Two minutes," Elizabeth called after them, and gnawed at her lip.

At the trunk of the tree Thomas turned so that he faced the small knot of women and the priest, and Laura had her back to them. "How are you, my dear?" he asked. "Have you been enjoying your new friends?"

"What do you want with me?"

He smiled pleasantly down at her. "Only to remind you that you yourself confessed to me you're a heretic. There are still some hot coals ready for you on Smithfield Plain if you don't come with me."

"You can't turn me in as a heretic," Laura said bravely, "because Cecil says 'tis against the law to wed a heretic. And you have to marry me to get my money."

He arched a brow. "You are growing up, little Laura. You're quite right. But it isn't only against the law to wed a heretic. It is also against the law to give one aid or comfort or shelter. And as you know, Queen Mary has long been looking for an excuse to clap her beloved sister in prison once and for all. I suspect she would be willing to reward anyone who provided her with such an excuse, very richly indeed."

Laura started to whirl back to Elizabeth, but he grasped her hands and held them tight, speaking softly. "Now, my dear. If you are indeed fond of your new friends, of Elizabeth and her ladies and teachers, of Father Burton and William Cecil, I'd advise you to turn around, smile, and tell the princess that you will be delighted to return to Guilford Hall with me. If you don't, I shall get on my horse, ride back to London, and inform Queen Mary that her sister is sheltering a heretic."

Laura's knees started to crumple beneath her. Thomas

slipped a chivalrous arm around her waist. "I'd say you have thirty seconds left in which to decide. What will it be, my dear?"

"Damn you," Laura whispered.

"Twenty-five seconds," he said implacably.

Sweet Jesus, Laura prayed, if you love me, then strike him down right where he stands, strike him dead! But no lightning bolt split the heavens; Thomas grinned cheerfully.

"I won't—" she started to say, then clamped her mouth shut. Hatfield House was a house of cards, balanced so precariously. Kate Ashley, Roger Ascham, Father Burton—all had already spent time in prison because of Mary's suspicions. The queen might not get away with burning her sister on the strength of such charges, but her ministers would have no qualms about convicting a Greek instructor or a renegade priest. And Elizabeth would go again to the Tower . . . to the room in which her mother had once been kept, waiting to die.

"Ten seconds," said Thomas Guilford.

Kate, Roger, Father Burton—maybe even Cecil and Nicholas Throckmorton. All their blood would be on her hands. But how could she go with Thomas? How could she marry the man who'd informed on her father?

"Five."

In the back of her mind Laura heard John Guilford's voice: *Laura Darby, what a vain little thing you are. . . . You think you're the center of the cosmos. . . . All else revolves around you . . .* Through the branches of the oak tree beyond Thomas's shoulders she could see the first stars flickering low on the horizon. All those lives in the balance, she thought. He was right. I am vain . . .

One hand still in Thomas's, she turned back to Elizabeth. "Thank you, milady," she called, smiling brightly, "for all your kindness. But I am ready to go home with Thomas now."

Laura rode away quietly with Thomas, ensconced in front of him in the bay's saddle, but the instant Hatfield House was out of sight she yanked on the reins. "What guarantee do I have that you'll not inform on the princess even though I come with you?"

His eyes glinted in the moonlight. "You are growing up very quickly indeed." There was admiration in his tone. "But you yourself are the guarantee, my dear. As you said, it is against the law to marry a heretic. Once we are wed, it will be as dangerous for me as for your new friends to reveal what I know."

Once we are wed... Laura leaned over the horse's withers and was suddenly, violently ill. Thomas waited on the shadowy road until she had finished retching, then they rode on.

The five miles that had seemed so impossibly lengthy to Laura during her escape passed in the space of a heartbeat. She saw the silvery dome and dark towers of Guilford Hall rise up before her, and then they were through the gates and pounding over the courtyard bricks. "I've invited a few guests to witness our nuptials," Thomas told her as he pulled her down from the horse.

"Who?" Laura whispered.

"Your family, naturally. I knew you would want to share this joyous occasion with them." Laura shivered as Theodore, his face pinched and hate-filled, threw open the doors. "Thank you, Theo," Thomas said smoothly. "You might lock up now. We are not expecting any more visitors tonight."

Laura's heart sank as Thomas pulled her straight down the corridor to the chapel. "Am I not even to have time to wash, and change my dress?" she asked. If she could only delay him, think of some way out of this awful plight...

"I think not, my dear. You've been proving surprisingly resourceful of late. And if you have any notions of escaping, let me remind you of the Princess Elizabeth."

The small stone chapel was ablaze with candles. Laura stopped on the threshold, blinking in the sudden bright light. Flames all around her... another reminder, she thought, hatred welling up in her soul.

Blanche and Humphrey were sitting in a front pew; her half brother rose abruptly when he turned and saw her. So did Blanche; Laura noted that her sister-in-law wore a new diamond throatpiece and a gorgeous rose taffeta gown. "Laura," she cried, "how unspeakably naughty of you to run off and cause Lord Guilford such trouble! You ought to be ashamed of yourself!"

Laura stood without moving as Humphrey came to kiss her. "You—you look well, Laura," he said nervously, his bald pate shining with sweat.

"Whose idea was it, Humphrey?" she demanded, her voice sounding harsh and strange in her ears.

"I don't know what you're talking about—"

"Come, come, of course you do. Whose idea was it to tell Thomas about Papa? I would like to think 'twas Blanche's, knowing how honestly Papa loved you. But I am not quite sure."

Humphrey licked his thick lips. "Laura," he began.

"We are wasting time," Thomas broke in abruptly. "Where is Father Devereaux?"

"Right—right here, Thomas, my good man." A short, fat fellow in clerical robes rose up from the pew on which he lay, a bottle clutched in his hand. His voice was thick with drink; Humphrey eyed the bottle longingly.

Thomas clenched Laura's arm in a grip as cold and final as death, leading her to the altar. "Let the Mass begin."

It doesn't count, Laura told herself as the drunken priest began to mumble in Latin. It doesn't count, because I have no choice. I don't believe in the Mass; I don't believe in the pope's authority—oh, God, I don't believe this is happening to me . . .

She did her best. She didn't speak any vows, did not plight her troth to him or vow to love and honor him. She did not say "I will." But the priest, pausing now and again to guzzle from his bottle, never noticed. He went on reciting the words between hiccups and giggles, and when Laura refused the host he held to her mouth he shrugged and swallowed it himself.

And then it was finished. The priest pronounced them man and wife, his palm thick and moist against her forehead. She turned her face away from Thomas's kiss. He and Humphrey shook hands; then Laura's brother, not meeting her eyes, hustled Blanche out of the chapel. Thomas gave the priest a purse; the man thanked him and then collapsed onto his pew, snoring deliriously.

"I hope you are satisfied," Laura spat at Thomas.

He smiled his charming, detestable smile. "Not quite, my dear."

"You have got what you wanted."

"No. One thing more remains before we are man and wife in the eyes of the law."

"What is that?"

"The consummation," said Thomas, taking a step toward her. "We are going upstairs to make love."

She laughed in his face. "Not likely."

He caught her arm and wrenched it behind her back with

such force that she fell to her knees. "I assure you, my dear, this will be as distasteful for me as for you."

"No!" Laura screamed as he dragged her from the chapel where the priest lay mumbling in his sleep. "No, I won't—" He clapped a hand across her face, and she bit his fingers. Cursing, he slung her up over his shoulder. She clawed at his back, kicking, crying out as loudly as she could.

She lunged for the railing as he started up the front staircase, clinging to it with desperate strength. "Polly!" she screamed, seeing the cook's ashen face peering out from the kitchens. "Oh, God, Polly, help me, please!"

"Go back to the kitchens, Polly," Thomas said calmly, and when the stunned woman did not move, he bellowed at her, "Get back to the kitchens or I'll beat you senseless, you worthless cow!"

Polly ducked through the doorway without a word.

Laura screamed until she was faint for lack of breath. She saw the paintings and hangings flash by upside-down as Thomas hauled her through the corridors, saw the patterns on the rugs, the table with the mosaic top. There was an ornate spider's web stretched between its legs. I must remember to dust that, she thought incongruously, her mind rebelling against what was happening. It was a bad dream; the past months had been only a nightmare. At any moment she would waken in her own bed at Howarth Manor and hear her father calling to her, "Get up, lazybones!"

But the bed she was thrust toward was covered in white linen, hung with drapes red as blood. With a curse Thomas tore aside the crimson hangings and shoved her facedown onto the feather mattress. She scrambled across the coverlet on her hands and knees, then cried out in terror as he yanked her skirts over her head with a whoosh. Beneath the sea of red silk she fought for air. He splayed a hand across the back of her head, shoving her down; with the other he pushed between her knees, forcing them apart, ripping her pettiskirts aside and reaching for her drawers.

Oh, God, Laura prayed, sprawled helpless beneath him, dear God, let me die now and not know this shame. His weight was suffocating; he was kneeling between her legs, scrabbling at his hose. She could hear his harsh breath through her tangled skirts; a horrible picture rose up in her mind of Theodore in this same posture, teeth bared, letting out those animal groans.

"Here's to you, wife," Thomas grunted, grabbing her

waist and raising her up, ready to plunge himself between her bared thighs. There was a pause that seemed to last forever—

And then she heard a strangled, feral cry and the bright, sharp crash of shattering glass. His hands, his weight were gone from her. Stunned, disbelieving, she fell against the bed, then screamed as a hand groped toward her face beneath her skirts.

"Laura." The voice was quiet and controlled. "Laura, get up."

She opened her eyes and saw John Guilford standing over her, his face taut and drawn. "What—"

"Get up, Laura," he said again, "we haven't much time." Dazed, she let him pull her from the bed and lead her to the doorway. The huge mirror on the far wall had been broken; Thomas was slumped on the floor beneath the smashed glass, blood flowing from a gash on the back of his head.

"It's all right," John told her patiently. "He can't hurt you now."

She stared at the motionless figure. "Did you—is he dead?"

"Do you care?" he asked, his voice suddenly harsh.

Laura began to cry.

John lifted her into his arms and carried her down the servants' stairs to the kitchens. Polly was cowering by the table. When she saw Laura, she too burst into tears. "Fetch the doctor for my brother," John told her brusquely. "He's had a nasty fall. And Theodore is hurt as well; he's in the front courtyard."

"Aye, Master John," she blubbered, then cried to Laura, "I'm sorry, missy! I didn't want to lose my place. I didn't know what to do—"

"All right, Polly," said John. "There's no harm done."

Laura stopped crying and began to laugh.

John frowned and carried her out to the kitchen gardens, then set her down. "Stop that," he ordered as she went on laughing, clutching her sides.

"No harm done," she gasped out. "No harm done—"

He slapped her sharply across the cheek.

Shocked into silence, she reached up and touched her palm to the spot where he'd struck her; the skin burned beneath her hand.

"Why did you go with him?" he demanded. She stared at him dumbly, and he grabbed her elbows and shook her.

"Damn you, tell me! Why did you leave Hatfield House with him?"

Laura had the strange sensation that she was under water. She tried to answer, but none of her muscles was working. Her throat was swollen; her tongue seemed frozen in place.

His eyes burned in the starlight. "You went with him willingly, didn't you? You thought it worth marrying him. You wanted this house; you've grown to like it here. It didn't matter to you, what he is—"

Under water. Everything moving so slowly. . .

When she did not answer he turned from her in disgust. "God help you, Laura Darby. I can do no more." He walked off through the ranks of sweet-scented herbs toward the horse he'd left at the back gate.

"I—"

He whirled around so quickly. "Why, Laura? *Why?*"

She reached out her hands to him; they were heavy as lead. She tried to take a step and swayed, a reed in the wind . . .

He caught her as she fell, somehow covering the distance between them before she reached the ground. As his arms closed around her, the words burst out in a sob: "I had no choice! He said Elizabeth would go to the Tower! He said the others would be burned—Jesus in heaven, what else could I do?"

He let out a long, ragged sigh and smoothed back her hair with his hand. "Laura—"

"How could you think I would want to marry him? How could you say that?"

"I am getting you away from here."

"I can't go! Don't you understand? I had to marry him to save the others! I married him," she cried. "God help me, I'm his wife . . ."

John jerked up his head as a sudden commotion broke out in the house; he heard Theodore screaming, and from his brother came an outraged roar. "Come on." He swept Laura up again and carried her to his horse, setting her onto the saddle. She tried frantically to climb back down.

"No. I can't go away—"

He leaped up behind her, pinning her in place, and caught up the reins. "I'll think of something, Laura, I swear it. Don't be afraid."

She wanted to protest, to insist that she stay for Elizabeth's sake, but the arm he tucked around her was so strong and warm that she gave up, swaying back against his chest. He urged the horse off across the fields toward the stream, past the strawberry patch. The night sky stretched above them, rich and dark as obsidian; the stars were a million far-off candles, a million miles away.

Laura saw them revolving slowly around her, while the earth went spinning in the opposite direction beneath the horse's hooves. She struggled to sit up, to ask one last question: "Why did you come after me?"

"What?" Her voice had been a tiny wisp; John bent his head to hear. "What did you ask?"

"Why you . . . came after me."

"Elizabeth asked me to."

"Oh," Laura whispered.

The horse galloped on beneath the black sea of sky.

"And because—" John Guilford began, then stopped as he heard the faint, steady rhythm of her sleeping breath.

It was just as well, he thought, shifting in the saddle.

He turned his attention back to the distant stars.

Part II

Chapter 9

The reflection of the late-day sun off the English Channel was so powerful that John Guilford, unaccustomed to such brightness, had to shield his eyes with his hand and narrow them to slits to see the cliffs of Dover in the distance. They gleamed above the sea like cuffs of fine bleached linen, perfectly crisped with starch. At the sight of them John felt as though all that chalk had been lifted from his shoulders. Their sparkling bulk signified that his voyage aboard the *White Lion* was nearly over—his "mission of mercy," as William Cecil had termed it, arranging for him to accompany Laura to Calais.

John had tried to argue that his presence wasn't needed on the journey, that anyone—a servant, the captain of the ship—could deliver the girl to the community of English Protestants who'd taken refuge from Mary's policies in the fortified city that was England's last foothold in France. But Sir William had been adamant. "Think of all the poor child has been through, John," he'd argued, lowering his voice so that Laura, sitting staring into the hearth in his house in London, might not hear him. "She knows you. She trusts you. 'Twill take you no more than four days—two there, two back."

"I've work to do," John told him. "Venus will be occulting Regulus early next week. And there's a total eclipse of the moon on the twenty-fifth, the only one this decade—"

"John." Cecil put a hand on his arm. "For once, just once, take an interest in something here on earth. Your own brother did this to her."

"I'm not my brother's keeper."

"Nor shall you be hers, once you get her to Calais."

Of course Cecil had won the argument. He was so damnably honest and upright that he always won arguments; he made a soul ashamed to be arguing with him. Not that it mattered now, thought John. The captain of the *White Lion* had assured him they'd be docked in Calais harbor by nine that night. Another hour or two to take her to the family Cecil had told him of, and his responsibility would be discharged, once and for all.

From beneath lowered lids he watched as she chattered with Captain Wainwright, who was demonstrating the use of the tiller. A crowd of sailors had gathered around her, preening for their lovely guest. All she had been through indeed. John's mouth twisted. Look at her. She still wore the red silk gown in which he'd carried her from Guilford Hall, but she'd tucked the overskirts up into her girdle and taken off her boots and stockings, so that anyone who cared to might see her small ankles and white feet. She was laughing now as one of the sailors made a jest, her golden eyes sparkling, brown-red curls shining bright as the sun. Not one whit the worse for wear she was. But then, that was females for you, thought John. Sloughing off everything the same way a snake shed its skin.

She reminded him of his mother, of Estelle, the glorious dark star that Paul Guilford had fallen in love with and then offered everything to. But everything had never been enough for Estelle. An insatiable sponge, she sopped up all he had and then went after more, flaunting lovers before her husband like so many changes of clothes.

John had watched and suffered along with the father he worshipped, whom he'd nicknamed Apollo for the magical, godlike wonders he could do. He'd helped, silent and uncomplaining, on the midnight forays to add a roof, a room, a wall to the shifting house Apollo had bought as a gift for his bride, while Estelle's mocking laughter floated from the windows. He'd taken refuge with his father in the glass dome they built when even the overgrown house became too small to hide in. He understood what had driven his father mad, spurred his bizarre quest to fly away from his wife and her lovers, to sail over the hills and trees. That was what love did to a man.

All Laura Darby had been through indeed. John watched her toss back her gleaming curls, laughing as Captain Wainwright let her take the wheel. Like skin from a snake, like water off oil . . . and still as lovely as a star. The only decent women in this world, he thought angrily, are the bawds at Meg Christie's whorehouse. They gave a man what he paid for and never asked more, constant as the moon in its phases. With them, in the dark, amid blankets and pillows and linens, there was never any talk of love.

Look at her. She was skipping toward him across the deck, calling his name while the sailors stared after her, tongues damned near hanging from their mouths. Her hips swayed; her breasts were full and ripe in the cherry-red gown. He shut his eyes, blocking out the sight of her, leaning against the ship's rail.

"John! Come and take a turn at steering; 'tis marvelous exciting. You can feel the whole ship shift when you move the tiller!"

He shook his head, eyes still closed, then flinched as he felt her small hand prying his fingers from the cold railing. "Do come on," she urged. "It will give you something to do besides stand about looking cross."

"If I look cross," he said, extricating his hand from hers, "'tis because I've better ways of spending time than nursemaiding you to Calais."

There was no answer for so long that he thought she'd gone and he warily opened his eyes. She was staring down at the deck through her lashes, tracing a pattern on the planks with her toe. "I am sorry," she mumbled at last. "I told Sir William I could manage alone. It was not my idea."

Tell her you are sorry. "I should think you'd have better things to do with your time too, besides distracting the crew," he said instead.

"Distracting the— How am I doing that?"

He laughed, then stopped as she raised wounded gold eyes to him. Was it possible she didn't know? He dismissed the question abruptly. Of course she knew. It was born in them, in women. She was just like Estelle.

"Excuse me, I asked how am I distracting them?"

"Go away, little Laura. Go back to your games." The only wonder was that it had taken Apollo so long to put an end to the torment Estelle enjoyed inflicting, thought John. He himself had understood that torment only too well; he too had loved his mother, desperate and unrequited, for years and years.

"I don't know what you have to be out of sorts about," Laura told him. "I have never seen the stars look so splendid from land as they did last night, over the water."

"There will be no stars tonight."

For an instant uncertainty flickered in her eyes. Good,

John thought. Let her be afraid. Let her keep her distance. "What do you mean?"

"There will be a storm."

She tilted her head at him. "How can you tell?"

"Sorcery."

She laughed. "Oh, bosh."

Her laughter rankled. He struck back the way life had taught him, swift and hard. "It is fine to see you laughing. I shall have to give the Reformed religion a try, if it lets you forget what my brother did to you so easily."

"Your brother did nothing to me," she said, and he thought, There, I knew it—before she added, "compared to what he did to my father." She whirled on her heel and crossed to where the captain and his men were waiting. Good, thought John. Keep your distance. Good.

The storm whose warning signs he had read on the wind and in the sky blew in just at dusk. Captain Wainwright cursed as a huge bank of roiling black clouds loomed on the horizon, belched out of the northeast.

"We'll make Calais tonight, won't we?" John asked him, unnerved at the prospect of a delay.

"Aye," said the gruff old seaman. "Ye'd best get below and tell the little lady. We'll land in an hour."

John started along the gangway to the leeward hatch, then stopped as the lookout in the mizzenmast cried, "Sails, cap'n, off starboard stern!"

Wainwright squinted across the darkening water, then called up into the rigging, "Under what flag?"

"Can't tell yet, sir, they're too far away!"

"French," John said quietly, catching sight of the scarlet oriflammes against the black clouds.

Wainwright regarded him in surprise. "Can ye make that out from here?"

John nodded. "I spend my time staring at things a good deal farther off than that."

"Do ye, now? And what might they be?"

"The stars."

"Ye don't say." Wainwright scratched his ribs. "Astrologer, are ye? I had my fortune told once by an astrologer in Tangiers. He said I'd meet my own true love on my next voyage to Africa." He shook his head. "Never should have told my wife, that's certain. Ever since, she won't let me sail nowheres but Calais to London, London to Calais!" He gazed at the ships again. "Well, if they're French we've got naught to fear; that bastard Philip ain't dragged England into his bloody war with 'em yet. And Queen Mary must know the first thing ye do when ye does declare war, ye warns yer shipping. Steady as she goes, boys! Hold course for Calais!"

In the gathering shadows of night and storm, John stood at the rail and watched the foreign ships sail closer. Sailors—the only damned ones with any sense, he thought. They'd always known the world was round. Look at how the tips of the French masts appeared first, coming over the horizon, then the topsails, the spreaders, and last of all the decks and hulls.

No stars tonight, not with this storm. Back in Hertfordshire he could be plotting the occultation of Venus and Regulus, preparing for the lunar eclipse . . .

Except there was a star—no, by God, it was a comet. He stared in wonder at the ball of fire streaking through the sky in a soaring arc. The biggest bloody comet he'd ever seen, with a tail that rumbled like thunder—

"Cap'n," the mizzenmast lookout screeched, "we're bein' fired on!"

The foredeck of the *White Lion* shattered as the cannonball hit. Two men were blown to pieces by the explosion, and flames leaped up from the planks. The captain whirled on John. "Ye said those flags were French!"

"Another shot comin', cap'n!" the terrified lookout cried, scrambling down from his post. "They're French ships, sir, but that ain't stoppin' 'em!"

"All hands on deck!" the captain bellowed. "Man the buckets! Wash down that fire!" A crowd of sailors poured through the break to work the bucket winches. "Set a new tack!" Wainwright shouted above the babble of voices and roaring flames. "Hard for south-southwest!" He ran for the tiller.

Southwest! John rushed to his side. "You said we were only an hour from Calais!"

"So we are, man," said the captain grimly, hauling at the wheel, "but I cannot fight the wind and the bleedin' Frogs both. We'll run ahead of the storm. We ought to make Portsmouth by dawn."

"What can I do to help?"

"Ye might pray, assumin' ye're inclined that way."

"And if I'm not?"

Wainwright grinned. "Then help with the fire."

John tore off his shirt, tying it at his waist, and started

toward the blaze on the foredeck while the sails cracked
above him, catching the breeze that was becoming a gale.
The ropes slipping through the pulleys sang in a high, wild
whine; the scent of acrid smoke swallowed that of clean salt
air. As he ran past the forecastle hatch, he caught a glimpse
of a small heart-shaped face, stark white in the glare of the
flames. Laura. "Get below," he called to her. She didn't
move. "Dammit, Laura, get below!"

How wide and frightened her eyes were, their gold reflecting the blazing flames. *The flames* . . . Christ, she was
afraid of the fire. "Laura, it will be all right, I swear it," he
told her. "We'll put it out. Get below."

A sailor rolled screaming across the deck, his leather leg-
gings ablaze. Several men went to help him. "Papa," Laura
whispered. "Papa—"

John froze, immobilized by the war raging wild and fierce
within him. Don't touch her, his mind cried, while his heart
told him, Take her into your arms . . .

You'll be lost.

You'll be found.

I don't want to be found . . .

But his hands had already reached for her of their own
accord. He drew her to him and felt the mad pounding of her
heart against his chest. "Laura, nothing will hurt you," he
promised. "I won't let the fire hurt you."

She was so fragile, so slight in his grasp, trembling like a
bird. He ran his hand over her shining hair, and stronger
than the sulphur or smoke, the night air burned with her
essence, volatile as powder, sweeter than bergamot.

She screamed as the heavens rumbled with thunder, as
cold lightning slashed the black sky. "Hush, Laura. Hush,
love," he whispered, knowing that in the tumult of wind and
fire and waves she would never hear.

The rain began, slashing down in drops as long as the
ship's ropes, rattling onto the deck and sweeping across it in
sheets whipped by the wind. The fire hissed and spat and
then smothered down to smoke; John led Laura beneath the
overhang of the hatch. "There, you see?" He wrapped his
soaked shirt over the dripping shoulders of her gown and
pushed sopping hair from her forehead. "Everything will be
fine." He spoke to her the way he always thought, always
wished, a mother should speak to her child.

"Don't leave me—"

So sweet, so small. There was a fire burning in his loins;

his blood was hot and bright as a star exploding. His soul seethed; his manhood was rock-hard and smoldering. Never in all the times he'd held a woman had he known such desire—

And never had he been so filled with dread. He pushed her away from him, moving his hands to her shoulders, shaking her angrily. "There is nothing to be afraid of," he said, his voice sharp and loud. "Go back to your cabin. Go below."

"I can't."

I will be cold and distant. A star... "Don't be such a damned child, Laura," he told her. "Go to your bed."

She stared at him for a moment, eyes mirroring the wretched disillusionment in her soul. Then she let out a strangled sob and stumbled down the ladder to the midship hold.

His urge to follow was stronger than the pull of the moon on the tides at its fullness. He went so far as to put one boot on the ladder; then a sailor shouted to him from the mouth of the hatch:

"Ye there!"

He wheeled about. "What?"

"Cap'n Wainwright's compass is smashed." The sailor wore a taunting grin. "He says if ye can read fortunes, can ye tell where we might be bound?"

John felt in his doublet for the needle he kept there. "I can indeed," he told the cocky sailor and went out into the driving rain.

He spent the night at the captain's side, struggling to keep hold of the bowl of water in which his magnetized needle floated precariously. Wainwright hadn't much choice about where the storm sent him, but, as he grunted to John, "Least with that there thing I can tell if we're going to run into France. Jeez, but I'd give my eyeteeth to wind up at dawn with some notion of where I am."

"You've a sandglass on board, to tell the ship's bells, haven't you?" John asked.

"Aye, there's a boy downstairs turnin' it—leastways he'd better damned be."

"Well, then, once the sun comes up you can figure your latitude."

Wainwright snorted. "Ain't got no declination tables on board. Never needed 'em to get myself to Calais."

"I know them by heart," said John. "But you don't need

the tables, not really. You can always figure latitude by the circumference of the earth."

The captain peered at him in the lantern light. "Can ye now," he said dubiously. "What sort of astrologer are ye, anyway?"

"The newfangled sort," said John.

Through the long hours of darkness the storm pushed the *White Lion* onward with wild bluster, making her skim along the tops of the waves like a child's toy. John felt fear as he struggled to keep his footing on the rain-slick deck, with the masts creaking and groaning while the ship pitched frantically up and down. But he also felt a breathtaking exhilaration as the vessel careened through the inky night. The realization that at any moment the entire ship might splinter to bits on a bar or crag made his senses tingle; the proximity of death threw the fact that he was alive into sharp focus. Simply clinging to the lantern, merely taking in and releasing his breath, seemed defiant and brave.

Even as a sudden huge swell engulfed the foredeck and very nearly swept him headlong into the sea, he found himself thinking, I am safer here than I am below, because she is there.

"Close call," Wainwright grunted, hauling him back over the rail by his boot heels.

John laughed, flush with confidence. Beneath the crushing water he had made a realization: he feared death less than he feared love. And that set him free at last from the power of Laura Darby's golden eyes. "You'll never know," he told the captain, "how close it was."

At long last the darkness paled to thick mist. The storm's fury was played out; the winds died; the seas turned a smooth gray. Still grinning at the memory of his narrow escape, John shook hands with the captain, gauged the angle of the thin streaks of light in the western sky with the ease of long practice, and went below to find the boy who'd had the task of staying awake all night to turn the hourglass. "Just a trickle past six," he told John smartly, despite his drooping eyelids.

"Good lad. Get some sleep now." As he climbed back up to the deck, John calculated the difference in the sun's altitude at that hour here with what he knew from his observatory at Guilford Hall. Not more than one and a half degrees. Circumference of the earth, twenty-four thousand, nine hundred miles. Three hundred and sixty degrees to the circle. One and a half times the circumference divided by three hundred and sixty. One hundred and three miles. He reported the result to Captain Wainwright, who pulled at his beard.

"How accurate is that method?"

John shrugged. "I don't know. I never put it to use before."

"Hmph. Well, if we're a hundred miles west of Hertford, we've blown way past Portsmouth. We should be off Lyme Bay, then, near Exmouth. We can put in there to fix that hole in the deck—and find out if Bloody Mary's declared war on France without warning her ships."

"I need to ask a favor, captain," John told him.

"Sure, man, go on, name it. If 'tweren't for ye and that needle, we'd prob'ly have crashed into Normandy."

John glanced at the midship hatch and lowered his voice. "The truth is, I got roped into taking that girl to Calais by a friend. I've got a hell of a lot of work to get back to in Hertford. And so I was wondering—"

"Hell, man." Wainwright grinned. "If ye wants to leave ship at Exmouth, ye're free to go. I'll see the lass safe to Calais. But if ye don't mind me sayin' so, I think ye're daft."

"I just don't have the time."

"Most fellows would make time for her sake, I reckon."

"I guess I'm just not most fellows, then." John noticed that Wainwright was staring over his shoulder, a look of utter disbelief stamped on his grizzled face.

"Jesus bloody Christ," the seaman whispered.

John turned and saw the French fleet lying not half a mile off the larboard bow. "Battle stations!" Wainwright roared across the empty deck. "All hands to battle stations! Prepare to ward off attack! Mitchell, Yarborough, Scott, get yer butts over to the guns!"

"How could they have stayed with us through that storm?" John asked in amazement.

"Ask yer bloody stars, man, not me. Mitchell, where are those guns?"

"Sir," one of the sleepy-eyed soldiers cried, "'tis six ships to one!"

"I can count, lad! But I ain't handin' over the *White Lion* without a fight!"

John winced as he saw the two paltry cannon the crew dragged forth from the quarterdeck. The French ships were closing the gap with impossible quickness; already he could see the black bores of the rows of guns lining the ports. "Don't just stand there, mate," one of the sailors shouted at him. "Draw yer sword, draw yer sword!" John looked down at the weapon he wore and felt an urge to laugh. What use would swords be against those guns? Across the water the linstocks of the French rammers were shining like little stars.

"Duck!" someone shouted beside him. "They're going to fire!" The sailors pressed down flat to the deck behind the bulwarks. From the hatchway at his back, John heard a small, strangled sound. He turned. Laura was standing there in her bloodred gown, long hair unbound and tumbling to her knees.

"Get down!" he shouted, taking a step toward her, trying to shield her from the view of the French. Lord, what would they do to her if they found her? It wasn't hard to guess. "Get down!" he shouted again, but his voice was drowned by the deafening explosion of the long French guns. The deck rocked beneath him. He felt a gust of hot air blast him. He smelled fire.

Then he felt fire, licking at his leg. He looked down. His leg was ablaze. But the water would put it out—for he could feel warm water coursing over his breeches. Thick warm water, red as blood . . .

My God, he thought, I am dead. He laughed, remembering how he'd tempted fate by choosing death over love. Now he'd got his wish. The planks of the deck were tilting up to meet him. He staggered backward and felt the press of the cool brass rail at his thighs.

He looked up one last time and saw Laura running toward him, screaming, reaching out her hands. Star, he thought, bright, bright star. Then the railing slipped away behind him and he was falling, falling through deep, black space toward a distant light.

Laura could not seem to stop screaming, even though she knew no one could possibly hear her above the roar of the guns. The expression on John's face when the shell hit his leg had been so horribly calm, bemused, as though he shared some private jest with destiny.

The deck was spattered with his blood. She ran to the railing beneath a hail of shot and sparks and stared down into the sea where he'd fallen, but she could not find him. She turned, searching the chaos aboard the *White Lion* for Captain Wainwright. He was sprawled across the tiller, the back of his head a pulp of hair and tissue and blood. Retching, she leaned over the rail again and saw John's body bob up on a white-crested wave, eyes closed, head lolling back.

He was dead. The shell had killed him. Oh, God, thought Laura, beginning to cry. Another shell blasted the hatchway behind her, splintering the wood. One of the masts had been hit; it came hurtling downward, draping the sailors, the bulkheads, the deck in a tangle of burning canvas shroud. Fires were flaring up everywhere, fed by tarred wood, pitched line, varnish. Backing slowly away, Laura stared as the flames swept toward her. A thick, burning log fell at her feet; she tried to stamp it out, failed, and kicked it beneath the rail. The log tilted and went flying into the murky water, and the sea quenched its flames with a sharp hiss.

Laura looked down. Her petticoats were smoking.

She crawled over the bulwark and jumped.

She surfaced through the green sea, kicking and clawing toward the light above her. The piece of mast that had fallen bobbed on the waves a few yards away. She swam toward it, red silk swirling around her, and curled one arm tight around the charred wood. She hung there, panting, looking back at the *White Lion*, and saw the French swarming over its sides, an army of bloodthirsty ants.

The sea raised her on a swell, spinning the log she clutched away from the ship, then bumped her into something with a soft, shuddering jolt. A body—John's body—floating facedown in the foam; she could see his broad shoulders and soaked blue-black hair. Swallowing a scream, she tried to kick his corpse away and saw something more: a thin stream of bubbles rising from the water beneath his head.

Oh, God, he was still alive! Disbelieving, Laura reached for his shoulder, trying to turn him over, but lost her grip on his salt-slick skin. He slipped away with a splash; she made a wild grab for his hair and caught it, wresting him back. Slowly she managed to haul one of his limp arms up over the mast, raising his face from the water. A trickle of brine ran from his nose.

The ocean around them was turning a sickly brown from his blood. Laura knew she should staunch the bleeding, but she could not bear to reach for his leg beneath the surface; she was terrified she would find a stump, not smooth and healed over like her father's arm, but ragged and raw. Instead she clung to the log and to him, and let the sea lead

them farther from the *White Lion*. As they emerged from the
cloud of smoke around the ships, the water glittered with
light so searing that it burned her eyes. She closed them wearily, leaning her cheek against the log.

How strange, she thought. Instead of dying by fire, I shall
die by water. And so much water! Until two days ago, she'd
never even seen the sea.

They drifted, no sign of life or of land anywhere around
them. The sun rose high in the sky and started down again,
then set in a blaze of gold that stretched forever across the
skies. Laura heard a chorus of rude squawks and looked up;
a long line of big white birds flapped past overhead, their
noisy cries like raucous laughter above waves tipped with
fire. Beside her John was breathing in faint, rasping gasps.
Laura followed the flight of the birds as long as she could;
they flew into a thick bank of clouds on the distant horizon,
and then there was nothing around her but the sea.

She must have fallen asleep, for she woke in darkness,
with the eerie sensation that the log had stopped moving.
She could feel water all around her; the tide was flowing, but
it was not carrying them. Puzzled, she shoved at the wood
with her hand. It resisted, spinning in a slow circle with
John's figure at the center. As if he anchored us, Laura
thought dizzily. She tugged at his arm and heard a faint
scraping sound.

Land—could it be? Not quite believing, she ducked beneath the water, reaching downward. Her bare toes touched
cold rock.

"John," she whispered to her oblivious companion.
"John, we've saved. It is land, we've reached land!" She gave
the log a mighty push forward, until she could stand in the
water. Then she caught John under his arms and dragged him
toward shore.

The coastline that rose from the sea was steep and rocky.
She hauled John up onto the rocks as far as she could. His
breathing was frighteningly shallow; she put one hand over
his heart and the other on her own to compare. His seemed
scarcely to be beating. I have to bring help, she thought, and
climbed higher on the rocks, looking for light.

She saw only the stars, distant, white, and dazzling.
"Hello!" she cried out. "Hello, is anybody there?" Her voice
echoed back to her, hollow and forlorn. She searched the sky
for the Pole Star and found it, straight ahead over the sea.
Nothing but water that way. She would strike out south.

She groped across the slippery rocks through the darkness. Sharp shells and barnacles tore at the soles of her shoes, and she could hear faint slithering sounds all around her. She shivered as some sort of spiny thing scuttled from her hand.

Her toes touched water, and a burst of cold spray brushed her cheek. More ocean, she thought, and glanced back over her shoulder at Ursa Major and the Pole Star. North to south—she'd circled west. She would have to go east.

She waded back onto the rocks, keeping them on her left, the ocean on her right. Her fingers touched something cold and yielding. Flesh, she realized, and stumbled over John's arm. A horrible suspicion began to form in her mind.

She climbed past John and started out again. Rocks on the left, ocean on the right—but this time she knew that she moved in a circle. They'd found land, yes, but it was only a jagged spur of stone rising from the sea.

"Never mind," she told John's oblivious form, crawling back to him, crouching on the rock beside him. "We're alive; that's what matters. Someone will come for us. You'll see. Come morning, someone will find us." Holding his hand, she settled back to wait.

Chapter 10

The sound of swift-rushing water woke Laura. For an instant, before she opened her eyes, she dreamed she was in the lavatory at Guilford Hall. The chamber pot was overflowing; the cool water was lapping over her knees . . .

She sat up, looked about, and blinked in the blaze of sunlight. Rocks. She was sitting on black rocks, and the water rushing toward her was the sea. John was stretched out beside her, cold and pale as death, the tide already up to his waist. Laura leaned over him, checking his heartbeat. Still there—but how faint!

The black rocks rose above her in a steep peak. Laura scrambled upward on her hands and knees, perching near the top. Not more than five hundred yards to the east was a tall cliff, its peak dotted with white birds. As she scanned the steep face of the precipice, she saw something more: a figure, white-shirted, windblown, climbing down toward a small skiff anchored at the cliff base.

"Thank you, Lord," she whispered, and stood up as tall as she could in her soaked red dress, waving frantically, calling toward the shore, "Hello! Hello, help! Help us, please!" The figure turned toward her, stared. She waved more wildly. "Hello! Help! Rescue us!" He'd heard her; she could tell by the way he jerked up his head. But instead of climbing down toward the skiff, the figure—it was a man, she was sure of it—turned and scrambled back up to the top of the cliff. Then he disappeared.

What on earth? Laura watched as the seagulls flapped into the sky where the man had run past them. The sound of rushing water was growing louder; she glanced down at John and gasped. The tide was past his chest now, almost to his chin.

Quickly she scrambled back down the black hulk of rock and caught him under his shoulders, dragging him up and away from the water, still averting her eyes; she did not want to see his right leg. Damn that man on the cliff, she thought angrily. Where could he have got to? It was plain as day that she needed help.

Perhaps she could swim to the skiff and row out for John afterward. Gingerly she picked her way down to the sea. The water was sending up great sprays of white foam as it closed around the rock she stood on. She stepped in, holding to an outcropping, and was nearly dragged under; the current was swift and hard.

Choking on salt, she fought her way back onto the rock. The tide would certainly carry her to the cliff—and then smash her to pieces there. She would never be able to row the boat back for John against that flood. And if she left him here—already the water had risen another two feet.

What in the world was she going to do? She peered up at the rock above her. If the tide rose another five yards, it would be swallowed up. Perhaps the water wouldn't come that high, but from the way it was rushing past now that didn't seem likely. She clambered back to John and yanked him higher still, struggling to raise his dead weight.

Where had that man on the cliff disappeared to? Laura climbed to the peak of the rock again and shouted for all she was worth. "Hello! Help! Hello!" Not even a seagull answered. "Oh, this is absurd!" Laura said aloud. "We are going to drown with all of that land right there!"

She peered down at the sea again, at the swift eddies and whirlpools it formed as the tide rushed in. She *might* make it to the shore safely through its currents—but what about John? She couldn't leave him stranded here, unconscious, helpless. He'd saved her from Thomas; she owed him more than her life for that.

And still the water was rising. She went back for John, pulling him up over the coarse black stone, then hesitated, looking down at him. He was practically dead already. He'd smiled when that cannonball hit him—as though he'd wanted to die. Perhaps she should just leave him here and save herself. Really, what more could anyone expect her to do?

"Hello! Are you out there?"

Laura raised her head at the shout. The man on the cliff! She crawled back around the increasingly narrow spit of rock and looked. Someone was coming down the steep face of the rock. A different man, though—this one was dressed all in black.

"Hello! Help me!" she screamed at him, waving her arms.

"I'm coming!" he called. "Stay high up on the rock!" He scrambled down the cliff; Laura watched, her heart in her throat, as he untied the skiff from its mooring. Could anyone row a boat against the force of that tide?

The man stepped into the rocking skiff, set the oars, and, his back to Laura, began to haul, his progress so slow that he scarcely seemed to move at all. "Oh, hurry," Laura whispered, wringing her hands as the tiny boat pushed through the onrushing water. "Please, please hurry!" He was coming closer, fighting for every foot. She could see muscles straining through his black shirt. The bald shining crown of his head gleamed with sweat.

"There are two of us here!" she shouted to him, and thought she saw him nod in acknowledgment. How hard he was working! Above the roar of the waves she heard his labored breath. Closer. Closer. And then the skiff was so close she could nearly touch it. "What should I do?" she cried.

"Catch this!" He turned, flinging her a rope, and she stared. He wasn't bald after all; he was tonsured. A Catholic priest.

The rope fell into the water; she was too stunned to reach for it. "Try again!" the priest shouted cheerily, hauling it in and throwing it once more. This time Laura managed to grasp it. "Hook it over the rock!" he told her. Laura took the loop he'd made and climbed up the fast-diminishing peak. He stood up and leaped out beside her, leaving the boat to stream out along the line and stop with a jolting snap.

"The trip back will be a lot quicker," the priest assured her. She took a quick look at him. His hair was brown, his complexion pale, his merry eyes hazel, crinkling at the corners. "Who else is here?" he asked, glancing about.

"John." She pointed around the rock. "He's hurt; he can't walk."

The priest frowned at the oncoming tide. "We haven't got much time. Let's bring him around to this side." He followed her over the rock and saw John's limp, pale body. "He's a big one, isn't he? How did you—well, never mind that." He bent over John quickly and felt his heart, then rolled his eyes. "Where is he hurt?"

"His—his leg." Laura pointed; it was still under the water. The priest grunted, lifting him up.

"Oh, dear God," Laura heard her rescuer say.

"Is it gone?" she asked fearfully, not looking.

"No, but it isn't good." As gently as he could he dragged John to the other side of the rock. "All right," he said, somewhat short of breath, laying his burden down. "I'm going to haul the boat back, and then I want you to jump in and go to the front. Then I'll lift John in, and then I'll get in, and then I'll cut the rope. Do you understand?"

Laura nodded. Hand over hand, he pulled the skiff back against the tide. When it had nearly reached the rock, he told her "Go!" and she clambered in, holding the sides. He wrapped the rope around his waist, bent for John, and shoved him down past the seat. Then, the rope still circling his waist, he stepped into the boat and grasped the oars. "Hold on!" he warned above the rushing water. He took a knife from his boot and slashed the rope.

The skiff sprang forward with a ferocious lurch and careened wildly right toward the cliff. Laura screamed as that huge, blunt wall of rock loomed up overhead. Just when it seemed absolutely certain they'd be smashed to bits, the sea pushed them back gently; they rocked a few feet off shore, caught between ebb and flow.

"Strange tides here, eh?" the priest called, as Laura pulled her hands away from her face. He unwrapped the rope from his waist, made another loop, and cast it up over a jutting crag. "We natives say there's a certain point, just as the tide changes, when a man can walk on the water. I must admit, I've never seen anyone try."

"Natives?" said Laura. But he was talking again.

"There are stairs cut into the cliff; do you see them?" She nodded. "Go up to the top then and tell Guy I need his help." He pronounced the name very strangely, so that it rhymed with "we."

Cautiously Laura climbed out of the boat and started up the cliff face. The stairs were steep and slippery, and if she had not been so grateful to be on solid high ground, she'd have been terrified. As it was, she made a point of not looking down.

It was a hard climb. As she cleared the very top at last she saw a big burly man in a flapping white shirt and jean trousers. His skin was so sunburned it was nearly black; he had bright blue eyes and a tangle of bushy gray beard. "Are you Guy—I mean—" She pronounced it again, the way the priest had. He nodded. "Well, the man down there asked me to tell you he needs your help." He bobbed his head again and bounded past her down the stone staircase, surefooted as a mountain goat.

Laura's head was spinning from the climb. She moved away from the edge of the treacherous cliff and sat down, feeling suddenly faint. She looked out over the ocean and shivered. The rock on which she and John had been stranded had been swallowed up by the sea.

It was half an hour or more before the priest and the man called Guy appeared, carrying John between them. "Are you all right?" asked the priest, seeing her sitting down, holding her head.

"Aye," she said faintly. "Just dizzy." She realized she had not thanked him. "I'm ever so grateful to you, sir—I mean, Father."

"And you are most welcome. I have to attend to this leg. Guy." Again he gave the name the strange foreign twist. And then, to Laura's horror, he let out a long stream of French.

Guy asked a quick question in the same language, then headed down from the cliff, through a lush green meadow toward a little stone cottage. There was a donkey cart tied up at the gate; he leaped in, clucking his tongue at the donkey, and they trotted off. Good Lord, thought Laura, a priest and a Frenchman! What have I got myself into now?

The priest had slung one of John's arms around his shoulders; now he gestured to Laura. "Can you grab the other arm, please? We've got to get him inside." Together they hauled him across the meadow to the cottage, through a small front room, into a bedchamber and onto a bed.

With infinite care the priest eased off John's bloodied boot and stocking and pried away what was left of his breeches leg. "I know I should help," Laura said shakily, "but I just cannot bear to."

"That's all right," he told her, "just sit. Guy has gone for help; he'll be back soon."

"I wish he wouldn't come back." Laura sank onto a stool by the bed. "It was his countrymen did that to John."

"Aren't you English, mistress— I don't know your name," said the priest, probing John's wound.

"Laura. Laura Darby. Of course I am English."

"Well, so is Guy. Laura Darby, do you know where you are?"

"Why, somewhere in the south of England, I suppose."

"Very far south," he said, looking up from John's leg with a grin. "You're on Guernsey, in the Channel Isles. Four little

English gnats in the armpit of France—I beg your pardon; that's what a French king once called them. Everyone here speaks French, even though the islands belong to England. They're much closer to France, you see. If you look out the door you can see Normandy."

"Englishmen who speak French," Laura said slowly. "Will wonders never cease!"

"I don't think so," he told her cheerfully. "It was a wonder Guy saw you out there today. He was drunk again last night and overslept. Otherwise he'd have been out fishing hours ago. The Lord does work in mysterious ways."

"I thought he'd run away when he disappeared from the cliff. Why didn't he come out and save us himself? Was he afraid of the tide?"

"What, Guy? Lord, no, he knows the tides better than any man on Guernsey." The priest fetched a basin of water from the outer room and began to wash off John's leg. "But he's afraid of that rock. There's a legend on Guernsey that when St. Patrick came to the island he found the devil holding court here and hurled him off that cliff. When he hit the water, he turned into that stone. 'L'An Drio,' Guy calls it. The Arch Druid."

"If that's not the silliest thing I ever heard," said Laura. "Why, we might have drowned!"

"Don't you believe in the devil, Mistress Darby?"

"I surely don't believe he's cooped up in that rock." For a moment her conscience pricked her, as she remembered how she'd contemplated leaving John there and saving herself. But that hadn't been the devil; that had been despair. She looked at the Catholic. "Do you?"

"I think," he said, "he is there for Guy. By the by, my name is Talbot. Père Talbot, the islanders call me—you know, Father."

"I speak French," Laura assured him. "Were you born on Guernsey?"

He nodded. "I got my university degree in England, though. Tell me, how did you and your husband manage to end up on our Arch Druid?"

Her husband! Laura started to correct his mistake, then paused. She knew nothing about these people, except that they were certainly Catholic. Perhaps it would be better, safer, if they believed she and John were wed.

The priest was regarding her expectantly. "We—we were on a ship, going to Calais," she said carefully. She wouldn't be telling a lie if she didn't actually say she and John were husband and wife. "Some French ships came up and started shooting at us, and John's leg got hit and he fell in the sea, and I jumped overboard. I think everyone else was killed by the French."

The priest nodded solemnly. "Queen Mary has finally declared war on King Henri; it was posted at St. Peter Port this morning. But the French beat her to it, I suppose. I'm sorry for your shipmates. We'll have to have a Mass for their souls."

Laura froze. But she was saved from making any reply by a burst of excited French chatter from the cottage doorway. "That will be Guy come back," said Talbot. "With his sister, Hannay."

"Talbot?" Guy called.

"In here," the priest called in English, then explained to Laura, "I've taught them some English, though the rest of the island doesn't speak it at all. Oh, except for Helier Gosselin, the seigneur." The burly fisherman came into the bed-chamber, followed by a woman much younger than he.

She was lovely. Her face was a perfect oval, her complexion olive. Her dark hair was drawn behind her small ears in a shiny bun. It was easy to tell she and Guy were sister and brother; they had the same bright, deep-set blue eyes.

The priest had turned his attention back to his patient. So Laura said, "How do you do? I am Laura Darby, and this is John."

The woman smiled. "I am Hannay de Carteret. You have met my brother."

"How does it look, Talbot?" the burly fisherman boomed, peering at John's leg.

"There are a lot of splinters of wood and some pieces of shell. We will have to cut them out."

"*Eh bien,* I bring the good knives. Hannay?" Guy gestured her toward the bed.

She knelt down on the opposite side from Talbot, taking the basin. Guy brought a tray of lethal-looking equipment, and the priest set to work. It was uncanny for Laura to see how the woman anticipated his needs as he probed the bloody flesh of John's leg. He would reach for a cloth to mop away the blood and she would have it ready; he would need a smaller knife or a set of pincers and she'd have it there. Yet Laura could not help noticing that they never, not once, touched each other. It was as though their busy hands danced some weird, courtly arabesque in which they were permitted to circle and curtsy but no more.

The priest knew his business. A half hour, perhaps less, had passed when, with a little pile of metal fragments and wood slivers on the floor beside him, he set down his tools. The woman, Hannay, brought him a bottle of lotion, and he bathed the wound and bound the leg in boiled linen. *"C'est fini,"* he said, and washed his hands. "Your husband is lucky. The shell must have hit the ship's deck just before it hit him. And the salt water acted as a purgative."

With the job finished, the woman seemed in a terrible rush to leave. She hastily gathered up the bloody linen, pincers, and knives, carrying them from the room. Talbot pulled a cloth bundle out of his shirt and handed it to Laura. "Give him some of this in a bit of ale when he needs it for pain. Chop it fine. About a pinch to a cup."

"What is it?" Laura asked, unwrapping the bundle and peering at the gnarled contents.

"Mandragora root. It will make him sleep."

Hannay ducked back into the bedchamber and squeezed Laura's hand. "It will be well, you see," she said reassuringly. "I will come by to see you."

"Thank you very much!" Laura called as the woman ran out the door.

Once she'd gone, the priest seemed to relax a little. "Change the dressing every four hours," he told Laura. "I'll check on him tomorrow morning. Meantime, Guy will look after you. You did say you spoke French."

"Oh, yes," Laura assured him.

"Good. I must be off to Mass. *Au revoir,* Guy."

"Au revoir, Talbot."

The priest left the cottage. Laura heard the jangle of the bells on his pony cart as he drove away.

John had not moved a muscle on the bed. That left Laura and the big fisherman staring at one another. He needs a haircut rather badly, she thought, as those bright blue eyes perused her curiously. His hands, she saw, were huge and knotted, the knuckles crisscrossed with bumps and scars.

"Avez-vous faim?" he asked, in a low, quiet voice much unlike the boom he'd used when the others were present.

Laura nodded hesitantly. *"Oui, je suis affamée."* It was true, she was starved.

He didn't laugh at her accent, though he did raise a bushy

gray brow. *"Eh bien,"* he said, crooking a gnarled finger. "We eat."

She followed him into the outer room of the cottage, taking a closer look at her surroundings. The stone building was shaped like a square; the long front room served as kitchen and sitting place, and besides the bedchamber in which John slept there was one other in the back. There were few furnishings: the long oak table, a couple of stools, a chest of drawers. The floor was made of packed dirt, the stone walls were bare. A bachelor's cottage, Laura thought, noting the absence of even a single feminine touch.

They sat at the table. He brought out two wooden bowls and a heel of bread, then served her some sort of fish stew from a pot at the hearth. There was a big ale barrel in a corner; he poured her a cup and then swallowed one quickly himself and poured out another.

"C'est très bon, ce ragoût," she told him, complimenting the stew.

He smiled at her, rather bashfully. *"Merci.* But if you do not mind, madame, could we speak in English? I would like the practice." And that, thought Laura, was the nicest possible way anyone could have told her how atrocious her accent was.

She smiled back. "If you like. What sort of fish is this?"

"Anguille." At her blank look he went on. "What you call conger. Eel."

"Eel!" Laura peered dubiously into her bowl. "Isn't that like a snake?"

He laughed. "No, no. No snakes on Guernsey. St. Patrick took them all away."

"I thought that was Ireland," said Laura, tasting the stew again.

Guy de Carteret gave a bit of a sniff. "St. Patrick came here to the Isles long before he went to Ireland. After he threw our Arch Druid into the sea, he took all the nasty creatures here—snakes and toads and vermin—put them in his pockets, swam over to Jersey—the other big island—and left them there. At least, that is how we tell the story on Guernsey."

"How do they tell it on Jersey?"

He shrugged. "The other way around."

Laura laughed. "Well, for something made of something that is like a snake, this is still good stew."

"It is what we eat here on Guernsey. There is not much

else but the eels and the fish. I make it myself. I am my own cook. Except for *le pain*—the bread. Hannay makes that for me. Somehow I have never gotten the knick—the knick?"

"The knack."

"The knack, *oui,* to make bread."

"That's odd," said Laura. "I know a woman in England who is just the opposite. The only decent thing she can make is bread."

"She and I—we would be like Jersey and Guernsey, *n'est-ce pas?*" he said, and chuckled.

Laura laughed too, warming to the jolly man. "If these islands are English, why do the people here speak French?" she asked.

His blue eyes shone. "I tell you the story. Once, far far back in time, so far back that no one knows when, the two giants who made the earth were fighting with slingshots. The rocks they shot that missed fell here, in the Channel, and they were the Isles. But nothing good would come to live on such bad rocks—"

"Bad rocks? How can a rock be bad?"

Guy de Carteret spread out his hands. "Every rock has its spirit, *oui?* Good rock, good spirit. Bad rock, bad spirit. These rocks had bad spirits, because the evil giants had played with them. So only bad things would live here—wizards and demons. *Les monstres.* But then St. Patrick came, and he fought with the Arch Druid, the great wizard who commanded the evil things. St. Patrick captured him and dragged him across the island and threw him into the sea. And from every rock that St. Patrick touched while he fought with the Arch Druid, the evil spirits flew out, and good spirits flew in."

"I see," said Laura, biting her lip at the Guernseyman's earnest rendition of this outlandish tale.

"Eh bien," he went on, not noticing her bemusement, "now there were good spirits on the islands, and people came from Normandy to live here. And St. Patrick told them, I will give you a way to live, to keep the good spirits in the rocks and to keep the evil spirits at bay. And he gave to the islanders Le Droit Ancien. The Ancient Way."

"What is the Ancient Way?"

The Guernseyman wrinkled his sunburned nose. "The rules, *oui?* The right way of doing things. And all the islanders learned the Ancient Way, and it was our way of life. And because the people on the islands had come from Normandy, we belonged to France." He got up and poured himself a third cup of ale. "Do you want more to drink?"

"Oh, no. No, thank you." Laura found the harsh black brew nearly as hard to swallow as Guy de Carteret's tale. He took his seat at the table again.

"Many, many years later," he continued, "there was a mighty king in France, Philip Augustus. He resented the privileges the islanders had under the Ancient Way, so he tried to take it away. We were very angry, so we sent emissaries to the King of England, King John."

"King John was a bad king," said Laura, remembering her English history.

He winked. "For England, yes. For the Isles, no. The islanders asked King John, if we belong to England instead of to France, will you let us keep our Ancient Way? And he said yes, and he gave us a charter that said our Ancient Way should never be broken so long as we belonged to England. And so from that day we became Englishmen."

"I'm certainly glad you did!" said Laura, remembering the French soldiers swarming over the decks of the *White Lion*. "It was French sailors who attacked the ship John and I were on."

Guy de Carteret nodded. "Queen Mary has declared war on France. It is bad, very bad. All the world is at war."

"Still," Laura mused, "you are not exactly English, are you, if you speak French. And if you've got your Ancient Way."

He frowned, his blue eyes no longer merry. "No more. The Ancient Way is past now. The seigneur we have now, Helier Gosselin, convinced the people of Guernsey it was a bad way."

"What is a seigneur?" Laura asked, struggling to pronounce it the way he did.

"Our overlord, *oui?* Our master. He told the Guernseymen, the Ancient Way is foolish. There are no spirits in the stones, he says. We are Englishmen, we must be modern. No more superstition, no more foolish customs. No more Ancient Way."

"Well," said Laura, "perhaps he is right. It is superstition, after all. There aren't really spirits in stones."

"Oh, yes, there are," Guy de Carteret said very gravely. "And Helier knows they are there. That is not why he tells the people the Ancient Way is bad. It is because he is greedy. Under the Ancient Way, we paid the seigneur his tributes in eels and chickens and hay. Helier does not want eels and chickens. He wants gold. And the people here, they are stupid. They listen to him. But the day will come when they will be sorry. The day will come when they see."

"See what?" asked Laura, looking into his solemn blue eyes.

"That what St. Patrick said was true. That without the Ancient Way, the evil spirits will seep back into the stones. They are coming back now, every day. More and more. And someday soon, unless the people bring back the old customs, the evil will grow so strong that the Arch Druid will break loose from his rock and rule over this island again."

Despite the bright sunlight that poured through the cottage windows, Laura felt a chill creep up her spine. She shrugged the eerie sensation away impatiently. She'd never heard such a pack of nonsense in her life! She regarded the big man who sat across from her, sipping his ale. "You don't *really* believe that, do you?"

His voice dropped to a whisper. "Wait and see. Wait and see," he crooned softly, wagging his head. Then he got up abruptly to clear away their bowls. "You had better go and look if your husband's dressing needs to be changed."

Chapter 11

For the next two days and nights, Laura watched over John and nursed his wound. She had made up a potion of mandragora root and ale according to Père Talbot's directions, but she never used it. John showed no signs of being in pain, though she could not believe the mess beneath his bandages was not agonizing. He slept for hour after hour, so soundly that he did not even wake to eat; she had to slip water and broth down his throat from a spoon. She slept on a chair beside the bed, with the door to the common room closed, keeping up the pretense that they were man and wife.

She'd been frantic at the prospect of having to empty his bedpan or change the linens, of seeing naked the parts of him that had looked so horrible on Thomas and Theodore. But Père Talbot, who came by each morning and evening, took over those chores without even being asked. "He is such a big man," he told Laura, smiling, "and you are so small." Laura was terrified that he would mention the Mass for the dead sailors again, but the subject never arose. Instead they talked of herbal medicines, of his bad-tempered pony, Gris-Gris, or of the children he taught in his school, while John lay sleeping silently.

As for Guy, their host, Laura found him utterly charming despite his peculiar superstitions. He worked very hard indeed, going out in the skiff to his boat at dawn, not returning until the light was nearly gone. Still, he was never too tired to sit by the hearth in the evening and tell her stories, while he downed cup after cup of the bitter island ale.

He'd built this stone cottage himself, he told her, checking first to see that the rocks beneath the spot he'd chosen were good. "How can you tell a good rock from a bad one?" she'd asked, hiding a smile.

He put his nose in the air and sniffed. "You smell them. Evil has a smell all its own. There is a rock here on the west part of Guernsey, the Catioroc, that is evil. It has a bad smell. The witches and wizards used to gather there at midnight on the Sabbath. There was a chapel to the Holy Virgin on Lihou Island, out in the bay, and the witches and wizards would stand on the rock and look out at the chapel, and all night long they would dance and sing: '*Qui hou hou, Marie Lihou!*'"

"What would happen if you built a house on a bad rock?"

"*Ça dépend.* Sometimes the good spirits help you," he said. "Many hundreds of years ago, the English bishop came here to build St. Martin's Church. He chose a place near Saint's Bay that was on very bad rock. The islanders tried to tell him, but he would not listen. He brought everything to build the church to the place. But then," Guy went on, eyes glowing in the firelight, "on the very night before the workmen were to start building, all the wood and tools and stones were moved miles and miles away to a new place, by the good spirits, because they did not want a church to be built on an evil rock. Then the bishop believed, and he built his church where they had moved the wood and tools. It is still there now."

He got up to pour himself more ale. "There is another way, too, to tell if a rock is good. You strike it with a hammer. If the rock is good, it will sing. There was a rock in Vale Parish long ago. La Rocque Qui Sonne, it was called. 'The Rock That Rings.' Like a bell, *oui?* A very good stone. A man named Hocart ordered it broken up for a house he was building. He made the workmen smash it. You could hear the good spirits in it crying all over the island. He built the house, and it fell down. Stupid Hocart, he would not believe it was because he broke a good stone. He loaded the pieces onto a ship to sail them to Jersey and build his house there. The ships sank. The rigging fell on him and he died. This is what happens when you do not pay attention to the spirits in the stones."

Though Laura knew the old tales were so much stuff and nonsense, every once in a while, sitting by the hearth with the night wind whistling up the cliff, she would feel that little tingle run along her spine as Guy spoke of the spirits, and of the wicked wizard who'd held sway on Guernsey before St. Patrick came.

Not all the stories were about such creatures. When he had drunk enough ale, he sometimes told tales of his own derring-do: how he'd sailed his fishing boat, the *Marie-Hélène*, through a terrible storm with waves twice as high as the cliff outside the door; how he'd sailed through a place called "The Needle," on the neighboring island of Sark, where the rocks were only inches apart; how he'd once caught a whale in his nets and been dragged halfway across the Channel; how he lost his mast to a lightning bolt and had to row home with a spoon. "And do you know, Laura, why it is that I, Guy de Carteret, could do all these things?" he would always ask at the end. "Because I believe. I believe in the Ancient Way."

On the afternoon of the third day, while Guy was out fishing, Hannay arrived at the cottage bearing a big brown sack. *"Bonjour!"* she called through the doorway. "Hello! Are you there?"

"Bonjour!" Laura emerged from the bedchamber where she'd just finished checking the bandages on John's leg. She suddenly realized how eager she was for feminine company. "Come in, come in!"

"Talbot is not here, is he?" the Guernseywoman asked, peering about.

"No, you've missed him. He comes early in the morning and again at night." They stood staring at one another. Feeling awkward, Laura beckoned her toward the table. "Won't you sit down? Would you care for something to drink?" Then she laughed. "It seems strange to invite you into your own brother's house."

Hannay smiled, offering her the sack. "I brought Guy his bread. I also brought some clothes for you. Nothing fancy like that." She nodded toward Laura's bedraggled red gown. "Just smocks, like we wear here."

"Bless you," Laura declared, laughing. "You can't imagine how glad I shall be to put on a plain, decent smock!"

Hannay laughed too. "Tell me, how is your husband?"

"I hardly know; all he does is sleep. But Talbot says his leg is healing. He knows a lot about medicine, doesn't he?"

"Père Talbot," said Hannay, with a small, wry smile, "is a remarkable man."

"So is your brother Guy," Laura told her. "It is so kind of him to have taken us in."

"I think he must be glad for the company. Has he been telling you stories?"

"Oh, yes. I think I must know the name of every spirit that lives in every rock on Guernsey!"

Hannay sighed. "Poor Guy."

"I don't know why you should say that. He really is most

entertaining. I cannot believe some lucky woman has not snatched him up for her husband."

"He was married once. Her name was Marie-Hélène. Has he mentioned her?" Laura shook her head. "So, that is one story he still does not tell. She died a long time ago."

Laura looked and saw a gold band on Hannay's right hand. "Are you married to a fisherman?"

Hannay laughed. "One might say that. I am married to Talbot."

Laura blinked. "In England, priests are not allowed to marry!"

"Nor can they here, not now. But ten years ago, in the reign of King Henry, the laws were different. That is when we were wed. When Queen Mary came to the throne, she decreed that all priests must put away their wives or else leave the church. Talbot could not leave the church, so it is almost five years now that we have lived apart. I have a cottage on the other side of the valley. He has one behind his church."

"But why don't you live here with Guy?" Laura asked curiously.

"Because Talbot comes to visit Guy, and no one else on the island does. Guy needs Talbot. And I do not want to see Talbot. The day he rescued you and your husband was the first time I have seen him in months. I would not have come then, but he sent Guy and said he needed me for the doctoring."

"Dear me." Laura was wishing they'd never gotten onto this subject. She remembered now how careful Hannay and Talbot had been not to greet or speak to each other, or even to touch. "Queen Mary's decree must have come as quite a relief."

"*Pardonne?*" said Hannay.

"I mean—" Laura felt herself blushing. "If you hate him so much that you can't stand to see him, it must have been a most unhappy marriage."

To Laura's atonishment, the woman burst out laughing. "Oh, *chérie*, I don't hate him! I love him! I love him madly."

"But then why on earth do you avoid each other?"

Hannay leaned her chin on her hand, groping to explain. "Not to see Talbot, this is a very hard thing, yes? A *very* hard thing. But to see him, to be near him as I was here the other day, and not to be able to *make* love to him—that is agony."

To Laura, still recoiling from Thomas's brutal attack on

their wedding night, from the memory of him on his bed with Theo, this notion was incomprehensible. "Do you mean," she blurted, "that you miss *that* as much as all *that?*"

Hannay wagged her head. "Oh, it is easy for you to say, with your own husband there in the next room and nothing to stop you from going in to him, *oui?* But think of it, *chérie.* Five years since I held my husband against me, since I felt him inside me!"

Laura wished more than ever that they'd stuck to the topic of, perhaps, the weather. "Couldn't you just—you know, meet in secret?" she asked tentatively.

Hannay let out a heartfelt sigh. "*Chérie,* if I could persuade Talbot to do that, I would have been able to persuade him to leave the church. *Non, ce n'est pas possible.* He is one of those men—beware lest you fall in love with one—who loves something else more than he loves me."

"Well, I am certainly sorry for you," said Laura, and realized how terribly prim that sounded.

"*Attendez,*" Hannay said knowingly. "You wait. You wait until, heaven forfend, you are ever parted from that big, handsome fellow in there. Then you know what sorry is, *n'est-ce pas?*" She winked. "But let us talk of happier things. Your husband—tell me, what does he do?"

"John? I'm not certain what the word is in French, but he's an astron—" She leaped up from her stool as, from the bedroom, there came a loud crash. "What on earth—" She ran in and saw that somehow John had managed to knock over the chair by the bed, though he was still sleeping soundly. She set the chair upright and turned to Hannay. "Do you know, I think that is the first time he has moved in three days!"

"That is the mandragora Talbot gave you."

Laura shook her head. "It can't be that. I haven't had to use any. He just keeps sleeping."

"*Vraiment?*" Hannay pinched his cheek. "His color is good." She raised her head suddenly. "Guy is coming home."

"How can you tell?"

"*Les mouettes.* The seabirds. Listen." Laura cocked her head. The cries of the gulls outside were growing louder. "He gives them scraps from the catch," Hannay explained, "so they follow him home. Come, we meet him out on the cliff."

"Hannay!" Guy waved, climbing up the cliff face with his nets over his arm. "Stay with us for supper!"

"I can't," his sister said wistfully. "Talbot will be coming."

Puffing, Guy looked at Laura as he reached the top. "The patient, how is he?"

"Sleeping," she said.

"*Bien,* I go to the church and tell Talbot not to come until morning. If that is all right with you, Laura?" She nodded, and he headed off down the hill.

It was a merry meal, the conversation a melange of English and French, helped along by the vast quantities of ale Guy poured. Laura noticed Hannay frowning as her brother gulped down his sixth cup, but she couldn't understand why. Guy never got angry or rough when he drank, the way Humphrey had; he only seemed to grow jollier.

Even when the meal was finished, Guy kept drinking. He vanished inside his bedchamber and returned with a big triple-strung harp. "The *télen,*" he told Laura, and sat down to play. The instrument sounded like no harp Laura had ever heard—or maybe it was merely the songs he sang that were strange and exotic. They were in French, but a French so twisted and archaic that she could not make out the words.

"It is the Old French," he told her. "La Normande, that the troubadours used to sing for the kings and queens of Provence and Aquitaine." He sang in a rich, sweet tenor and played beautifully, his thick, scarred fingers flying over the strings. Even though Laura could not comprehend the words, the songs made her sad.

"That is because they are old songs," said Guy. "Songs of when we Guernseymen still had the Ancient Way."

His sister snorted. "No. It is because they are love songs." She stood up, smoothing down her skirts. "It is late, and Talbot will come early in the morning. I must go home."

Guy stood up too and nearly stumbled. "I will walk you home," he offered grandly.

She laughed. "If you do, you will spend the night! I know what you are like when you drink this much ale."

"*Bien,* then I stay the night. Laura will be safe. She has her husband here." He staggered toward the door, then came back for a refill of his ale cup. "*Bonne nuit,* Laura!"

Hannay hurried to take his arm, winking back at Laura. "He is walking me, eh, do you hear him?" She rolled her eyes. "*Bonne nuit!*"

Laura could hear Guy singing as they set off down the

road to the valley. She heard Hannay too, trying unsuccessfully to get him to hush. She smiled to herself; then the smile
faded as she thought of what Hannay had said about the old
French songs: they were sad because they were love songs. It
is true, she thought; love doesn't seem to bring anyone anything but unhappiness. Look at poor Hannay and Talbot,
stuck here on this little island, avoiding each other. Look at
John's father and mother; look at old King Henry and his six
wives. The more she got to know of love, the more she suspected her parents had had the only happy marriage in the
entire world.

The ale had made her terribly sleepy. She knew she ought
to get up to change John's bandages, but she could not find
the will. She leaned over, cradling her head in her arms atop
the table, and closed her eyes. Just for a moment, she promised herself. I'll just rest for a moment, right here.

She awoke in pitch-darkness, stiff-necked and thirsty. The
water pitcher at her elbow was empty; grumbling, she got up
to refill it at the well outside, thinking longingly of the magical privies at Guilford Hall. The cottage door opened to a
flood of moonlight so bright that she blinked. She made her
way to the well, filled the pitcher, and drank eagerly, the cool
water clearing her aching head.

As she walked back to the cottage, she glanced up at the
cliff to see the moon. It was full and ghost white, adrift far
out over the ocean in a sea of stars. A bit of movement high
atop the rocks caught her attention. A gull, she thought, and
then realized it was a man.

"Guy!" she called. Lord, he would fall and kill himself,
drunk as he was! In the soft, dreamy moonlight the figure
turned toward her—not Guy, but John.

Barefoot, in the loose smock that Hannay had lent her,
she ran through the dew-soaked grass toward the rocks. How
in heaven's name had he climbed all that way on his leg?
"John, what are you doing?" she called, scrambling up to
him.

He nodded toward the western sky. "There is going to be
an eclipse of the moon." His voice sounded strange, husky
with disuse.

"An eclipse of the—oh, for God's sake." She reached for
his arm. "You're ill! You should not be walking. Come back
to the house."

He shook her off with surprising strength. "It happens

once, twice perhaps, in a man's whole lifetime. I don't intend to miss this one."

"At the cost of your life?" she asked angrily.

He laughed, the sound low and grating. "And just how much is that? What is my life worth?"

Laura looked up into his cold wolf's eyes, remembering the small, calm smile he'd worn when the shell hit his leg. *As though he shared some private jest with destiny. . .* "It is worth something to Père Talbot, who has worked so hard to save it! And to Guy, who has taken us in!"

"The fools ought to turn us over to their seigneur. They would probably get a reward; I'm sure my brother has one posted for you."

"Turn us in to the—" Laura paused. "How do you know about the seigneur? You've been sleeping."

He shook his head. "I've been listening."

"Listening . . ." Blushing, Laura looked away, remembering her conversation with Hannay earlier that day. "To everything?"

"Aye. Do you remember Elizabeth's motto—*Video et tacit?* It is what has kept her alive; I learned from her. I couldn't watch, but I could listen."

Laura was dumbfounded. She'd seen the wound on his leg, had pulled the bloodied bandages away from it time and again. She could not imagine the will it must have taken to feign sleep through such pain.

He was looking out at the sky again. "Why did you tell them that we were married?"

"I didn't tell them. They assumed it. And I thought it would be easier—safer—to let them go on thinking we were."

"I thought it was perhaps because you wished we were married."

"Certainly not!"

He stared at the stars. "I have never understood why some men feel compelled to marry."

"Did you hear Hannay today?" she asked curiously.

"One can get that better from a harlot. And at less cost."

"I don't know much about harlots," Laura declared, stung by his detached, superior tone, "but I know this: it was horribly rude for you to pretend to be asleep without telling me. Didn't you trust me?"

"I've found it best," said John Guilford, "never to trust anyone."

"My, what a pleasant way to live," Laura said coolly.

"Who ever said life was pleasant? What did God tell Adam—'In the sweat of thy face shalt thou eat bread, until thou returnest to dust.'" He scuffed the rock on which he stood. "Dust. That is all any of it is."

"Surely you must trust Guy and Talbot and Hannay by now, if you've been listening to them!"

"Not at all."

"Is that why you kicked over that chair today when Hannay asked what you do?"

He nodded. "You're not the only heretic on Guernsey, Laura Darby. I'll thank you to remember that."

"Why do you care," Laura demanded furiously, "if it's all just dust? Why not announce to the world that you're a heretic and burn at the stake? You don't care a fig about staying alive. I saw you when that cannon shell hit you. You smiled. You were glad."

"Maybe I will tell the world I'm a heretic."

Laura stamped her foot. "Oh, you are impossible. Don't you believe in anything?"

"What should I believe in?"

"You have to believe in something," she told him. "Otherwise men would be just the same as beasts."

"I believe," said John Guilford, "the eclipse is about to begin."

Laura looked up. At the right-hand edge of the glowing white moon she saw a hint of shadow. "What is an eclipse?"

"The shadow of the earth falls across the face of the moon."

"I've never seen one. Have you?"

"Once. A long time ago. With my father. Before you were even born."

The night wind bore a heavy fragrance of salt mixed with meadow flowers: eglantine, honeysuckle, sea lavender. As Laura breathed it in, she started at a sudden realization. "I was born today. I mean—it is my birthday. If it is after midnight."

"It is. The eclipse began at just past two."

The shadow in the sky became more defined, until it seemed there were two sixpences hanging there, one white, one black, moving toward each other. "How can that be the shadow of the earth?" Laura asked.

"Because the earth is directly in between the sun and the moon. Here." Wincing, he knelt on the cliff and found three stones. Laura crouched beside him, hiking up the edge of her smock. "Sun, earth, moon." He pointed, assigning each stone an identity. "The earth goes around the sun, and the moon goes around the earth. And every once in a great while, the three are perfectly aligned, like so, so that the earth's shadow from the sun, here, falls across the moon."

Laura glanced up at him. His eyes glowed as they always did when he spoke of the stars; his deep voice rang with intensity. "Why is it," she asked wistfully, "that you care so much more about what goes on way up there than about what goes on right here?"

He gathered the stones in his hand and tossed them over the cliff. "I don't know. For the same reason you let these people go on thinking we are married, I suppose. Because it is easier. Safer."

The shadow that was the earth's crept across the moon's surface. "It is wondrous to watch, isn't it?" Laura breathed, chin tilted to the sky. "It makes me think of that psalm: 'When I consider the heavens, the moon and the stars which thou hast ordained, What is man, that thou art mindful of him?'"

Inch by slow inch, the earth moved the moon toward darkness. "'Yet thou hast made him a little lower than the angels,'" John said softly, continuing the psalm.

"That is hardly dust," Laura pointed out, for some reason still whispering.

"Some of us are closer to angels than others."

The moon disappeared.

Laura felt the stirring of the air before he touched her. His hand, so soft it might have been the wind, brushed her cheek. A circle of white light marked the spot beyond his shoulder where the moon had shone. His mouth found hers, and the circle vanished from her sight.

His arm slipped around her waist, drawing her against his chest. His mouth was warm and strong; he tasted of sea salt and the herbs she'd fed him: sweet bay, sorrel, thyme. He pushed at her mouth with his tongue, coaxing it to open. His fingertips brushed her breast, and the heat that flared in her belly was so hot she might have touched the sun.

He is swallowing me, thought Laura, as the ocean swallows the Arch Druid at morning and evening. As the earth's shadow swallowed the moon. He is a wolf, he is devouring me . . .

He moved his mouth to her ear, whispering, "Laura. Laura."

"Stop," she said, fighting back the tide of her blood that pulled her to him.

"Why?" His voice was soft as his caresses.

"You are only doing this to hurt your brother," she said angrily.

"I would to God that were true." And now there was in his voice something of the force, the spark it had when he spoke of his stars. "Touch me, Laura," he whispered. He was the teacher, she his pupil, and she obeyed, letting him take her hand and put it to his cheek. She felt the stubble of stiff black beard there, the taut skin stretched across bone, the smooth line of his upper lip. "Again," he urged. "Touch me again. Touch me here." He moved her hand down over his throat to his chest. Her fingers trailed through the thick black curls there, and then over his linen shirt, the leather of his belt, the rough twill of his breeches. "Laura. Laura, here..."

Something thick, hard as the rock they knelt on, but not cold like rock, not unyielding; it was hot and beating with life, pulsing beneath her fingers in a surge like the sea. His whole body seemed to quicken, shuddering, beneath her hand. "Oh, Laura." His voice was a ragged moan. "Let me touch you too."

In the sky above them, light was uncovering the moon, inch by slow inch. Just as slowly, he slipped her smock from her shoulders to bare her breasts.

She wrapped her arms across her body, shivering. He pried her hands away and replaced them with his own, stroking her moon-white flesh. The wind rushed up over the cliff, flattening the grass in the meadow, releasing its cool, sweet scent. Laura began to cry.

"God." He moved to release her, then held her more tightly instead, cradling her in his long arms with awkward gentleness. "Don't cry," he murmured against her hair. "Like holding a star..."

He raised her face to the sky and kissed her, slowly, softly, her breasts crushed against his chest. Laura felt her nipples growing round and hard where he pressed them, felt the heat flare again in her belly as his tongue touched hers. She knew she ought to pull away from him, run from him, but her will had eroded beneath the flood of longing his touch unleashed in her soul. "Let me teach you, Laura," he whispered. "I can teach you . . ."

Caught halfway between dread and fascination, she heard herself answer, "Yes . . ."

He caught her in his arms and tumbled her down from the rocks into the billowing grass, lying in the meadow, his face to the sky. He pulled her atop him, and against her thigh she felt that urgent pressure again. "Kiss me," he commanded. Hesitantly she touched his mouth with hers and felt him move beneath her, against her, groaning. He put his hands on her waist, raising her up, and touched his mouth to her breast.

At any moment, she told herself, this will turn hateful and ugly. He will shove me down with my face in the grass; he will make me scream. But as his warm tongue traced the tip of her breast, a sigh rose from her, soft and shivering; what he was doing was heavenly.

His mouth pulled at her nipple with hot, slow intensity; he stroked her bared shoulders with his fingertips, moaning with each new caress, rocking back and forth against her like the waves of the sea. "I need you," he said out of the darkness. "God, how I need you."

"No. No more. Please," she tried to tell him, but he reached back and found the hem of her smock, drawing it up over her thighs, past her waist, her breasts, and over her head in a tangle of curls. Laura wanted to run and stay at the same time; she was mortified by her near-nakedness, by the liberties she had already let him take, and yet stronger than her shame was the longing in her soul, in her heart for knowledge. *And Adam knew Eve his wife* . . . So this was the knowing the Bible spoke of, time and again.

"Laura," he whispered, and it was as though he had read her mind. "This is Eden. I am Adam. You are Eve."

"It is wrong!"

"How can this be wrong?" he asked, his hand running through her hair, over her breast.

"I am married to your brother," she said desperately.

"You don't believe that." He brushed her thick curls back over her shoulders, and the moonlight shimmered on her white skin. "God, you are beautiful." She turned away from the reflection she saw in his midnight eyes: two naked Lauras, strangers, twins. He cupped her chin in his hand, pulling her back to face him. "Don't be ashamed."

He lifted her up and laid her down beside him, then knelt,

pulling off his shirt, unbuckling his belt. She saw the black curls on his chest leading down in a trail, and then, as he tugged off his breeches with rough impatience, she saw the thick, pulsing rod of his desire. At the sight her fear returned with a vengeance. "No!" she cried, scrambling away through the long, cool grass.

He caught her by the waist and pulled her back, crushing her against him, hands tangled in her loose hair. She felt the wild beating of his heart and the smooth, round head of his manhood press at her drawers. He kissed her, no longer gentle, his tongue thrusting inside her in swift, hard strokes. He found the string of her drawers and yanked at the knot, slipping the soft linen down to her knees.

Now, Laura thought. Now he will hurt me. But instead he whispered her name, bending his head to hers; she felt the sweep of his black hair against her throat. He ran his hand over her shoulder, down to her breast, then lower still, to her waist, and lower, until his fingers brushed the soft curls between her thighs.

"Ah," he breathed, closing his eyes, "ah, Laura. So sweet—" His hand caressed her belly in feathery strokes, faster and faster, and he found her breast with his mouth and sucked the nipple with hungry insistence. His hand slipped between her thighs, fingers probing, exploring, touching her where no one had ever touched her before.

Laura lay trembling beneath him, the most absurd thoughts whirling through her head. Horses don't have fingers; how do they do this? He is looking for something. What is he looking for? "Oh, God," she cried suddenly. He had found a spot, a tiny bud that stiffened at his touch, letting loose a river of warmth that spread through her blood and bone.

"Hush," he murmured, mouth seeking hers in the darkness. "Hush . . ." He shifted in the grass, kneeling, arching above her to block out the moon. He pushed up on his hands; she felt the head of his manhood slide over her belly and between her legs.

Back and forth he glided, over and over again, teasing the sweet bud of her desire with his hard rod until Laura, flesh tingling, blood swirling, began to move with him. He groaned and slipped his palms under her buttocks, raising her up, his head against her breast. With the last shred of self-control she possessed, Laura begged him again, "Stop. Please, don't—"

"So help me God," he cried, "I cannot stop now." He drew back and then drove inside her, bearing down into her, pushing past her weak resistance. She felt a flash of pain and gasped. "Your maidenhead," he whispered, hands cupping her face.

"No!" she cried, too late, trying to push his weight from her.

"Laura. Laura. Wait." He leaned back to the stars, his face in shadow, and then that hard, thick shaft thrust into her again. His loins ground against her in a slow, hot rhythm; his hands molded her to him, tighter than skin to flesh, flesh to bone.

Laura shut her eyes, shut out the moon and the stars and his wild wolf's face, his harsh breathing and ragged groans, the pulse of his thighs against hers. I will not move, she vowed. I will be cold stone; I will shut this out too—

But how could she shut out the strange, shimmering aching he had awakened in her? She was matching his groans with her sighs even as she resisted; her body strained to meet his as he towered over her, thrusting into her again and again. *And Adam knew Eve his wife.* She felt as though the sky overhead was opening. "Oh," she whispered, "oh—" Her fingers closed on his shoulders, nails raking his flesh as the aching took hold.

"Love," he groaned. "Oh, God, Laura. Oh, my love—" Together they were spinning skyward, blazing like a star. Sun, moon, planets all whirled around them, nearer and nearer, settling in Laura's belly, shattering into shards of light so bright that nothing, no secret, could stay hidden between them. They were one being, one flesh . . .

And Adam knew Eve.

He thrust into her one last time, shuddering; then he fell against her, exhausted, drained. Laura clung to him, awed by this miraculous joining. She wanted to weep with joy; she wanted him to lie atop her forever, for that night to last for all time.

But he did roll away, stretching out in the grass beside her, arms clasped behind his head, staring up at the stars. Laura lay close to him, fingers caught in the crown of black curls on his chest. "We are one now," she whispered.

"What's that?"

"It is just as it says in Genesis," she said dreamily. "'Therefore shall a man leave his father and mother and cleave unto his wife, and they shall be one flesh.'"

"Seems to me we are still quite separate," said John. "And God knows I'm not about to marry you."

Laura pulled back her hand, staring at his harsh profile in the moonlight. "But I thought—"

"What did you think?"

"You—you said you wanted me! You said you loved me!"

"Did I really? What a man won't do in the heat of passion."

She regarded him uncertainly. "Don't tease me, John."

"Why should I tease you? I've no more intention of marrying you than of flying to the moon. I gave you a little present for your birthday, that's all. Don't pretend you didn't enjoy it."

"But you said—"

"A man with a bulge in his breeches," he told her coldly, "doesn't mean all he says."

"No," Laura whispered. "No. I don't believe you. I don't believe you would do that to me."

"Do that *to* you?" He laughed again. "You begged me for it. You were hot as a whore."

Laura cringed as she realized the awful, irrevocable thing he had done—that she had let him do. "My soul," she whispered, moonlight flooding her stark, ravaged face. "My soul . . . is lost."

"Don't think yourself singled out, Laura Darby," John Guilford told her. "We are all lost souls."

Sobbing, Laura caught up her clothes and ran to the cottage, leaving him lying there naked, staring at the stars.

Chapter 12

When Père Talbot came to the cottage early the next morning, Laura had already decided what she must do. She had washed the smocks and drawers that Hannay had lent her and hung them to dry outside. She had washed herself as well and put on her red silk gown. The sea water had stained and spotted it and left the rich folds of the fabric stiff with salt; it scratched like a hairshirt against her skin.

"*Bonjour,*" said the priest from the doorway, tipping his black hat.

Laura drew a deep breath. "Père Talbot. I must speak with you."

"Of course, my dear." He took a seat at the table, pulling off his hat. Laura sat across from him. "Well?" he asked gently.

"Yes. Well." Laura folded her hands in her lap and stared at them. "Would you care for something to eat?"

"*Non, merci.* I had my breakfast at home."

"Perhaps a cup of water?"

He shook his head. "No, I am fine."

"You're fine. Perhaps I'll just get some for myself, then." She rose from her seat. This was even harder than she'd imagined it would be. "It is very warm in here, don't you think, Père Talbot? Let me open a window—"

"Laura." He caught her wrist, tugging her back to her stool. "What did you want to speak to me about?"

"I—I have a confession to make."

He nodded encouragingly. "I'm in the business of hearing them. Go ahead."

"That's part of the confession. You see, Père Talbot, I'm a her—" She swallowed. "A heretic."

"Yes, I know."

"How did you know?" she asked in dismay.

"The first thing any good Catholic rescued from a ship-wreck would do," he told her wryly, "is light fifty candles to

Our Lady of the Sea. Guy and I have already discussed the matter. You have nothing to fear from us. We won't give you away." He picked up his hat.

"Wait," said Laura, with a little gulp. "There's more." He put the hat down. "I—well, it's about John. You know John."

"I'm well acquainted with his right leg."

Laura felt a bright red blush crawling over her cheeks. "I don't quite know how to put this. The simple fact is, he isn't my husband. We aren't married—at least, he's not. I am, in a way, only not to him—to his twin brother. Thomas. Only Thomas and I never—but you see, now John and I have." She got up and paced across the cottage floor, then whirled back to face him. "Père Talbot, I must leave this place. Now. Today. I must go to Calais."

The priest's forehead furrowed. "That would be very difficult, my dear, with England and France at war. I said as much to John this morning."

"You saw John?" Laura's golden eyes widened. "What did he say?"

"He too made a confession. Confessing seems to be rather in the air; I find that often happens after a full moon. One of those unexplainable phenomena."

"What did he confess to you?" Laura asked in dread.

"The secrets of the confessional are just that—secrets. Even a heretic must know that. I can tell you this much, though—he too was looking for some means to get you to Calais."

"I am sure he was." Laura turned from him, her voice bitter. "I'm sure he thought that would solve everything."

"Well, not exactly. You see, he wanted to make sure you could get to Calais once he threw himself off the cliff."

She whipped back to face him. "After he what?"

"After he killed himself. Right there in front of that rock we islanders call the Arch Druid." The priest was frowning. "I told you there was something evil about that stone."

"John—is dead?" Laura whispered.

"No, no, no. Forgive me; I didn't mean to frighten you. No, he was going to kill himself, but then I came along."

"Why would John want to kill himself?" she asked angrily. "He wasn't sorry for what he did!"

"What he did?"

"What he did to me last night! Clearly he didn't confess *that* to you."

"Oh, yes," said the priest, his face grave. "Yes, he did. He told me."

"Not everything, I'll wager! How he—how he laughed at me afterward and called me a whore—"

"He told me all that."

"I'm surprised you didn't tell him to jump off that cliff then!"

"*Chérie*. Would you want me to have told him that—"

"Yes, I would!" Laura sobbed.

"—when he loves you with all his heart?"

"He doesn't love me!" she cried harshly.

"Oh, yes, he does." Père Talbot sighed. "Laura, what John did last night was a terrible thing, a desperate thing. No one knows that better than he. But unless you can find it in your heart to forgive him, I very much fear he will climb right back out on that cliff."

"Forgive him? For having ruined me?"

"No, no. Not for that. For having lied to you."

"Lying to me is the *least* of it!" Laura said after a pause.

Père Talbot traced the empty spot on his finger where he'd once worn a wedding band. "Laura, when you were growing up, did you ever have a cat with kittens?" She nodded, perplexed. "Do you remember how helpless the little ones at first were? They could do nothing for themselves; the mother cat had to teach them. They watched her, and they learned to drink milk from a bowl, to wash themselves, to catch the mouse—"

"I don't see what that has to do with anything," Laura broke in crossly.

"We are no different from kittens, *cherie*. When we are children, we watch and we learn. We see our parents together, joyous, caring, giving, and that is how we learn about love." He leaned back in his chair. "Only some of us are not so lucky. Some of us watch our parents, and instead of joy and love, we see other things. Bad things—ugliness, bitterness. Hopelessness. That is what happened to John. He watched and saw his mother with her lovers, Thomas with his lovers. He watched his father; he saw a man's love for a woman drive him to madness and finally to murder and suicide. Is it any wonder, then, that he is afraid of love? That when at long last he finds this terrifying thing stirring in his heart he should run from it, even if the path he is on leads straight off a cliff?"

"Well," Laura said coldly, "that is too bad for him. I don't know what you expect me to do."

"He needs something to live for, *chérie*. Something to believe in."

"Let him believe in God."

"Child, listen to me. For John, God is like—like a star. More distant than the Milky Way. He can't even see God. His only religion is his suffering. But you—do you know what he calls you? 'A star that is fallen to earth.' And he loves you, yes—with whatever goodness and decency and honor this hard world has not stripped from him."

He got up then, putting on his black hat. "I don't know what you expect me to do about that," Laura said again.

The priest smiled. "I would not presume to tell you what to do, Laura Darby. Only your heart can do that. But for his sake—and yours—won't you try looking there?" He went out, pulling the door shut with a click. Laura heard the jangling bells of his donkey cart as he drove away.

Laura leaned her head in her hands, closing her eyes. He is wrong, she thought. John doesn't love me. She remembered the wonderful, romantic story her mother had told her over and over again, about kneeling in the strawberry patch and looking up and seeing Charles Darby, and knowing right away, from that moment, that she was in love. That was the way it was supposed to happen—in an instant. A bolt from heaven. That was love, plain and simple, easy and direct, not all tangled up like a Gordian knot. Love couldn't possibly be such hard work as loving John Guilford would be.

She sat up suddenly as a distant memory floated into her mind. How old had she been? Perhaps six or seven. She'd found a beautiful butterfly in the yard and came running into Howarth Manor, bearing it proudly in her cupped hands. "Papa?" she heard her own child-high voice call. "Papa, Mama, see what I have!"

She couldn't find them right away; then she heard her father shouting at the top of the stairs. She crept up cautiously, peeking around the baluster. He stood in the doorway to her parents' bedchamber, legs akimbo, his only hand clenched in a fist.

She couldn't see her mother, but she heard her crying from within the room, "I didn't mean to hurt you, Charles. I simply wanted to dance—"

"Did you also want to make a spectacle of me?" Charles

Darby roared. "You knew what I was when you wed me. You knew I was maimed. A cripple—"

"Charles, stop!"

"You knew your dancing days were done!"

"Damn you, Charles Darby," her mother had sobbed, "sometimes you make it so hard to be in love with you!"

Laura could feel the way her pulse had raced at that moment, the sudden stickiness on her palms as she cupped the butterfly's frail wings. *Don't stop loving him, Mama,* she'd prayed. *Papa, don't hurt her this way! What will happen to me?*

And then her father had started to chuckle. "All right, then, pet," he said, "all right, don't cry. 'Tis God's truth, I do make it hard, don't I? Lord knows why you stick with a gnarled old bear like me."

"A gnarled old one-armed bear," Dorrity corrected him, sniffling back tears. "And neither do I."

Laughing, he held out his arm to her. "Come here, pet." Dorrity ran to him, clinging to him while he gave her a long, slow kiss. Then he looked down and saw Laura. "Hello, little thing. What have you got there?"

"Butterfly," she'd told him shyly, opening her cupped hands. And the beautiful, delicate creature had fluttered away...

She heard her father's voice again, years later, on the night the queen's soldiers had come to take him away: *Sometimes the people whom it is hardest to love need our love the most.* It hadn't been just words, then. It was something he'd learned, something he knew.

Laura got up slowly from the table, went to the cottage door, opened it onto a flood of warm summer wind. She could see John sitting high atop the cliff, his back turned toward her, and beyond his black head the Arch Druid, rising out of the sea.

She walked toward him through the long green grass, red skirts caught in her hands. The wind billowed his white shirt over his back like a sail, like a fluttering gull. She sat beside him on the rock where St. Patrick had hurled the devil into the sea. She reached for his hand. He would not look at her; he stared over the edge of the cliff with haggard, hooded eyes.

"Tell me, John," she said quietly. "Tell me what it was like for you, growing up."

His broad back was bent beneath the weight of his memories. "Does that matter?" he asked, still not meeting her gaze, his voice strangled and low.

"I think it does."

The story came out slowly at first, like blood from an old wound reopened, but then the words built to a flood. He spoke of his mother's brutal preference for his brother, her even more brutal disdain for the man she had wed. He described how she'd paraded her lovers up to her chambers shamelessly, boastfully, and how his father, tortured by her brazen infidelity, sought hopelessly for solace in his building, his books, and his stars.

He told her of Thomas's cruelty, childish at first, more subtle in time as Estelle spurred him on. How he'd lain, silent, shaking, in the dark bedchamber he shared with his brother while Thomas copulated with fieldboys, schoolmates, stablehands, laughing at him from across the room. He spoke of his father's growing, brooding madness, of the pain of watching as the man he'd thought was a god, was Apollo, had his mind turned twisted and impotent, reduced to pondering plumbing problems and trying to shore up his crumbling house, and the bizarre quest to learn to fly.

Very quietly he told her how, when he grew older, Estelle, ghastly and insatiable, would summon him to her rooms, how she would try to stroke him, bare her breasts to him, taunt him, seeking to seduce her own son.

Through it all, through all those years, he had lived with his overwhelming guilt, with the horrible conviction that the madness around him was his fault, that if somehow he could be different, wiser, stronger, he could change his family, hold the center together, make everything all right.

In the end he'd failed. The madness soared inescapably, feeding on itself, burgeoning, swelling, until on a cold winter's night he'd stood in his mother's bloodied bedchamber, watching her life seep away, hearing from the top of the tower his father's final, anguished cry as at long last he flew. "And I was glad," John Guilford said fiercely. "God help me, but I was happy. For Apollo. For him."

He was crying. Laura was crying. She could think of nothing to say to soothe him, no words of comfort, but she turned to him and opened her arms. He hesitated, eyes hooded: a wolf, hunted, wild, and fearful. Then he lowered his heavy head onto her breast and sobbed.

She held him, rocking him, stroking his tangled black

hair. Far out to sea, the tide rose up over the Arch Druid and swallowed it, leaving no trace.

A long time later he pulled away from her embrace and stood up awkwardly, favoring his wounded leg. He rubbed his face impatiently on his sleeve and turned, pacing to the very edge of the cliff with slow, unsteady steps. Laura watched him, waiting, knowing he would turn back.

He did, finally, the sun pouring over his wide shoulders like thick, golden butter. He pushed back his hair with one hand. His shirt was open to the waist; his skin bore a sheen of sweat. I have seen him stand like that once before, thought Laura, with the sun behind him. Where had it been?

"Laura," he said. "About last night. I never meant to— God, I would do anything to make it up to you, if only I could."

Once before. At Guilford Hall, by the stream. When he'd yanked off his doublet and shirt there in the strawberry patch.

In a strawberry patch. Just like her mother and father. She began to laugh. Oh, heavens, she thought. I ought to have known right then—

"Not that there is any way to make it up," John rushed on miserably, mistaking her laughter. "So that's why I've got to kill myself. Talbot will find some way to get you to Calais. But I wanted you to know, before I— I wanted to tell you, I lied last night. I do love you, Laura. I love you with all my heart." He said this very quickly, looking down at her, then away, then back again. "Are you laughing at me?"

"Oh, John, no! I'm sorry." She bit her lip, but another giggle slipped out. "It is just that—of course you love me. It's the strawberry patch, you see."

"What are you talking about?" he asked uncertainly.

"It is God, I suppose. Or fate, if you'd rather. Perhaps you could even find it written in those stars of yours, beside that bear that doesn't look like a bear."

"Find what written?"

"Why, that you would fall in love with me, and I with you. Only sometimes, just as you said, you can't see it all clearly at first. Sometimes you have to squint a bit."

There was still that uncertainty in his blue eyes, but now there was something more too. Something like hope, beautiful and delicate as a butterfly. "Laura, did you say that—that you love me?"

"I did. I do."

"Why?" he asked, with such complete bewilderment that she burst out laughing again.

"I don't know," she told him at last. "But perhaps if you were to come and kiss me, I might recall."

He came across the rocks on which St. Patrick had walked, slowly limping. "Don't change your mind before I get there," he warned.

"I won't," she promised, and ran to meet him halfway.

Chapter 13

The loud, eager squawks of hundreds of hungry seagulls shattered the stillness of twilight. Laura tried to sit up, but John would not let her; he lay stretched out on the cliff with his head in her lap, his arm circling her waist.

"Those birds," said Laura, "mean that Guy is bringing the boat in. And that means we have work to do."

"I am working," said John.

"At what, pray tell?"

"I am counting your heartbeats. Hush, or I'll lose track. Thirteen thousand and five. Thirteen thousand and six—"

Laura snorted, wriggling out of his grasp. "A productive use of your time."

"Oh, I agree." He lunged for her ankle and pulled her back, catching her off balance so that she teetered and then fell across his chest. "Come here, you. This has been a perfect day, and I am not yet ready for it to end."

"Perfect? We haven't done anything except lie about in the sun."

"That's what made it perfect," he told her, capturing her in a languorous kiss.

"You are a terrible influence on me, John Guilford," she whispered, her mouth against his.

"You need someone to moderate that Protestant industriousness."

"Are you trying to convert me?" she teased.

"Why not? You converted me."

"How did I do that?"

"I don't believe any more that the universe revolves around the sun."

"You don't?" she asked in astonishment.

He shook his head, tracing her cheekbones with his fingertip. "No. It revolves around you." For a moment his warm eyes darkened with shadow. "I want to marry you."

"Oh, love." Laura seized his finger and kissed it. "I've told you I don't care about that."

"And I've told you I don't believe you. A good, pious creature like you doesn't care that we're living in sin?"

"Not when there's no help for it. It is better I should go against my conscience than ask Talbot to go against his."

"There, you see, it is against your conscience." He sat up, frowning at the blazing sunset. "I don't see what difference a piece of paper from the pope should make when neither of us recognizes his authority."

"Talbot says that under the law of England I am still married to your brother unless I get an annulment."

"Then let him write to Rome for an annulment."

"And risk having Thomas learn where I am? I'd sooner live in sin. Anyway, it's a very nice sort of sin, don't you think, here on this beautiful island?" She looked over his shoulder at the meadow grass dotted with bright wildflowers, the green trees in the valley far below the cottage, the tall stone spire of Talbot's church. "It really is remarkably kind of Guy to let us stay on this way until your leg is healed."

He pinched her. "He likes you."

She laughed. "He just likes having someone to tell his stories to." She contemplated the thatch-roofed cottages in the valley below. "He must be very lonely living way up here. Why do you suppose no one ever comes to visit him except Hannay and Talbot?"

"Talbot says everyone else is tired of hearing him talk about the Ancient Way and the spirits in the stones."

"What do you think about all that?" Laura asked curiously.

"I don't know. If you asked me a month ago, I would have said— What's that expression you use? Ah, yes. Bosh."

"And now?"

He hesitated a moment. "Now I am not so sure. That night of the eclipse, after you ran back to the cottage—" He flushed. "You'll think this is silly."

"No, I won't. Tell me."

"Well, it's just that I thought—I imagined, I guess—that the Arch Druid was . . . pulling at me. That it wanted me to jump off the cliff."

"Oh, really, John." Laura bit her lip.

He made a face at her. "I knew you would laugh. But why should it seem outlandish that there are spirits—good or evil—that inhabit certain places? Think of all the stories there are about trolls that lurk under bridges, or marsh-monsters that live in bogs, or fairy-rings—how do you think all those tales got started?"

"By ignorant, superstitious people who didn't know any better." Her gold gaze slanted toward him. "I'm surprised at you."

"Elizabeth says we only fear what we don't understand. I think we ought at least to respect such things. Look at Guilford Hall, Laura. That's an unhappy place if there ever was one. And the walls and floors were always shifting around. Maybe it's built on bad rock." He saw her incredulous expression and grinned. "Say what you like, but if I were building a house, I'd ask Guy about the spirits in the stones first. Here he comes."

Hearing Guy puffing his way up the cliff face, John pushed to his feet. Laura stood by, offering a hand, but he shook it off. "I'm all right, dammit. Just a little stiffness. Here, Guy, let me help with those nets."

"There's a barrel of ale down in the skiff," said Guy, handing over the tangle of rope netting. "I'll go back and get it soon as I've caught my breath."

"I'll go," John offered, limping toward the steps.

"John, no!" Laura went to stop him, but Guy caught her arm.

"Let him go," he said softly. "If you watch, you'll only make him nervous. The cliff is good rock."

"But he should wait until his leg is healed!" she objected.

"He must make a start, *oui?* Tell me, what is for our supper?"

"Eel stew. What else?" With a last worried glance at the cliff, Laura followed Guy to the gate.

He spread the nets on the wall to dry, then stood frowning down into a steep, dark ravine that ran behind the cottage. "Le Chemin du Sanctuaire, it is all overgrown," he muttered, and scrambled down into the gully. Pulling a knife from his belt, he began to hack at the branches of an old, gnarled pine.

"The Road of Sanctuary?" Laura peered down at him.

"*Oui, oui.* The Sanctuary Path. Do you see the stones?" He yanked back the tangled underbrush to show her the flat, worn slabs of slate that lay beneath. "The stones St. Patrick walked on when he dragged the Arch Druid across the island. It runs all the way from the castle at St. Peter Port to the cliff."

"Why do you call it the Sanctuary Path?"

"In the old days, under the Ancient Way, if a man was found guilty of a crime for which he must be killed, he could claim the right of *perquage*. The Sanctuary Path. With a priest beside him, he must walk all the way from the castle to the cliff, on the day he is to die, following the stones. No one could touch him or help him, not even the priest. And if he reached the cliff by nightfall, instead of being put to death he became *exilé*. It gave to him one last chance, *n'est-ce pas?*"

"It sounds very civilized," Laura said wistfully, thinking of her father.

"The Ancient Way was civilized." Guy chopped at another wayward branch. "Helier Gosselin, the seigneur—he tells the people that English law is better than the Ancient Way, but this is not so. When we had the Ancient Way, everything was settled *entre nous*, between us. Say you have a neighbor and you see him cutting down oats from your field. Today you must go to St. Peter Port and file many papers with the seigneur. The papers go to England, and many months later some papers come back, and they say, *Voilà*, you are right. The oats are in your field; your neighbor must not cut them. *Eh bien*, you win—but too late for your oats!"

Laura laughed. "What happened under the Ancient Way?"

"Ah! Back then if you see your neighbor cutting your oats, you kneel down and say, *'Haro! Haro! A l'aide, mon prince, on me fait tort'*—one wrongs me, you understand. And the neighbor must stop cutting down your oats."

"Did that really work? I mean, would the neighbor stop?" Laura asked dubiously.

"Of course. Everyone respected the Ancient Way. It was our way of life." He sighed, looking at the moss-covered stones beneath his boots. "Now no one remembers anymore. No one keeps the Sanctuary Path clear. It is all long gone."

John, out of breath but grinning, had made it to the cottage with the ale barrel. "Let's eat!" he said.

"Phut." With an air of futility, Guy gathered up the branches he'd cut.

"At least you have got some firewood," said Laura, trying to cheer him.

He shook his head, climbing out of the ravine. "These are holy branches. They have touched the good stones. I put them up in the thatch for luck."

Talbot came to visit after supper. He took John into the bedroom to examine his leg, while Laura washed the dishes and Guy sat by the fire, drinking ale and plucking his *télen*. Talbot's examination took longer than usual; Laura looked up from her washing as the two men emerged. "Is everything all right?" she asked.

"Fine, fine," the priest assured her. "By the by, Guy, there is to be a wedding in a fortnight. Robert de Boutin, Antoine and Eloise's son, is to wed Isobel Monteil. Everyone in the parish is invited."

"Are you going to go, Guy?" asked Laura. He shook his head and went on playing his harp.

"Are you certain, Guy?" Talbot asked gently. "You and Antoine are old friends."

"I stay home," said Guy, in a tone clearly indicating that was that.

"Well, there's no reason why you and John shouldn't come if you like," Talbot told Laura. "If not to the church, then to the celebration afterward, at the groom's house. You could meet some of your neighbors."

"A fortnight." Laura looked dubious. "John's leg will be all better by then. We will probably be in Calais."

"Give it some thought," the priest suggested. "If you're still here, of course." He bade them good night.

When he'd gone, Guy drained his cup of ale and got up to draw another. "Why don't you want to go to the wedding?" Laura asked.

"Wedding? Hah." The Guernseyman scowled into his cup. "An English wedding, in a church—that is no way to marry." He struck a jarring chord on the *télen*.

"What other way is there of getting married?"

"The old way, *bien sûr.*"

"And how was that?"

Guy strummed his harp. "I talk too much about the old ways. Talbot tells me so."

"I like your stories," Laura told him. "Please?"

Guy's sad face brightened slightly. *"Eh bien.* In those days—" His big hands flew over the harp strings, plucking them softly. "In those days, once a year everyone would go to a place we call La Roque Balan. A good rock, with a good spirit. We would go on the night of *le solstice d'été.*"

"The what?" asked Laura.

"The summer solstice," John translated rather absently.

"When the sun reaches the point on its ecliptic at the highest declination south."

"I beg your pardon?"

"When the sun is closest to the earth—or the earth to the sun, if you're a heretic." She stared at him blankly, and he laughed. "Midsummer's Eve."

Guy nodded. *"Oui, oui.* The Midsummer's Eve. That was *le plus grand jour du fête de toute l'année."*

"Bigger than Easter or Christmas?" Laura asked in surprise.

He nodded. "Bigger. And older. Older than anyone can remember. Older than the time of Christ."

"How did you celebrate?" Laura asked.

"We would build a huge fire in the middle of the rock. If you go there, you can still see where the fire was built. That was to make the rock spirit happy. And then we would dance."

"Oh, I adore dancing!" Laura declared.

Guy laughed. "I do not think you would like this dancing, *chérie.* It was not pretty English dancing."

"What was it like? Can you show me?"

"Non. I am too old and too drunk. But I play you the music we danced to." He fiddled with the pegs of his harp, changing the tuning, and then he began to play.

The song he played was eerie, unearthly, like nothing Laura had ever heard before, stranger even than the old French love songs she'd heard him sing. The notes seemed to fly after one another like sparks, higher and higher, while the bottom strings twanged in a slow, steady rhythm of drums. There were no words to go with it; it needed none. The mystical sounds rippled and flowed, spreading out until the walls of the cottage seemed too small to hold it, moving in tides dark and strong as the sea. Laura stared into the flames of the hearth fire as the song swirled around her, engulfed her, and imagined that in the red-gold glow she could see dark dancers, leaping and twirling, their naked bodies shimmering with sweat. Around and around they spun, chasing one another in a circle of fire.

Guy ended the song abruptly on a high, wild chord. The log in the fireplace cracked and fell in a flurry of sparks. And though Laura knew the dark dancers had been only an illusion, she was sad when they disappeared. They'd been so beautiful . . .

"When that song was finished," said Guy, his gruff voice a

whisper, "if a young man wanted a girl, he would lift her up in his arms and carry her through the bonfire three times."

"Through the fire?" Laura asked, wide-eyed. "Wouldn't they be burned?"

"Not on the Midsummer's Eve. The spirit in the rock would protect them. Then the young man would carry his beloved down to the sea. They would make their vows in the water, and then they would make love."

"And then they were *married*? Without any priest or witnesses?" Laura demanded dubiously.

"If they want to be." Guy shrugged. "If not, the young man could always pick a new wife at the next *solstice d'été*. But there were not many mistakes, if the young man listened to his heart, for the good spirit would tell him which girl to choose."

"Lord," said Laura, "little wonder Helier Gosselin put an end to the Ancient Way! Is that how you and your wife were married?"

"My wife?" Guy echoed.

"Aye. Marie-Hélène, whom you named your boat for. Hannay told me about her."

Guy set down his *télen*. "What did she tell you?"

"That's all. Just her name."

Guy rocked back on his stool, staring into the fire. "That is all long past. Gone, like the Ancient Way."

"But were you married like that, on Midsummer's Eve?"

Guy did not seem to have heard her; he'd picked up his harp and was lost in his music again.

That night in their borrowed bed, John made love to Laura with slow, sweet passion, while Guy, befuddled with ale, snored beside the hearth. "That was beautiful," John told her when at last, both sated, they lay in the darkness, holding tight to each other. "You are beautiful."

"Mm. So are you." She curled against him. "We have to start thinking of some way to get to Calais, John. We've been imposing on Guy for far too long."

"I talked to him about that today, love. He honestly does seem glad to have us here. He said we should stay as long as we please."

"Guy is very kind, but we can't. We haven't got any money to pay him."

"He says I can earn my keep. He wants to teach me to fish."

"You, a fisherman?" Laura giggled. "You would have to get up at dawn! You'd never see the stars."

"I have all the stars I need." He kissed her eyelids. "Right here."

"You're serious, aren't you?" she asked in astonishment.

"I am. We're safer here than in Calais. Thomas would never think to look for you here. No one knows us. They don't even know my real name. They think it's John Darby, because that's the name you gave and you said we were married. As far as anyone in England knows, we've dropped right off the end of the earth."

"You can say that again." Laura laughed ruefully. "Can you imagine what the end of the earth must be like in wintertime?"

"It wouldn't be forever, love. Just until the war settles down."

"But what would I do all day?"

"Cook eel stew. Listen for the birds that mean I am coming home to you."

"It sounds absolutely deadly."

He rolled over in the bed. "You're right. It was a stupid idea. I'll start working on a way to get to Calais."

He sounded so disappointed that Laura tucked her arm around him and kissed his cheek. "I don't know how you ever came up with such a strange notion. What in the world makes you think you'd enjoy living on Guernsey and being a fisherman?"

"Laura, don't you see? Nobody knows me here. No one knows about my family. No one has that look in their eyes when they meet me, that pity, that fear. It's as though—as though I've been reborn. As though I've been handed a whole new life."

"Oh, John." Laura thought of all those years he'd spent hidden away in the dome atop Guilford Hall. "I never realized..." How wretched his life in the darkness must have been!

He shrugged in her arms. "It doesn't matter. You're right; you would be unhappy here."

"How could I possibly ever be unhappy," she whispered, "when I have you? I should like to see you burned brown like Guy. You'll make a splendid fisherman!"

He turned to her. "Laura. Are you sure?"

"You said yourself it wouldn't be forever. And now we

can go to that wedding Talbot told us about. We'll meet the neighbors and dance—"

"I may not be ready for dancing, you know," he said a trifle gruffly. "Not with this leg—"

"Nonsense, darling. In another two weeks you'll be hopping up and down that cliff just like Guy."

"We'll see," said John, and kissed her. "We'll see."

The very next morning, John went out fishing. Laura watched from the cottage doorway as he and Guy set out together in the thin light of dawn, the seagulls swooping and diving over their heads. The sun broke through the mist as Guy rowed the skiff out from the cliff, circling the big black bulk of the Arch Druid and cutting through the silver-tipped waves to the *Marie-Hélène*.

John came home at dusk, filthy and bedraggled, but in great good spirits, laughing with Guy about the beginner's mistakes he had made, limping from the cliff to grab her in a mighty hug. And Laura thought, Well, in all labor there is profit, though she could not help wishing he'd chosen some labor that did not leave his clothes stinking so.

She occupied herself with cleaning the cottage, though there was little enough of it to clean, with cooking and laundry, and with a special project of her own. Though grateful to Hannay for the plain homespun smocks that the woman had lent her, she wanted something special to wear to the wedding of Robert de Boutin and Isobel Monteil. Having no other fabric to work with, she was remaking the red silk gown she'd worn from England, cutting out the stained parts, raising the bodice, removing the gaudy cloth-of-gold in the sleeves. She kept the work a secret from John, telling herself it was because she wanted the gown to be a surprise. In truth, she thought he might not be pleased to see her in Thomas's gift again.

On the day before the wedding, Hannay came to visit. "How is your husband the fisherman?" the Guernseywoman asked with a smile.

"I can't understand it," Laura confessed, "but he seems to enjoy it."

"Work is good for men, *oui?*"

"For women too." Gold eyes sparkling, Laura brought forth her reworked gown. "What do you think? I thought I would wear it to the wedding tomorrow."

"It is lovely." The Guernseywoman ran her hand over the

luxe fabric admiringly. "I wish I could be there to see you in it."

"Aren't you going?"

"I cannot. Talbot will be there."

"Oh, Hannay." Laura felt a twinge of guilt over her own anticipation of the affair. "What a terribly lonely way this is for you to live."

"Talbot said it would not be forever. If Queen Mary and King Philip have no children, and the Princess Elizabeth comes to the throne, then we will be able to live together again."

"But that could take years!" Laura said in dismay.

Hannay shrugged. "Talbot is worth it. I will wait for him."

Laura, sensing the conversation was making Hannay sad, quickly changed the subject. "Guy was telling us about the way people used to get married here on the island. You know, about the Ancient Way."

"My brother." Hannay made a wry face. "He lives too much in the past."

"He ought to remarry."

"He never will," Hannay said with certainty.

"What was his wife like? He never talks about her."

"Marie-Hélène? Ah, she was a great beauty. The greatest beauty in all the Isles. All the men wanted to marry her, but she chose Guy." Hannay's lovely face bore a faraway smile. "You would not believe it, but he was a handsome man then. He did not drink all the time. He took care of himself. And he was so brave! There was nothing he would not do."

"The stories he tells then—about the whale he caught and sailing his boat through the Needle on Sark—they're true?"

"*Oui,* all true. But all a long time ago."

"What did Marie-Hélène die of?" asked Laura.

"She drowned."

"Oh, how tragic. No wonder her death changed Guy."

"It changed Guy, yes. It changed—a lot of things."

"What do you mean?"

Hannay shrugged. "Talk of the past—it is no good. *C'est futile, n'est-ce pas?* Tell Guy I will visit tomorrow night while you and John are at the wedding. I keep him company."

At dusk Laura heard the gulls and walked out in the soft evening air to the cliffs to welcome home the men. Every other night they had climbed up together, laughing and jesting, but on this night neither was laughing. Guy came up the stone stairs first, mumbling to himself, barely greeting Laura, and marched straight to the cottage for a cup of ale. John hauled himself up the steep slope with more difficulty, carrying the nets, his expression grim.

Laura ran to kiss him and take some of the nets from him. "What is the matter?" she asked as he limped to the wall to hang the nets to dry. "Did you and Guy have a fight?"

"It's nothing. Just a minor disagreement."

"Over what?" she asked curiously. They usually got along together so well . . .

"It's nothing, I told you," he said a trifle sharply, and she thought it best to let the subject pass.

"Hannay came by," she told him, "but would not stay for supper. I feel so sorry for her, John. Do you know, she is not even going to the wedding because Talbot will be there."

"Have you still got your heart set on going to that silly thing?"

"What do you mean, silly? I think it will be splendid to get out of the cottage, meet some more of the islanders, hear some music besides Guy's harp for a change. And don't forget, there is to be dancing!"

"I've been working hard lately," said John. "I would rather just stay here."

"But, John, that's not fair! Why, I even made myself a new dress just for this wedding. Sort of new, that is."

"Made a new dress? Out of what?"

"Out of my old red silk gown. You would hardly even recognize it; I cut out the spoiled parts and remade the bodice and sleeves—"

"The dress Thomas gave you," he broke in, a trace of the wolf in his eyes.

"It was all I had. I didn't think it should go to waste."

"Perhaps you wish Thomas was here to dance with you as well," said John. She stared at him, hurt, as he heaved the last net over the wall. "Is supper ready? I'm starved."

"Aye," Laura said faintly, taken aback.

From within the cottage came the sound of Guy's harp above the crash of the waves, fierce and wild and sad.

Chapter 14

Though barely speaking to each other the next morning,
John and Guy still set out early to fish. Laura put the final
touches to her gown, took a bath and washed her hair, made
Guy his supper, and waited impatiently for them to return.
Talbot had pointed out the cottage of the de Boutins down in
the valley; as dusk fell she could see a flurry of activity there,
and then a long procession winding its way along the island
roads from the house to Talbot's church. She turned, searching for some sign of the gulls or the *Marie-Hélène*, but all she
saw were the waves and the tip of the Arch Druid's black
head.

"Laura!" It was Hannay, climbing the hill from the road
below. "The wedding is starting! What are you still doing
here?"

"Waiting for John," Laura told her crossly. "I can't understand why he is so late. He knew how I was looking forward to this. And he and Guy have had some sort of
argument, and they're hardly talking. All in all, it has not
been pleasant around here."

"Poor Laura," said Hannay, with a hint of a smile. "Put
on your pretty dress and go on to the church. I will send John
after you when he comes home."

"I believe I shall do just that," said Laura, tossing her
bright hair. "That will teach him to keep me waiting!"

A few minutes later she was on her way down to the valley, red skirts gathered up in her hands. She was late indeed;
she did not even arrive at the small stone church until the
bride and groom were emerging, to joyous shouts and a
flurry of flower petals. Laura hung back, suddenly shy
among this crowd of strangers, studying their faces. The
groom, Robert, was a handsome, sturdy youth, sunburned,
black-haired, and blue-eyed. The bride was lovely in her simple gown of yellow linen, a wreath of wildflowers circling her
dark head.

"Isobel looks radiant, doesn't she?" asked a voice at Laura's shoulder, speaking English with only a trace of French accent. Surprised, Laura turned around and saw a tall, older gentleman smiling fondly at the bridal couple. He looked down at her, still smiling, and noticed her surprise. "I beg your pardon; we have not been introduced. But I know everyone on the island, and I don't know you, so I assume you must be the Englishwoman Talbot mentioned, who is staying with Guy de Carteret." He winked at her. "Talbot did not tell me how lovely you are, though."

"Laura!" That was Talbot, waving to her from the church stairs. He pushed his way through the throng of jocular islanders to reach her side. "I see you have met Helier."

"Oh!" Laura looked again at the tall man. "You must be the seigneur Guy told us of."

He bowed. "Helier Gosselin, at your service, Madame Darby."

"Please, you must call me Laura."

"I should be delighted, if you will do me the honor of calling me Helier." He glanced around the churchyard. "I see no other strangers. Is your husband here?"

"He was late getting home from his fishing tonight," she explained.

"Ah. Are you coming to the reception?" Laura nodded, rather tentatively. He offered his arm. "Then perhaps you will allow me to escort you."

"Splendid!" said Talbot, clapping the seigneur on the shoulder. "I'll meet you there." He hurried off again.

"Well," said Laura, casting a last look about for John, then smiling at the man beside her. "It appears you are stuck with me."

"I cannot imagine a more pleasant duty," he told her gallantly. "Shall we go?"

For her part, Laura could not imagine a more charming escort. Helier Gosselin did know everyone on the island, or at least everyone who'd come to the wedding, and as the procession made its way back to the groom's house, he introduced her to a steady stream of Guernseymen and women. She greeted them as well as she could in her fractured French, and they made her feel at ease immediately. Most were fishermen or farmers; strong hardy folk, shortish, dark-haired, most with blue eyes. Their wives were more shy, but their faces were friendly as they welcomed her to the island.

"You speak English far better than I speak French, Helier," she said, laughing, struggling to pronounce the names of the islanders as he did.

"I went to Oxford, a long time ago," he explained. Covertly she studied his face as he spoke with one of the islanders about a problem the farmer was having with his crop of wheat. It was a good face, wide and open; he had a long hooked nose, well-fed jowls, and a broad mouth that seemed always to be smiling.

"What exactly does a seigneur do?" she asked, as the farmer, satisfied, took his leave.

He gave a small, self-deprecating chuckle. "Nothing much, actually, now that we are living under English law. Keep up appearances, mostly. *Bonjour, Alec, Louis!*" he called, waving to friends.

"Guy does not seem very happy that the islanders have given up the Ancient Way."

"Guy lives in the past," the seigneur said gently. "He would see Guernsey stuck in the past as well. We all must move forward with the times, don't you agree?"

"I don't know. I am only an outsider. But I like the old stories Guy tells."

He nodded. "The Ancient Way was very quaint. The islanders paid the seigneur so many chickens per hearth, so many bushels of wheat for each cow. Now they pay me shillings. It is not so different."

"What about the rights the islanders used to have under the Ancient Way?"

"Now we have rights under English law. *Ma chère,* you must understand. The Ancient Way is based on foolish notions, superstitions. It held this island back. I could not put up a dovecote without checking first with Guy to see that the 'spirits in the rocks' were favorable. Such nonsense!" They had reached the groom's house. "Come," said Helier Gosselin, "I will introduce you to the family."

Antoine de Boutin, the father of the groom, was a compact man with bright eyes and a jolly laugh. His wife, Eloise, was bustling madly about in the neat, spare house, but she took time from her hostessing duties to greet Laura with a warm smile. "Can I help you?" Laura offered in French, watching the Guernseywoman filling a big basket with cakes and wine.

"Non, non, merci. C'est bien, c'est bien," Eloise de Boutin assured her.

"The basket is for Robert and Isobel to take around the

island, to anyone who could not come to the wedding," Helier Gosselin explained.

"What a lovely custom!"

"They'll be leaving now." He took her elbow. "Let us go
out to the yard and see them off."

The bride, laughing and blushing, was already sitting on
the driver's seat of Père Talbot's donkey cart, which had
been festooned with chains of leaves and flowers. Robert de
Boutin accepted the basket and a kiss on each cheek from his
mother, then clambered up beside Isobel, waving and ac-
knowledging the shouts of the other young men. "Whom
shall we go see, Papa?" he called to Antoine, who searched
the faces in the crowd.

"Martine Albert is sick in bed," someone shouted.

"And my Jacquetta is at home with the baby," another
man cried. "But don't give her too much cake; she is big
enough as it is!" The islanders laughed.

"Who else?" Robert asked, setting the basket in the back
of the cart, one arm around his bride.

"Old Violette d'Estaing and her Léon!"

"The Dantons have a cow that's calving—"

"Joseph and Madeleine could not come; his gout is very
bad."

Robert counted them up on his fingers and nudged Isobel. "Will you remember all of these?" She nodded and
laughed.

"Robert," his father called above the commotion, "go and
see Guy de Carteret." The laughter and jests died away.

"Oh, Papa." Robert was frowning. "Do I *have* to? That
crazy old drunk?"

"He did not come to your wedding. That is the tradition."

"He was afraid to come, I'll wager," shouted a youth in
the back of the crowd, to a round of appreciative hoots.

"Robert." His father's voice was stern. "Go and see
Guy."

"Hannay is there too, Robert," Talbot told him.

"Well, all right then," the groom grumbled, "just so I
don't have to be alone with him." He settled into the driver's
seat, arm wrapped around Isobel, and away they drove, to
more shouts of congratulations and a jangling of bridle bells.
Eloise de Boutin cried on her husband's shoulder, and Madame Monteil, mother of the bride, burst into tears as well.

"Come, come, my Eloise," said Anotine de Boutin, hugging his wife's shaking shoulders. "Let us have a dance." A

drummer and a piper began to play, and before long the yard was filled with music and cheer.

"Still looking for your husband?" asked Helier Gosselin, noticing Laura standing on tiptoe. "I don't see him. Perhaps you would honor me with this dance?"

"You're very kind, Helier," she said with a smile. "But I don't know the steps to this one, I'm afraid."

"It is a very simple country dance, like your English May dance," he told her. "I will teach it to you. Come along."

She followed him into the line of dancers. He was right; the steps were simple, and within two turns she was laughing and clapping along with the beat. He was a splendid dancer, elegant and quick, and he made it easy to follow his lead. Laura had just completed a whirling circle with him when from the corner of her eye she saw John at last, leaning against the wall surrounding the yard, still in his fishing clothes. Oh, honestly, she thought, he might at least have changed. She waved to him, but he did not wave back.

"Your husband?" asked Gosselin, looking where she was waving.

"Aye," she said with a sigh. "That's John."

"Shall we stop?"

"Oh, no, please. Let's finish out the dance, now that I have finally learned it!" Laughing, he led her on.

When the tune came to an end, Laura curtsied, giggling, slightly breathless. "I am out of practice," she told the seigneur.

"*Pas du tout.* You are the soul of grace."

"Well, thank you very much. Would you like to come and meet John?"

"Certainly."

"John!" Laura called, as they made their way through the regrouping dancers to the wall where he stood. "What on earth took you so long to get here? You've completely missed the bride and groom." She stood on tiptoe to kiss him, then stood back, waiting for him to compliment her on the red gown. Disappointed when he did not, she gestured to the man at her side. "John, this is Helier Gosselin, the seigneur."

John inclined his head one-quarter inch. "How do you do?"

Gosselin bowed from the waist. "I'm very glad to meet you, Monsieur Darby. May I say, you have a most charming wife."

"Glad you think so," John said, scowling at the man. "If you'd excuse us, I'd like to talk with her." He grabbed Laura's elbow and yanked her out of the yard.

"John! What is the matter with you?" she demanded, casting an apologetic glance back at Gosselin. "You were horribly rude to him!"

"Guy doesn't like him."

"Well, I happen to find him quite nice! And anyway, what do you care whether Guy likes him? You aren't speaking to Guy."

"That doesn't mean I don't respect his opinion of Helier Gosselin."

"Why are you in such a temper?" Laura demanded. "Have I done something wrong? Are you angry with me?"

"No." He stood looking down at her in the moonlight. "No. I just want to go home."

"Go home? But you've only just got here! Why, we haven't even danced!"

"I cannot dance." He turned, taking a hobbling step away from her. Laura caught his arm.

"Darling, if you are worried about your leg, that is just plain silly. You may not be able to dance so well as Helier this time, but we'll make a start. And soon your leg will be all better!"

"It isn't getting any better."

"Why, what do you mean?"

He would not meet her gaze. "Talbot had already told me, but I didn't want to believe him. I got Guy to sail me to Alderney today, to a surgeon there. He said the same. My leg has healed as well as it's going to, Laura. I'll always be lame."

"You can't know that for certain!" she cried. "You must give it time!"

"I know for certain," he said quietly. "Believe me, I know." He reached out to touch her cheek. "The good part, of course, is that we haven't been married. That you haven't tied yourself to a—a cripple for life."

Laura was silent, remembering the looks that used to greet her father on the few occasions when he ventured out in public. The outright curiosity: "'Ey, mister, where's yer arm?" The murmured comments. The whispers. The stares. The village children who'd chased after him, arms tucked behind their backs.

It had never occurred to her that John's wound might be

permanent, that he too faced a lifetime of whispers and stares. And for her there would be...no more dancing. Beyond his broad shoulder she could see the couples in the yard, whirling and leaping to the rhythm of the pipe and the drum...Just like Mama and Papa, she thought, and then, remembering the ugly scene between Charles and Dorrity that she'd witnessed as a child, she added: I don't know if I am strong enough.

John had pulled back his hand. "If I'd known, Laura, I swear, I never would have spoken of my love for you. If I'd known before, I would have—" He left the thought unfinished, but she knew what he meant to say, and at the realization all her uncertainty fled.

"Would have what? Thrown yourself off that cliff?" she demanded fiercely. "Let me tell you something, John Guilford. You are only as much a cripple as you think you are. As for me, I would marry you still if you had but one leg and one arm and no eyes, for even then you would be the only man I have ever loved. So if you want to have someone pity you, you will have to do it for yourself; I don't intend to. Do I make myself clear?"

There was a moment of silence. Then John chuckled.

"You didn't answer my question," Laura said sternly. "Is that quite clear?"

"Perfectly," said John, and gathered her into his arms. He kissed her, slowly and passionately, running his hands through her hair. "I love you so much—"

"I love you too. Now tell me, does having a little limp—"

"It is not so little."

"Oh, honestly. Now you are boasting about it." Laura rolled her eyes. "Does it keep you from drinking ale or meeting our neighbors?"

"Absolutely not."

"Then come along."

After that, they had a wonderful time. Laura muddled her way through the introductions, and John, with his perfect French, took over from there, charming the women, befriending the men. He and Talbot put on an impromptu skit of an Englishman trying to ask directions from an islander that made Antoine de Boutin laugh until he cried.

Helier Gosselin invited Laura to dance again, but she thanked him and declined, staying at John's side; there were plenty of other partners for the seigneur. At one point John asked her to refill his ale cup for him; when she returned he was deep in conversation with Antoine and another of the fishermen, a gnarled fellow named Alec Forret. When the men saw her coming, their intent expressions changed; by the time she reached them, they were laughing at some jest John had made.

"What were you discussing so seriously?" she whispered to John.

"The best spots to catch eel, of course," he said, and pulled her close to him.

Not long after that, the guests began to take their leave. "Farmers and fishermen—we are early risers, yes?" Antoine de Boutin told Laura, grinning, as she and John thanked him and his wife and bade them *bonne nuit*.

"You come back anytime, my dear," Eloise urged Laura, with a rueful glance at her husband. "I know what it is like, when your man is away all day!"

They walked with Talbot as far as his church, leaving him at the door. Then Laura started up the hill to the cottage. "Do you want to go home right away?" John asked. "Are you tired?"

She shook her head, smiling. "Not a bit. Just stuffed full of cakes and ale."

"Come for a walk with me, then. I want to show you something."

"What?"

He would not say, but only offered her his arm, grinning mysteriously.

He led her westward through the forest. The pine needles beneath their feet gave off a cool green scent, and the air was quiet and soft beneath the arching trees. Then the ground rose steeply, and the woods gave way to a huge flat rock that shone like silver in the light of the moon. "What's this?" Laura whispered, loath to break the silence.

"La Roque Balan. Where the islanders used to dance on Midsummer's Eve."

"Really?" Laura started to climb up on it, but John held her back.

"Wait. Guy says one must only walk on it barefoot, so as not to perturb the spirit." Laura would have laughed, but there was something oddly hushed and holy about the place. John knelt down and pulled off first her boots and stockings and then his own. As she watched curiously, he gathered some brush from the forest and carried it onto the stone.

"What are you doing?"

"Guy said you could see where they built the bonfires, remember? Ah, this must be it—the rock is burned black." He laid down the pile of brushwood and groped in his girdle for his flint. He struck a spark, and a few crackling twigs ignited; cupping his hands around them, he blew until the fire flared.

"Actually," he said, "Guy told me if we wanted to do it right, we shouldn't wear any clothes at all."

"Do what right?"

"Get married, of course."

Laura laughed. "You can't really intend—"

"Why not?"

"It won't mean anything!"

"It will to me. Anyway, I asked Talbot. It's still a legal way to get married in the Isles, even if English law doesn't recognize it."

Laura put her hand to her mouth, swallowing a hiccup. She really had drunk too much ale. Over her fingertips she looked up at John. "You want me to take off all my clothes so that you can carry me through that fire and down to the sea?"

"I do." He reached for her bodice laces and untied them. Laura laughed, pushing his hands away.

"What if someone comes by and sees us?"

"No one will. The spirit in the rock will protect us." He slipped the gown from her shoulders, baring her breasts.

"Your brother was right about you after all," Laura told him. "You are a madman."

"Marry me," said John, his blue eyes ablaze. He drew the gown down further, over her waist and hips, until it fluttered to the forest floor. Her drawers soon followed; then he unpinned her braids from the nape of her neck and unwound them, letting the red-brown waves tumble to her knees.

"Heathen," she whispered, but she stood unmoving while he stripped his own clothing off hurriedly. The sky above them was a black quilt stitched through with stars; the pounding of the sea on the shore was like distant drums, and borne on the gentle night breeze she imagined she could hear Guy's harp, high and driving and wild.

John swept her up in his arms and carried her onto La Roque Balan.

Laura caught her breath as a sweet, fresh scent wafted toward them; it was as though the rock was strewn with honeysuckle blossoms. The fire John had built seemed somehow to have grown larger. As he walked steadily toward the blaze, she was suddenly afraid. "Stop, please," she begged, burying her face against his chest. "We'll be burned—"

"We're already through."

In disbelief, Laura raised her head. They stood on the opposite side of the rock. She could see John's footprints, damp from the moist earth of the woods, leading right up to the fire and out again . . . and she knew he hadn't jumped. He couldn't jump, not with his bad leg; she would have felt it if he'd tried.

She looked into John's dark eyes, shivering. He smiled and carried her through the flames again.

The sea sounded more like drums than ever. Every tree in the forest seemed a harp that the wind played on. In the shadows cast by the flickering firelight Laura saw pairs of dancers leaping and whirling across the great silver stone. Too much ale! she thought, shaking her head to clear it. No wonder Guy believes in the spirits of the stones, with all he drinks . . .

John carried her through the bonfire one last time. As the red-gold flames engulfed them, Laura dreamed she heard voices laughing, calling one to another above the music of the harps and drums. The scent of honeysuckle hung on the wind, so sweet and strong that one could almost see the fragrance dangling in small, bright crystals that sparkled and turned. The silver rock was a great heart beating beneath them; John's blue eyes were fiery stars.

They passed out of the flames and over the rock to the sea.

The water was a soft, salt-scented blanket, warm and welcoming, showered with moonstones of foam. John's gaze never left Laura's face as he held her tight in his arms, bearing her through the waves until they reached his waist. He stood looking down at her, grave and solemn, then took her hand and raised it to cover her fast-beating heart. He laid his hand atop hers. "On this night," he whispered, "in the name of all that is holy, I take thee, Laura, to my wife." He covered his own heart with his hand. Hesitantly Laura put her fingers to his.

"On this night," she whispered back, "in the name of all that is holy, I take thee, John, to my husband."

He bent down and kissed her beneath the shimmering stars. And as his mouth closed over hers, she knew he was right; it did matter; it was all they needed, for everything around them—sea, strand, sky, forest, moon, and stars—was holy on this mystical night.

She opened her mouth to him, and he slipped his tongue inside her, tasting her essence and the savor of salt from the sea. He ran his hands over her breasts; the nipples were tight and hard beneath his fingers. She leaned back in the water, and he moved his mouth to her throat, tongue trailing over her shoulder and then lower still. She wrapped her legs around his and floated, hair spread out like a fan of bright seaweed, while he sucked the buds of her nipples. The waves broke around them; their bodies were slick and wet and gleaming like stars.

"Wife," he murmured, cupping her small face in his hands, moving them down over the soft, white mounds of her breasts to her waist. He pulled her tight against him, raising her up so that his burning manhood was between her thighs. "Laura. Love." She caught her fists in his hair as he pushed inside her; his palms caressed her buttocks, guiding her back and forth atop him while she clung to his shoulders. He covered her eyes, her throat, her face with his kisses, wild and fierce.

The sea wove her hair around them in a silken net. His breath was quick and fast, his fierce pleasure firing hers. He pushed into her again, deeper, and again, groaning as her warm flesh tightened around him. She moved with him, wanton and eager, legs clasping his loins. His hands tightened on her buttocks, plunging her down again, and she cried out as waves of shimmering light burst inside her with his every thrust. Faster and faster they moved together, glistening, glowing, until the light within her was so bright that all else went dark. "Laura!" he cried, and she cried out as his fire exploded within her, thick and hot as molten gold.

He held her there for a long moment, panting, shaken. "Oh, my love," he murmured against her soaked hair.

She clung to him, fraught with wonder. "Did you feel that?" she whispered, heart still pounding like the sea. "Do you feel that when we make love too? It's as though—"

He laughed raggedly, kissing the tip of her nose. "I know. As though the earth is falling away. Yes, I feel it too."

He withdrew from her slowly, shifting her in his arms, carrying her to shore. Laura looked up, and the masses of stars in the heavens seemed to shift, resolving into constellations before her eyes. Taurus rampaged through fields of fire while Orion pursued him with a taut-strung bow; Perseus sighed for Andromeda, hung by a chain of flame just out of his reach. Cancer scuttled toward Hydra on claws of light; Leo pranced and preened; Castor and Pollux spurred their ethereal horses across the sky—and wondrously, miraculously, she recognized them all.

"Wife," said John, "you are mine for so long as these stars shine. You are mine—forever."

Laura blushed, coming to her senses, realizing she was standing stark naked in the moonlit night. "I don't know what I could have been thinking," she mumbled, "to do such a thing!" Dripping, she darted back toward the rock for her clothes.

John followed, grinning, not one whit dismayed by her sudden display of modesty. "Just you wait," he told the silver bulk of La Roque Balan as he crossed it. "In the morning she'll try to blame all of this on the ale. Just you wait and see!"

Chapter 15

Summer was all soft blue and green on the Isle of Guernsey, but autumn announced itself in a blaze of bright colors: the primrose of the linden leaves, ocher beeches, grand oaks turned the glorious russet of Laura's hair. Though the rest of Europe was wracked by King Philip's wars, the tiny islands caught halfway between England and France seemed suspended, a world apart, placid and serene as the fat, dappled cattle foraging beneath the indigo skies.

John and Guy had mended their quarrel, and neither ever spoke to Laura of what it had been about. The days settled into an easy pattern of fishing and chores and sleep and making love. John came home each night stinking of eel, limping up the cliff stripped to the waist, burned brown as a butternut; against his darkened skin his eyes glowed like rich blue jewels. When Laura heard the frantic cries of the gulls that signaled the *Marie-Hélène*'s arrival, she dropped cooking or laundering or mending to run to the cliff and greet him with a kiss.

In the evenings she and John sometimes visited the neighbors, though Guy never budged from his cottage. In one or another of the small stone houses, the fishermen from the west end of the island would gather: John; Antoine de Boutin and his impetuous son, Robert; Jean d'Armand; old Alec Forret; and half a dozen more. They would drink the dark island ale and tell their tall tales while the wives gossiped and sewed and traded recipes for eel. Laura's French accent improved a bit, or perhaps the islanders simply adjusted to the way she mangled their language; she was never sure. They were the kindest people she had ever known; she told John that her father would have felt at home on Guernsey, and it was true. Since all were poor, anyone's good fortune was a source of rejoicing rather than jealousy, and when any of the fishermen found a treasure in the sea—a barrel of salt cod, a crate of Spanish oranges—it was shared evenly.

One night in mid-September when Laura met John on the cliff he was whistling gaily, carring amid the usual tangle of nets a leather sack. "What is that?" she asked curiously as he grabbed and kissed her.

"Presents."

"Presents? Whatever for?"

"For our anniversary. Do you know, Laura Darby, it is five months exactly tonight since I first saw you? Come into the house."

She peered down the cliff. "But where is Guy?"

"At Hannay's for the night."

"He let you sail the *Marie-Hélène* home by yourself?" Laura asked, wide-eyed, knowing how Guy doted on his boat.

John laughed. "He didn't have any choice; he'd drunk himself to sleep." He pulled her toward the house.

"Drunk himself—on what?"

He closed the cottage door behind them and reached into the sack, pulling out a bottle. "On this."

Laura held the bottle up to the lamp. "John, is this wine?" He nodded, grinning. *"French* wine?" she asked incredulously. He nodded again. "But where on earth did you get it?"

"Antoine found a whole case of it bobbing in Vazon Bay. *And* look what else he found." Out of the sack came a length of midnight-blue satin. "A sky to go with my favorite star."

"Oh, John!" Laura touched the shining fabric in wonder; it was soft as a cloud. "It doesn't look as though it has been in the sea."

"There were yards and yards of it, packed up tight in a pitched barrel. All the wives got a length; you must make yourself a gown for the holidays."

Laura giggled. "We will look like the Sisters of the Blue Satin, all dressed alike. Have you any idea how much this would cost to buy? It is like the stuff Humphrey used to order for Blanche from France, at thirty pounds the yard!"

"Well, it didn't cost me a cent. Now you can get rid of that red silk that Thomas gave you. I have never liked seeing you in that."

"This is still terribly fancy."

He laughed and chucked her chin. "I would have had Antoine find plain gray fustian if I could have managed it, pet."

Laura's sly gold gaze slanted up to meet his. "Then I suppose"—she sighed—"I am stuck with this." Then, all pretense of scruples vanished, she asked, "Did he find anything else?"

"Greedy little Protestant!" He sat at the table, pulling her onto his lap. "Look for yourself," he invited, giving her the sack.

She reached into its depths and felt a small paper-wrapped bundle. "What is in here?" she asked, drawing it forth.

"Open it and see."

She sat up on his knee and untied the knotted twine. "Give me a hint, please."

"It is something I have wanted you to have for a very long time."

"How long a time?"

His fingertips traced the shadows in the hollows of her throat. "From the very first moment I saw you."

"That's no hint," she scoffed, and pried at the paper. Inside was a bit of rolled-up velvet; she unwound it eagerly and saw against the dark fabric the rich gleam of gold. "Oh, John," she breathed.

It was a ring, a plain gold band set with a small gold star, exquisite in its simplicity. "I thought it the sort of ornament even a Protestant might wear," he told her. "Look inside."

She tilted the band to the lamp and saw the words engraved within it: "From John to Laura: my morning star."

Eyes brimming with tears, she sat while he kissed her and slipped the ring onto the third finger of her right hand. "There," he said with satisfaction, "official and permanent. You're my wife—so long as we stay on this island."

"It's so beautiful," she whispered, turning her hand, admiring the play of the lamplight on the shining star. Then she looked up at him. "You cannot tell me you found this, though!"

"Astonishing coincidence, isn't it? I mean, the names and all."

Laura pinched him. "I'll have you know I'm not at all sure Antoine found that satin in the ocean either."

"Where else could he have gotten it?" he asked, blue eyes perfectly innocent. "We are all only poor Guernsey fishermen, after all." He pulled the cork from a wine bottle with his teeth.

"John Guilford, what are you and the rest of the poor Guernsey fishermen up to?" Laura demanded suspiciously.

"I can't speak for all of us." He took a swallow of wine,

rolling it in his mouth, and then kissed her, sharing the savor while he slipped his hands beneath her smock. "But I am up to this." And then he made love to her.

Laura showed the ring and the satin to Hannay when next she came to visit. "Where do you suppose John got them?" she asked Guy's sister. "He told me he found them."

Hannay laughed. "Don't you have the saying in English not to look at a gift horse's teeth? I cannot speak of the ring, but Eloise de Boutin has got a piece of cloth just like this. She is making a new gown for Christmas. It is nearly done."

Laura sighed, sitting down on a stool. "I keep meaning to start a dress from it myself, but I don't have the energy. All I seem to want to do lately is sleep." She lowered her eyes. "I've been wanting to ask Talbot about it, but I am too embarrassed. I think there is something wrong inside of me. That I've gotten—stopped up."

"Stopped up?"

Laura nodded, blushing. "I haven't had my bleeding this month at all."

"*Chérie!*" Hannay took her hands excitedly. "Perhaps you are with child!"

"With child?" Laura blinked. "How could that be?"

"The better question would be, what took you so long?" Hannay smiled slyly. "I have seen the way John looks at you in the evenings. As though he cannot wait to get you to bed and make love to you!"

"Oh, Hannay, honestly. What has that got to do with anything?"

"Laura," her friend said after a pause, "don't you know how babies are made?"

"Of course I do!" Laura said indignantly. "Sort of. I think."

"*Bien.* You tell me, then." Hannay sat across from her, blue eyes twinkling.

"Well . . ."

"Well?"

"Well, a man and a woman get married and then they have babies."

"*Mon Dieu,*" Hannay said with a rueful laugh. "If it were as simple as that, Talbot and I could have a family of ten. *Écoutes. chérie.* When you and John make love, he puts a seed inside you, and the seed grows into a child. In here." She tapped Laura's belly.

"Hannay, that's ridiculous! How would it get out?"

"The same way it got in. It pushes out, right down there."

"A baby," said Laura, "could *never* get out that way."

"It hurts. But it comes out."

Laura pondered this bizarre notion. "How long does it take before it comes out?" she asked at last.

"A long time. Nine months."

"Really," Laura said politely, not believing a word of it.

"You think I am lying to you, *chérie?* That is why Talbot and I do not have any babies. Because we do not make love. You have got a baby inside you. Just you wait. You will see."

Laura gave Hannay the benefit of the doubt. She waited a month. By that time she didn't feel tired or sick any longer. She had a little bleeding, and that settled that. Her appetite returned with a vengeance, and then she was more embarrassed than ever to say anything to Talbot or John, because she knew what was wrong with her: she was getting fat.

The first snow fell in late November. Laura stood by the cottage window watching the big soft flakes drift over the yard and cover the cliff. The sight made her think of home, something she rarely did nowadays. England, Queen Mary, Thomas—they all might have been a million miles away instead of a hundred. John had been right when, that night on the cliffs, he had called Guernsey "Eden." They were Adam and Eve, newborn on this small spit of Paradise. The old world of hate and deceit and war could not touch them here...

She heard the squawking gulls on the cliff and wrapped herself in a cloak, walking out through the swirling snow to welcome John and Guy home. To her surprise, Antoine de Boutin and his son Robert were with them; John and Robert were supporting Antoine between them, staggering up the cliff. Antoine was singing, head thrown back to the sky:

> *J'aime la fille*
> *Qui est si jolie*
> *Et une grande bouteille du vin—ooph!*

The song ended in a startled grunt as they reached the top of the cliff. "What on earth—" Laura stared at the sodden quartet.

"Drunk," John told her briefly, as he and Robert dragged Antoine toward the house. "We found some more wine."

"Drunk—" That was odd, thought Laura. The other men all looked cold sober, even Guy—though now that she noticed it, he also looked terrified out of his wits. She followed the men into the cottage, where they deposited Antoine, groaning, on the floor. "My Lord, he looks awful," she said, and laughed.

"Laura." John had knelt by Antoine's prostrate body and was struggling to pull off the Guernseyman's wet jacket. "Could you go down the hill, please, and fetch Talbot? Tell him we need his donkey cart to get Antoine home."

"Wouldn't it be best just to let him sleep it off here?"

"Do as I say, Laura. Please." His voice was unaccustomedly sharp, and she shrugged and wrapped her cloak more tightly around her shoulders, heading out into the snow again.

She found the priest in his tiny cottage behind the church, reading by the fire. When he heard Laura's message he scrambled to hitch up the pony with alarming speed. "I hardly think there's any need to rush so," Laura told him, laughing. "From what I saw, all he needs is a good night's sleep."

"Nonetheless," said Talbot, helping her into the cart, "Eloise will be worried if he comes home late in this storm." He clucked his tongue at the donkey, starting up the hill.

When they reached the cottage, Talbot jumped from the cart and ran in, leaving Laura to climb down herself and hitch the pony at the gate. By the time she had stomped the snow from her boots and gone inside, the men had Antoine all wrapped in blankets and were hoisting him onto their shoulders to carry him out. Not all the men, though—Guy was sitting on his stool at the hearth, gulping down ale. At the doorway Robert turned and shook a fist at him. "This is your fault, old man," he shouted. "Old drunken coward."

Guy spun around on his stool. "I told you there was evil there," he said stolidly. "There were bad rocks—"

"Oh, shut up about your damned bloody rocks!" Robert cried. "The only evil there was you!"

"Hush, Robert," Talbot said quickly. "Let's get your father home." He and John carried Antoine out; Robert followed, with a final glare at Guy, and slammed the door.

"Fool," Guy muttered, and turned back to the fire.

John returned a moment later, brushing snow from his hair. "Guy, what Robert said—he didn't mean it. You lost your head for a moment, that's all. You panicked—"

"I did—not—panic," Guy said very distinctly. "It was a bad place, where we were. The rocks were bad. But if no one listens to me, I tell you what. I do not go with you anymore."

"Guy, hold on! You're the best sailor on all of Guernsey!" John told him urgently. "We need you with us."

"I should come with you so that boy, that fool, can call me such names?" Guy slammed down his ale cup. "No! If no one listens, I will not go with you anymore."

Laura looked from one man to the other and started to ask a question. John shook his head at her, motioning her toward their bedchamber. Puzzled, she started toward it, then noticed Antoine's discarded jacket lying in a heap on the floor. "See here," she said, shaking it out, "Eloise will be cross with him after all." She blinked, seeing a jagged hole in the back of the jacket, and a dark, sticky blotch. She put her finger to the stain, and it came away marked with red. Blood...

Her startled gaze flew to John. He yanked her into the bedroom and closed the door.

"You told me Antoine was drunk!" she said, bewildered, clutching the bloodied jacket.

"Hush. Don't let Guy hear you. Antoine is drunk. We poured a whole bottle of sherry into him."

"But then—how—" She stared at the jacket in her hands.

John sighed. "It's very simple. We were all of us sailing over on the Normandy coast when some French ships came up behind us. We got the boats into a cove to hide, but Guy got spooked by the rocks there and insisted on sailing out. That drew their attention, and Antoine took an arrow in his back."

"Oh, dear God!"

"He'll be all right," John said quickly. "Talbot's going to take out the arrowhead once they get him home. It's nothing to worry about."

"Nothing to worry about?" Laura heard her voice rising. "What in the world were you doing on the Normandy coast?"

He sat down heavily on the bed. "I didn't want to tell you about this before. And it honestly isn't anything to fret about. But we've been sailing over to France for the past few months to—well, to reconnoiter."

"To reconnoiter? Do you mean to spy? On the French?"

"Aye. Something is going on over there, Laura, something big. King Henri has ships and men pouring into those ports—St. Malo, Paimpol, La Haye. There are more every time we look."

"You're spying for Queen Mary," she said accusingly. "You are helping the woman who murdered my father!"

"I'm helping England," he corrected her gently.

"What do you care about England? England would burn both of us if it could."

"No, love, no. England doesn't burn people. Queen Mary and her ministers do. You can't blame a nation because it's leaders do cruel, foolish things." He reached for her hands. "If the French defeat Queen Mary, if they conquer England, what do you think will become of Elizabeth Tudor?"

"What has that got to do with anything?"

"Do you remember you once asked me what I believed in? Well, I believe in Elizabeth. She could be a great queen; I know that. With her as ruler, England could be the kind of nation that the rest of the world would look up to. A nation where people are free to believe anything they want, to explore God and the heavens and anything else however they see fit."

Laura was silent, remembering what Father Burton had once said to her at Hatfield House: *In the England I dream of someday seeing, no man or woman would have to choose whether to heed conscience or to die*... Her own father had said much the same thing when he told her the martyrs' fires were candles, lighting the way...

But still. "Antoine could have been killed," she said stubbornly. "You could have been killed!"

"It was sheer bad luck that the French ever saw us, Laura. If Guy hadn't tried to sail out—"

"But he did!"

"You heard him tonight. He won't be coming with us again. He never wanted to anyway."

She looked at him. "Was that what you and he argued about this past summer?"

He nodded. "We've been giving our reports on the movements of the French to Helier Gosselin. You know how Guy feels about the seigneur."

"You told me once that you thought he might be right."

"He may be. But we haven't got any other way of making sure the information gets to Queen Mary and her ministers."

At his mention of the queen, Laura's eyes filled with

tears. "I cannot believe you would risk your life for her sake."

"It's for England's sake, Laura. Anyway, it isn't as though we are fighting. All we do is sail a little closer to Normandy to fish than we usually would."

"Close enough to snag bolts of satin and cases of wine from the docks?" she demanded.

He laughed at the shrewd guess. "That was Robert; he's a daredevil, that young man is. You wouldn't catch me trying that."

Laura looked into his deep blue eyes. "Would you stop if I asked you to?"

He returned her gaze steadily. "Are you going to ask me that?"

Beware, Hannay had told Laura, *lest you fall in love with a man who loves something more than you . . .*

But John wasn't that kind of man, Laura argued to herself. He'd told her she was the center of his universe. He loved her more than anything, more than life itself—didn't he?

"You're all I have now, John," she said softly. "If anything were ever to happen to you—"

"Oh, love." He opened his arms, and she ran to him; he held her tightly, stroking her hair. "Nothing will happen to me. I swear it. I promise."

And Laura believed him, because it was what she wanted to hear.

For the next few weeks, while Antoine recuperated, John sailed with Robert on the de Boutins' fishing boat. Guy went out alone on the *Marie-Hélène,* true to his word. Laura worried about him; since Antoine had been shot, Guy was drinking more than ever. Through the long winter nights he sat by the hearth with his ale cup and his *télen,* mumbling of wizards and demons and the Arch Druid.

A fortnight before Christmas, Helier Gosselin paid a call at the cottage while the men were out on the boats, riding up to the gate through the snow atop a splendid black steed. Laura saw him through the window and ran to open the door. *"Bonjour!* Come in, come in, you must be frozen. I'll make you something warm to drink."

The seigneur stomped in, peeling off gloves and wrappings, and Laura set a stool for him at the hearth and put the kettle to boil. He looked about the common room curiously. "It has been a long time since I was in this house."

"Guy doesn't have many visitors way up here," Laura said ruefully. "I don't know why not. It's true he does drink too much, but he's a very sweet man."

Gosselin smiled. "I suppose we have all grown tired of hearing his dire talk about what will become of us because we have given up the Ancient Way. You're a newcomer still; you forget we have been hearing his silly warnings for twenty years. 'The Arch Druid will come out of the rock and rule over Guernsey again'—what nonsense!" He rubbed his red hands together above the coals.

Laura was tempted to put in a good word for Guy, but instead changed the subject. "What a lot of snow there has been! Are the winters always like this here?"

"This is a bad one," the seigneur agreed. "Still, it is milder here than in England, yes?"

Laura laughed. "Perhaps it is, in a thatch-roofed cottage. I wouldn't know."

"Will you be going back to see your family for the holidays?" Gosselin asked.

"Oh, I haven't got any family except for John." Laura measured out chamomile for a tisane.

"No one?" he asked in surprise. "No mother? No father?"

"Well, I have a half brother." Laura poured hot water over the herbs, strained the brew, and handed him a cup. "But we are estranged. No, I'm the last of the Darby line, as my father once said." The seigneur let out a strange little grunt, and she glanced at him.

"I spilled my tisane," he explained, brushing a spot from his black breeches knee. "Very hot!"

"Let me get you a towel—"

"No, no, no. It is nothing." He took a cautious sip. "I came by because I must make a crossing to England. I thought perhaps if you weren't going home, there might be someone you would wish me to convey holiday greetings to."

"Oh, that's very kind of you, Helier. But thank you, no." Laura took her own cup and perched on a stool beside him. "Will it be safe for you to cross the Channel with this war going on?"

The seigneur chuckled. "Wars have a way of dying down when the weather is this bad. Nothing will happen until the spring."

Laura found his certainty reassuring. "Do you really think

so? John says there are an awful lot of ships and men gathering in Normandy."

He stirred his tisane with the tip of his finger and winked. "With all due respect, Laura—what do Guernsey fishermen know about matters of state? Trust me. King Henri's soldiers are going to stay safe and warm and close to a fire!" As she set down her cup and picked up the blue satin gown she was hemming, his face lit up. "What a magnificent dress! You must wear it to Castle Cornet for Christmas Day."

"Are you having a party?" Laura asked eagerly.

"*Bien sûr.* I have one every year, for all my islanders."

"Then John and I will certainly be there!"

Gosselin smiled and drained his cup. "You think of yourselves as islanders now. I am glad. *Eh bien,* if you are quite sure there is no one I can give your regards to in Shropshire—"

"Hertfordshire," she corrected him. "Must you leave so soon?"

"I'm afraid I must, or my poor horse will turn to ice. Speaking of which—you haven't any horses here, have you? I shall send my carriage to fetch you on Christmas Day."

"You mustn't go to such trouble," Laura said quickly.

"No trouble," he assured her. "You could hardly walk all the way to St. Peter Port in winter! And if you did, you would be too tired to dance with me."

"I'm afraid, Helier, that my dancing days are done."

"Ah, your husband's leg. I forgot. Well, we will share a cup of punch then, you and me and John." He made a face. "I do not think Guy will come."

Laura laughed. "No, I don't think he will! Do have a safe trip to England."

"Give my best regards to John." He bowed and kissed her hand. "And until I see you again—*joyeux Noel.*"

"And a very merry Christmas to you, Helier."

Chapter 16

"More ivy, I think," said Laura, standing back to examine the cottage mantelpiece with a critical eye. "Don't you think so, Hannay?"

"You are the expert, *chérie.*" Hannay sat at the table bemusedly stringing holly berries with a needle and thread according to Laura's directions. "After all, this is to be an English Christmas Eve."

"Not English," Laura said quickly. "Just the sort I remember from home. A Howarth Manor Christmas, if you will." She added another loop of ivy to the arrangement and adjusted a hemlock twig.

"Here are your berries." Hannay handed her the string and watched as Laura draped it over the deep green ivy leaves. "Is there anything else you need?"

"Just this." Gold eyes glinting mischievously, Laura pulled a small bundle of gray leaves and creamy berries from her girdle and climbed onto a stool to hang it from the top of the doorframe. Hannay peered at it curiously.

"Le gui? What is that for?"

"We call it mistletoe. If you kiss your true love underneath it on Christmas Eve, you will have good luck for the New Year." She looked down at the Guernseywoman quickly. "I'm sorry—I wasn't thinking. About you and Talbot, I mean. Shall I take it down?"

"No, no." Hannay planted a kiss on the wooden frame. "When Talbot comes to the cottage next, you tell him to kiss the door right there. And who knows? Perhaps we will be lucky in the New Year."

Laura climbed down from the stool and hugged her friend. "I hope so, Hannay. Are you going to Helier Gosselin's fête at the castle tomorrow?"

"I have not decided. I must ask Guy what Talbot plans to do. Do you and John go?"

Laura made a face. "John doesn't want to. I think he is

afraid I will want to dance—you know how silly he is about
his leg. But with my new gown, and this mistletoe, *and* the
apple pies I made, I'm pretty sure I can change his mind!"
She raised her head. "Was that the gulls? No, only the wind.
Such a bitter night!" She went and put another log in the
hearth, stirring the coals. "I'll be glad when John and Guy
are both safe home."

"Does John still sail with the de Boutins?" Hannay asked
with a frown.

Laura nodded. "If you ask me, your brother is the only
fisherman on Guernsey who has any sense, refusing to go
along on those spying jaunts. Still, there hasn't been any
trouble since Antoine got shot. I suppose that's because of
this wretched weather. Helier Gosselin says the French will
stay put in Normandy until spring." The December wind rattled the shutters, and Laura shivered, setting down the fire
tongs. "Do you know, Hannay, it was the most peculiar
thing. When Guy came into the cottage after Helier visited,
he knew right away who had been here. He said Helier has
an evil smell to him, just like the bad rocks. Why does Guy
hate him so much?"

"He blames Helier for convincing the people to give up
the Ancient Way. You know how superstitious my brother
is."

"He told me that the power of the Arch Druid is getting
stronger. He says he feels it more and more each day as he
rows out to his boat."

"Sometimes," Hannay said darkly, "I think poor Guy is
losing his mind." She let out a sigh. "I wish he would stop
drinking. That is where all this nonsense about spirits comes
from."

"I must say, I think you are right about that." Laura was
remembering Midsummer's Eve on La Roque Balan, and the
shadowy dancers that she had seen.

Hannay cocked her head at the ceiling. *"Les mouettes.*
That will be Guy. You had better get into your new gown!"

She helped Laura lift the heavy satin skirts over her head
and settled the bodice and shoulders. *"C'est très belle, cette
robe,"* said the Guernseywoman, admiring the rich fabric,
the wide sleeves, and tiny tucked waist. "Turn about so I
fasten the buttons." Laura spun around, wide skirts swirling.
"Breathe in, *chérie,"* Hannay directed. "You have made *la
ceinture* too tight."

"I don't see how that can be." Laura peered back over

her shoulder. "It fit perfectly the last time I tried it on!"

"And when was that?"

"A few weeks ago. Try again, Hannay; I'll breathe in harder." Laura put her hands on her waist, stood up very straight, and took the longest, deepest breath she could. "Oh!" she cried suddenly, letting it out in a gasp.

"*Qu'est-ce que c'est?*"

"I don't know!" Laura turned to stare at her, hands on her belly, golden eyes wide. "The most extraordinary feeling —as though a bird were beating its wings inside me!"

Relieved, Hannay began to laugh. "Not a bird, *mon petite chou*—the baby! Didn't I tell you so? That is why your gown does not fit."

"There isn't any baby—oh, my!" Laura clapped her hands to her stomach. "There it goes again!"

Hannay wagged her head. "*Chérie,* why will you not believe me? This is how babies grow! You have not had your bleeding since when?"

"I don't know. September? October?"

Exasperated, Hannay shook her by the shoulders. "And you say nothing to John?"

"I don't understand how a baby can grow inside a person," Laura confessed sheepishly.

"Who can understand such a thing? It is one of God's miracles, *chérie.*"

"Hannay, are you certain that's what's wrong with me?"

"I stake my life on it."

"A baby." Laura sat down on the bed. "I am going to have a baby! Fancy that."

Hannay came and hugged her. "Such a fine Christmas gift for John!" As she pulled away, Laura saw tears shining in her bright blue eyes.

"Oh, Hannay, you and Talbot will have children someday. I know you will."

"Not while Queen Mary rules England." Hannay rubbed her eyes on her sleeve, hearing her brother's whistle at the cottage door. "Well," she said with brave cheer, "you will have to move these buttons before you can wear your new gown."

Laura struggled out of the voluminous blue satin and back into her old smock. "I suppose it is worth moving buttons to have a baby!" she said with a laugh.

Guy was already at the ale barrel when they emerged from the bedchamber. "It is very strong tonight," he mumbled, gulping down his drink, his beard dripping ice. *"Très forte. Très forte."*

"Guy, can't that wait until after supper?" his sister asked of the ale. "What is strong, the wind?"

He shook his head, scattering beads of water over the floor. "The evil in the rock. The Arch Druid."

"Don't be a fool, Guy," Hannay snapped. "There's no evil in that rock. It is all in your mind."

"Evil," he repeated. "The devil. I feel it. I smell it." Laura felt her spine tingle as she looked at his wizened face, his grizzled tangle of beard.

"You smell of fish, old man," said Hannay, fingering his filthy shirt. "Fish and ale on your breath—" She stopped, glancing toward the rafters.

"My Lord," said Laura, "listen to the gulls!" In all her months on Guernsey she'd never heard the birds so loud. She ran to the door and opened it a crack, letting in a blast of frigid night air. "Hannay, Guy, come and see! The whole sky is filled with gulls!" It was true: in the pale bluish light of the gibbous moon, thousands upon thousands of birds were wheeling and diving over the cliff.

"Laura!" Above the raucous chatter of the gulls a distant drawn-out cry floated from the cliff.

"That's John!" Laura caught up her cloak from a peg by the door, unable to wait to give him her news of the baby.

Hannay was listening to the frantic gulls. "I wonder—" She grabbed her own cloak, tugging at her brother's sleeve. "Come on. Come out to the cliffs, old man."

As Laura and Hannay left the cottage he trailed after them through the snow, muttering beneath his breath.

Laura could see John's tall figure high on the rocks in the moonlight, and someone else standing beside him. "Is that Talbot?" she asked Hannay, climbing up through the frozen meadow.

"Oui," said Hannay, keeping right at her side.

Laura glanced at her curiously. "And you are coming to meet him?"

"Oui," said Hannay. "Watch your step on this ice."

"Why are you going to see him?" Laura asked. The Guernseywoman didn't answer; she just kept pushing toward the cliff against the wind. Above them the gulls swept around and around, their frenzied cries nearly drowning out the sound of the crashing waves.

Hannay reached the cliff and ran to Talbot, who opened

his arms to embrace her. As Laura climbed onto the rocks she saw half a dozen fishing boats bobbing on the black water beyond the Arch Druid. "Laura." John caught and held her, mouth brushing her spray-damp hair. She could feel his heart racing in his chest, the thumping pulse at the side of her throat as he crushed her against him. "Laura, love, I have to go away for a little while."

"Go away?" She pulled back from his embrace. "Go away where? Now? On Christmas Eve?"

Talbot, his arm circling Hannay's waist, was talking to Guy. "The French have set sail from Normandy," he said urgently. "They're headed for Calais. No one will expect them in weather like this. We're going to try and get through to warn the English garrison. We need you with us, Guy."

"Hah!" Guy stumbled to the edge of the cliff and peered down at the boats. "Who else is out there? Is Robert de Boutin with you? Does he want me to come—an old drunk, a coward?"

"Guy, you are still the best sailor on Guernsey," John told him. "And the more of us that go, the more chance—"

He stopped, seeing Laura's wide, horrified gaze.

"*You're* not going," she whispered.

"They need me to navigate."

"You can't go!" She searched his shadowy face. "You're not going with them!"

"Laura, if the French take Calais—"

"I don't care about the French or Calais or anything else. I care about you!"

"John! Talbot!" A shout echoed over the water. "Guy—is he coming?"

"Guy." Talbot turned to him. "We need you. Won't you come along?"

The gruff old Guernseyman shook his head, staring out at the black rock that reared its head above the waves. "It is no good. The evil is too strong." His nose probed the air, sniffing, and for an instant Laura thought she caught on the cold salt air a scent that was dank and strange.

"For God's sake, Guy," Hannay cried, "for the love of God, go with them! If you stay behind, don't you know what people will say?"

In the stark moonlight, Guy's rough-hewn face and scraggy beard made him look like an ancient prophet. "They can say what they like," he told Hannay, his voice ringing from the rocks. "It is no good. I stay here. You should all stay here." And he stumbled back to the cottage through the snow.

"John! Talbot! Come on, then. Hurry!" someone cried from the boats.

"Laura." John look a limping step toward her. "I have to go. Try to understand—"

Laura looked at Talbot and Hannay, who clung to each other, kissing, and then back at John. "You've been planning this all along, haven't you?" Her golden eyes flashed. "Hannay knew about it, didn't she? Everyone knew but me!"

"We didn't think—we hoped it wouldn't come to this. Laura, if we don't get warning to those English soldiers, they'll be sitting like lambs for the slaughter! What would you have me do?"

"Leave them," she said in a terrible voice. "Let them die for their bloodthirsty queen."

Robert de Boutin shouted up from the sea, "We can't wait any longer!" The gulls swooped and screamed overhead. John held out his arms.

"Come, love. Kiss me farewell."

"You cannot leave me!" Laura cried in desperation. "I—I have your baby inside me!"

His gaze dropped from hers for a moment. Then he said. "I know."

"Oh, John." She stared at him, stricken, betrayed. "You knew and you didn't tell me. You didn't tell me . . . because you were going away."

"I love you, Laura."

"Do you love England more?" she raged at him.

"I love . . . what England could be. It's for you that I'm going, Laura. For you and our child."

"And would you stay, for me, for our child, if I ask you to?"

"Don't ask me that, love—"

"I am asking you now."

"Laura. I have to go."

It had been her last lure to hold him, and as she heard his words, as she realized it would not be enough, her frightened anger exploded. "Go then!" she screamed at him. "Go and don't ever come back! I hope the French get your heart and not your leg this time!" She wrenched off the ring he had given her and flung it down in the snow.

He bent awkwardly to retrieve it, and the moon showed

tears in his eyes. "I do love you, Laura," he said hoarsely, "for so long as the stars shine."

"Damn you," she told him. "Damn you to hell."

Talbot was already halfway down the cliff. John started after him. From far out over the water, Robert called to them again. *"Nous venons,"* John called back, sounding lost and sad. At the foot of the rocks he and Talbot stepped into the skiff; John took the oars, and the tiny boat cut through the waves. The salt spray glistened like diamonds. The moon rolled into the clouds. Snow began to fall. In the cove far below, the Arch Druid reared its head, hideous and black.

The gulls streamed out after the boats as they set their sails. Hannay stood on the cliff, staring after them, but Laura ran back to the cottage.

Guy was crouched on his stool by the hearth, drinking as fast as he could. Laura went to his side. "You were right not to go with them," she told him fiercely.

Hannay slammed the door against the wind behind them. "Old man," she said harshly. "Old man, you shame me."

"Leave him alone," Laura cried.

"Coward." Hannay went to her brother and shook him by the back of his soiled jacket. "Why don't you tell her why you live in the past, why you cling to the Ancient Way?"

Laura pushed her away. "He was right not to go with them! He's not a coward!"

"No?" Hannay's blue eyes were bright and hard. "Will you tell her, Guy, or shall I?"

"Hannay," he mumbled, "no—"

She turned to Laura. "Ask him about his wife. Ask him how his wife died."

"Hannay, no!" He put up his hands as though to ward off her words.

"I tell her, then." Hannay brushed past Laura and stood, arms crossed over her breasts, her back to the fire. "His Marie-Hélène. His wife. His love. How beautiful was she, Guy? How much did you love her?"

"I loved her!"

"But not enough, did you?"

"It was the rock, the rock!"

"The rock is evil. You'd like everyone to believe that, wouldn't you, Guy? It was the big black Arch Druid."

"But it was!"

Hannay looked at Laura. "Marie-Hélène, she had a little dog that Guy bought her. A pretty little dog, black and white, to keep her company while he was fishing all day. What did Marie-Hélène call the dog, Guy? What was its name?"

"Cocotte. She called her Cocotte," he mumbled miserably.

"Cocotte. And one day, when the tide was just at that place where the fishermen say a man can walk on the water, Cocotte got out on the Arch Druid. Perhaps she was chasing a gull, who knows? Marie-Hélène begged Guy to go out and save her pretty little dog. But you wouldn't go, would you, Guy?"

"I told her. I warned her."

"You told her the rock was evil, didn't you, you superstitious old man? But the truth is that you were afraid."

"Evil is a thing to be feared," Guy insisted.

"So Marie-Hélène had to row herself out in the skiff," Hannay went on relentlessly. "She rowed herself out, and she drowned."

"Oh, Guy, no!" Laura whispered.

"And that," said Hannay, eyes flashing, "was when the islanders listened to Helier Gosselin and gave up the Ancient Way. Because they saw how stupid it was, that it cost Marie-Hélène her life."

"What cost her life," Guy said stubbornly, "was the evil spirit in that rock."

"There is nothing wrong with that rock," said Hannay. "But there is something wrong with my brother. He is a coward, just as all the Guernseymen say."

"I am going," said Laura, "and you can't stop me." Defiantly she tied a strip of leftover satin around her waist, covering the place in the back of her gown where the buttons did not quite meet.

"Laura. No. Do not go to the castle," Guy pleaded. "There is a great evil loose. I know it. I feel it."

"Oh, do shut up about that!" Laura told him harshly. The story Hannay had revealed the night before had quite changed her mind about Guy. Any man that would let his wife drown because he was afraid of a rock *was* a coward—and crazy too. "I am sick to death of all your prattling about evil and doom. I am going to the castle, to Helier's party, and I am going to drink wine and dance and make merry." She twisted her long red-brown curls back into a chignon, then looked up, hearing carriage wheels clattering on the hill.

"'Twill be a treat to ride in a coach again, by God." She glared at her sturdy boots. "I wish to hell I had some decent shoes."

Guy grabbed her hands. "Laura, listen to me, please. I have a bad feeling. A very bad feeling."

"So have I," Laura snapped. "But not about rocks. About John." For a moment, seeing the old man looking so desolate, Laura pitied him. "You've been a good friend to me, Guy. I wish—" The carriage driver rang his bell. Impulsively Laura kissed Guy's weather-battered cheek. "Never mind. Goodbye."

The seats of the carriage were of padded leather, glove soft and cozy. Laura sank back onto them, determined not to think about John. She was young. Some people said she was beautiful. She was going to a party. Going dancing. As for her husband, he could go to hell.

She tapped her feet impatiently, staring through the coach window as the gray hills and winter-drear fields rolled past. Eden, John had called this island once. Paradise—hah! It was a miserable, pathetic little place, filled with miserable pathetic little people. She wished they had never come here.

Night fell as she rode, and the thin moon seemed to shiver as it rose above the town of St. Peter Port. Castle Cornet loomed high above the tiled roofs of the houses, every window in its towers and turrets ablaze with candles. Laura's anticipation mounted as the carriage lurched to a stop. The driver helped her down. Already she could hear on the night wind the cheery strains of viols and flutes and pipes.

A footman in a handsome green livery opened the castle doors to her. The grand hall within was filled with islanders, unbundling themselves from wraps and hats and gloves. Their mood seemed strangely unfestive, subdued. News of the fishermen's mission to Calais, thought Laura, must have spread fast. She saw Hannay murmuring in a corner with Eloise de Boutin and Robert's lovely young wife, Isobel. The sadness that clouded their faces aroused Laura's ire. What was the matter with them? They ought not to be sad: they ought to be furious with their men for leaving this way.

"Mistress Darby." At the sound of the smooth, low voice Laura turned and saw Helier Gosselin, looking tall and elegant in a fine dark doublet trimmed with gold braid. He smiled down at her. "How was your carriage ride?"

She smiled back. "I can't tell you how much I enjoyed it! Thank you ever so much for sending it for me."

"I'm delighted I did." His dark eyes raked over her blue satin gown. "That dress was made for dancing, my dear."

"Alas, I am without a partner," she said coquettishly.

"But where is your charming husband?"

"On a wild goose chase."

"Ah." He nodded. "Gone to Calais with the others, has he? They might have saved their time. Henri of France would never launch an attack in the dead of winter."

"I wish you had convinced John of that. He insists he and the others saw the French ships leaving Normandy."

Helier Gosselin gave a deprecating laugh. "Ah, yes, the reports of our little band of Guernsey spies. I found them quaint indeed. Well, since you find yourself abandoned, lovely Laura, perhaps you will dance with me."

Laura gave the seigneur her most charming smile. "I would be delighted, Helier."

He took her arm and led her into a huge ballroom. There were chandeliers of crystal and a floor of polished marble. Statues posed in the corners, and a silver fountain spouted red wine. The islanders were huddled on the edges of the room, whispering together, but the musicians were playing. "It seems we shall have to take the lead, my dear," Gosselin told her, guiding her into the center of the floor.

Laura had forgotten how fine a dancer he was. She had nearly forgotten how to dance, she thought wistfully, following him through the intricate steps of a sarabande. Forgotten how marvelous it was to glide across gleaming marble with full skirts swirling and a man's strong hand at her waist. Forgotten the gay pleasure of leaping and whirling beneath the sparkle of crystal, while painted walls and rich tapestries flew past . . .

"What a ravishing creature you are, Laura," her partner murmured at her ear, his arm tightening around her. Laura laughed, gaily tossing her head.

"You mustn't say such things, Helier," she reproved him. "I am a married woman."

"Your husband is a dolt to have left you. Were you mine, I should never stray an inch from your side."

"Why, Helier." Laura curtsied as the sarabande ended, gazing up at him from beneath the sweep of her lashes. "Are you flirting with me?"

He laughed and signaled to the musicians. "Shall we have another dance, *chérie?*"

Around the vast hall they went, the candles blazing above

them. Laura could see Hannay and Eloise watching her with silent disapproval, but why should she care? If they chose to stand about being miserable, then let them. She intended to enjoy this night.

She and Helier shared two more dances. Then he proposed a cup of wine, and they stood together by the silver fountain. He poured her a cup of sparkling bloodred burgundy, filled another for himself, and touched his cup to hers. "To you, *ma chère* Laura. The most beautiful woman on Guernsey."

"Isobel de Boutin is very lovely, don't you think?" Laura asked, watching Robert's wife across the room.

"If one likes peasants." Helier sipped his wine, his dark eyes never leaving her face. "You—you are different from these foolish people. You were never meant to be a fisherman's wife. You ought always to be dressed in satin, to walk across marble floors."

Laura laughed; the strong wine had gone straight to her head. "Believe it or not, I had a chance at that once. But I gave it all up—for John." The thought made her angry again. Look at the sacrifices she had made for him! And what did he do in return? Run off and abandon her! And to help Queen Mary—the woman who'd murdered her father.

Helier bent down, leaning very close to her. "There is a fine collection of portraiture here in the castle. Perhaps you would like me to show it to you."

Laura glanced around the ballroom and saw Hannay frowning in her direction. The Guernseywoman's unspoken reprimand of her flirtatious behavior only irritated her more. She smiled up at the handsome seigneur. "I would enjoy that very much. Thank you, Helier."

He took her arm again, escorting her through a set of double glass-paned doors at the end of the room. Laura heard Hannay call her name and ignored it defiantly. Her heart was beating fast. She remembered the couples she'd seen slip off just this way from the receiving room of Guilford Hall, going into the gardens. She knew now what they had been doing: kissing in the shadowy arbors, out of sight of the other guests. She wondered if the seigneur intended to kiss her and what she would do if he tried. He really was so charming. How much harm could there be in a kiss?

He led her down a long, echoing corridor lit by sconced torches. The walls were lined with huge, dark paintings in gilded frames. "My predecessors," he told her softly. "All the seigneurs of Guernsey, back five hundred years." She admired them absently, far more aware of the live seigneur close beside her than these portraits of those long dead.

They reached the end of the gallery and stood before a red door. "My private offices," said Helier Gosselin, smiling. "Would you like to come in? I have some fine French brandy in here—too good to share with the others."

"Certainly," said Laura, feeling very naughty and daring. This would teach John to run off and leave her, she thought bemusedly. Hannay would be sure to tell him she had left the ballroom alone with the seigneur.

Gosselin pushed open the door and ushered her inside, then closed the door behind them with a little click. Laura stood admiring the rich dark paneled walls, the tiled floors. In the center of the room was a long, polished oak desk; the wall behind it was covered with splendid crimson velvet drapes. One corner of the desk was heaped with a huge pile of gold coins. Laura eyed them curiously. "I did not realize the post of seigneur was so lucrative," she said with a laugh.

"It isn't," the man behind her said briskly. "I had thought getting rid of the Ancient Way would improve my fortunes, but the fact is, this island is a godforsaken place." He circled around her and sat in the chair behind the desk, letting the gold run through his fingers and onto the oak with a sound like showers of hard spring rain.

"It was clever of you and John to use your last name, little Mistress Laura," he said idly. "I kept looking for information about a John Darby, you see. That slowed me down considerably."

"Slowed you down at what?" Laura asked, puzzled.

"Fortunately, I'm a patient man." The coins dripped from his palms. "I knew that sooner or later you'd slip. And so you did. You told me you were the last of the Darby line. And about your half brother. And Hertfordshire. After that it was easy."

"I am not very good at riddles, Helier," Laura said with a nervous smile. The satisfaction on his dark face as he toyed with the gold was alarming. "What was easy for you?"

"Strange," the seigneur mused. "Guernsey is a small island. But England is very small too." He looked up at her, smiling. "Do you know how much gold there is in this pile?"

"I wouldn't have any idea."

"Ten thousand pounds," he told her, weighing sovereigns and crowns in his hands. "I thought it a large amount to offer for so small a person. Until your husband told me your father's estate is worth four times this much a year."

"John told you that?" Laura echoed, bewildered.

"No, no, my dear. Your husband, I said. I believe it is time he joined us now."

The red curtains at his back parted soundlessly.

"*Bonjour,* Laura," Thomas Guilford said.

Part III

Chapter 17

If she played the chain out as far as it reached, stood on one leg, and lunged, Laura had discovered, on an average of one in three tries she could push the drapes aside just long enough to catch a glimpse of sky. When she missed, the iron shackle cut into her right ankle, but the effort to view the outside world at least gave her something to do. Since her father's death she'd always imagined hell as an inferno of fire and brimstone, but after a week she was beginning to suspect it might consist instead of being chained to the elegant bed in her old chambers at Guilford Hall.

She leaned forward, holding her breath, and grabbed for the curtains. Her fingers closed for an instant on the linen, revealing a flash of glorious sunlit blue, before she let go. She might have held on and torn the drapes away, but that was too risky; if Theo found out about the little game she played, he'd only find some way of ruining it for her.

She heard soft padding footfalls coming down the corridor and scrambled back to the bed. Theo could move as quietly as a cat, but she'd grown accustomed to listening for him. By the time he turned the key in the lock she was lying atop the rose-splattered coverlet, staring up at the canopy above her head.

"Good afternoon, Mistress Laura," he sang out in his reedy voice. "I've brought you your dinner."

"Oh, is it dinnertime already?" Laura asked airily.

Thomas's butler-secretary-lover set down the tray he carried and laughed. "Time does pass quickly, doesn't it, Mistress Laura, when one is amusing oneself?" With a moue of distaste he picked up the lidded chamber pot, carried it to the lavatory, and emptied it. Laura heard the whoosh of water as he pulled the chain on the privy and thought, When John comes to rescue me, I must remember to ask him what makes that work.

Theo replaced the chamber pot at the foot of the bed and

233

bowed. "Will there be anything else, Mistress Laura?"

"Yes, Theodore. You might unchain me."

He wagged a finger. "Ah, ah, ah. You know I can't do that."

Laura adjusted the pillows at her back with languid unconcern. "You and Thomas are mad if you think you can keep me locked up in here forever."

"Perhaps," said Theodore, grinning, "Thomas and I *are* mad." Laura could not repress a shiver as his eyes, green as a grass snake, met hers. She tried a different ploy.

"Theo," she said, fingers tracing the roses on the coverlet, "it doesn't make any sense for you to want to keep me here. If you were to let me go, if I got away, then you would have Thomas all to yourself."

"I have him all to myself now, haven't I?" Theodore purred. "I find the current arrangement quite satisfactory. Until tomorrow, Mistress Laura." He picked up the tray that held her half-eaten breakfast and went out, locking the door again.

Laura chewed her lip, listening to his soft footfalls as they faded away. Of course he was right. She hadn't even seen Thomas since he'd deposited her here on his return from Guernsey. What a great deal of trouble he'd gone to to get her back! The ten thousand pounds paid to Helier Gosselin, the ship with diplomat's flags and passes to get through the Channel, the closed carriage from London—the extent of his determination astonished and frightened her. She hadn't realized how much her money meant to him.

At least he hadn't tried to touch her. For that, she was heartily grateful. What did he hope to accomplish by keeping her prisoner this way? she wondered. He could hardly hold her there for the rest of her life. He and Theo will both be good and sorry, she thought fiercely, when John comes to rescue me.

John would be sorry too—that he'd sailed off to Calais and left her to fall right into Gosselin's trap. If he'd been with her at Castle Cornet on Christmas Day, none of this would have happened. When he came for her, she would have a few choice words for him!

She lifted the covers on the tray Theodore had brought and peered beneath them. Boiled plovers' eggs in a lumpy cream sauce, some sort of mess of parsnips and onions, a custard with its skin burned black—Polly's cooking had lapsed to its usual state in the months Laura had been away.

She wondered what Thomas had told the cook about her return. Of course, he had the poor woman so completely cowed that he could have told her anything he liked.

She picked up a slice of brown bread, knowing she could rely on Polly's touch with that, at least. She wasn't hungry, but she knew she ought to eat, for the sake of the child. She hadn't mentioned the baby to Thomas; she saw no reason to. John would be coming to rescue her soon enough.

She looked up from her meal. Footsteps coming down the hallway again—not Theo's soft, mincing walk, but another, heavy and bold. John, she thought, heart fluttering. He's come for me at last. He's here!

She watched, trying to decide whether she would kiss him first or chide him, as the door swung open. "Good evening, dear wife," Thomas said.

Laura sank back against the pillows. "What do you want?"

He smiled, the smile she'd once thought so charming but that now made her blood run cold. "I thought you might be interested to know," he said easily, casually. "Calais has fallen to the French."

"Liar," said Laura, and stabbed a plover's egg.

"Oh, it's quite true," he assured her. "The news reached London this morning. The Duke of Guise has claimed the city for Henri of France. The surprise attack the French launched fooled the English completely."

"It wasn't a surprise," said Laura. "John and the Guernsey fishermen went to warn them. I watched them go."

Thomas went to the window, pulling the drapes aside, looking out at the snow-covered gardens. "There's a curious story making the rounds in London about that. It seems a fleet of fishing boats did manage to beat the French blockade to the harbor. It was a valiant effort, but in the end quite futile. You see, King Philip had withdrawn nearly all of Mary's troops from Calais to fight for him in the Netherlands."

"He would never have done that. John sent Queen Mary reports about the French ships and men gathering in Normandy!"

"Did he really? Odd. Mary never got them. She is said to be terribly distraught over the loss of the city."

Laura was about to make some angry retort when she suddenly remembered Helier Gosselin at his Christmas party: *Ah, yes, the reports of our little band of Guernsey spies. I found them quaint indeed* . . . My God. Was it possible he hadn't sent them on to England?

"The garrison held out for seven days," Thomas went on smoothly. "Less than eight hundred English against thirty thousand French. Cardinal Pole and Bishop Bonner are preaching that the Protestants betrayed the city. I expect they are gathering wood over on Smithfield Plain."

That had a frightening ring of truth to it. If Calais had fallen, it would be just like Queen Mary's ministers to blame it on the Protestants. Laura put her hands together to hide their sudden trembling, and said coldly, carefully, "Is that why you came to see me, to inform me of current events?"

"What else are husbands for? Here's more news for you. Queen Mary's with child."

Laura looked up at him. "How can that be? King Philip has been on the Continent for a year."

"He came back briefly for a visit four months ago. Which would make the child due in late May or early June."

The same time my child will be born, thought Laura, if what Hannay told me—nine months—is true. But, "Queen Mary is too old to have children," she told Thomas.

"What's the matter, Laura dear, don't you believe in miracles?" he asked with a taunting grin. "Such a child is the answer to all good Englishmen's prayers. A Catholic heir to the throne, a new dynasty begun—" He turned back to the window. "Rather a pity for Elizabeth Tudor, though. I imagine the minute the baby's born, she will lose her head."

"If you're quite finished playing your little game, Thomas," said Laura, "would you please leave?"

He let the drapes drop. "Certainly, my pet." He started for the door, then faced her again. "By the by, those Guernsey fishermen who tried to warn Calais? There's talk in Parliament of awarding them knighthoods. Posthumous, of course."

"Posthumous—" Laura stared up at him and saw he was laughing. "Liar," she spat.

"Imagine it, won't you? My own little brother, Sir John. Of course, posthumous knighthoods don't cost the queen a penny—"

"Shut up," said Laura.

"They tell me he was one of the first to die. His body was too badly mangled to be brought back, alas. They've buried him there at Calais, in the Church of Notre Dame."

"Shut up. Shut *up*," Laura cried. "It is all lies, lies!"

"A fellow Englishman did manage to salvage this somehow." He pulled something out of his waistcoat and tossed it onto the bed by her knee. "I thought you might like it as a remembrance. The devil knows I've no use for it. Sweet dreams, Laura dearest." He went out, locking the door.

Laura stared in horror at the small circlet of gold, inlaid with a star, that lay on the coverlet. She reached out a trembling hand, pulling it toward her, and tilted the tiny circle so the polished inner surface caught the candlelight.

The words graven there seared her soul like a brand: "From John to Laura: my morning star."

"No," she whispered in disbelief, feeling the gold cold as ice in her hand. "No . . ." He couldn't be dead, it was impossible. She thought of the way she had seen him last, on the cliff by the cottage, tears in his eyes: *I do love you, Laura, for so long as the stars shine . . .* And she—she had screamed at him, she had wished him dead. *I hope the French get your heart and not your leg this time!*

God in heaven, she thought, all the prayers I have prayed, and *that* is the one you answer . . . John was dead. A thousand images of him crowded into her mind. The sound of the gulls on the cliff as she ran through warm summer sun to welcome him home from fishing. Long evenings she'd spent curled in his lap by the fire, while Guy strummed his *télen*. The night they'd stood in the sea beneath a black sky quilted with stars and pledged their love for all time . . .

And now he was dead. Laura felt coldness creep through her. Dead. Killed on a wild goose chase, trying to save England for Elizabeth Tudor—

And Queen Mary was with child.

"Oh, John," she whispered. "Oh, John, my dear heart. My sweet, dead fool." She began to laugh.

She laughed until tears streamed down her cheeks and splashed onto the coverlet, until she had to double over, sides aching, shoulders quaking, until the bed rocked against the floor. And what was so terrifically, so monstrously amusing, of course, was the utter futility of the dream he had died for, his dream for England that never even had a chance of coming true.

When Theodore brought up her breakfast the following morning, he stopped in the doorway and stared at the small, hard-eyed woman who sat on the edge of the bed. "Is something amiss?" Laura demanded, arching a brow.

"N-no—"

"Very well. Put the tray down and go and tell your master I want to speak to him."

He stood motionless. "Thomas is occupied."

"Tell him to unoccupy himself."

Theodore set down the tray and went out, looking back at her with wary grass-green eyes.

"You sent for me, my dear?" That was Thomas, lounging in the doorway, toying with a key ring that hung from his girdle.

"I've a proposition for you."

He crossed the room and sat in the armchair by the window. "I am, as they say, all ears."

"I am four months' along with child." He started to say something, and Laura held up her hand. "Spare me your felicitations. John and I were never married under English law, so legally my child will be born illegitimate. The world is a harsh enough place without that stigma. Here is what I propose. I will live here at Guilford Hall as your wife. We will, of course, maintain separate rooms. You will provide my child with a name. You will not enforce your physical marital rights upon me, nor shall I, of course, on you. Neither shall you interfere with the upbringing of the child. One-third of the yearly income from my estates will go to you, one-third to me, and one-third will remain in trust for my child."

"I could take it all, you know," said Thomas.

"You could, but you won't. If you try, I shall see that your relationship with Theodore is brought to the attention of the queen's ministers. The Bible calls what you do together 'sodomy.' And it is a crime."

"What, pray tell, is to keep me from countercharging you with heresy?" Thomas demanded, pulling at his beard.

Laura smiled. "Have you forgotten, Thomas? It is against the law to marry a heretic."

"Very neat," he grunted. "Is that all?"

"All save one thing. My child inherits Guilford Hall."

Again he tugged at his beard. "Separate rooms, you say."

"Don't be coy, Thomas; it doesn't suit you. Sexual relations were never one of your purposes in marrying me."

He eyed her curiously. "What do you think my purposes were?"

Laura ticked them off on her fingers. "My lands and money, of course. A pliant hostess to further your social ambitions. And a gull, to cover your sexual proclivities."

"You are most perceptive," he told her, nodding. "And under the terms of your proposition, am I to gain those things?"

"I've already told you—one-third of the money. I've no objections to helping you entertain; if I wanted to live like a nun I'd join a nunnery. As for the last, you will have a child. How better to dispel any rumors about your behavior that might arise?"

"I've underestimated you, my dear," he said with frank approval. "I'm delighted to accept your terms." He unhooked a key from the ring at his girdle and tossed it to her. "This unfastens your chain." He turned to go.

"One thing more, Thomas." He turned back. "The one hundred pounds per year that my brother and his wife pay as rent for Howarth Manor. Increase it to a thousand."

"They'll never be able to pay that."

Laura shrugged, unfastening the cuff on her leg. "Then I'd suggest you begin looking for a tenant who can."

Thomas smiled slowly. "I do hope you'll let me offer my congratulations, dear wife. Both for your happy condition and for your having truly grown up at last."

Chapter 18

So it was that Laura began a new life—the strangest of all the incarnations she had known so far. To the world, or as much of the world as might care, she was Thomas Guilford's wife; when he entertained she sat at his right hand, draped with jewels, dressed in fabulous gowns. She took over from Polly in the kitchens, and Guilford Hall developed a reputation in Thomas's circle for fine cuisine. Under her direction Theodore replanted the estate gardens; she made changes in the house decor as well. Her bedchamber was done over completely, the white and red hangings and linens exchanged for blue and gold.

The sole room to escape her improvements was John's observatory. Despite her newfound resoluteness, which delighted Thomas and made Theodore surlily resentful, she did not trust herself to touch John's belongings any more than she trusted herself to look up at the night sky.

On a crisp, clear morning in late February, she had a visitor. Theodore came to her bedchamber to announce the arrival, a speculative gleam in his eyes. "Sir William Cecil to see you, madame," he said, giving the last word a twist that showed what he thought of her arrangement with Thomas.

"I am indisposed."

"He says it is urgent."

Laura sighed. She had not contacted any of her old friends from Hatfield House since her return to England; she'd had no desire to. Fools and dreamers, the lot of them. Still, Cecil had some influence; she or Thomas might need something from him someday. "You may show him up," she told Theodore.

The rings around Sir William's eyes were deeper and darker than she remembered. When Theodore ushered him in he stood uncertainly on the threshold, his hat in his hands. "You may go, Theo," Laura said shortly. "Sir William. How kind of you to call."

"Laura." He blinked, coming forward. "I heard from Lord Dacre that you'd come back. I couldn't believe it. I had to see for myself."

"Well, here I am, as you can see." Laura gestured to a chair. "Won't you sit down?"

He nodded, coming very close to her, lowering his voice. "We're being spied on, is that it?"

"Spied on? In my own home?" Laura laughed.

"But surely you are being held here against your will," he insisted.

"Oh, really, Sir William. How absurd! Held against my will? I think you must be working too hard."

Sir William's broad brow was furrowed with incomprehension. "But the last time I saw you, you were desperate to get away from Thomas Guilford!"

"The last time you saw me, Sir William," said Laura, poking her needle through the cloth she was embroidering, "I was a foolish child. I've grown up now. And as you can see, Thomas and I are expecting. So is Queen Mary, Thomas tells me. Isn't it splendid news?"

"Laura, where in God's name is John?" Cecil asked in bewilderment.

"Oh, hadn't you heard? He was at Calais when it fell."

"My God, I had no idea!"

"Can you stay for dinner, Sir William?" asked Laura, setting her needlework down. "We are having a roast of lamb."

Cecil stumbled to his feet. "No. No, thank you. I only wanted to— Look here, Laura, are you all right?"

"Oh—" Laura smiled. "I have a touch of swelling in my ankles from time to time, and my back is sore. But the physician Thomas has engaged for me, Dr. Mason, assures me those are common complaints for a woman in my condition. If not dinner, then perhaps some wine?"

"Dammit, Laura," he said in a low tone, "that's not what I meant! What I want to know is—"

"Yes?" Laura arched her brows above disinterested gold eyes.

"Never mind," he muttered, and clapped his hat back on his head. "Goodbye, Laura."

"Goodbye, Sir William. Do tell the Lady Elizabeth that Mistress Laura Guilford sends her regards."

It was as though someone else was inhabiting her body: that same Mistress Laura Guilford, cool, poised, imperious. From time to time, though the times grew fewer and farther between, she would wake in her bed in the middle of the night and once more she would be Laura Darby, sobbing wildly at the memory of John. She would remember his warm blue eyes brimming with love as he held her, caressed her, whispering the sweet endearments that turned her heart to flame. But that was only in the dark, in solitude; come morning she would wash the tearstains from her face and become the mistress of Guilford Hall again.

Polly must have wondered what had brought Laura home, just as she must have realized that Thomas could not be the father of her mistress's child. But fear, either of losing her place or of something darker, deeper, made her hold her tongue against asking questions. Now and again Laura would look up from shelling peas or stirring a custard and find the woman staring at her as though she secretly suspected the devil had fathered the babe.

When Laura entered her seventh month of pregnancy she informed Thomas that she would not be appearing in public or receiving guests until the child was born. She was surprised, then, a few weeks later when he called upon her in their rooms; they no longer dined together and had not spoken since early March. But she admitted him, and he greeted her with a peck on the cheek. "How are you, wife?"

She had long since learned that Thomas had no real wish to hear about her health; he had a peculiar horror of the changes affecting her body. She answered simply, "Well."

"Good, good." He rubbed his hands together, darting a nervous glance at her burgeoning belly before looking away. "You must find it tedious, I'd wager, to be cooped up here day after day. Don't you think it would serve you well to get out and about now and then?"

"What did you have in mind, Thomas, a bout of lawn tennis?" she inquired drily.

He laughed, though with a slight edge. "No, actually, I thought perhaps a trip to London might suit you."

"Really. And what purpose might such a journey serve— besides, of course, providing me with enjoyment?"

"You have grown shrewd, haven't you? Well, the truth is, Queen Mary has asked for an audience with you."

It was a measure of how great were the changes in Laura that at this utterly astounding information she said merely, "I hardly think either Queen Mary or myself is in any condition for an audience."

"That's just it, you see. The queen knows you are due to

deliver at about the same time she is. Apparently she wants to—well, to compare."

"There must be five thousand women in England who are due to have children in late May," said Laura.

"Aye, but only one happens to be my wife. Now listen here, Laura. I can't really say I expect you to agree to this, but if you care as much about the future of that—that thing in there"—he pointed to her stomach—"as I think you do, you'll recognize this audience could do it a world of good. Who knows? The queen might even agree to serve as its godmother."

"That would certainly be intriguing," said Laura. "What is in it for you?"

"Just that. The good it would do the thing—the baby."

"Honestly, Thomas. And when you yourself just called me shrewd."

"Well, it would not hurt my career at court," he said snappishly. "Not that I expect you'll take the opportunity, knowing how you feel about the queen."

How *did* she feel about the queen? Laura wondered idly. At that moment, she did not seem to feel much of anything. She knew she should have all manner of emotions at the prospect of meeting the woman who was responsible for her father's death and for John's. But those emotions belonged to the night, to her private darkness, and it was daylight now.

"I'll go," she told Thomas. His jaw dropped open. "On the condition that we take the closed carriage, and that the driver go slow. You're quite right; it could be advantageous to our child."

Thomas closed his jaw with an audible click. "You never cease to amaze me, Laura darling. I'll make the arrangements as quickly as I can."

Exactly one week later they set out for London, on a drab, gray afternoon. Thomas was unusually solicitous, packing the carriage with cushions and warm fur robes, bringing a hamper of food in case Laura got hungry along the way. Theodore traveled with them, for they'd been invited to spend the night at the queen's residence, Hampton Court. He sat beside Thomas in the coach and watched through narrowed eyes as his master settled Laura in with gingerly care.

Thomas had made a list of notes about the forthcoming meeting, which he pulled out and consulted as the carriage rolled south. "You will have to kneel when you are presented," he told Laura, and eyed her stomach dubiously. "Can you kneel like that?"

"Of course I can."

"We've brought a gift for her baby." He rooted inside his doublet and produced a foil-wrapped package. "A rattle. Solid gold, with a sapphire at each end. Do you think she will like it?"

"I'm sure King Philip will. He can always pawn it to pay for his wars."

"Oh, Christ, Laura, that's another thing. Whatever you do, don't mention Calais. Or—" He consulted the list. "Miscarriage, religion, the pope, the course of the war, money, the Princess Elizabeth, Parliament, hair—"

"Hair?" Laura repeated.

"Mary's lost hers."

"I see. Anything else?"

"Well—your father, of course."

"Of course," Laura said gravely. "That would never do."

They arrived at the palace just as dusk was falling, draping the handsome building in shadows of black and gray. A swarm of footmen and grooms ran to meet them. Thomas straightened his hat and cloak and checked the list he'd made. "Theodore."

"Yes, Thomas?" he asked eagerly.

"Stay with the baggage and see that it gets to our rooms. No, no. I'll get her." Thomas waved back the footman who'd opened the door, climbed down, and reached for Laura. "Careful, now," he cautioned. "These cobbles are slippery. Damn, it's beginning to rain. You there!" He commandeered a passing groom. "Fetch a canopy to hold over my wife, and make it quick. The queen is expecting us."

"Yes, sir, right away!"

As Thomas lifted her from the coach, Laura thought she heard Theo let out a low, angry growl.

The interior of Hampton Court looked the way Laura imagined the chapel at Howarth Manor must have before her family turned Protestant. Everywhere one turned there were crucifixes and statues of Jesus and the Virgin Mother and the saints. A huge portrait flanked by massive gold candlesticks caught her eye as they were led through a gloomy reception chamber. "Who is that?" she asked Thomas, pointing.

"King Philip," he whispered, and yanked her hand back to her side. She stared over her shoulder at the painting. A short man, in black armor trimmed with gold and great wide pantaloons that made his legs look spindly. He had light hair and thick eyebrows that nearly met over wide pale eyes; beneath a thin moustache his mouth was oddly large, with a heavy, drooping underlip. "That vicious little husband of hers," Elizabeth had called him. He did not look vicious to Laura so much as bland.

Together she and Thomas trailed after a line of servants, through a series of dim passages into the palace's interior. The windows were covered with layer upon layer of hangings, and the lighting was so faint that when they reached a step, the servant in the front of the line turned to whisper, "Down, please." The warning was passed in a quiet murmur all the way back to Thomas and Laura.

The air smelled of sandalwood incense and herbs: bitter tansy, soapwort, samphire. Dampness hung everywhere, seeming to seep from the stone floors and walls. I wonder what Guy de Carteret would have thought of the spirits of this place, Laura thought idly, as the long line of servants stopped at last, moving back against the walls. Thomas squinted at Laura in the ghostly light, straightened the ruffed collar of her gown. "Ready?" he asked. She shrugged. A door opened in the passageway.

"Her Most Regal Highness, Mary, Queen of England, Ireland, Wales, Scotland, Normandy—" A herald ran through a long list of places, some of which hadn't seen English rule for centuries. "Thomas, Lord Guilford." Thomas approached the doorway and knelt, bowing to the floor. "Laura, Lady Guilford," the herald intoned. Laura stepped forward and knelt beside Thomas in the entranceway. The room within was even darker than the corridors had been.

"Proceed," said a voice, low and deep as a man's, yet somehow womanish. Thomas nudged Laura and moved ahead into the darkness, still on his knees. Laura followed, thinking, My word, there's a vile stench in this place. Her head brushed against dark satin, then touched something bumpy and moist, like the skin of a toad. The queen's hand, she realized, and kissed the ring that Mary wore. "So, Thomas," the deep, rolling voice went on. "We meet your wife at last."

"Yes, Your Majesty."

That cold, moist hand groped over Laura's face. "Mary," said another voice, "let us have a candle."

"Must we, Reginald?" the queen asked peevishly.

"I believe we must."

"Oh, very well. One candle. A small one." The shadowy figure who'd spoken snapped his fingers, and one of the servants brought a taper into the room. In its flickering light Laura looked up at the queen and understood why she preferred the dark.

The woman who sat before her in a jeweled throne looked decades older than her forty years. Her sallow cheeks sagged; the flesh on her chin hung in loose folds. Her hands lay in her lap, swollen like sausages bound by rich rings. Ropes of pearls circled her pasty neck, and a dazzling array of diamonds and rubies was set into her cap. Her crimson satin gown was more opulent than any Laura had ever seen, but its huge sleeves and wide skirts could not disguise the grotesquely distended figure within its folds.

"Mary." The tall, thin man beside the throne spoke again. "Lady Guilford should have a chair. That cold floor, in her condition—"

"Quite right, Reginald," Mary said. "Thomas, of course you know my cousin Reginald, Cardinal Pole."

"Excellency." Thomas knelt again to kiss the ring of the Archbishop of Canterbury.

"And Bishop Bonner of London."

Another man came forward, short and stout. Pole and Bonner, Laura thought. Architects of the queen's policy against the Protestants. The men who had burned her father to death were fetching her a chair.

She sat in it and folded her hands in her lap. Pole brought the candle closer and tipped her chin to the light with a long, thin finger. "She is lovely, Thomas," he said. His eyes were small and dark, feverishly intense. A zealot's eyes . . .

"She is rather small, isn't she?" Bonner asked, looking down at her.

"She is perfectly healthy, Excellency," Thomas said.

"Has she been attended by a physician?" Pole asked.

"Certainly. By Dr. Mason. I am sure you have heard of him."

"They say he is good," Bonner acknowledged.

Laura had the peculiar feeling she might as well not have been in the room at all.

The queen reached out her fat beringed hand and touched Laura's coiled braids. "Lovely hair," she crooned, "such lovely hair. I had lovely hair too, once upon a time." She patted her bulging stomach. "My child will have lovely hair. There! Just now, I felt him move! It is a boy, you know, a great healthy boy. Would you like to touch him?"

Uncertain what to do, Laura glanced at Thomas. He gave her a quick, impatient nod. Slowly she stretched out her own hand and let the queen lay it on her crimson silk gown.

A shivering chill ran up her spine as she felt squashy, yielding flesh beneath her fingers, like unbaked dough. Whatever lay in Queen Mary's abdomen, it was not a child.

"Did you feel it kick? Did you?" the queen demanded. Larua looked into her pale jaundiced eyes. She could feel Thomas watching her, and Pole, and Bonner.

"Aye, I did," she said.

The queen crowed triumphantly. "Philip will be so pleased, so proud. Here, this is the ring he gave me when we were betrothed." She flapped her spongy hand in Laura's face, and Laura caught a glimpse of bright black and gold between the folds of flesh. "He used to write me long, long letters every single day." Her deep voice turned petulant. "Now he scarcely ever writes me anymore."

"Now, Mary," Reginald Pole said soothingly, "His Majesty is very busy with his wars."

"With his whores!" the queen cried, thin lips curving downward between her sagging cheeks. "I knew it! Busy with Flemish strumpets. I know what he's up to." Her eyes narrowed with cunning. "But all that will change, won't it, Reginald, once I give him a son?"

"That's right, Mary."

"Once I give him his son," Mary declared with great satisfaction, "he'll come back to me."

Laura saw the two prelates exchange quick glances. Mary's small, bejeweled head lolled forward onto her chest. Suddenly she jerked upright again, her gaze surprisingly sharp as she fixed Laura with her pale eyes. "Have you met my husband the king?"

"No, Your Majesty."

"Then you must be presented to him. Dawson, Hatcher!" she called to the servants. "Bid His Majesty join us, if he will."

Pole tried to forestall her. "Mary, I hardly think—"

Mary leaned back complacently in her throne. "I say he shall come in."

Two of the servants trotted off down the corridor, while Laura, bewildered, tried to understand how King Philip could be at Hampton Court when he was supposed to be in the Netherlands. "Move the candle back, Reginald," Mary ordered, misshapen hands primping at her cap, fussing with her jewels. "I don't like him to see me this way. Ah, Philip!" she called suddenly, her deep voice ghoulishly coquettish. Laura turned, following the queen's gaze, and saw the servants enter with the portrait of Philip she'd glimpsed in the receiving chamber.

Mary beckoned them closer and barked at her guests, "Kneel down! Kneel and pay homage to the King of England!" Laura slid slowly out of the chair to her knees. "Philip, my pet," Mary crooned, rising from her throne. "Two loyal subjects. Thomas, Lord Guilford. His wife, Lady Guilford." She turned to them. "What, are you stones? Come and kiss his ring! You first, Lady Guilford."

Laura was filled with a growing sense that she'd wandered into someone else's bad dream. She knelt, rooted to the spot. Thomas elbowed her sharply. "Go kiss the bloody ring," he hissed in her ear.

Laura crawled forward on her knees through the inky chamber, until she reached the painted canvas in its golden frame. She touched her mouth to the ring of state on the king's right hand, tasting varnish and turpentine.

"That's enough!" the queen declared abruptly, yanking her back. "He cannot be trusted around pretty women. I know that. They told me it before we were wed." The pale eyes were tiny slits in her face. "He wishes I were like Elizabeth. Young and pretty. But I never have been beautiful like her. Not beautiful. Not witty or clever..." She turned back to the portrait, her deep voice a snarl. "You wish you had married her, don't you? That bastard daughter of a black-eyed slut—"

"Mary." Pole came quickly to take her arms. "You are tired, Mary. You must rest, for the sake of the baby."

"Rest," the queen whispered. "Rest. For the baby."

"That's right, Mary." The cardinal motioned to the servants in the doorway; three women came forward, murmuring to the queen in soft voices as they led her away.

"And Philip!" Mary cried, looking back over her shoulder. "He must come to bed with me—"

"Philip too," Pole told her with a hint of impatience. He nodded to the men who held the portrait. "Go with her, then."

For another moment Mary's pale, cunning gaze met Laura's. "Can't let him out of my sight," she giggled, with a ludicrous wink.

"Get her *out*," Pole told the women. With the queen babbling beneath her breath, they steered her into the corridor.

When they'd gone, the portrait after them, Pole helped Laura up from the floor. "You must understand," the old archbishop said softly. "Her doctors give her medication for her condition."

"She is overwrought," Bonner put in. "She wearies herself with matters of state."

"Of course," said Laura. Odd, she'd assumed the strange, sickly smell in the room had been due to the queen, but it seemed only to have grown stronger now she was gone. "Thomas, I should like to retire myself; our journey has exhausted me."

He moved quickly to her side. "If you will excuse us, Your Excellencies?"

The servants were gone from the corridor. Laura turned to Thomas in the dim torchlight. "She's mad, isn't she?"

"Shut up," he ordered, voice low and vehement.

"The queen of England is mad as a hatter," Laura repeated thoughtfully.

"I said shut up, you damned fool." He yanked her down the hall, though not before she heard a brief muttered exchange between the two men they'd left behind in the privy chamber.

"Will she do, do you think?" asked Bonner.

"She'll do," said Pole.

Alone that night in her borrowed bedchamber, Laura dreamed the strangest, most vivid dream she had had of John since she learned of his death. They were back on Guernsey, outside Guy de Carteret's cottage, walking hand in hand on the cliff overlooking the rock that was called the Arch Druid. The sun shone brightly; they were laughing, trading kisses, when the stones beneath their feet began to crumble to dust.

"Be careful," said John. "Be careful, Laura." Then he pushed her back from the edge and tumbled toward the sea.

He fell slowly, drifting like a leaf on the wind. He looked back at her. "Be careful, Laura," he called again. Then, right before her wide eyes, he changed into a huge white seagull and flapped away, alighting on the Arch Druid's head.

As he perched there, time began to pass very quickly. The sun careened across the sky and set behind the rock; the moon rose; the tide came roaring up over the Arch Druid. The gull threw back its head and began to squawk. "Careful! Careful!" it seemed to be crying again and again. The sea swallowed up the Arch Druid, and the great white bird soared into the sky, moonlight gleaming on his feathers. Higher and higher he rose, until he flew so high that he became a star.

Be careful, Laura.

She sat up in the unfamiliar bed, ghost-white, shaking. Be careful of what? she wondered, and in the whispering wind that rattled the shuttered windows thought she heard the voice of old Reginald Pole murmuring, "She'll do."

Chapter 19

Laura saw no more of Queen Mary or her bishops during that brief sojourn at Hampton Court. She left with Thomas early the next morning, under lowering skies that dripped dull, heavy rain. The carriage ride back to Hertfordshire was uneventful, unless one could call Theodore's even more churlish than ordinary behavior an event. Thomas had rearranged their seating so that he himself was next to Laura, Theodore across from them. Thomas's conduct was more than ever that of a doting husband and father-to-be; he settled cushions around Laura, offered her wine and sweetmeats he said were a gift to them from Mary, and was up from his seat every few moments adjusting the louvered windows lest she catch a chill. Theodore observed all these attentions through glowering eyes.

When they reached Guilford Hall, Thomas asked Laura into his study. "Sit down, my dear, please. No, no, this chair; 'tis far more comfortable. Would you like a pillow? Perhaps something warm to drink?"

"If you've aught on your mind, Thomas, out with it, please," she told him. "I'm weary with journeying. I would like to go up to my bed."

"Certainly, certainly. I wanted to thank you again for coming with me, for meeting Queen Mary. And to assure you I had no notion that Bishop Bonner or Cardinal Pole would be there. It must have been very difficult for you to meet them, considering—well, your father—" He was watching her carefully.

Laura shrugged. "My father was a fool. He died for a fool's dream." She meant the words, but as she said them she heard in her mind an echo of her own dream from the night before: John's voice. *Be careful, Laura . . .*

"Yes, well. As you say." Thomas folded his hands on his desk. "You understand of course that, next to Mary, Bonner and Pole are the two most powerful figures in England right now."

"From what I saw of the queen, I should rather think they are running England, not she. Thomas, is there a point?"

"Of course there is," he said quickly. "I hope you won't object, then, that I've invited the bishops here to the house. Next Saturday. For dinner."

Laura arched a brow. "And have they accepted?" He nodded. "My, my, Thomas, you are coming up in the world. Congratulations."

"Then you don't object?"

"Why should I? I won't be greeting them, not when I am this far along."

"No," he agreed. "I did hope, though, I might prevail upon you to prepare the meal. Polly has improved under your tutelage, but I should like the cardinal and the archbishop to be served a really fine dinner." He smiled.

"If you like," Laura said disinterestedly.

"I thought," Thomas proposed with his new tentativeness, "we might start off with those little cheese pasties you made so incomparably. And then—poached salmon with dill? And your stewed plums and apples, with a saddle of venison. If you think that suitable."

"If you like." Laura rose from her chair. "Excuse me."

"Laura. There is one thing more. About the queen. I'm sure you were shocked by her peculiar behavior. I just want you to know—I want to *assure* you—that her disability is only temporary."

"Pregnancy always is, isn't it? Good night, Thomas," Laura said.

"Cheese pasties is done, missy," said Polly, then glanced down uncertainly at the trayful of shapely crusts she'd filled with a mixture of rich cream, grated Cheshire cheese, eggs, almonds, and ginger spice. "Leastways they is if ye thinks they is suitable."

Laura wiped her hands on her apron and came to see. "Perfect," she pronounced, making the blond woman beam. "They can go in the oven just as soon as your bread is done."

"Aye, missy, what's next, then?"

Laura looked around the kitchens. The saddle of venison was roasting on a spit at the hearth, sending sizzling drops of fat flaring onto the embers. The two huge salmons had been poached and were cooling, wrapped in cheesecloth, on the windowsill. She'd made a sauce for them of egg yolks, butter, and dill that was in the cooler; the apples and plums, redolent with cinnamon and cloves, were stewing on the fireback. The bread was baking, the pasties were ready to, and three raisin pies, glazed like brightest gold, sat wafting their sweet, spicy fragrance into the air. Laura eased herself down on a bench. "I think we've earned ourselves a bit of breathing space."

Polly sighed gratefully and joined her at the table. "Must be mighty important folk Master Thomas is havin' to supper."

"Dinner," Laura said absently. "They are." Once more she looked about the kitchens with a critical eye. "Did Master Thomas tell you what wines he wanted served with the courses?"

"Aye, that he did. Just let me think now." She pursed her lips. "I think he said port with the pasties."

"Port before the fish?" Laura asked with a frown.

"Or was it white Bordeaux, then Rhenish, and then port?"

"Well, which was it?"

"I can't remember," said the cook, looking distressed. "Ye knows me, missy; I've no head on my shoulders."

"You will have to go and ask again, then," Laura said briskly. "I think he's in his study."

"But, mum, he's already told me once. If I asks again, he'll bite off my head!"

Laura looked into the woman's fearful brown eyes. "Polly, it is absolutely beyond my comprehension why you stay on here, considering how Thomas treats you."

"Because it's my place."

"You could easily find another place. One where you wouldn't have to work so hard. Where you wouldn't always be afraid of your master. There are such places, you know."

"Not fer me there ain't. I'm all thumbs, missy, ye knows that."

"That's not true, Polly. Those pasties you made are beautiful. You've improved immensely in these past months. Besides, don't you ever think about marrying, about having children?"

The cook blushed, looking down at her work-reddened hands. "There's none would want to marry me, missy. I'm no young lass, heaven only knows, and I've got no looks."

"Polly, why do you think of yourself that way?" Laura

demanded impatiently. "You're not old. And you're very pretty; just look at your hair! You are gentle and kind and generous—why, you've a great deal to offer any man. And God knows you deserve something better than living out your days in this overgrown tomb with Thomas and Theodore." She got up to open the oven and check on the bread.

"Mind if I asks ye a question, missy?"

"Go on," said Laura, probing the crust of a loaf.

"What are ye doin' here?"

The oven door sprang shut with a bang. "Take out the bread and put in the pasties," said Laura. "I'll go and ask Thomas about the wine."

As she left the kitchens and headed for Thomas's study, Laura ran over the details of the evening to come in her mind. Cardinal Pole would have the place of honor, Bishop Bonner the next highest place. The Duchess of Strathearn, Sir Frances Englefield, Lord and Lady Dacre—all the bright lights of the kingdom that Thomas had been cultivating for so long would be there. She was glad she had gone to see the queen, so she knew where the true power lay. Thomas had suggested having the cardinal baptize their child; that would be a fine beginning to its life. She must talk to Charlotte about a christening gown.

A slow, cold rain had been falling all day. Perhaps Thomas would like a hot punch served before the dinner, Laura thought, her mind turning back to the present. The ceiling above the corridor to his study had developed a leak, and she'd had the rugs pulled up to keep them from being ruined. The stones bore a slick sheen of water from the relentless leak. Be careful, Laura, she told herself as she tiptoed along. She probed the damp air with her nose. There was an off smell lingering in the hall, as though something had died within one of the walls. She would have to tell Theo to put some camphor down.

She heard shouting from behind the closed door to the study. Theodore and Thomas, arguing again. Ever since the journey to London, Theo had been impossibly uncivil to his master and mistress both. Whatever was bothering him, he was letting Thomas know about it now, shouting practically at the top of his lungs. I'll be damned if I intend to get involved with this, Laura thought crossly, turning around. I'll serve the Bordeaux, and if Thomas doesn't like it, he can blame Theodore.

As she made her way slowly back down the slippery corridor, their argument pursued her. "Keep your bloody voice down," she heard Thomas roar, "or you can find a new post!"

"Oh, that's right," Theo cried. "You don't need me anymore. You don't love me. You're in love with her."

"Don't be absurd," Thomas snapped.

"You do love her, you do!" Theo sounded as though he were in tears. "You're always looking after her, waiting on her hand and foot—"

"That's because she's with child."

"Aye, and the moment the bloody baby's born, don't you think I know what will happen to me? It will be 'So long, Theo. Nice to have known you, Theo.' Dammit, Thomas, I've given you the best years of my life!"

"And hardly suffered for it," Thomas roared. "You've got everything you need."

"But I haven't!" Theo wailed in despair. "I haven't got you any longer. I've lost you to her!"

Oh, really, thought Laura, rolling her eyes.

"Do you remember the way it used to be, Thomas?" Now Theo's voice was plaintive, eager. "Just the two of us. We could go away together. We could see Paris and Florence and Rome—"

"We will go to Paris, dammit!"

"How? How will we go when you're saddled with a wife and child?"

"I'm not going to *have* a wife and a child!"

Laura stopped dead in the hall. "What are you talking about?" Theo asked, and she wanted to ask the same thing.

Thomas lowered his voice abruptly. Laura walked back toward the study door. "When the bloody baby is born," he was saying, "it will be sneaked into Hampton Court and presented to the world as the new prince or princess. I came up with the idea and presented it to Pole and Bonner. They took it to King Philip, and he agreed."

"But—what about the child the queen is bearing?" Theo asked.

"The queen isn't bearing. She's dying," Thomas said bluntly. "If King Philip wants to hold on to England and keep it Catholic, he needs to keep Elizabeth from taking the throne. He needs an heir. That's why I've been looking after Laura, you damned fool. The brat's got to be healthy and strong, or Philip won't pay."

"Pay how much?" Theo wanted to know.

"Fifty thousand pounds." Theo let out a long, low whistle. "That ought to be enough, don't you think," Thomas went on, "for us to see Paris?"

"But what about *her?*" Theo demanded in an urgent whisper. "What makes you think she'll give up the child?"

"She won't have any say in the matter. She and the queen, alas, are both going to die in childbirth. It's a terribly risky business, you know."

Theo chuckled. "My God, Thomas. You are brilliant."

Laura could picture Thomas's negligent shrug. "The baby smuggled in in the chamber pot," he said carelessly. "One of the oldest tricks in the world."

Laura was remembering the snatch of conversation between Pole and Bonner that she'd overheard at Hampton Court. *Will she do, do you think? She'll do* . . . By God, it was a clever idea. Philip would rid himself of a queen whose madness had made her a liability. The English would surely rally to the motherless infant. The kingdom would stay Catholic; Philip would rule as regent. And the Princess Elizabeth? Once the new dynasty was established, she could be disposed of once and for all.

My child, Laura thought, and let out a hysterical giggle. My child, king or queen of England! Talk about a fine start in life! She would have to let Thomas know she'd overheard his plan and approved it; he wouldn't have to kill her. Who in the world wouldn't give up her baby under such circumstances? King or queen of England. She wondered which it would be.

A mouse skittered along the hallway in front of her. Aha, Laura thought, that must be what is dying in the walls and making that smell. What we need around here is a cat. I shall make Thomas get me one in return for my baby.

From another world, another lifetime, she heard a gentle, patient voice speaking to her. Père Talbot, sitting with his black hat in his hands: *When you were growing up, did you ever have a cat with kittens? Do you remember how helpless the little ones were at first? . . . The mother cat had to teach them. They watched her and they learned* . . . What a peculiar thing to remember now, thought Laura, staring at the wet stones beneath her toes. And in her mind's eye another image appeared: a white bird beating its wings against a black rock called the Arch Druid. *Be careful, Laura.* That silly dream about John—

The child she carried was his, too. But he'd abandoned

her and the baby, she remembered angrily. For the sake of an England where people could believe—as if it made any difference—that the earth moved around the sun. What a fine jest to play on him; their child would be brought up at Hampton Court, tutored by men like Pole and Bonner.

Men who believed the earth was the center of the universe despite the plain proof in the skies above them. Men with zealot's eyes. Men who burned anyone who dared to think otherwise.

We are no different from kittens, chérie. . . . *We watch and we learn.*

Her child would be just like Pole and Bonner.

Just like them . . .

Lord in heaven.

The fog that had engulfed her for so many months was suddenly lifted. Was that what she wanted her child, John's child, to become? All the kingdoms, all the crowns in the world would not be worth that! She sagged against the wall, numbed, shaking. "Jesus, forgive me," she whispered in horror, overcome with dread at the unspeakable tragedy she'd so nearly consented to. "Sweet Jesus in heaven, what has happened to me?"

"Missy?" Polly was peeking out of the kitchen doorway. "Missy, what is it? What's the matter?" She clucked her tongue in fright at the sight of Laura's pale, shocked face. "Didn't I say ye was doin' too much, now, missy?" She hurried to take Laura's arm. "Come on back to the fire, then! Sit down, sit down! Is it the baby?"

Laura nodded faintly, sinking onto the bench the woman led her to, hands clutched protectively over her belly. "Oh, Polly, aye. It's the baby. It is . . ."

"Land sakes, I'd best fetch Master Thomas!"

"No!" Laura took a deep breath, trying to regain her composure. She could not stop trembling at the thought of how close she'd come to giving her baby away! She thought of the strange, foul odor she'd noticed in the hallway to Thomas's study, and of what Guy had once told her: *Evil has a scent all its own* . . . God, she had to leave this dreadful house. She had to get away now, tonight!

"No," she said more calmly. "I am fine now, Polly, thank you." She looked up at the yellow-haired cook. "You asked me before why I was staying here. What would you do if I told you I was thinking of leaving?"

Polly stared down at her toes. "I reckon I'd have to tell

Master Thomas, missy. Otherwise I'd surely lose my place."
Then her dark gaze slanted to meet Laura's. "Is ye leavin',
missy?"

"Oh, no, not really," Laura said, forcing a laugh. "I just
wondered. That's all."

"Well, then." The cook's face brightened. "What did
Master Thomas say 'bout the wine?"

"White Bordeaux with the pasties, Rhenish with the fish,
port with the venison," Laura told her briskly. "And I am
going to make a hot wine cup to be served first thing when
our guests arrive." She went to the garden door and took
Polly's oiled cloak from its peg. "I must pick some fresh
herbs for it."

"Don't go out in this cold rain, missy! Let me go."

"I'll only be outside for a moment. Could you bring up a
small keg of malmsey from the cellars, please?"

Thinking of Père Talbot had given Laura the idea. She
took the kitchen lantern out to the herb bed and peered
down at Theo's neatly lettered signs. Mandragora, that was
what she wanted. The plant was right where she remembered
it, leaves withered and brown. She tugged on a bunch as
hard as she could, yanking up a great earthy ball of forked
roots. A pinch to a cup to make John sleep, the priest had
said. She had more than enough. To help cover the taste she
snipped some branches of winter-hardy rosemary and rue.
Then she tucked the herbs under her cloak, glancing up at
the sky.

The thick clouds had blotted out every star in the
heavens. In vain she searched for the Great and Little Bears
and Polaris; the blackness above nearly melted her resolve.
But if she put everyone in the house to sleep, she should get
a good start. Hatfield House was down in that valley somewhere. She flicked drops of icy rain from her forehead and
marched back inside.

The low doors to the wine cellar stood open; she could
hear Polly rummaging through the kegs, looking for malmsey. Hurriedly she dunked the bunch of mandragora root
into a bucket of water and swished it around. Polly grunted,
staggering up the ladder with her load. Laura waited until
she'd nearly reached the top, then called, "Polly, is that
you?"

"Why, who else would it be?"

"I'm sorry, Polly, but I said malmsey, didn't I? I meant
muscadel."

With patience born of long suffering, Polly sighed and started down the ladder again.

Like lightning Laura pulled the roots from their bath, shook off the water, and grabbed a knife, chopping them up in tiny pieces as quick as she could. Still she had barely finished before Polly came up the ladder with the muscadel. "What's that there?" she asked curiously, lowering the wine butt to the floor.

"Ginger," said Laura.

"Don't look like no ginger I've ever seen."

"It's special ginger. Guernsey ginger," Laura said, with a touch of dark humor. Polly reached for a piece to taste it. "No, don't!" Laura grabbed her hand. "It's horribly bitter until it is boiled with wine. You can have some then."

"Missy, ye knows Master Thomas don't let me drink nothin' but small beer," Polly said longingly.

"We shall make an exception tonight, in honor of our special guests." Laura scraped the mandragora root into a heavy iron kettle. "Now, add the wine if you please."

The drugged punch was burbling merrily on the hearth an hour later when Thomas entered the kitchens, smiling, sniffing the air. "Heavenly," he declared of the mélange of aromas. "You are a wonder, Laura. What's that in the kettle?"

"Wine punch. I thought since the day is so raw, it would be a nice touch to greet our visitors with it."

"You think of everything, don't you, Laura darling?"

"I hope I have."

"She's put that there special ginger in it, Master Thomas," Polly put in, "that comes from—"

"Polly," Laura said sharply, "I smell the pasties burning."

"Oh, Lord in heaven!" The cook rushed for the oven door.

From the courtyard the stableboy's bell jangled. "Well, here they come," said Thomas, and straightened his fine new doublet. "How do I look?"

"Very handsome indeed. Good luck, Thomas."

"Thank you, Laura, my dear."

But Laura was the lucky one. All twelve of the guests arrived almost at once, en masse. Polly held a tray loaded with silver cups while Laura ladled out the steaming punch. "Should I offer 'em seconds, missy, if any wants 'em?" the cook asked, heading for the receiving chamber.

Laura, a bit giddy now that her bold venture was actually

under way, stifled a giggle. "If any wants 'em, yes."

But her high humor faded as she watched the woman teeter down the hallway with the tray. What if she'd added too little mandragora to the mixture? Or too much? Or what if, God forbid, what she'd pulled in the dark garden wasn't mandragora after all, but something poisonous, and everyone died?

She looked up anxiously as Polly returned with the empty tray. "Did everyone take a cup?" she asked, trying to keep her voice steady.

"Oh, aye, missy, they did. That big loud lady—what's her name?"

"Lady Dacre."

"Aye, Lady Dacre, she said 'twas the finest punch she ever tasted. Master Thomas told me to send you his compliments, too. Did ye know there's some sort of bishops out there?"

"I certainly did." Laura's hands shook as she filled a tumbler with the punch. "Take this to Theo, Polly, will you? He must be chilled to the bone from standing at the door."

"Yes, missy." Polly trotted off down the hallway again. When she came back, Laura had another cup ready for her.

"Here, Polly. Why don't you try this and let me know what you think?"

"I'm sure 'tis right lovely, missy, but I'd better not, not with all them high-falutin' folks to serve supper—I mean, dinner—to."

"Drink it," Laura ordered. "It will relax me. I mean, relax you."

"Well, if ye insist." Polly gulped the punch down, set the cup on the table, let out a little belch, and giggled. "Whoo! If that don't warm a soul through to the toes. Well, what now, missy?"

"What now?" Laura echoed faintly. The punch didn't seem to have affected her even a whit.

"Fer the dinner, missy," said Polly, gazing at her as though she were daft. Laura turned away, tears burning her eyes. It hadn't worked after all. She'd been crazy even to try.

"Put some sprigs of watercress around the pasties," she told Polly wearily. "And then take out the—" She heard a muffled thump from the table behind her and whirled around.

Polly was sitting slumped over, face buried in the watercress.

"Polly!" Laura rushed to her side. "Polly, can you hear me?"

The cook smiled sleepily. "Aye, missy. I'm goin' to have a wee nap now. Just a wee one, mind ye . . ." Her voice trailed off, and she began to snore.

"Thank you, Lord, for Père Talbot!" Laura whispered. Gently she moved Polly's head from the watercress onto a dish towel. Then she caught up her oiled cloak and tiptoed into the corridor.

Theodore was lying in a crumpled heap by the front doorway, the tumbler still clutched in his hand. "Theo!" Laura whispered. He never moved. She crept to the entrance to the receiving chamber, holding her breath, and peeked inside.

Thomas's guests lay slumped in their chairs, draped over tables, curled up on rugs. Archbishop Pole sat with his legs akimbo, head thrown back, snoring contentedly. Bishop Bonner was sprawled facedown on a gaming table across from the fat, wheezing figure of Francis Englefield. The Marchioness of Salister had collapsed by the garden doors, though her bountiful golden curls—a wig—lay a few feet away. Thomas had dropped like a stone beside Lady Dacre, who slept with her mouth open, just as it always was when she was awake.

Murmuring a prayer of thanksgiving, Laura turned to go —and turned back, filled with dread, as she heard a voice call her name. One of the figures was moving, rising from his chair.

"Lord Dacre," she whispered.

The short, bald man nodded. "Aye. I've given up drinking, you see. My doctor says 'tis bad for my gout. I must say he's right. I haven't felt this well in years."

"What—what are you going to do to me?"

"I rather thought I'd ask where you were headed."

"That's none of your concern."

"If you thought to strike out for Hatfield House, you'll never make it."

Laura brought up her chin. "Just try to stop me."

To her astonishment he laughed. "No, no, I meant 'tis too dreadful a night out to walk that far. You were planning on walking, I take it? Or did you also slip something into the stableboy's drink?"

"I—" Laura stared at him.

"Um, I didn't think so." He rubbed his bald pate. "How would this be? I'll take this cup I didn't have out to him, then saddle two horses, and I'll take you to Hatfield House. What did you use? Poppies? Nightshade?"

"Mandragora," said Laura, still too startled to think straight. "I mean—what difference does that make?"

"I'll have to get back here before they wake up, naturally. I wouldn't want to miss that for the world."

Laura put her hands on her hips, completely dumbfounded. "Lord Dacre, why would you want to help me?"

The short little nobleman sighed, once more rubbing his head. "I sent William Cecil round to see you, you know. I couldn't believe you'd come back to Thomas of your own free will. You didn't belong in this house; you don't belong with these people. I knew that the first time I saw you; you were so fresh and lovely and pure. Then, when you came back, you were different. Hard. I hated seeing you that way."

"You don't belong here either," Laura told him softly.

He shrugged. "It's too late for me. I made the wrong choices a long time ago."

"And that's why you're helping me?"

Lord Dacre grinned and gestured to his wife. "Well—that and Matilda. This is the longest she's kept quiet at a dinner party in thirty years!"

Chapter 20

As she and Lord Dacre rode toward Hatfield House beneath the starless sky, Laura could not help but remember the last time she'd made this journey, reaching sanctuary only to have Thomas loom up at the gate. She tried to spur her horse faster, but the man beside her gripped her reins, slowing her pace. "Too much risk to the baby," he objected. "You'll make it, don't worry. Tell me, when are you due?"

"The—the end of May. Or the beginning of June."

"Ah. The same time as the queen." They rode for a time in silence. Then he observed softly, "Thomas is making quite a name for himself these days, isn't he? Bonner and Pole as his dinner guests, private audiences with the queen—it does make one wonder."

The dark walls of Hatfield House appeared through the trees. "Lord Dacre," Laura began, "I think you should know—"

"Stop," he said tersely. "I don't want to. There's little enough I could do about it anyway. See you tell the princess and Cecil. Cecil's a better head on him than any man I ever met. He'll know what to do." He reined in his horse at the edge of the wood. "I'd best be getting back before the others wake up."

"You saved my life," she told him quietly.

He laughed. "Nay, lass. That you did yourself." His voice turned grave. "He'll be coming after you, you know. And he'll be in a rage. You've made a fool of him and all his fancy friends. Be gone from here by morning if you can."

Laura searched the darkness for the nobleman's face and leaned from her saddle to kiss his cheek. "You're wrong about it being too late for you," she whispered. "It is never too late. Believe me, I know."

She thought she saw him smile faintly and shrug his shoulders. "Good luck to you, Laura Darby." He slapped his horse's rump, and the beast cantered toward the gate.

The sentry in the guardhouse heard hoofbeats in the night and raised his lantern, peering over the barbican. "Who goes there?"

Laura looked up at the full moon the lantern light made of his face. "Would you be so kind as to tell the Lady Elizabeth that Laura Darby is here?"

Not two minutes later Elizabeth herself came flying out in her nightclothes, flame-colored hair streaming. "Laura! Oh, I knew you would come to your senses and leave him!" she cried. "Guerrin, help her down and get her bags." She enveloped Laura in a huge hug.

"I haven't got any bags," Laura told her. "Is Sir William here?"

Elizabeth heard the urgency in her voice and nodded, taking her elbow, not asking questions. "Up in my rooms. Come along."

She and Cecil had been playing chess; the knight was still sitting at the board, pondering a move. He greeted Laura guardedly. "Surprised to see you out of Guilford Hall," he said. "Thomas has been boasting all over London about Pole and Bonner visiting tonight."

Laura sat across the board from him. "Do you know, Sir William, why Thomas is in such good standing with the bishops of a sudden?"

"Hmph. Like with like."

"I'm afraid it's something more than that." Briefly Laura outlined Thomas's plan.

"My God in heaven." Elizabeth's black eyes had grown wider and wider as Laura spoke. "Mary's not with child?"

"I know she isn't. Thomas took me to see her at Hampton Court, so that Bonner and Pole could have a look at me. She made me touch her stomach." Laura shivered, remembering the soft, pasty flesh of the queen's belly. "There isn't any baby in there."

"I never in my wildest dreams thought Philip would go so far." Elizabeth touched her throat as though she felt the edge of the headsman's axe.

Cecil eyed Laura suspiciously. "If what you're saying is true, why did Thomas let you leave Guilford Hall to come here?"

"He didn't. I made a punch out of mandragora for him and his guests and put them all to sleep."

"No!" cried Elizabeth, at once appalled and bemused.

Cecil tapped his fingertips on the chessboard, his heavy-lidded eyes narrowed and shrewd. "When last I saw you, Laura Darby, you seemed contented at Guilford Hall. I'm surprised you didn't agree to go along with Thomas's plan."

"And give up her baby to those—those vultures?" Elizabeth was indignant. "Sir William, how could you say such a thing?"

Laura had flushed beneath the knight's scrutiny. "No, Elizabeth. He's right. I nearly did agree. When I first heard Thomas's plan I thought, What better life could there possibly be for my child?"

"But you changed your mind." Cecil's voice still held a note of distrust. "Why?"

"It was something a priest once told me. About how children learn by watching the people around them. And I just couldn't bear the thought of what my child—John's child—would learn from those men." Her eyes filled with tears.

Cecil's harsh expression softened; he reached across the playing board to take her hand. "Well. Welcome back, my dear."

"Thomas is going to be absolutely *livid* when he finds out what you've done," Elizabeth said worriedly. "He is sure to suspect you came here. We have to get you away to a safer place."

"I can't help but think," said Laura, "that even without me, King Philip can carry out Thomas's plan. He will just have to find someone else's baby to use."

"That's true." Cecil rubbed his nose with his forefinger. "But the plan hinges on the queen's dying, supposedly in childbirth. Philip hasn't even been in England since late last summer. If Mary lives through this summer, not even Cardinal Pole could convince the English people that she is having a child." He nodded briskly. "She must have the best physicians, the best possible care. And we will have to guard against poisoning."

Elizabeth shuddered. "God knows I hate Philip, but I cannot believe even he would try to murder poor Mary."

"With the stakes so high as the future of England? I've no doubt, Bess, he would try anything. That he would even agree to Thomas's scheme shows how desperate he is. The nation's in an ugly mood since the loss of Calais."

"Oh!" Elizabeth looked at Laura. "I was so terribly sorry to hear about John."

Cecil jumped up from his chair. "That reminds me, Laura. Someone who said he knows you showed up here the other day. Wait, I'll go and find him." He hurried out, leaving Laura and Elizabeth alone.

The princess wrapped her arm around Laura's shoulders, seeing her tears spilling over. "Please don't cry, Laura; it must be bad for your baby." Laura buried her face in her hands, her composure shattered. "Hush, lovey, hush," Elizabeth said soothingly. "Everything will turn out for the best. You'll see."

"How can you say that?" Laura sobbed. "How can you say that when John is—"

"Laura?"

She raised her head. She would have recognized that French-shaded voice anywhere. "Guy! Oh, Guy!" She ran to throw her arms around the tall, burly fisherman, kissing his straggly gray beard, drinking in the scent of eels and salt and sea wind—the scent of home—that clung to him. "What in heaven's name are you doing here?"

Cecil cleared his throat in the doorway. "Monsieur de Carteret came to see Elizabeth, to try and raise the money."

"The money," Laura echoed.

Guy nodded. "To bring our fishermen home. I remember, John told me about the Princess Elizabeth while we would go fishing. I think, she must have money, *n'est-ce pas?* She is royalty."

"Of course," Elizabeth interjected, smiling wryly, "that was before Monsieur de Carteret saw how I live."

To bring the men home... Laura choked back her tears and nodded. "Oh, Guy, yes. We must. John would have wanted that. We could bury him up on the cliff, looking over the sea."

Elizabeth laughed. "I suppose you could, but shouldn't you wait 'til he's dead?"

Two things happened simultaneously to Laura. Her heart stopped beating, and in the sudden stillness she felt a brisk kick in her womb. "But he is dead," she said after a moment. "Thomas told me so."

Elizabeth blanched. "Oh, my poor Laura! No wonder you stayed at Guilford Hall!"

Cecil saw Laura swaying on her feet and hurriedly helped her back to her chair. "Child, child. He's not dead. He's being held for ransom."

"Held for—" Laura pulled at her wedding ring. "But Thomas had this! He showed it to me—"

"A token," Cecil explained. "It's customary when holding

hostages to send a token of proof. The French must have sent that to Thomas with their ransom demand."

"John is alive?" Laura whispered, still unable to grasp what he was saying.

"They are all alive," Guy told her. "All the Guernsey-men. But their families cannot pay the ransoms that the French ask. Hannay went to Helier Gosselin to beg him for the money, but he said he does not have that much gold."

That broke through Laura's daze. "Gosselin—what did he tell you had happened to me?"

Guy's forehead furrowed. "That you were so angry with John for going to Calais that you asked him for passage here to England."

"That's a lie! Gosselin found out who I was and told John's brother, Thomas, and Thomas kidnapped me from the castle! And what does Gosselin mean, he hasn't got any money? Thomas paid him ten thousand pounds!"

"*Sacré bleu.*" Guy's huge hands had balled into fists. "I told them. Again and again I told them—without the Ancient Way, the evil will come to Guernsey again. The Arch Druid will wake up. And he did! He is living there at the Castle Cornet!"

"That's not all, Guy. Those reports John and the others gave him about all those French ships on the Normandy coast—I don't think he ever sent them on to London."

"What's that?" Cecil asked quickly.

"The Guernsey fishermen were watching the Normandy coast all last autumn," Laura explained. "John said he knew King Henri was planning to attack Calais. But the fishermen gave their reports to the seigneur of the island—"

"They never reached Mary's council, that's certain," Cecil said grimly. "Dammit to hell! If we'd known about that, we never would have let King Philip pull out the queen's troops!"

"Now," said Guy, eyes shining. "Now the people will listen to me. Now we get back our Ancient Way."

Laura laughed. "I'm sure you will. But right now I'm more worried about getting John and Talbot and the others home from Calais. How much ransom are the French asking?"

"A thousand pounds for each." The way Guy said it, it might have been a million. "Twelve thousand pounds in all."

"If the French knew enough to send their demand for

John to Thomas," Cecil put in, "they are probably asking that much again for him."

"What about your father's money, Laura?" Elizabeth asked.

"I'm afraid I burned all my bridges to that when I put Thomas and his dinner party to sleep. Damn!" Laura wracked her brain. "Guy. What if you and I were to go to Calais?"

"But, *chérie,* we do not have the ransom."

"We could find some other way of getting them out."

"Such as what, pray tell?" Cecil asked, and Elizabeth echoed him: "How?"

"I don't know." Laura cast about frantically for an idea. "You speak French perfectly, Guy. You could—you could pretend you are French. You could say you were looking for work in the fortress!"

"That would get him in." Cecil was tapping his nose again. "And once you get in, you could try to break them out. It's been tried before."

"Sir William," Elizabeth warned him, "don't you dare encourage such insanity!"

"But what about Laura?" Guy asked, paying no attention to the princess as the idea took hold.

"What about Laura? She can't go to Calais," Elizabeth declared. "She is going to have a child!"

"So she is." Cecil nodded thoughtfully. "Do you know, that gives me a notion. Laura could get in too if Guy said she was his daughter. Laura, you could tell them you'd been raped and impregnated by an English soldier. The French get sentimental about that sort of thing. They'd be sure to believe you both hate Englishmen."

"Sir William," Elizabeth moaned.

"The only problem with that," said Laura, "is that my French is absolutely atrocious. Laughable. I'd never be able to convince anyone I was French."

"Mm. Pity," Sir William mused. "Still, if we put our heads together we can come up with some way round that."

"Stop it, all of you!" Elizabeth cried crossly, stamping her foot. "Laura is *not* going to Calais. It is far too dangerous. And if you think I am going to sit here quietly while you make these cockamamie plans—"

"Elizabeth. That's it!" said Laura.

"What's what?"

Laura pointed to the motto carved above the princess's

mantelpiece. *"Video et tacit.* I watch and am silent. That's how I'll get into Calais!" She looked at Guy. "If you are willing to take me, that is."

"Of course I take you, *chérie!"* Guy's tangle of beard could not hide his wide grin. "Do you think I would miss the chance to say to those fools, 'I told you so'?"

Laura scuffed the toes of her boots across the deck of the *Marie-Hélène* and straightened the fraying cuffs of the gown she'd borrowed from Elizabeth's scullery maid. The gray ramparts of Calais loomed on the horizon, rising up out of sheer rock, bolstered by peaked forts and high walls, batteries and parapets, surrounded on all sides by the murky black sea. She stole a glance at Guy. He was sniffing the air.

"Well? What sorts of spirits are waiting for us there?" she asked, only half jesting.

"Chut," he warned her quickly, nodding toward the fortress. A bargeful of French soldiers had poled off from beneath the towers and was coming to meet them. Someone fired a musket shot in warning. "Trim your sail!" the captain of the barge bellowed to Guy. He hauled at the lanyard.

Laura held her breath, suddenly terrified. What if Hannay and Robert de Boutin and the others had been right when they called Guy a coward? One misstep now and they would both be dead. The barge slipped closer, the captain in the prow, his men ranged behind him, guns at the ready. Their faces were so stern and forbidding! "What business in Calais?" the captain barked.

Laura looked at Guy and saw that he was trembling. Good God, that was it. They were dead. He was going to give them away—

"Oh, my friends!" Guy burst into loud sobs, throwing out his arms as if to embrace the soldiers. Laura blinked. "My dear comrades!" the fisherman went on. "A hundred thousand congratulations on your magnificent victory over the English dogs!"

The captain preened, just slightly. "Well. Thank you, my good man. But really, it was not so magnificent as that."

"Hah!" Guy turned to Laura. "Do you hear what this modest fellow says? Not so magnificent—why, at home in Normandy one hears talk of nothing, nothing but the valiant heroes who have brought the gem of Calais back into King Henri's crown!"

"The odds were on our side, my Norman friend," the captain admitted.

"Bah! Do not speak to me of odds, *mon capitaine!* Had there been a hundred million Englishmen, you would have crushed them like bugs. Oh, noble knights, I salute your bravery, your fortitude, your courage!"

"Are they really talking about us like that at home?" one of the musketeers asked, pleased but dubious.

"Honored sir, would I lie to you? Of course they are! You are the mightiest heroes France has seen since the days of the great Charlemagne! That is one reason why I, Guy de Carteret, come to offer my heart and my hands to you!"

"What exactly do you mean by that?" asked the captain.

Guy dropped to one knee on the deck. "I beg you, Monseiur le Capitaine. Let me serve you and your men. Let me work for you."

There was a bit of a stir among the musketeers, who had all been impressed into the military. The captain silenced them with a wave, regarding Guy more closely. "You said one of the reasons. What else?"

Guy gestured Laura forward. She came shyly, clinging to the rail, hoping she could play her role half as well as he had. *"Voilà,"* said Guy, and glowered. "My beloved, my only daughter. *Chérie,* open your cloak."

She did so, revealing the substantial bulge in the front of her gown. "Looks like someone's had his way with her," observed the captain.

"Someone has." Guy's scowl was fierce. "An English soldier. The bastard ravished her and beat her and left her to die."

This time the murmur from the soldiers was outraged. "Poor child," said the captain, leaning out from the barge for a better view. "What is your name, little one?"

Laura shrugged her shoulders at Guy, who told the man in mournful tones, "She is called Laura. She is dumb; she cannot speak. She has been this way from birth, may God have mercy on her. That is why I did not hear when the villainous Englishman stole from her what can never be recovered. She could not cry out to me." He drew out his kerchief and dabbed at his eyes.

There was another, louder clamor from the soldiers. Guy, sniffling, shook his fist at the distant Dover cliffs. "Do you see why I rejoice so greatly at the news you have taken

Calais?" he beseeched the captain. "Why I come here to offer my services to you?"

"Mm. Quite so, quite so," said the captain, looking him up and down. "Well, what can you do?"

"I do anything," Guy said passionately. "Anything to serve you noble gentlemen."

"Let him scrub the privies, sir," one of the soldiers suggested, anxious to be relieved of that chore.

"Hm. I suppose we could find him some work. But what about her?" He pointed to Laura. "This is an armed garrison. There's no room for one who does not work."

"She can work in the scullery," Guy suggested eagerly. "True, she cannot speak, but she hears and understands perfectly. Don't you, *chérie?*" Laura nodded vigorously. Guy looked at the captain with pleading eyes. "Give us a chance, I beg you. If not for my sake, for hers."

"Come on, captain," his men urged their leader. "Look at the poor girl. "What harm could it do?"

"It's not up to me, you know." He turned back to Guy. "You'll have to go and see the commandant."

"A thousand blessings on you and your men!" Guy cried, hugging Laura. "Did you hear him, dear little daughter? We go to see the commandant!"

Commandant Leger, a short, straight man with brilliantly polished black boots, was a tougher nut than the captain. He barked a long string of questions, but Guy answered them all. Whether it was Guy's patriotic fervor or Laura's pitiful plight, something won him over, and he gave them permission to stay. By nightfall they were installed in a tiny room in the nether reaches of the fortress, already with tasks assigned. Guy was indeed to scrub the French soldiers' privies, and Laura was to work in the kitchens for the chief cook, Monsieur Valotte.

"Guy, you were absolutely splendid," Laura whispered as they settled on their thin straw pallets. "Weren't you afraid?"

"What, me, Guy de Carteret, afraid of Frenchmen?" He snorted. "Certainly not. I was terrified!"

Laura was up at dawn to report to the kitchens. After meeting the chief cook, Monsieur Valotte, she would gladly have traded assignments with Guy. Valotte was big and heavyset, with a bright red face marked with smallpox scars and beady eyes. He carried a whip as he strode through the kitchens, cracking it at any minion who didn't do his bidding quick enough to suit him. Very few did. Laura was eternally grateful for the hint Elizabeth Tudor had given her: to keep a pebble tucked under her tongue to remind her not to speak. More than once that first day she felt the lash of Valotte's whip and wanted to tell the horrid bully what she thought of him.

Only the hope that Guy would find out where John and the others were being held kept her on her feet through the endless hours of drudgery. But when she dragged herself back in exhaustion to the cell they shared and saw his long face, she knew the news he had was bad. "Well, let's hear it anyway," she said, rubbing her aching back.

"There are hundreds of cells down in the prison, they tell me, but I could not get any closer than the privies at the top of the stairs that lead down to them. There are six guards stationed at every staircase. And at least twenty sets of stairs." He noticed a thin red stripe on her forearm and touched it gently. *"Qu'est-ce que c'est?"*

"Oh—" She tugged her sleeve down to hide the mark. "The head cook is a bully. With a whip."

"Chérie! Elizabeth Tudor was right. You should not have come."

"A little whipping is nothing compared to what John and the others must be going through." Laura shivered, thinking of them locked away somewhere in the maze of rock below. "Guy, we have got to find them!"

"We try, *chérie.* We try."

But four days later they were no closer to knowing in which of the myriad cells the Guernseymen were kept than they'd been that first night. The soldiers who guarded the stairways, Guy told Laura, were closemouthed and scornful to anyone who did not wear his uniform. As for Laura, all she had learned was how to stay one step ahead of Valotte and his whip. The chief cook's staff was a motley crew of women and youths from the mainland, seeking to earn a few extra sous for their families. They worked hard, but no matter how much they tried, Valotte was never satisfied.

On the fifth morning of their stay, Laura moved up from scrubbing pans into a long line assigned to wash and chop vegetables. Working beside her was a towheaded boy of perhaps fourteen, impossibly skinny, with big hazel eyes in his thin freckled face. He handled his paring knife clumsily—he had an air of not yet having grown into his gangly hands—and Laura tried wordlessly to show him how to grasp the hilt and use the thumb to push down on the onions and leeks. He nodded shy thanks at her and whispered his name: *"Je m'appelle Alain; comment vous appelez-vous?"* Laura pointed to her mouth, shaking her head to indicate that she could not speak. The boy gave her a quick, knowing glance of sympathy. She understood why when Valotte yanked him from the line to wash pots. One of his bare feet was horribly clubbed, shortened and turned inward, the heel drawn up, so that he limped along on the outer edge. He had recognized, in her, a companion in deformity.

That afternoon, Laura was set to making biscuits: thousands of biscuits, pressed from thick, sticky dough that she struggled to knead. Beside the table at which she worked, Alain was ladling painfully thin barley gruel for the prisoners into pots beneath Valotte's watchful, malevolent eye.

"More in that one, fool," the chief cook ordered, his lash flicking Alain's back. "That is a nobleman in that cell; Commandant Leger wants to keep him alive."

"Yes, sir," the boy whispered, scooping extra ladlefuls in. Laura darted a glance at the row of iron kettles. She had not realized all the prisoners were not fed the same. How could the guards tell which went to which?

Valotte answered her question, at the cost to Alain of another sting of the whip. "No, no, fool!" the chief cook cried, wresting the ladle from Alain's trembling hand, rapping it against the side of the pot. "This is marked seven—are you blind as well as a cripple? *This* is the nobleman—eight. Seven is for the Guernseymen. Take it out, take it out again. No one is going to ransom a parcel of stinking fishermen. The sooner they die, the better. They get half what the others do. Now get on with your work!" Valotte delivered a kick to the seat of the boy's pants that sent him sprawling across the stone floor.

"I'm sorry, sir," Alain whispered, crawling back across the stones, clubfoot dragging behind him.

Laura stared at the kettles in desperate excitement. Seven. That gruel was going to John and the others! If only she could get a message to them, let them know she was here. She needed some sort of token. something John would know had come only from her—

"You!" The crack of the whip made her jump. "What are you staring at?" Valotte, face red with rage, glowered down at her. Laura bobbed in a apologetic curtsy and hurried to roll out the biscuit dough.

"I'm not running a charity here," the cook roared in her

ear. "I don't need whores and cripples working for me!"
Laura nodded, bracing against the sting of the whip as it
lashed her cheek. "Now get to work! All of you, get to work!
Alain, take those bloody buckets down to the guards!"

Valotte waddled across the kitchens, twirling his crop in
his hands. Alain hastened to slip a staff through the handles
of four pots to lift them onto his back. The kettle marked
with the seven was one of them. Laura bit down on her lip.
Who knew when such a chance might come again—and she
was going to miss it. Tears springing in her eyes, she turned
back to her dough and saw, on the third finger of her floury
right hand, a spark of gold. Her wedding band...

Alain bent down, grunting, and struggled to hoist the staff
and its load onto his scrawny back. As he straightened up,
his eyes met Laura's: dark, gentle eyes filled with sympathy...

He might give her away—or he might not. It was a
chance she would have to take. Checking to make sure Valotte was not looking, she twisted the ring from her finger,
darted toward the boy, and dropped it into the pot.

"Alain, get moving!" Valotte bellowed.

Laura stared into the boy's hazel eyes.

His expression utterly blank, he staggered out the door to
the cells.

Chapter 21

In the squalid darkness of the prisons carved beneath the rocks of Calais, a single voice was singing softly in French:

> *J'aime la fille*
> *Qui est si jolie*
> *Et une grande bouteille du vin . . .*

"Shut up in there," a guard shouted from the top of the stairs, "or there'll be no supper for the lot of you!"

"And wouldn't that be a pity," muttered Antoine de Boutin, who'd been doing the singing.

"The fellow has a point, Antoine," Jean d'Armand said wryly. "If you must sing, for God's sake sing about something besides pretty girls and wine."

"All the songs I know are about girls and wine," Antoine objected.

"That's not so, Papa," his son Robert said out of the gloom. "You know the death song, the one we sing on the way to funerals. You should practice that."

"Hush, Robert," his father said sharply. "No one is going to die."

"Stop pretending, Papa. We are all going to die. The French know by now no one is going to ransom us. They are going to starve us to death."

"Then they'll have a rough time of it," Alec Forret said, chuckling, "considering a man don't eat much better back on Guernsey than he does here."

"Don't be so hasty, Alec," Antoine chided him. "My Eloise could do things with an eel 'twould make a man swear he was eating venison pie. Isn't that so, Robert?"

"What's the sense in talking about it?" his son demanded. "We're never going to see Guernsey or eat venison, much less eel, again. We're all going to—"

"We could sing a hymn," Père Talbot suggested quietly.

275

Robert moved in the darkness. "Don't make me laugh."

A key grated in the lock of the door. "Food," said a guard, thrusting a pail through and slamming the door shut again.

Alec Forret crawled toward the bucket. "Shall we see what is the speciality of the house this evening?" He sniffed the pail's contents. "Why, you'll never guess."

"It's gruel," said Robert. "And I'll wager not half so thin as that jest is getting to be."

The Guernseymen dug out their bowls and gathered round to be served. Robert dipped a finger into his portion. "Look here, Papa. Half of yesterday's. Didn't I tell you they would make us starve?"

Alec had been counting bowls as he filled them. "Eleven. Who is holding out on me, now? Who's missing his chance at this lovely gruel? You, John, where's your trencher?"

John shifted on the stones, trying to ease the constant throbbing in his bad leg. "I'm just not in the mood for gruel tonight, Alec; I had my heart set on kidney stew. Give it to Robert, if he can get it down."

"I'll take it!" the young man cried, thrusting his bowl back for more.

"Like hell you will, lad," said his father, pushing him back. "'Tis share and share alike in here, and those that groan most don't get the most."

"Antoine," John broke in, "I honestly can't eat it."

"You've got to eat it," the islander told him. "Give me your bowl."

John gritted his teeth and tried to reach the hand Antoine extended. The damp and cold of the prison had wreaked havoc on his old injury; it throbbed like bloody hell every time he moved. Talbot sensed his discomfort and took the bowl to Alec for him, then crawled back with it. "Is your leg worse?" he murmured in English.

"The same," John lied.

"Talbot, say the grace," Louis Vidal suggested.

"Give thanks for this?" Robert de Boutin made an inelegant noise.

Talbot led the men in grace anyway. Silence descended for a moment as they sipped the gruel.

"'Tis the perfect temperature tonight," old Alec called cheerily. "Not too hot, not too cool. And the consistency! Just like gritty sea water on the tongue!"

"Shut up, Alec," said Robert. "Nobody wants to hear your stale jests."

"They would rather that than your whining, boy," his father said angrily.

"Guy will have us out of here any day now, Robert," Jean d'Armand told him.

"That's right," Alec chimed in. "Guy won't forget about us, you can bet your hat. Why, I've seen Guy sail the *Marie-Hélène* through waves twice as high as this here fortress."

"Remember that time he threaded the Needle over on Sark?" another voice asked. "I'd swear on my life those rocks were only half so far apart as a man's chest, but Guy cut clean through without even a scratch!"

"How about when he caught that whale in his net and got dragged half across the Channel?"

"Or when he lost his mast off St. Malo and had to row home with a spoon?"

"It wasn't a spoon, you fool; it was the lid from his tackle basket."

"It was so a spoon!"

"Shut up, all of you!" Robert cried, banging his bowl on the stones. "Guy de Carteret is a drunk and a coward. He turned tail like a rabbit and ran when he saw those French ships off Normandy; you all know it's true. The man's afraid of rocks, for God's sake. He's not going to save us. No one is going to save us. No one gives a damn about us. We're all going to die."

There was silence for a moment in the dank, crowded cell. Then Alec said, "I remember Guy once made the run from St. Peter Port to Alderney in twenty minutes flat."

"Oh, Christ," Robert snapped, and picked up his bowl.

John sipped his thin porridge absently, thinking about Guy's repeated warnings not to trust the seigneur. He'd been right, God knew; they learned that when they ran the blockade and reached the fortress. Only eight hundred men.

"Didn't the queen get our reports," John had asked the English deputy, Wentworth, "about the French ships, the troops that were gathering in Normandy?" The man, quaking in his boots at the sight of the French forces assembled against him, mutely shook his head no.

It had been Wentworth who surrendered the fortress after seven days of siege. The situation was hopeless; all the men knew that. Fortunately, Henri's long wars with Philip had left him more in need of money than of dead enemies; he'd ordered the commandant to send out ransom demands.

The French had confiscated the ring Laura threw at John on the night he left Guernsey; when they asked whom to contact for his ransom, he gave them Thomas's name. He found a certain black humor in imagining what his brother's reaction to the demand must have been.

He found no amusement at all in thinking of Laura, only a dull, hard ache of pain sharper than that in his leg. There was irony, though, of a sort. It was she who had made him whole, taught him there were things in this world worth caring about, fighting for, even dying for. She had simply never expected that he would find England one of them.

She would be safe enough on Guernsey for a time, with Hannay and Guy to look after her. When Queen Mary died and Elizabeth took the throne, she could return to England and reclaim her inheritance. She would have friends in high places then. And she would have the child . . . his child. He tried not to think of the child. As for him—well, Robert de Boutin was right, and all the Guernseymen knew it. Helier Gosselin would hardly ransom the only people who knew he'd been responsible for the fall of Calais. And who else on Guernsey had any money?

Eventually Laura would remarry. Aye, that would be best for her—though the thought stabbed his heart like fire. Another man's arms around her. Another's hands wrapped in her hair, shining like russet oak leaves. Another's mouth at her breasts, so white and lovely, while the sweet buds of her nipples hardened to his touch . . .

Damn. Just the memories made his manhood swell; he was grateful for the darkness. God, he prayed, if only you could make her understand. Make her see why I had to leave her, Lord—or if you can't, at least let her forgive me.

"Is there any more gruel?" asked Robert de Boutin.

"Nah," Alec told him. "Just what's stuck to the bottom of the pot."

"I'll scrape it out. Pass it over." In the silence his bowl made a loud rasp against the iron kettle. Suddenly he let fly a curse and began to cough. Antoine found him in the dark and clapped his back, hard.

"What's the matter, boy?"

Robert spat noisily into his hand. "I take it back—the gruel isn't always the same. Some ass dropped his button into this lot; I damned near swallowed it. Wait, now, it isn't a button. It's some kind of ring." He grunted, trying it on.

"Too small for me. Must have fell off a kitchen girl." He let out a harsh laugh. "I'll keep it as a token. To show I've got a wench upstairs in love with me."

"Wait, boy. Pass it round," his father suggested.

"Why should I? I found it."

"So we can all pretend for a moment," Antoine said softly, "that we've got a wench upstairs in love with us."

"Well." Robert raised up his empty bowl. "A toast, then, to Isobel, who is waiting for me upstairs."

"To Isobel," the company said gravely, toasting with their bowls—all except John, who was still lost in thought.

Robert passed the ring to his father. "To Eloise," said Antoine, "and her myriad ways with an eel."

"To Eloise," said the rest.

"*And* eel," said Robert.

Antoine gave the ring to Alec. "To Micheline," the old man said hoarsely. "I never thought to join her in heaven so soon."

"To Micheline."

"To Hannay," said Talbot, taking the ring from Alec. "She deserved better than me. I hope she finds happiness once I am gone."

"To Hannay," said the Guernseymen. Talbot pressed the ring on John, who looked up from his reverie, blinking.

"What's this?" Unthinkingly he slipped it onto the small finger of his right hand. It fit into the groove of his first knuckle perfectly. He ran his thumb along the cool metal, felt the outline of a shape—a star. "Laura," he whispered, thunderstruck.

"To Laura," everyone began.

John shook his head. "No, you don't understand. This is Laura's ring, the one I gave her."

"Don't be stupid," Robert de Boutin said bluntly. "How can you tell in the dark?"

"It's got a star on it—here, you can feel it yourself. The French took it from me to send with their ransom demand!"

"Then it's some dirty French trick," Jean d'Armand suggested. "Anyway, John, you cannot be sure it is the same."

"I can prove it. There's an inscription engraved inside."

"And no light to read by," Alec pointed out.

"When the guard comes back for the bucket, he'll bring a lantern," Robert hissed.

"So he will," his father said thoughtfully. "You've the

youngest eyes, boy. Sit by the crack in the door and see if you can see anything when he comes."

"He's coming now," Louis warned. "John, give him the ring." John relinquished it to Robert, who crouched down by the hinges of the door. Louis thrust the empty bucket at Alec. "You're the best talker. Stall him."

"Stall him *how?*" Alec demanded as the key turned in the door.

"Bucket!" the French guard barked, thrusting his hand inside the cell.

"Ah," said Alec. "The bucket. The bucket. Would that be the gruel bucket you'd be wanting, sir?"

"Bastard." The guard shoved the old man's chest so that he went reeling backward onto the stones. "Now where's the bloody bucket?" Without another word, Talbot gave it to him. The door slammed shut.

The guard's heavy footsteps died away.

"Well?" Antoine demanded.

"He's bloody right!" Robert said excitedly. "'From John to Laura,' it said, and then something more—"

"My morning star," John whispered, and sweeter than the notion of rescue was that of redemption. So God had made her understand . . .

"Someone's come for us." Robert whispered it in wonder, then grabbed his father and kissed him on both cheeks. "Someone's come to get us!"

Old Alec, rubbing his sore ribs, laughed in the dark. "Looks like one of us might have a wench upstairs in love with him after all."

Guy was glum and exhausted as he opened the door to the tiny bedchamber that night. He rubbed his forehead with his thumb and forefinger, not meeting Laura's gaze. "It's no use, *chérie.* I begin to think it was useless to—"

"Guy." He looked at her in surprise and saw her gold eyes were shining. "I know where they are! And I got a message to them—at least I think I did." She told him about Alain and the bucket and ring.

"God smiles on us at last!" he said excitedly, then frowned. "The boy. You do not think he will give you away?"

"I don't think so. He was looking straight at me when I dropped the ring in. He didn't say anything to Valotte."

Guy sat down heavily on his pallet. "Now we know which staircase leads to their cell, true. But there are still all those guards. They have guns and swords. And after three months in prison, I do not think even Guernsey fishermen will be in any condition to fight their way out."

Laura chewed her lip. "What we need is some means of getting down to the sea without being seen. We will have to escape all the way to the harbor, to the *Marie-Hélène.*"

Guy patted her hand, no longer glum, but determined. "We will need darkness to sail. How long until the moon is new?"

Laura had seen the quartered, waning moon that night as she came from the kitchens. "Three days."

Guy grunted. "We will have to think of something fast."

Part of the answer came to him the next day, quite unexpectedly, as he stood emptying a bucket of soapy scrubwater into one of the privies. The stuff sloshed over the iron grate and into the black hole beneath. Curious, Guy held his nose against the stench and crouched down to peer into it.

"Hey, you!" Startled, Guy turned and saw a guard lounging in the door to the privy. "What in hell are you doing?"

"I—I dropped a sou."

The man laughed, yanking down his breeches. "Then you're lucky it wasn't a florin, for it's down at the bottom of the sea. Get out of my way."

That night Guy reported his discovery to Laura, and they devised an experiment. When Guy reported to work the next day, he carried a block of wood hidden in his shirt. Laura, risking a beating from Valotte, took the morning air on the parapet. As the bells of the Church of Notre Dame pealed the last stroke of seven, she was leaning over the western wall of the citadel, eyes trained on the water below, holding her breath.

For the longest time she saw nothing, and wondered whether the French soldier had been wrong when he told Guy the sewers went to the sea. But then far below the parapet a block of wood marked with a red tie bobbed to the surface. Laura drew in air with a mighty gasp. How long had it been? A minute and a half, two minutes. But some of that would not be under water; some would be in the sewer itself. It could be done.

Now there were only the guards to get past. "Six of them, at the top of the stairs to the cell," Guy said worriedly, as he and Laura met in their room that night. "And you will have to manage that yourself, for I must be in the harbor waiting."

Laura thought longingly of the mandragora at Guilford

Hall. There wasn't any here . . . but there was French wine, barrels of it locked in a room off the kitchens. And the key to that room was hanging on the ring at Valotte's belt. What was the chance of getting hold of that, with the new moon the very next night?

But another opportunity would not come for a month. Laura had seen the pitiful rations the Guernseymen were getting. They could not hold out that long. "Pray, Guy," she said. "Pray as hard as you can."

He gave her a weak grin. "One Catholic, one Protestant, eh? He will have to hear one of us!"

Valotte's temper was fouler than usual the following morning. All the help suffered for it, but poor Alain suffered most of all. Everything the boy did ignited his master's wrath; the more Valotte whipped him, the more nervous and clumsy he became. The final straw came when the head cook sent him to the wine cellar for a barrel of Bordeaux for the officers. Alain's clubfoot always troubled him on the ladder, and on this day, edgy and cowed, he slipped and let the barrel tumble from his shoulder to the floor below. It smashed into a hundred pieces, permeating the air with the scent of wine.

Everyone in the kitchens froze except Valotte, who lunged for the ladder, letting out a string of furious obscenities. He grabbed Alain by his shirt and hauled him up into the kitchens, then fell on him with the whip with furious energy.

Laura turned away, sickened by the brutal attack, desperate for some means of ending it; from the look of Valotte's red face and bulging eyes, he would kill the boy. Beside her on the table stood a tall stack of tin trays. She shoved them off the edge. They fell with a crash like heavy thunder that echoed through the room. Distracted, Valotte turned from Alain, whip raised; the boy dragged himself under the table, hugging his bleeding arms. Laura bent to pick up the trays; Valotte snarled and came toward her, then stopped as from across the kitchen there came the sound of shattering glass. One of the dairy women had dropped a basket filled with bottles of cream.

Speechless, sputtering with anger, the head cook turned on the cringing woman, flourishing the whip. In the opposite corner of the room, by the hearth, a scullion tipped a kettle of broth over onto the flames. The resultant hiss drowned out Valotte's scream of rage; the kitchens filled with acrid gray smoke. Beneath its cover, someone dumped a whole bushel of apples that went rolling crazily over the floor.

Surrounded on all sides by workers needing whipping, Valotte's fury surged to the point where it rendered him impotent. He stood for a moment in the midst of the mess, then roared, "Clean it up, damn you! Clean all of it!" and stomped out of the room.

The door slammed behind him. A nervous titter spread among the workers, then swelled to a roar. Laura helped Alain out of his hiding place. *"Merci, ma'moiselle,"* he whispered. Catching up a bucket and mop, he turned for the celler to wipe up the wine. Laura moved to help him—and saw the key sticking out from the lock in the door.

She looked at Alain, knowing he had seen it too. He stared back at her with blank hazel eyes.

When Valotte returned to the kitchens an hour later, the wine cellar was scrubbed and mopped, the door locked, and the key tucked into Laura's sleeve.

Guy was against the plan. He argued that she would not be able to carry the wine cask to the guards, that she couldn't speak French, that at least he should come with her. "But, Guy," she argued back, "you will have a hard enough time getting out through the gate and aboard the *Marie-Hélène*. And I can't sail the boat."

"Then we wait, and come up with a better plan."

"Wait how long, 'til the next new moon? They may all be dead by then."

"Get someone to help you," he said stubbornly. "The boy, Alain. He helped with the ring and the key."

"I can't ask his help with this. It's too dangerous. If we fail, we'll be hanged."

"I wish," said Guy, "you did not remind me of that."

She kissed him farewell. "Good luck. When next we see each other, we'll be on our way home."

"God willing," he muttered. *"Adieu."* He slipped off to talk his way through the gate and out to the quay where the *Marie-Hélène* had been anchored for the past week. Laura drew a deep breath and sneaked through the fortress to the kitchens, dodging the soldiers who roamed the halls.

The corridor leading to the kitchens was deserted, the door unlocked; Laura knew it would be, for the bakers started their work at two, while Valotte still slept. The big room was eerily silent, in stark contrast to the noise during the workday. Laura groped her way toward the long table in the center, found candles and flint, and lit a taper. In its flickering light shadows crept round the walls like thin, shivering ghosts.

She pulled the key to the wine cellar from her sleeve and picked up the candle. The lock opened smoothly, silently, and she threw back the heavy bar. She tugged at the iron handle of the hatch with one hand, found it was too heavy, and set the candle back on the table so as to be able to grasp it with both.

The door flew open with terrible suddenness. The candlelight fell on the harsh, ugly face of Valotte, rising up from below.

She stumbled back against the table as he came toward her, grinning, his hammy fist wrapped around the shaft of his whip. "So, my little sneak thief," he purred, small eyes gleaming. "Did you honestly think I would not miss that key?" He laughed, tickling her cheek with a teasing lash. "But, of course, you can't tell me that, can you? You can't tell anybody anything at all. Can't even cry for help—didn't Commandant Leger tell me that is what got you into your present predicament?"

Laura moved away from him, hands on the edge of the table. "The simplest thing to do with you, my pretty little thief," he went on, coming after her at a leisurely pace, "would be to turn you in to Leger. But I have a more interesting notion. Suppose you were to fall down that ladder there and break your neck—after, of course, I have a bit of sport with you?"

Laura ducked around the table, putting its width between them, her eyes grown wide. She wrapped an arm around her belly, then looked up at the menacing cook with silent pleading. He laughed again. "You want me to spare you for the sake of your child? Why? So that you can bring a mongrel half-English brat into the world? I should think that as a patriotic Frenchwoman, you would sooner die."

Laura, circling the table slowly, was torn by indecision. If she cried out, she could bring the guards. But they'd soon enough discover that she was English. She'd be imprisoned or hanged. Guy would be out in the harbor with no one to rescue. And John and the Guernseymen would die.

But if she kept silent, Valotte would kill her. The prisoners still would not be rescued. God, what was she to do?

Her frightened gaze caught on a gleam of silver—the long row of knives hanging from pegs on the wall behind Valotte.

He half turned, following her gaze, and grinned horribly, complacently. "What, will you try to kill me first? Despite the size of your stomach, little thief, I doubt you've enough for that." He stepped away from the wall. "Go on," he invited. "Make a try for one, if you like. I won't stop you."

Laura turned the corner of the table and feinted toward the knives. True to his word, he did not move. She feinted again, then darted over and yanked down a long, thin boning blade, grasping it tightly by the hilt, backing away.

All it will take is one hard thrust into his heart, she told herself as he came closer. I will aim for that button, the third one down. To save John and the others, I can kill him. But the very idea of it made her hands shake; she had never imagined actually taking another's life. Such an act went against everything she had ever been taught, all that she believed in. *Thou shalt not kill* ... What could be more direct than that command?

He was only a few yards from her now and lumbering closer. His eyes were like slits, glinting in the candlelight; she could hear him chuckling between each hot, wheezing breath.

To save John and the others, she told herself frantically. Do it, Laura! Do it! Kill him now! She drew back the knife—

One hand closed on her throat, pinning her against the table; the other tore the blade from her trembling grip. She closed her eyes in defeat, hearing the knife go skittering across the floor. "I told you so," Valotte muttered in grim satisfaction. His rough fingers caught in the throat of her bodice, ripping it open wide; his groin thrust against her belly, bending her backward beneath his weight. "I knew you couldn't kill me."

"No, Valotte," came a quiet voice from beyond his shoulder, "but I can."

Laura's eyes flew open just in time to see Alain, his young face grim and determined, raising the knife. "No, Alain, no!" she cried. Valotte, torn between surprises, had started to whirl around; now he turned back.

"You," he sputtered in astonishment, staring down at Laura. "You can speak—"

They were the last words he ever said. Alain plunged the knife into his back, and he fell against Laura like a stone, crushing her to the tabletop.

Alain pulled the body off her and lowered it to the floor. Blood oozed up around the hilt, the only part of the knife still showing. Laura turned her head, her stomach churning wildly.

The boy brought her a cup of water, his mutilated foot dragging over the stones. He made her drink it, his arms around her shoulders, holding her until she could catch her breath.

"You are English?" he asked softly in French. She nodded. "And you can talk—but in that language." She nodded again. He reached out and brushed her hair back from her face. "I thought perhaps God did not give you a voice because he could not find one lovely enough for your face."

"Oh, Alain," she whispered in her tortured French, "you should not have—" She averted her eyes from the corpse on the floor.

"I would do anything for you," he told her fiercely. And then, suddenly shy, he drew back his hand. "The man below, the one you are trying to rescue—I don't suppose it might be your father. Or your brother?"

She shook her head. "My husband."

"I was afraid of that. But then, I could not expect—" He glanced down at his maimed foot. "It does not matter. I help you anyway."

"Alain. No. You can't."

He grinned crookedly. "The trouble is, I can't very well stay here now, not with—" He gestured toward Valotte's body. "Perhaps—if it is not too much to ask—I could come with you?"

"Oh, Alain," Laura said again, and began to cry.

He pulled off his shirt and drew it over her, covering the torn bodice. "At least now I learn your name, yes?"

"Laura," she told him.

"*Eh bien,* Laura, now you tell me your plan."

A few minutes later the six soldiers sitting playing *l'ambigu* at the top of the stairway leading to dungeons five through ten looked up from their cards to see a skinny clubfooted boy staggering toward them beneath the weight of a wine cask nearly as big as he. "What have you got there, boy?" one barked as he emerged from the gloom of the passage into their circle of lantern light.

Alain set the barrel down with a thud. "Keg of wine, sir, for the nobleman in number eight. Compliments of Commandant Leger."

"Keg of wine for that snooty son of a bitch?"

"Aye, sir."

The soldier shook his head. "Well, go on. Take it down."

Alain grunted, shouldering the keg up again. "'Tis a strange world, sir, if you'll pardon my saying so, where English prisoners drink good wine and brave Frenchmen go without."

"That it is, boy," said the soldier, and spat onto the floor.

"You know, Jacques," said one of his mates, a speculative gleam in his eye, "'tis a big keg of wine."

"That it is," said Jacques. "Go on, man, play a card."

"You know what else, Jacques?" said another soldier. "'Tis a very small Englishman."

Jacques looked up from his hand. "Don't tell me you're thinking of—"

"Well, what would be the harm," his mate asked, "just in topping it off?"

Alain clutched the barrel protectively. "If you'd be thinking of having some, sirs, I ought to warn you, I should have to report you to Commandant Leger."

"Well, of course you would, my good lad," said Jacques, ruffling Alain's hair. "You're a good, honest Frenchman, and so are we. But look here. You're just about done in, I reckon, from toting that heavy keg all the way down here. Doesn't he look done in, men?" There was a chorus of *ouis*. "Suppose you leave it right here, there's a good lad, and we'll take it down to Sir Such-and-Such just as soon as we finish this hand."

"You swear you'll take it to him straight off?" Alain asked, with the proper hint of dubiousness.

Jacques grabbed the hilt of his sword. "On my honor as a French soldier, true and brave."

"Well—" Alain hesitated a moment, then gave the men a salute. "Very good, then, sirs."

Jacques tousled his hair again. "Go on to your bed, lad. You'll make a fine soldier someday." Alain limped back down the dark passageway. When Jacques thought him out of earshot, he muttered, "If France has ever got an army made up of dimwit cripples ... Who's got a dagger to get out this bung?"

"Never mind," Laura whispered, squeezing Alain's hand as he knelt beside her in the darkness. "We'll show who's dim-witted, won't we?"

When Laura had lived with Humphrey at Howarth

Manor, she had always been amazed at how quickly he could
drink himself into a stupor. An hour after dinner, with half a
dozen cups of port under his belt, he'd be snoring away. The
French soldiers in Calais prison, alas, were made of sterner
stuff—or so it seemed as she and Alain crouched uncomfortably in the corridor.

"Are you sure that was wine you brought and not water?"
she whispered, when she was certain that hours had passed.

"They aren't complaining, are they?" he muttered back.
She had to agree that the soldiers were having a marvelous
time, laughing and joking, telling ribald jests about each
other's wives and sisters. Now and again she could see one
leave the circle of lantern light to relieve himself in the privy
off to their right. Once in a great while someone would propose that perhaps it was time to take the barrel to the prisoner, but whenever the suggestion was raised it was promptly
hooted down again.

"They are never going to go to sleep," Laura moaned to
her companion.

"It is a law of nature, *n'est-ce pas?* They must."

Finally, just when Laura was certain the men would go on
drinking past dawn, when she was frantic the escape would
be ruined, their voices began to grow thicker, slower, the
merriment less boisterous. "Well," one muttered. "Well.
Time to take that barrel down now, I suppose."

"*You* take it down," said Jacques, and began to snore.

"Just . . . just give a hand here, friends." Laura and Alain
heard a grunt, a thud, and a jumble of curses. "What do you
say," someone proposed, "that first we rest a bit?"

"Hear . . . hear. Rest." And then the only sound was a
muddle of sighs.

Alain stood up, grabbing Laura's hand. "Come on."

The soldiers were clustered around their makeshift table
and the lantern, cards and cups strewn over the floor.
Jacques wore the keys on his belt; as quietly as he could,
Alain slipped off the ring. The soldier mumbled and stirred,
but he did not wake. Laura reached for the lantern, but
Alain shook his head.

"No. If they wake up and find it's gone, they'll know
something is wrong." He tried the keys in the lock of the
thick iron door until one fit. Then he reached for her hand
again. "Come on. Stay close to me." He nudged the door
with his shoulder; it opened with a wrenching clank. Miraculously, the soldiers slept on.

Alain pushed the door shut when they had passed through, and thick darkness enveloped them. Laura clung to his arm as slowly, awkwardly, he groped his way down the steep staircase. The air was dense and stale and smelled of unwashed bodies and excrement. Except for their own hesitant footsteps, the prison was so silent that Laura had the sudden terrifying thought they would find nothing in the seventh cell but a pile of blackened corpses, decaying slowly, adding their stench to the goatish stink.

Even as she thought that, she heard a voice, old, weary, begin to sing:

> *J'aime la fille*
> *Qui est si jolie—*

"Frenchmen?" Alain whispered in confusion.

"No," Laura told him, smiling, running toward the sound. "Guernseymen!"

"Laura." She had blundered straight into an iron door but felt no pain; it was John who had spoken her name. She began to cry, tearing at the door with her hands, and then Alain was beside her, fumbling with the keys, and then somehow the door was open—

And she was in John's arms again.

He was crying too, his hands running over her face and throat and hair. "Oh, God. Oh, Laura. You're so beautiful—"

"You can't even see me," she said between a sob and a laugh.

"I have seen you every moment of every hour."

His mouth covered hers, drawing breath, drawing life from her, and she returned the kiss with passionate abandon, wondering how in the world she had ever thought she'd stopped loving him.

Antoine de Boutin cleared his throat behind them in the darkness. *"Pardon,* you two, but there are some of us who are ready to get out of here."

John drew back reluctantly, his arm still around her. "Sorry, Antoine. Who is with you, love?"

"His name is Alain, John. He saved my life."

"Is he a Frenchie?" Robert growled.

"He is French," Laura told him, "and he is my friend."

"That's good enough for me," Robert's father rumbled. "Quiet, everyone. Let's go."

In absolute silence they crept through the darkness to the stairs. Though the prisoners were stiff and aching, none made the slightest groan. Alain was in the lead; he pushed open the door at the top, finger pressed to his mouth. In the shaft of light that fell through Laura looked at John. He was gaunt and ghost pale, naught but drawn skin and bone—and he had never looked more wonderful. "I love you," he mouthed to her, and she mouthed back, "I love you too."

Alain waved them on, and one by one they stepped into the guardroom. The prisoners stood for a moment staring down at their jailors, still sprawled drunkenly amid their cards. Then Robert moved, grabbing a sword and aiming it at the throat of one unheeding guard.

With startling swiftness John wrenched the weapon from his grasp. Robert turned on him in fury. "They tried to kill us, didn't they?" he demanded, and looked to the others for assent.

John's voice was very quiet but rock steady as he answered, "The war is over for us, Robert."

Robert sputtered in protest, but his father grabbed him by his tattered collar and turned to Alain. "Where next?"

He beckoned them on, and they crept through the doorway to the privy. "Down there," Laura whispered, indicating the hole. John knelt and pulled away the grate, staring into the fetid void.

"Are you sure we can fit?" he asked Laura.

"I—I think so."

From the guardroom behind them came the muddled sounds of heavy-headed men stirring.

"I'll go first," John said grimly. "Give me half a minute lead. Then come after me, with half a minute between." He kissed Laura swiftly and lowered himself into the hole.

His legs, then his shoulders, then his head, and finally his hands disappeared. They heard a sort of whoosh, then a bang and a muffled curse. "John?" Laura called anxiously. His voice floated out of the darkness, eerie, disembodied. "Be careful! There's a sort of a—" That was all he said.

"John!" Laura cried, suddenly frightened. She started to climb into the hole, but Antoine held her back.

"No. I go. In case there is trouble."

"No, Papa," Robert told him. "I'm stronger. I'll go."

He slipped into the tunnel, while the others gathered uneasily around the opening. Again they heard the sound like rushing wind, and then a definite thud. Antoine called his son's name, but this time there was no response. The remaining would-be escapers looked at one another.

"Who's next?" old Alec whispered.

"I think we all are." Alain, eyes wide, gestured toward the door. Jacques was standing there, breeches halfway to his knees, blinking uncertainly.

"What the—Who in—What's going on here?" he bellowed, reaching behind him for a harquebus. There was a blinding flash of light, and a ball of fire whizzed over their heads. "Help Laura in," Alain said urgently, as the soldier fumbled to reload his gun.

"John said wait half a minute," she protested.

"We haven't got half a minute." Louis lifted her bodily and thrust her into the hole. "Come on! Next!"

As she slipped into the darkness, Laura thought she would choke on the vile stench. She was sliding down a steep, slippery incline; she tried to slow herself by bracing her feet against the sides of the tunnel, but they were too damp and slick. She could hear the others tumbling into the chute behind her and the distant roar of the gun. Then her feet rammed against something that felt at once firm and giving. *"Chut!"* someone exclaimed right in her face, and clamped his hand over her mouth.

Robert! He took his hand away, and she started to ask where John was, but he hushed her again and caught old Alec, who was skidding down the slope behind her. Startled, Laura realized she could see. She looked up to find the source of the light that streamed down from overhead.

Silhouetted against the glare of a lantern were the highly polished boots of Commandant Leger, who was standing on a grating relieving himself, not four feet away.

She moved back against the wall, away from the stream of his urine. He was humming a little tune, beating out the time with those gleaming boots. Behind Laura the rest of the prisoners were piling up atop one another, craning to see why they'd stopped and, once they saw, frantically trying to silence those coming after them. John was clinging by his fingertips to a tiny outcrop of rock on the far side of the grate.

The scene was so impossibly ludicrous that Laura had to bite down on her hand to keep from laughing. Commandant Leger finally finished his business, still humming, and buttoned up his breeches again. Then he picked up his lantern; his boots disappeared from the grating, and the tunnel was plunged into darkness once more.

"Jesus Christ," John muttered, "if *that* didn't take me by surprise!" A chuckle ran through the cramped pile of men. Above the smell of sewage Laura caught a faint whiff of salt air. They were nearly there . . .

"Here goes nothing," said John, stepping back into the hole. Not five seconds later came a loud, gratifying splash that sprinkled Laura's gown.

"Everybody in!" Robert cried, shoving Laura from behind. She fell down, slid over bumpy rocks, and then she was in the sea. She kicked off into the darkness, down and then up, up through the black water, fighting, crawling. At last she broke the surface and hung there, gasping for air.

"Laura!" John called from somewhere to her left. She swam a few strokes toward him. A steady stream of coughs and sputters behind her signaled the arrival of the rest of the men. She found John, and they clung to each other, treading water. John threw back his head; the stars shimmered above.

"Did you think you would never see them again?" Laura whispered.

He found her mouth with his. "Believe it or not, I wasn't thinking about the stars."

Robert, followed by the others, paddled toward them. "What do we do now?"

Laura searched the darkness around them. "Guy is here with his boat somewhere."

"Guy?" The name exploded from Robert's mouth in a spray of salt. "Jesus, if I'd known we were depending on that bleeding coward to be rescued, I'd—"

"You'd what, lad?" asked a quiet voice from over his head. The hull of the *Marie-Hélène* glided silently toward them beneath the stars.

"Be the first to shake his hand?" John suggested, and reached up to do so. "Hello, Guy. Come and help me get my wife on board."

Three hours later the *Marie-Hélène* had cleared the Straits of Dover and, hugging tight to the shore of England, was headed south-southwest, to Guernsey and home. Dawn broke, and sunlight spilled over the railing and onto the deck, illuminating the pallid, upturned faces of the escaped prisoners. "Never thought I'd see another such morning." Old Alec sighed, leaning against the rail.

"Never thought I'd be so eager for a taste of eel," said Robert de Boutin.

Only Alain kept glancing back nervously at the rocky shore of France. "Why don't they come after us?" he asked Guy, crouched beside him at the rudder.

The Guernseyman laughed. "That's the wonder of it, boy. We were never worth anything to them anyway. Is there somewhere over there"—he nodded toward France—"where you'd want to be left off?"

"Oh, I don't know. My family always sort of thought the same about me as you say the French did about Guernseymen."

Guy glanced down at the sad-eyed boy. "Ever do any fishing? Off a boat, I mean?"

Alain blushed. "I wouldn't be any good. I'm not much good at anything, with this foot of mine."

"Alain!" That was John, calling to them from across the deck where he and Laura were sitting. He pushed himself up slowly, gingerly, and walked toward them with unsteady step, favoring his right leg. Alain's eyes grew immensely wide as he watched him; in the darkened prison he had not been able to see John limp.

"Laura's been telling me what you did for her," John said, leaning against the mast. "How you saved her from the cook, killed a man to help us."

"It wasn't much, really," the boy said shyly, unable to tear his gaze from John's leg.

"Not much? There aren't any words to tell you how much I owe you. How much we all owe you."

"Who, me, sir?"

"John. Yes, you." John held out his hand, and Alain, still blushing, shook it gingerly.

Guy clapped Alain's skinny shoulders. "Can't you see you're embarrassing the lad, John Guilford? Go on, now. Get back to your wife."

"I just wanted Alain to know—if there's any way I can repay the debt—"

"Well, he knows it now. Go on, go on." Guy gave John a playful shove, and he grinned, limping back across the planks. Alain watched him go with those same disbelieving eyes. When John had eased himself back down at Laura's side, Alain turned to Guy.

"I suppose that happened to him in prison?" he whispered.

"What's that, boy?" Guy boomed.

Alain's blush was beet red. "You know," he whispered. "His—" He nodded toward John.

"His what?" Guy glanced over his shoulder at John and laughed. "Oh, you mean his leg! No, no, that didn't happen in prison. It's been that way for ages. Odd, you know, I don't even notice it. He used to be my fishing partner. No, lad, the leg never held him back."

Beneath lowered lashes Alain watched Laura smile and snuggle against John in a long, loving kiss. "But it *must* have happened," he whispered, "after he was married to her."

"Mm?" Guy scratched his nose and gave the rudder a slight turn to port. "Oh, my, no, lad. John got hurt before they fell in love."

"Before," the boy breathed, and looked down at his own foot. "What do you make of that?"

"Make of it what you will," Guy told him cheerfully. "And think about fishing, why don't you? It's not a bad life."

John was smiling down at Laura. "I didn't think you'd ever understand why I had to leave you."

She leaned her head against his chest, drinking in the familiar, long-missed scent he bore now, of salt sea and clean wind and sweat. "I don't know that I do understand. But I am trying to."

He wrapped his arm around her shoulders, running his hand over her belly, and beneath his fingers felt a hard, quick shove. "What in hell was that?"

Laura smiled, remembering how he'd once believed his family was doomed to extinction. "The next generation of the house of Guilford, saying good morning to you."

"It feels strong," he said with a touch of awe. "Strong and solid."

She turned to kiss him. "It is."

Part IV

Chapter 22

The sun overhead was at the very peak of its circuit, so bright it seemed to shower fistfuls of diamonds onto the rippling waves. Laura sat propped with pillows against the doorway to Guy's cottage, shaded by the eaves and the wide straw brim of a *bordier*'s hat. Paul had at long last lost interest in the breast he'd been suckling and was playing with her bodice strings, catching them in his small, strong fists and tugging them gleefully, making delighted burbling sounds.

John in miniature, she thought, and told her son so, smiling into his sky-colored eyes. Right down to the fierce black brows and that stubborn little mouth, its full upper lip set in a comical baby sneer. "I've never in my life seen such a haughty little god, Apollo," she cooed, and giggled as one brow arched imperiously. "I have already bet your father twenty shillings that the first word you learn will be 'no.'" He gazed steadily back at her along his straight Roman nose.

Nothing in Laura's experience or imagination had prepared her for the way she loved this child—a love so fiercely powerful and protective that at times, when she held him this way, she wanted to cry just from the wonder of it. John teased her and called her a lioness, but she'd seen the same sense of awe on his face when he held his son.

Or his daughter. Hannay, seeing that Paul had finished nursing, brought Elizabeth from the willow cradle and exchanged the babies. "And this one's first word will be 'princess,' I suppose, from all the times John has called her that."

"I know." Laura suppressed a shudder. "I wish he wouldn't. It always reminds me of how close she came to becoming one."

"She is one," Hannay corrected her. "The Princess of Guernsey."

Laura laughed, surveying the toy-strewn yard with rueful resignation. "So she is. They are both going to become spoiled rotten by all this attention."

"Nonsense. A child can never have too much love."

"You may be right. But you must admit, Hannay, they have quite enough balls and hoops and poppets and tops."

"Tell that to Guy. He is whittling them a set of bowling pins."

"Oh, for glory's sake. They can't even walk!"

Hannay giggled, but the sound was wistful as she watched Laura settle her daughter against her breast. "It was worth it, yes? Just as Eloise and I kept telling you."

"I didn't think anything could be worth that. But yes. God, yes."

The birth of the twins had been a nightmare Laura thought would never end. She'd felt the first pangs of impending labor early in the morning of the fourth of June, just moments before John and Guy and Alain set out to fish. The men flew into the routine John had been drilling them in for two entire months, ever since their return from Calais. Guy ran to fetch his sister, Alain for Eloise de Boutin, while John put vast quantities of water on the hearth to boil and began tearing up linen sheets.

Twelve hours later both women were still hovering by Laura's bedside. Guy had taken Alain out on the boat in the dead of night just for something to do, and every bit of linen in the cottage had been ripped to shreds. Laura had screamed and cried to the point of exhaustion and still had produced nothing but tears and sweat. That was when Eloise, who'd birthed more babies on the island than anyone living, took John aside and told him to fetch Père Talbot.

The moment Laura saw the priest, she knew she was dying. She remembered what Bishop Bonner had said at Hampton Court when she'd gone to see the queen—*She is rather small, isn't she?*—and for the first time understood the reason for his qualms. The strange forces inside her were going to tear her apart, blood and bone and sinew, and there was nothing anyone could do. "Save the baby, Eloise," she'd pleaded. "Save the baby and let me die—"

"No one is dying while I am in charge," the midwife told her. "You save your breath."

The hours dragged on. Dawn came. Bereft of linen to tear, John started chewing his nails. Hannay emerged from the bedchamber to brew some lady's mantle tisane at Talbot's direction. "How is she?" John demanded.

"She is laughing," Hannay told him. "She keeps laughing

and saying Thomas was right about childbirth. Do you know what she means?"

John nodded miserably, remembering what Laura had told him about his brother's plot to claim that both she and the queen had died giving birth. *A terribly risky business,* Thomas had called it. John looked at Talbot. "Do something, dammit! Isn't there something you can do?"

The priest put an arm around him. "All we can do is pray."

So pray John did, as he'd never prayed before in his lifetime, to the God he knew was not distant or cold like a star, but watchful and caring, a fellow fisherman. "You know how I love her, Lord," he prayed, "and I know that you love her too..."

When the bells in Talbot's church rang out ten o'clock, a tiny head covered in downy black hair began to emerge. Eloise de Boutin crossed herself, rolling her eyes toward heaven. *"Bien,* Laura, here it comes. Just a little more— that's a good girl. *Attends, attends—"* Laura opened her tight-clenched eyes and, through a haze of blood and tears, saw the two women hovering over her, and then a small, shiny bundle. And then she heard a tiny hiccupping sound—

"That's it, Laura!" Eloise cried excitedly. "You have a son! It is finished!"

Laura sank back on the bed, weeping with exhaustion and accomplishment, and within her womb she felt a sudden stirring—a foot, a hand. Her eyes flew open. "Oh, Eloise," she whispered, "it's not finished yet..."

Hannay went to break the news to John. "Congratulations, *mon ami.* You have a fine lusty boy. A son."

"A son—" He shook his head dazedly. "Laura—can I see her?"

"Not just yet."

"But why not? The baby has come."

"Because another baby is coming. You are having twins."

Talbot told Laura later that he'd never seen another human being turn so pale. Without another word John walked straight out the cottage door.

John himself told Laura what his thoughts had been as he walked along the cliffs on that fine summer morning. He was remembering his lifelong rivalry with Thomas, his mother's brutal preference for her older son, the way it had split his family in two and begun the twisted journey of love and hate that finally erupted into tragedy. He'd looked out over the glistening Channel to the grim black figure of the Arch Druid and shook his fist. "Once wasn't enough for you, was it?" he'd cried to the devil stone. "You let me think it was a new beginning, but it is only beginning again . . ."

And then, tears streaming down his face, he'd seen a mother gull out on the rock, teaching her chicks to dive, while the father bird soared above them, keeping watch over his brood, wings spread to the sky, and he realized: It did not have to begin again.

Hannay shouted up to him from the cottage doorway: "John! *Viens, viens,—tu as une belle fille!*"

And he laughed. It had never occurred to him that the second child might be a girl.

Laura stared down at her daughter's tiny, perfect face and wondered for the millionth time how Estelle Guilford had managed to love one of her children more than the other. Paul and Elizabeth were as different as night and day, but she could no more imagine living without one of them than she could imagine life without John.

Elizabeth had Laura's coloring: brown hair with a sheen of red; wide-set eyes, framed by impossibly long black lashes, which were turning golden brown. While her brother was cool and stoic, she had a temper that flared at the slightest provocation, causing her to erupt in outraged cries of "Bwah-ah!" "That's the Darby in her," John had teased once, and when Laura turned on him indignantly, stamping her foot, to cry "It is not!" he laughed until he thought he would burst.

Now Hannay was bouncing Paul on her knee, singing a nonsense song in French and trying vainly to make him smile. "Such a solemn little boy," she exclaimed as he watched her antic faces with disdain.

"The great god Apollo probably needs his linen changed, though he won't deign to cry and tell us that," Laura said with a sigh.

"You are right," said Hannay, feeling his bottom. "Who ever heard of a baby that did not cry? Still, it makes for more peaceful nights, no? I hope that when Talbot and I—" She stopped.

"Oh, Hannay." Laura regarded her sadly. "Queen Mary won't live forever."

"I know," the Guernseywoman agreed. "It only seems that way."

Cecil's work to prolong the queen's life and thus thwart

King Philip's bedchamber plot had proven successful. Though Laura, remembering Mary's grossly swollen limbs, her rambling mind, would not have thought it possible, the queen lived through the summer, putting to rest any lingering Catholic hopes that she might still produce an heir. But even the finest physicians could only do so much. England was a nation in a state of suspension, waiting for the inevitable death of its unhappy queen.

"Anyway," said Laura, getting up to change Paul's diaper, "good always does triumph over evil, just as Talbot says. Just look at what happened to Helier Gosselin."

That made Hannay smile. "And to think Guy did that all on his own! How my brother has changed."

"He never was a coward, you know," Laura mused, wiping Paul's bare bottom. "But everyone had told him he was for so long, he had started to believe it himself. He's just like that cook of Thomas's that I told you about—Polly. Thomas told her over and over again that she was clumsy and stupid and hopeless, until now she really thinks she is."

Hannay laughed. "Well, now everyone tells Guy he is a hero, and God knows he believes that!"

"All that really matters to him, though," said Laura, kissing Paul's nose, "is that he's got back his Ancient Way."

The very day Guy had returned to Guernsey, he'd sailed to St. Peter Port, marched to the castle doors, and demanded an audience with Helier Gosselin. He told the seigneur that the islanders knew he had sold Laura to John's brother, and that he'd had the money to ransom the Guernseymen from prison but had not paid. Then he informed Gosselin that unless he left Guernsey and never set foot on it again, he, Guy de Carteret, would personally tell Queen Mary's council that Gosselin's failure to forward the fishermen's reports had caused the fall of Calais.

That same day Gosselin had boarded a ship for England. He had not been seen or heard of since. Guy had sailed back to his cove and stood on the cliff, hands on his hips, grinning out at the Arch Druid. "So there," he told the rock. "I kick you off again!" And on Midsummer's Eve of the year 1558, the bonfires on La Roque Balan had burned all through the night, while Guy de Carteret played his *télen*.

Laura looked up as a stream of seagulls appeared in the sky. "Is that the men?" she asked in surprise, watching as the birds swooped down from the cliff to the sea. "It is only noon! What do you suppose brings them home so early?"

"It cannot be anything bad," Hannay observed. "Just listen to them!"

Bursts of excited laughter preceded the fishermen over the cliff. Then they came into sight: first John, his prison-pale skin once more burned deep bronze, then Guy, his arms wrapped around a huge cuttlefish, and then, doing a sort of hobbling jig over the rocks, Alain. "Laura, Hannay, look!" the boy cried, pointing to Guy's hideous catch. "Ten legs and it still cannot walk so well as me!"

"Guy!" Hannay screamed as her brother tossed the cuttlefish toward her. It landed with a splat, suckered legs slapping the dirt. Paul eyed the ugly thing with his usual aplomb, but Elizabeth promptly let out a horrendous wail.

"What is wrong? Don't you like the present I brought you?" Guy grinned at his sister and wiped his hands on Alain's shirt, tickling him until he collapsed in a giggling fit. John administered a thorough hugging and kissing to his wife, then his daughter, and then his son, scooping up the twins in his arms.

"Oh, John, do throw that ghastly thing back in the water!" Laura begged him. "It is making Elizabeth cry."

"Paul likes it, though. Don't you, baby?" John crouched down beside the squid. Elizabeth's screams intensified, but Paul blew a bubble and touched his fist to the slimy creature's wet skin.

"What do you propose to do with it, Guy?" Hannay asked, circling it warily.

"Make a stew, of course."

"Are you mad? It would feed a hundred!"

"More, I hope," said Guy.

"Hannay, Hannay, guess what?" Alain, recovered from his giggles, was leaping about as though he had Saint Vitus' dance.

"Ah, let me see. Leonie Richet smiled at you."

"No, really, Hannay. This is important," said the boy, blushing at her mention of his latest sweetheart.

"Wait!" Guy cried. "We must announce this properly. John, where is that last bottle of French wine we found last fall?"

"Guy! You have given up drinking!" his sister cried.

"This is for the rest of you. Go on, John. Fetch it." Grinning from ear to ear, John ducked into the cottage and emerged with the bottle. "Cups, boy!" Guy commanded Alain. "And stop hopping about or you will wet your breeches!" He popped the cork with his teeth. Laura and Hannay exchanged mystified glances. Alain brought the cups, and Guy filled them to the brim. When everyone but the babies had been served, he struck a distinguished pose, head thrown back, one hand on his hip. "A toast," he proclaimed.

"To what, pray tell?" Hannay inquired.

Alain could stand it no longer. "To Sir Guy de Carteret!"

"*Sir* Guy?" Laura echoed.

"*Pardon?*" Hannay said blankly.

Guy straightened his fish-scented collar with great dignity. "You heard him. Me, myself. Sir Guy de Carteret." He extended a boot. "You may kiss my feet."

"I'll kiss your derrière, you outrageous liar!" Hannay told him. "Who in his right mind would make you a knight?"

"Nobody," Guy admitted. "But Queen Mary is not in her right mind."

"There's to be a ceremony of induction," Alain said proudly, struggling to pronounce the unfamiliar terms, "on the second Sunday in October, in the chapel at Castle Cornet."

Laura looked at John in amazement. "Is it true?"

He shrugged and nodded, the babies shifting in his arms. "There's a proclamation posted in St. Peter Port, big and bright as day."

"The paper says, 'In honor of his outstanding bravery and service to the crown,'" Alain put in, "'in rescuing Her Majesty's subjects from the prison at Calais.'"

"But how did Queen Mary find out about that?" Laura demanded.

John laughed. "Who in the Isles has talked about anything else since we got back?"

"Well, I'll be damned," said Hannay.

"I don't see why you should be so surprised," said Guy, his tone highly offended. Then he burst out laughing. "Though no one was more surprised than me!"

"Sir Guy de Carteret!" Hannay shook her head in wonder. "Who would ever have believed it?"

"Believe it, woman," Guy told her gruffly. "Now come and give me a kiss." She threw her arms around him, laughing too. "By the by, I've invited the island to supper. That's what the cuttlefish is for. Oh, and Hannay, now that I am to be a knight, I intend to eat only white bread."

"You don't like white bread, Guy!"

"No, but I shall eat it on principle."

Hannay pinched him. "I don't care if you've been made a duke. I am still not cleaning that cuttlefish!"

By sundown the neighbors had begun to stream up the road, bursting with proud excitement. Never in anyone's memory had a Guernseyman been knighted by the crown. Guy opened the keg of malty double ale he'd been saving for Christmas and poured with great gusto. Everyone who wasn't fussing over the knight-to-be was fussing over the babies; John, quick to grasp an opportunity, asked Eloise de Boutin to keep her eye on the twins. Then he grabbed a pitcher of ale and two cups and pulled Laura through the crowded yard and out the gate.

"Where do you think you are taking me?" she demanded, dodging arriving well-wishers.

"Stargazing. I adore my children, but they don't leave us much leisure for old pastimes. Look!" He waved the pitcher at the blazing heavens. "There's the Great Bear—hello, old friend! And Casseopeia and Cepheus and Perseus and Andromeda, and, oh, my Lord, look, Vulpecula and Anser!"

"And Laura," said Laura, tugging his arm.

"Where?" he asked, still gazing upward.

"Down here."

"Ah, yes, Laura. It is all coming back to me. A very small star, but exceedingly bright. I think I just might have a better view of her out by the cliff."

They settled in the long green meadow grass at the edge of the rocks. John poured beakers of the foaming ale, and they sat side by side looking over the sea. The tide was full; the Arch Druid was nowhere to be seen.

John stretched out his legs, leaning back in the whispering grass. Laura caught the tiny grimace he made as he moved his right ankle. "Does it bother you much still?"

He drew her near. "Nothing could bother me on a night like this."

"What do you suppose it means, that Guy is made a knight?"

"That our troubles are over." His fingers played with her bodice strings. "I have been thinking. I don't believe Laura is a star after all."

"What is she, then?"

"A planet. With two white moons." The strings fell open, loosing her breasts to the sky.

"I should rather be a star than a planet."

"Stars don't have moons."

"I suppose that would disappoint Paul and Elizabeth."

"Not only Paul and Elizabeth," he said, and buried his face against her sweet flesh. Laura caught her fingers in his hair and held him tight against her, pulse quickening at the touch of his tongue. The stars made a bright corona behind his head.

He loosened the bands on her skirts and pulled her atop him, so that she felt his hard rod of desire against her thighs. She could see the lights of the cottage down the hill from the meadow, illuminating the long row of linen diapers she and Hannay had washed that morning and forgotten to take in. Such a lot of washing! "John," she said suddenly, "there is something I've been meaning to ask you for ages."

"Mm?" he murmured, mouth tracing her throat.

"How did your father make water run into the privies at Guilford Hall?"

"What in God's name made you think of that?"

"Laundry. An ocean of it." She nodded toward the diapers strung up on the line.

"Laundry." With a bit of a sigh he sat up, lifting her onto the grass, and cleared a bit of dirt for a sketching pad. "There are two tanks on the roof, one on each of the towers," he told her, drawing an outline with a stick. "They catch rainwater from gutters that Apollo laid along the parapets. There are pipes with stoppers running down from the tanks to the privies, like so. Above each privy, there's a chamber in the wall. When you pull the chain, stoppers open here and here. The water in the chamber flows into the bowl and drains down to the sewers through more piping. When you let go the chain, the chamber stops up again."

"What makes the water flow through the house?" Laura wanted to know.

"Water always flows from high point to low point. That's why the tanks are on the roof."

"Where did he get the idea to do that?"

"He was sitting watching rain drip off the eaves one day."

Laura studied the sketch he'd made her. "Could you put pipes like that in the cottage?"

"I don't see how. The roof isn't high enough."

"But if you were to build a house with a tower—out of good-spirited rocks, of course—"

He sat back, staring at her. "On Guernsey?"

"It is just a thought. I would like for Paul and Elizabeth

to grow up with better French accents than mine."

"It took my father eight years to get those privies to work." He scratched his chin. "Surely they'll be out of diapers by then."

"Ah," said Laura. "But there will be others coming along."

"Not if you keep talking about privies there won't."

He began his caresses again, his touch gentle as the brush of a goosedown feather. Laura shivered with delight as he kissed her, his arm cradling her head, his tongue exploring hers in quick, darting strokes. "God, I love the taste of you," he whispered, trailing kisses between her breasts.

"I taste of milk."

"Mm. No. Of honey and bergamot. But I know where you taste even sweeter." He tugged her skirts down over her hips.

"John, what if someone sees us?" she whispered, blushing.

"I hardly think it's any secret I am passionately in love with my wife." He pulled off her bodice and then her drawers. "Look at you. You glow like alabaster. I could look at you this way forever."

She reached for the buttons of his breeches. "At least let me look at you too."

Starlight and sea-sound wound them in a shell of seclusion. Laura arched back, hands thrown above her head, and surrendered to hs artful tongue. His hands smoothed her thighs, parting them inch by inch, then ran up her waist to her breasts, cupping them, teasing their roseate tips. His black hair swept her white belly; he dipped his head, and she let out her breath in a shivering sigh.

"Oh, love—" His tongue flicked against her, a white-hard diamond. She writhed as the first bolt of lightning shot through her womb, and as always she was astonished at its intensity.

He plotted the course of her passion as surely as he'd once plotted the stars; he knew just when to touch her more forcefully and when to draw away, bringing her again and again to the cliff edge of consummation, leaving her quivering there until, at last, aching for release, she brought her hands down to clench his shoulders, and he slid up to bestride her. She was never certain if she said the words—"Now, love"—or merely thought them, but always, always he was there at that moment, his manhood driving into her.

Then his own groans began, one for each pounding thrust, while she wrapped her legs around his buttocks and followed his movements. He began with tormenting slowness, arching up, holding back, while all her nerves flared and sparked in anticipation of what was to come. His breathing turned harsh and hollow, matching the growing pace of his pounding loins—

And then they were moving together, pulling earth, sea, moon, stars after them in a dazzling wake. The light within them blazed to blinding; the circle tightened; time dropped away, and they were the center of the universe.

They tumbled back slowly. Laura felt the incandescence drain from his loins, his seed like a thousand sparks of light. But always, always when he raised his head and kissed her afterward, the fire still shone in his sky-dark eyes. "Love," he whispered, voice catching on stardust. His arms still around her, he rolled over so that she sprawled half across him, half across the crushed meadow grass. His fingers made idle patterns against her white buttocks. "Four moons, not two," he murmured, and laughed.

The tide was receding now; far out in the black water the Arch Druid raised his black head. John saw it and looked away, up at the Pole Star that pointed a path to England across the waves. "Just stay here, eh? I wonder if they will let us."

"If who will let us?"

"I don't know. Our stars."

Once Laura would have said—had said, in fact—"I don't put any stock in such things." But she had learned since then; it was better to respect what one could not understand. She lay back and stared at the heavens. "We won't know until we try." The strains of Guy's *télen* floated from the cottage: a love song, old as the rocks and sea and sky.

"Dance with me," John whispered, wrapping her again in his arms. As his mouth closed over hers, she heard a rustle in the long grass far off to their left. She pulled back, cocking her head at the sound.

"What is it?" John whispered.

"Shh." She put a finger to his lips. From across the face of the cliffs a boy's voice drifted, fervent and low.

"Oh, Leonie. Look at you. You glow like alabaster. I could look at you this way forever."

"My God," John muttered. "Alain."

"I love the taste of you, Leonie."

Laura stuffed her fist into her mouth to keep from laughing at the utter disbelief that crossed John's face as he realized the boy's sweet French words had been translated from his own. "That young man's understanding of English is certainly coming along splendidly, isn't it, darling?" she asked.

"I'll kill him. I swear, I'll kill him." John lunged for his breeches, tugging them on as he stomped across the meadow, roaring, "Alain!"

Chapter 23

The second Sunday in October, the date set for the ceremony inducting Guy de Carteret into the Most Noble Order
of the Garter, dawned sodden and gray. A drear rain was
falling, and thick sea mist had swept up the cliffs and
wrapped the cottage in its glove. But nothing, least of all the
weather, could dampen the high spirits of those inside. The
common room was a shambles, littered with tried-on and
cast-off articles of clothing, remnants of breakfast, and
crumpled drafts of the speech Guy had been perfecting for
the past month. Alain was trying to coax an overexcited Elizabeth out of tears with the help of a rattle; little Paul, imper-
vious to the pandemonium around him, sat like a swaddled
Buddha and watched his sister's histrionics with a jaded eye.
John and Laura were stumbling over and around each other
in their bedchamber, searching for stockings and boots and
capes. Guy was walking through the house, clearing his
throat, tugging his newly waxed and parted beard and saying, "My fellow Guernseymen, I come before you today—"

"Drat," John muttered as his boot lace broke in his
hands. "Have I got another of these?"

"Oh, darling, I don't know. Why don't you get one from
Guy?"

"Guy has enough on his mind without worrying about my
boot laces. How would it be if I tied it together?"

"I'm sure it would be fine. No one is going to be looking
at your feet, for heaven's sake." Laura moaned in exasperation as the braids she'd coiled over her ears slipped down.
"*What* is the matter with my hair today?"

"I thought you were wearing a hat," said John.

"It could blow off," Laura said with patent female logic.

"If it does, your hair will look one hell of a lot worse than
it does now. Alain!" John bellowed, switching to French as
Elizabeth's wails shook the rafters. "Are you teasing that
child?"

Alain, doing his best to keep her quiet, replied with an indignant "*Non!*"

Laura nibbled her lip. "Maybe she's hungry, John. Maybe I should try to feed her again." Her daughter, caught up in the feverish excitement, had refused to nurse that morning.

"You can always feed her in the wagon if you have to; there's no time now." Triumphantly John pulled the knot in his boot lace tight. "There!" He glanced at his wife. "God, you're a gorgeous creature."

Laura smoothed down the skirts of her brand-new gray gown. "Do you honestly like this outfit?"

"The only one I like you in better, you couldn't wear in a chapel," he told her with a lascivious wink. "Oh, Lord, I nearly forgot." He rummaged beneath the bed. "I've a present for you."

"What is it?" she asked in wonder, taking the bundle he proffered.

"To go with your gown."

Laura eyed him askance, then pulled away the wrappings. Inside the plain brown paper was a pair of slippers, of glove-soft gray kid. The toes sparkled with sequins, and the soles were supple as baby's skin. "What are these?" she asked, holding them up, admiring the delicate craftsmanship.

"What in hell do they look like? They're dancing shoes."

"Oh, but John—"

"I've been thinking it over," he told her gruffly. "There'll be dancing tonight at the castle. God knows I'll look a fool, but I'm willing to try."

She threw her arms around his neck and kissed him all over his face. He pushed her away, hiding his pleasure in roughness. "Go on. Put them on."

Delightedly Laura kicked off her boots and slipped on the dainty shoes. "Heavenly." She sighed, wriggling her toes. "And you are the most wonderful husband in the entire—"

"Guy! Laura! John!" Alain called from the front room. "Talbot is here!"

There ensued a half hour of magnificent chaos as the household struggled to wedge itself into the priest's donkey cart in the pouring rain. "We should have just sailed to St. Peter Port," Alain grumbled, scrunched tight against the side of the wagon, knees touching his chin.

"Can't sail in this pea soup, lad," Guy told him, climbing in with his speech in one hand and *télen* in the other. "Here, Laura, pass one of those babies up."

Somehow they all squeezed in, covered with oiled cloaks, laughing and squirming. Talbot clicked the reins, and the donkey trotted off down the hill. *"Eh bien,"* said Guy, "who wants to hear me practice my speech again?"

"No one!" The answer arose as a chorus. Not put out in the least, Guy began anyway. Elizabeth started to cry.

"Is Guy going to get robes of velvet and a hat of gold?" Alain wanted to know.

"He's going to get a Garter," Talbot called back from the driver's seat.

"A garter like Laura uses to hold up her stockings?"

"How do you know what Laura holds up her stockings with?" John growled, giving the boy a mock cuff. "Who's conferring this knighthood, anyway, Talbot?"

"I hear it's to be the deputy of Calais—former deputy of Calais."

"Wentworth?" John groaned.

"Do you know him?" asked Talbot.

"Aye. I thought he'd been taken to France as a prisoner of war."

"Well, the queen must have got him back."

They followed the road through Vale and St. Andrew to the east coast—the same route, Laura remembered, soothing Elizabeth's wails, that she had taken to Castle Cornet on Christmas Eve past, riding in Gosselin's carriage. How furious she had been with John that night for abandoning her on Guernsey! She had danced then—danced right into the seigneur's trap. It all seemed a lifetime ago now, with John beside her, the twins in her arms.

The journey took nearly three hours, thanks to the muddy roads and the rain, but as they rattled at last over the high-banked bridge into the city, all discomfort was forgotten. The islanders thronged the streets, cheering them on their way. Guy climbed onto the seat beside Talbot and was hailed as a hero by the swelling crowds.

The old iron gates to the castle yards had been festooned with garlands of pine, and the chapel bells pealed out as the procession passed through. Hannay worked her way through the tumultuous throng and grinned at her brother, now standing on the driver's seat, waving grandly to right and left. "Sit down, you big fool," she cried affectionately, "before your puffed chest bursts the buttons on your shirt!"

John held Paul up so he could see the crowd. "Look at this, Laura." She turned and burst out laughing; her son, as sternly serene as ever, was mimicking *Oncle Guy* by waving to the upturned faces below.

Virtually the entire population of Guernsey was gathered in the castle courtyard. With help from Antoine and Robert de Boutin, Guy dismounted from the cart at the foot of the chapel steps beneath a shower of damp rose petals. The rain still had not let up. Laura had hoped to find a quiet spot in which to nurse Elizabeth, but clearly there was to be no such place at Castle Cornet that day.

"Where's Wentworth, John?" Talbot called above the uproar. John shrugged, shaking his head; though the walls were lined with English soldiers, he didn't see the queen's deputy among them. Holding tight to Paul, he moved to Laura's side.

"Guy's enjoying himself, isn't he?" he asked.

Laura laughed. "He has a right to. He earned it." The fisherman, a huge grin splitting his waxed whiskers, had mounted the steps to the chapel while the islanders roared his name. He raised his hands for silence and, when he got it, turned and pounded on the heavy doors. "Where's this fellow Wentworth," he bellowed, "that's supposed to make me a knight?"

"Oh, Lord!" Laura laughed, hiding her face against Elizabeth's hair.

"You tell 'em, Guy!" shouted Alain.

The chapel doors swung open. Guy, who'd turned his back to them, heard a sudden hush descend on the crowd.

Helier Gosselin, dressed all in black, stepped out of the chapel, a dozen armed men behind him. "I regret to inform you, Guy, that there's been a change in plans."

Guy whirled at the sound of the voice, blinking in confusion. "Helier! What's going on here?"

"One moment, if you please." The Seigneur of Guernsey gestured to the guards at the castle gates, who slammed the iron bars shut, then stood before them, pikestaffs lowered at the bewildered multitude. "Now then, Guy, you had something to say?"

Guy had recovered his tongue. This was his day in the sun, even if it *was* raining, and he was in no mood for interference. "I sure in hell do," he said angrily. "You may not like the idea of my becoming a knight, Helier, but there's naught you can do about it, seeing as it's by order of the queen!"

"The queen gave no such order."

Guy's wide jaw dropped. "That's not true! I saw the proclamation right on that gate, with these two eyes! Everyone else did too!"

"That's right!" a hundred voices chorused.

"We saw it!"

"I saw it!"

"I did!"

"I wrote the proclamation myself," Gosselin said smoothly, silkily, "and had it put there."

"But why?" Guy stammered, staring at the black-clad man.

"Because I could think of no better way of gathering all my dear fellow Guernseymen and women together than by pretending to honor the great hero of the prison break at Calais."

John, listening, caught Laura's eye above the head of the crowd and motioned her close to him. As unobtrusively as she could, she crept that way. Gosselin drew a sheaf of parchment from within his cloak and perused it slowly. "What's that?" Guy demanded.

"An order for the arrest of one Laura Darby, heretic."

"Let me see that!" Guy cried.

"It's all in proper order," said Gosselin, an ugly edge to his unctuous tone. His dark gaze flicked over the crowd like the tongue of a lizard. "So, if you'll just surrender her to me—"

"Never!" Guy shouted, and the crowd echoed him in a roar. Gosselin signaled to the soldiers on the wall; they fired a volley from their muskets that stunned everyone into silence, except for baby Elizabeth. Gosselin beckoned forward one of the guards who stood beside him. "Would you please read out, my good man, the statute of Her Majesty Queen Mary regarding the sheltering of heretics?"

In halting French, the soldier struggled through the document Helier gave him. "Any man or woman who knowingly provides aid, shelter, comfort . . . to enemies against the true religion of God anywhere in the realm . . ." Laura heard the words with a sick sensation spreading in her stomach. Gosselin was smiling thinly, triumphantly. When the soldier had finished, the seigneur elbowed him rudely back into place.

"Now. I'll give you all one last chance to surrender her to me."

"Go to hell, Gosselin." Guy spat.

"Very well." The seigneur scanned the heads of the crowd.

"Père Talbot!" he called. The priest stepped forward. "Did you know that this woman, Laura Darby, was a heretic?"

There was a gasp from Hannay. Talbot bowed his tonsured head. "Aye," he said. "I did."

Gosselin licked his lips and turned to Guy. "You, Guy de Carteret, did you know the woman Laura Darby was a—"

"Wait! Guy, say nothing!" Laura, shaking off John's restraining hand, pushed through the sea of heads and shoulders around her to the foot of the steps.

The seigneur's eyes positively glittered. "Well, well, well. Mistress Laura Darby. You have any number of prominent Englishmen incensed with you, from the Archbishop of Canterbury on down."

"Not as incensed as they will be with you," said John, calm and steady at her side, "when they learn it was through your negligence that the queen lost Calais."

"That problem stymied me for a time," Gosselin said with a careless shrug. "But I've spent these past months in England wisely. Laying a foundation, one might say. And I doubt the queen or her ministers will accept your version of that incident over mine. So—" He contemplated his manicured fingers. "I am ready to take Mistress Darby back to England to burn. Along with anyone else who cares to admit he knew she was a heretic."

"Then you'll be taking me, Gosselin," John told him.

"And me, by God!" Guy cried angrily.

"No, please!" Laura tried to tell him, but Alain had darted out of the crowd.

"Me too!" he piped up.

"And me," Hannay said proudly.

Robert de Boutin, his arm around Isobel, moved to the front of the steps. "We knew as well."

"So did I," his father announced, beaming at his son as he joined them.

"And I," said Eloise.

One after another the islanders shouted it out: "I knew! I knew!"

"You'll have to take me too!"

"Sir," said the goggle-eyed soldier beside Gosselin, "you can't mean to burn them all!"

"I don't," the seigneur snapped. "Shut up, all of you! All I want is the woman. What do you care about her? She's not one of you!"

"She's more one of us than you, you bloody-fingered Janus," Guy growled.

"Seize her," Gosselin told his soldiers blandly.

"Hold on," said Guy, stepping between them. "You can't take her. She's an islander now. And she's got rights under the Ancient Way."

The seigneur's lip curled in a sneer. "The Ancient Way? Don't be ridiculous. No one but you believes in that antique nonsense, you cowardly drunk."

His scornful words brought a roar of outrage from the crowd. The soldiers, seeing the sheer number of islanders, regarded one another nervously. "What in hell's the Ancient Way, sir?" the captain beside Gosselin asked.

"*Merde,*" he said bluntly. "Superstitious crap."

The captain nodded toward the furious crowd. "There's one hell of a lot more of them than there is of us, sir. Maybe you'd best give in to what they say."

Rolling his eyes, Gosselin raised his hands for quiet. When it finally descended, he gave Guy a bored smile. "What right did you have in mind to claim for her? Paying taxes in chickens?"

"*Perquage,*" Guy said stoutly.

"*Perquage. Perquage.*" Gosselin frowned. "I don't believe I recall—"

"Of course you don't," Guy interrupted him. "You told us the Ancient Way was a way of oppression. But it was the way of clemency too. *Perquage.* The Sanctuary Path."

"The Sanctuary Path. Ah, yes." Gosselin glanced down at Laura. "She would have to walk all the way across the island, from here to the cliff by your cottage, by nightfall. Unaided. She could never make it."

Guy stared at him steadily. "She has the right to try."

Gosselin scratched his chin. "If I remember correctly, even if by some miracle she should reach the cliff, she would be exiled." He waved a hand. "But there's no reason even to be discussing this. The Ancient Way no longer exists."

"The Ancient Way," Guy told him, chin held high, "will exist so long as Guernsey exists."

Gosselin laughed and beckoned the soldiers toward Laura. "Take her."

The angry rumble of the crowd swelled once more. "*Perquage!*" they shouted, fists raised. "*Perquage! The Sanctuary Path!*" With Antoine and Robert in the lead, they surged toward the chapel doors in a riotous mass.

"Sir," said the nervous captain of the soldiers, "please!"

"All right, then! Let her have her damned *perquage!*" Gosselin bellowed, and glared at the captain. "You and your men go with her. If she sets one foot off those rocks —if she stumbles and anyone aids her—bring her back to me." His eyes, bitter and malevolent, fixed on Laura. "I'll have the chapel bells rung at sundown. See you soon, my dear."

The gates to the castle swung open. Guy ran down the stairs to Laura. "You know what you must do?"

She nodded, handing baby Elizabeth to him as the soldiers gathered around. "Walk the path to the cliff by the Arch Druid."

"No one can help you," Guy warned. "Not me. Not John. Only St. Patrick. You follow his stones." He winked. "Very good stones."

Laura stared at the long line of flat, worn stones leading out from the gates. She glanced at John, who held Paul tight to his chest. He nodded encouragingly. "Go on, love. You'll make it. I know you will."

Head held high, Laura went through the gates and stepped onto the first stone. Its surface was slick and cold beneath the thin soles of her new dancing shoes. She stretched to reach the next stone, John close at her side. Hannay and Talbot were right behind them, and Guy and Alain brought up the rear—

But not quite the rear. As the little entourage passed by, the islanders closed in behind Alain in neat double-file. Laura, jumping from stone to stone, was halfway across the town before, hearing the stamp of marching feet behind her, she thought to look back. Only three score soldiers? It sounded like hundreds more!

The Guernseymen and women smiled and waved and cheered, stretching all the way back to the castle. In the distant ranks of the long procession, Robert de Boutin began to sing:

> *J'aime la fille*
> *Qui est si jolie—*

"Hey. You." One of the soldiers jabed his ribs with a pike. "You heard the seigneur. No helping."

"We're not helping," Robert told him. "We're just walking too."

"Do you know, darling," Laura observed an hour later, lifting her icy skirts to jump onto a stone that lay beneath water up to her knees, "these dancing shoes were a splendid gift, but I can't help wishing I had my boots."

"Timing was never my strongest virtue," he acknowledged ruefully, watching with anxious eyes as she landed safely.

Laura saw his concern and smiled. "Don't worry. They are good rocks, just as Guy said." She gathered her skirts to jump again. "Though St. Patrick must have had awfully long legs. Still, ten miles is really nothing. I walked from Guilford Hall to Hatfield House once in the dead of night, without all these people to encourage me." She looked up at the dreary sky. "Though not in the rain, of course."

From stone to stone she went, splashing and sodden. Some were close enough together that she could step, but for most she had to jump. Her ankles were sore, and her thighs were sorer, but even so she was pleased with her progress as they reached the parish line between St. Andrew's and Vale. Then the air turned sharply colder, and the rain became not snow, which might have been a welcome change, but driving sleet. In the dim light the stones gleamed with ice, and she had to move carefully indeed.

"Look on the bright side," John offered, tramping sturdily at her side despite his bad leg, shielding Paul from the sleet with his cloak. " 'Twill make it that much harder to tell when the sun goes down.' "

Laura spoke softly, so the soldiers around them would not hear. "What time *does* the sun go down today?"

"Oh, you've plenty of time."

"John. When?"

"A little past five," he answered reluctantly.

She had that to mull over while the stones led up and down the hills that had given her such pleasure when she gazed from the cottage windows. What time had it been when they arrived at the castle? Noon? Half past? And then half an hour with Gosselin talking—one o'clock. Four hours to walk—no, to jump—ten miles.

Elizabeth was crying. Laura wished uselessly that she'd fed her daughter before they set out for St. Peter Port. She perched on a rock and scanned the faces of the soldiers, searching out one who might have babes of his own. "Please," she begged a fellow with warm brown eyes and a soft, kindly mouth, "if I could just nurse her—"

He opened the mouth, and his voice wasn't kindly at all. "Lady, if 'twere up to me there'd be none of this peek-widge nonsense, and ye'd be on yer way t' England in chains."

John stiffened, taking a step toward the surly soldier, but Guy yanked him back. "Save it, man. Laura needs you alive."

For a time he and Talbot took turns, walking backward in front of Laura, holding Elizabeth so she could see her mother's face, but the baby wasn't having any of that. She knew what she wanted, knew where it was, and wailed that it was forbidden to her. Laura listened to her fruitless screams in agony, hoping the grim soldiers might relent out of concern for their eardrums if not out of pity, but they simply marched on.

Paul, for his part, took this forced frigid outing with his usual haughty composure, matching the English guards glower for glower, sneer for sneer. They seemed to find his miniature superciliousness unnerving, and gave him and Hannay a wide berth. "*Voici,*" Alain whispered to Laura, nodding toward her disdainful son, "he is fiercer than the Arch Druid!" Laura laughed until her sides ached—a dishearteningly short period of time.

Time was on her mind. She bemoaned her wet shoes and soggy stockings, her frozen fingers and nose. She fretted over each slippery stone. But most of all she worried about the time. Every few minutes she started to ask John what time he thought it was, but always she stopped herself. What was the use? She was going as fast as she could.

It was all the more alarming, then, when, panting for breath, she leaped onto a stone at the crest of a short, steep hill and heard him murmur quietly, "Can you go faster, love?" She stared at him, gold eyes wide and frightened, and the captain of the soldiers quickly stepped between them.

"You heard the seigneur," he grunted. "No aid."

"I was telling her a jest, if you must know," John said jauntily. "The one about the English soldier and his pet sow —oof!" He winced as the man's boot crunched his bad shin. "I see you have already heard it."

"Ye're pretty damned cheeky, bud," another soldier told him, "considerin' the trouble yer wife is puttin' us to. I hope to hell I'm on the boat takes the both of ye back to England to burn when this farce is through."

But John's question had accomplished its purpose. Though she would not have believed it possible, Laura found that she could go faster, when the cost of not doing so was her life. The islanders were still singing, stretched out in a long line behind her, but their voices were faint now; everyone was conserving his breath. Laura concentrated on the stones beneath her feet, not daring to look up into the skies, certain that if she did she would see night falling, and hear the slow tolling of the chapel bells.

Elizabeth had at long last stopped crying, exhausted with despair. Laura looked at her daughter's tiny, woebegone face and found herself thinking of her father and the way he had gone with another corps of English soldiers to meet his death. How she had hated those grim men! But Charles Darby had been right when he said they were only doing their duty. Odd. She didn't feel hatred for the soldiers who walked beside her now, despite their jibes. *Father, forgive them,* she prayed, *for they know not what they do . . .*

She peered through the driving sleet and saw she had reached the foot of another hill. "Steady," Talbot murmured, "you're almost there." Laura stared at the gnarled pine tree tilting out over the path and recognized it. The tree Guy had kept trimming back, in the faith that someday someone would need to walk over these stones again . . .

At the top of this rise was the cottage. The realization made her heart pound, turned her leaden feet light again. The stones that lined the steep ravine were covered with ice; she fumbled for holds among them, scrabbling up. John was climbing beside her, while the soldiers muttered and cursed this new hazard in the trail. Far back in the line, she heard Robert de Boutin singing in a high, clear voice.

Laura didn't feel as if she were climbing; she thought she was flying. She was going to make it! The sleet slashed at her unnoticed, leaving ice crinkling on her lashes, forcing back her hood. Hand over hand, foot by foot, she stretched for the summit, higher and higher, clinging by her fingertips to the frigid stones—

And then she was reaching up for the last stone above her. Her hand closed over it; she balanced herself on her toes and pulled—

The stone slipped loose from the earth with a wrenching crack.

She was flying again, backward, head over heels, down the ravine into darkness. She heard two voices as she fell: one, an English soldier's, roared "Don't touch her! Don't nobody touch her!" The other, French, Guy's, cried "*Mon Dieu*, don't leave the path!"

Don't leave the path! Laura would have laughed if she'd the breath for it. She crashed over the stones, ribs ramming her lungs, while the islanders and soldiers dashed out of her way. She caught a glimpse of Hannay screaming, and of little Paul, one black eyebrow raised. My Lord, she thought, he almost looks concerned!

How long the fall seemed to be taking! Climbing up, she thought dizzily, had gone much faster than this—

She landed on her back, square on a stone, with a jolting thump that sent her heart careening into her throat. The sky above her went black. Sundown, she thought, and then, tasting blood, I have bitten my tongue. Through the thick haze that covered her she heard Guy shouting again: "John, for God's sake, don't touch her! You can't; that's the law. That's the Ancient Way!" And John, low and vehement: "To hell with your bloody way. She's my wife."

With a fortitude she had never imagined she possessed, Laura pushed herself up on her elbows. The sleet was falling in circles around her head. Coming toward her, spinning, whirling, she saw John, his arms outstretched. "Laura," he called, "Laura, love—"

She heard herself say "No."

He stopped or, rather, he went on spinning, though at the same distance. "Laura?"

"I can make it," she said distinctly, dragging herself to her knees.

"Forget it," he growled, spinning closer, an angry moon.

"John, it's their way. It is our way now."

"Christ, Laura." She thought he was crying, but it might only have been the sleet crashing down. "Christ, love. You're bleeding."

"I can make it," she said again. If only she could stand up, he would have to believe her. She tried, knees buckling, and tried again.

"There, you see?" She took a teetering step forward to the next stone, and then another, through the rows of silent, staring soldiers, past the frightened islanders. Talbot crossed himself as she reached the bottom of the ravine, his lips moving in prayer.

"I can make it," she said, and swayed, hearing above the clatter of pounding sleet the far-off tolling of a bell. "I can make it." Her hands clawed the stones at her head. "I can make it." But all her strength had gone; she slithered down in a heap, the death bell ringing in her head. Guy's tragic face hovered above her. "Oh, Guy," she whispered. "I am sorry. They are—good stones."

Strong, gentle hands grasped her and lifted her heavenward. She fell back against a broad, ice-speckled chest. "Well, what the hell," the captain of the English guard growled, starting up the hill with her in his arms. "It ain't our bloody way, now, is it? Anyone breathes a word of this to that bastard seigneur, and I'll have yer head."

Chapter 24

Though the gruff English captain went so far as to carry Laura down the cliff to Guy's skiff, John did not dare test his compassion by suggesting a stop at the cottage for provisions and dry clothes. Talbot, fearing for Hannay's safety once Gosselin learned Laura had made it off the island, insisted that she go with the exiles; she had tearfully refused unless he came too. With Guy and Alain and the babies that made eight all together, John realized, and they would have to make two trips out to the *Marie-Hélène*.

"That's it," the English soldier barked, laying Laura in the bottom of the skiff. "All that's goin', get off with you."

John looked at the man. "We won't all fit. We'll need to go out and come back again."

"Hurry and be done with it, then!" Already the captain seemed to be regretting his instance of mercy.

John issued orders in a low, tight voice. "Hannay, Talbot. Go now with Guy and Laura and take the babies. Where the devil's Alain?"

Guy blinked. "I have not seen him since we reached the ravine. Alain!" he called up the cliff. "Alain, *viens vitement!*"

There was no answer from the rocks overhead, where the islanders peered down at them through the icy storm. "Go on, Guy," John said grimly, wading into the churning water to push the skiff from shore. He was suddenly terrified that the English captain would change his mind. "I'll wait for him here. Send the skiff back for us." Guy nodded and hauled at the oars. The tiny craft slipped into the maelstrom of spray and sleet, and a mighty cheer rose up from the islanders on the cliff.

But John held his breath until he heard the skiff scrape the gunnel of the *Marie-Hélène*, far out in the dark harbor. "All safe on board!" Guy shouted above the crashing waves. "Here is the skiff for you and Alain!" John saw the prow come hurtling toward him, borne on the rushing tide, and snatched up the rope fastened there.

Where the devil had Alain got to? He turned back to the cliffs, roaring his name. Far up against the face of the rocks he saw a pinpoint of light, moving downward with a strange, jerky gait. "Alain!" he shouted again.

"Ici, ici!" The light swung in an arc.

"Damn you, Alain!" John called sharply. "Get down here before you—" His words of reproach died as he saw the huge sack the boy strained to haul after him on the steps. "What's that?"

"Food," Alain gasped. "Clothes. The nets. Linens for the twins—"

"Where did you get it?" John asked in disbelief.

"The cottage." The boy had reached the foot of the cliff, and John relieved him of the unwieldy bag.

"When did you go to the cottage?" he demanded, grunting as he shoved the sack down in the skiff.

"When Laura got to the ravine."

John turned to stare at the boy. "You didn't wait to see if she would make it?"

"Why? I knew she would. Laura can do anything."

John grinned, cuffing his shoulder, shoving him into the skiff. Blind faith, he thought. Holding aloft the lantern Alain had brought, he caught the English captain's eye. "We'll not forget this," he promised, thrusting out his hand.

The man ignored the gesture of friendship. "Thanks, but 'twould suit me just fine if ye did."

The skiff's prow was scraping on the rocks. Standing waist-deep in the icy water, John shoved it around and leaped in. The Guernseymen on the cliff stamped and roared and waved. John pulled at the oars, and the skiff shot out into the darkness. Past the glowering bulk of the Arch Druid he rowed, straight to the *Marie-Hélène*.

He and Alain pushed the sack up to Guy and then clambered aboard. "How is she?" John asked Talbot anxiously, bringing the lantern to where the priest knelt beside Laura, gently probing her ribs and back.

"Only bruises," Talbot assured him. "Nothing is broken."

"Pah! Nothing but that rock she held to!" Guy shook his head dejectedly. "And I thought those were good stones!"

Laura's eyes, bright as new-minted gold in the lantern light, fluttered open. "Guy," she whispered, "they were..."

"How can you say that? You were nearly killed!"

She was shaking her head. "St. Patrick made that stone break, Guy. That's what I think. So the English captain could show mercy to me."

"Hm." Guy pondered this for a moment, then nodded. *"Eh bien.* You are right. Good rocks!" Delighted to have his faith restored, he busied himself preparing makeshift beds from piles of netting and sails.

The exiles were on their way. The question was, where?

"The New World?" Talbot suggested, only half in jest, his voice low. Laura and Hannay and the babies were sound asleep, exhausted, beneath coarse canvas sheets.

Guy grunted. "There's not a doubt in my mind the *Marie-Hélène* would make it, mind you. But we have only a few days' stores. And in this weather, we would all freeze to death."

"Very well," said Talbot. "What would you suggest?"

"There are the other Channel Islands. But—" Guy looked at John, who nodded, his rugged face grim in the lantern's glow.

"You're right, Guy. Gosselin will be madder than hell when he hears Laura made it. I'd lay odds the first thing he'll do is send his men out to look for her in the other Isles."

"C'est ça." Guy scratched his beard absently; the wax he'd used to groom it that morning was damp and itching. "That and this blasted weather narrow it down. France—but she's out. What about the Low Countries?"

"I don't relish trying to shoot the Dover Straits in this storm." John stared at the lantern. "One wrong move and we'd be right back at Calais. Anyway, it would take us three days just to reach the straits."

"We might make the Scilly Isles by nightfall tomorrow," Guy said thoughtfully. "Never been there, though. I've heard tell the reefs are fierce."

"And the Scillys are English," Talbot pointed out glumly. "We would be out of the frying pan and into the fire."

Alain, curled beside the men on the deck, let out a mighty sneeze. "Wherever we go, I hope it's someplace peaceful. I've had enough adventure to last 'til I die."

Guy got up to fasten a flapping line. "Where's the most peaceful place you've ever been, John Guilford—besides Guernsey, of course?"

John considered the question, frowning up at the leaden skies. Sleet slabbered over his face. He missed the stars. It was nearly winter—in another few weeks the Leonids would begin. Not the richest of meteor showers, but the shooting stars flew so fast that they made a magnificent sight. In his mind's eye he pictured a warm summer's night, not so long ago, when he'd stood beside Laura in her fluttering white nightdress, on a dew-swept lawn in Hertfordshire—

"What is it, John?" Talbot asked, seeing the softening in those fierce wolf's eyes.

John shrugged away the image. "Nothing. I was thinking of Hatfield House."

"Where Guy went to see the Princess Elizabeth?" The priest blinked. "Well, it's a novel notion."

John laughed. "I wasn't suggesting that we go there!"

Guy came back from securing the line. "That was one fine young lady, that Princess Elizabeth. She'd give the bodice right off her back to help a friend in need."

"I'm sure she would take us in," John agreed. "But Hatfield is only a few miles away from Guilford Hall. If my brother found out that Laura was there—"

"We've a saying on Guernsey." Guy crouched on the icy deck. "Hide a jewel in the crown, *tu comprends?* Not that anyone on Guernsey has ever had any jewels."

"There is something to be said in Hatfield's favor," Talbot mused. "It's one thing for us, and even the women, to be on the run in such weather. But what about the twins?"

John frowned, looking over at his sleeping wife and children. "I won't say it's not risky, John," Guy allowed, "but it does have a certain perverse appeal."

Alain, sleepy-eyed and shy, spoke up again. "I'd give my right leg for the chance to meet a princess—not that she'd want it."

"This one might," Guy told him. "She's a special sort of princess, she is."

John's blue gaze met Guy's. "Perverse appeal, eh? Well, I'll grant you that. And England's the last place in the world Gosselin would think to look for us." He glanced at Talbot. "What do you say?"

"It's been twenty years since I was in England. But I remember seeing Elizabeth once when she was just a child. She was riding with her sister Mary in a procession. I seem to recall that Elizabeth had a poppet that Mary was trying to get away from her." He grinned. "If the princess holds on to her friends the way she held to that doll, I'd say

Hatfield House is the safest place we could go in the entire world!"

Five days later, Elizabeth Tudor was playing ruff-and-honours with Sir William Cecil and Sir Nicholas Throckmorton—and beating both badly—when the chief of her household guard appeared at her chamber door. "Hah! A timely interruption," Cecil declared, folding up his hand.

"Timely for whom?" Elizabeth inquired sweetly, leading a heart. "Go on, Guerrin. *I* can listen *and* play."

Guerrin grinned at Cecil. "There is a whole parcel of folk at thy door, mum, asking to see thee." He ticked off on his fingers. "Three fellows, two maids, a lad, and a brace of bairns, all cold and wet as can be."

"Fancy that," said the princess. "Sir William, your play."

"Dammit, Bess, you know perfectly well I can't follow suit," Cecil growled.

"Pity. Then I believe you owe me—" She tallied it on her notepad. "Two more shillings. Guerrin, has this strange band of tinkers got names?"

"I reckon they've all got 'em, mum, but the only ones as they'd tell me was the two babes. Apollo and Elizabeth."

"Apollo," Nicholas Throckmorton mused. "Isn't that what John Guilford called his father?"

"So it is. *And* Elizabeth." To Cecil's great relief, the princess let her cards slip to the floor. "My Lord in heaven. Do you suppose John and Laura had twins?"

Scrubbed, combed, clothed, fed, and diapered where applicable, the party from Guernsey was ushered into Elizabeth's chamber an hour later. "The first item I shall attend to if I ever am queen," the princess declared, "is to have calling cards made up for you, Laura Darby. Have you never heard of the custom of sending them ahead?" Laura laughed, running to hug her. "You never do anything by halves, my pet, do you? Well, well, let's see them."

John grinned. "Which first?"

"The one you named for me, naturally."

John presented Elizabeth the elder with Elizabeth the younger, who promptly began to bawl. The princess arched a thin red brow at the wailing child. "Is it me, or does she do this often?"

John laughed. "Her motto is: 'I watch and I cry.'"

Elizabeth peered down at the baby she held. "It is rather

hard to tell what she looks like with her face all scrunched up like that. She surely is loud, though. Do you suppose I might have the other one instead?" Laura took her daughter, and John preferred Paul to Elizabeth. The princess stared bemusedly at his fierce expression. "That's more like it! My God, he has got the court manner pat, hasn't he? Sir William, come see."

Cecil came close, and Paul turned his cool blue gaze on the knight, who burst out laughing. "So he has! Dammit, John Guilford, why didn't you let us know what had happened to you? We were worried sick!"

"Blame it on Laura," John told him. "She wouldn't let me write; she was afraid a letter might fall into the wrong hands. But as you can see, she and Guy managed to get us all out of Calais."

The princess beamed at Guy. "How splendid to see you again, Monsieur de Carteret! Prithee, what did you think of Calais?"

"Bad rocks," Guy said briefly. "Leave it to the French."

Elizabeth laughed. "I shall pass your advice on to Mary. Who's this?" she asked of Hannay.

"My sister, milady. Hannay. And this is her—" Guy glanced at Talbot, still in his priest's habit, and then at John.

"Hannay's husband," John finished for him. "Père Talbot. They've been living apart since your sister took the throne."

"I see. Madame, monsieur, you have my sympathies." She sighed. "As does my sister. Cecil says she is wretchedly ill."

John nodded. "We heard at Weymouth when we landed. In fact, there were rumors she was dead."

"The kingdom's all in a muddle," the princess acknowledged. "No one seems to know what is happening from one day to the next." Just then she caught sight of Alain, hanging back shyly in the doorway. "Well, well. What have we here?"

"Alain, *venais,*" Laura urged, coaxing him forward. "Allow me to present our good friend Alain to you, milady. He killed a man to save my life—all of our lives—in the prison at Calais."

"He did, did he?" Elizabeth considered the skinny, crippled boy and smiled. "I take it back, Laura. The first thing

I'll do won't be having your calling cards made. I shall make Alain a knight instead."

"Moi?" Alain whispered, English failing him in his awed excitement.

"Oui, vous," Elizabeth declared in her crisp, perfect French. "Well, I am absolutely ecstatic to have you all here, and I insist you stay as long as you please. I don't suppose any of you knows how to play ruff-and-honours?"

Later that night, John and Laura had a long audience with the princess, Cecil, and Throckmorton. Cecil took copious notes as John recounted what he'd seen of the siege of Calais. "Damn that Guernsey seigneur for not sending those bloody reports," Cecil said angrily when John finished. "And damn King Philip for pulling out Mary's men; he might as soon have handed the French the keys." His dark-ringed eyes slanted slyly toward Elizabeth. "I beg your pardon, Bess; I meant no disrespect."

Elizabeth laughed as John and Laura exchanged puzzled glances. "Oh, I quite forgot to tell you. I've had a visit from the Count of Feria, Philip's Imperial Ambassador. He's just come from seeing his master at Flanders. He brought me a proposal of marriage."

Laura let out a sympathetic sigh. "From whom this time?"

"From my brother-in-law. From Philip."

John choked on the wine he was drinking. "Talk about putting the cart before the horse! I was under the impression Philip had a wife!"

"Did this Count of Feria seem embarrassed to be discussing the king's remarriage while the queen is still alive?" Laura wondered.

"Not a bit. He kept mentioning children. A dynasty to unite England and the Empire against France, to crush her once and for all." The princess made a moue. "Sir William thinks I should entertain the proposal."

"Now, Bess," the courtier contradicted her, "I didn't say that. All I said was it was time to face the fact that you shall have to marry someday."

"Why shall I?"

"Why? You fool girl, you need a man to help you govern!"

Again that red brow arched. "I was under the impression I should always have you for that."

"'Tain't natural for a woman to go unmarried," Throckmorton said gruffly.

"Do tell," Elizabeth cooed. "And why is that?"

Throckmorton's face reddened. "You know. Urges," he mumbled.

Elizabeth grinned. "Urges, as you so quaintly put it, Sir Nicholas, have been satisfied out of wedlock since the world began. Men do it all the time. Why shouldn't I?"

"You're talking nonsense, Bess." Cecil's stiff, gray whiskers were stuck out like a flag. "Urges have nothing to do with it. It's a question of the succession. When you're laid out in Westminister Abbey, who's to carry on?"

"Marriage is no guarantee of children. Look at Mary."

"Aye, Bess, but she was old when she wed!"

"I feel old myself these days," Elizabeth mused. "As old as the mountains." She took a sip of wine. "My not marrying would hardly be the end of the world, you know. It would not even be the end of the Tudors. My father's sister Margaret—her son has that daughter. William, what's her name?"

"Mary, as you know perfectly well," he said after a pause. "Mary, Queen of Scots. Look here, Bess, you can't seriously propose—"

"Why not? The union of England and Scotland was always my father's fondest dream. Had my brother Edward lived, he would have married this queen of the Scots. So, outside the question of the succession, which I've just resolved, who can give me any reason why I should marry?"

"What about your happiness?" Laura said softly.

For the briefest instant Elizabeth's shell of self-assurance threatened to crack. She picked up her wine, took a long swallow, and set it down. "Well," she said. "Well, there is that. But if marriage is bliss, then I reckon my father ought to have been blissful six times over. And somehow I don't think he was."

"There are happy marriages," John pointed out.

"Oh, of course there are," Elizabeth said impatiently. "But common sense will tell you, precious few are those arranged between heads of state for the purpose of politics. Who in God's name *would* I marry? Some prancing French fop? One of those dullard Flemish princes? A Spanish grandee? I'm not a giddy girl, you know, who is likely to have my head turned by some smooth-tongued fellow with fine calves. I am twenty-five years old. I have learned to look after myself. The problem is, no one ever lets me. Ever since my poor mother laid herself down on that chopping block, other people have been pushing me about like a pawn."

She paused for breath, examining one long, manicured finger. Then she said steadily. "Now I have a few plans of my own. Plans for me, and plans for England. And I don't intend for those plans to be checked and thwarted and bungled at every turn"—her voice swelled in power; her black eyes were blazing—"by some fancy-dance foreign husband who hasn't got half the brains I was born with. *Do I make myself clear?*"

Cecil shifted uncomfortably in his chair. Throckmorton peered into his wine cup. Laura stared, fascinated by the force of will crackling in Elizabeth's black eyes. Here at last, she thought, is King Henry's true successor. Not sickly Edward, or poor mad Mary, but Elizabeth Tudor, the motherless child the Catholics had once called "The Little Bastard." Queen Elizabeth . . . She remembered what the princess had said of her father: *He remade the whole world according to his own will* . . .

Elizabeth broke the spell, laughing, pinching Cecil. "Frightened you for a moment, didn't I, sweet William? Good. Get used to it."

"You'll throw off the whole balance of power in Europe," Cecil moaned, shaking his head, "when word gets out that you don't intend to wed."

"Why should word get out? I am only telling the four of you." Those midnight eyes sparkled. "Just think, sweet William, of the fun we shall have watching every eligible prince in the world come a-courting me! And as for children, well, I shall be nursemaid and mother to four million Englishmen. That's enough of a brood for one woman, don't you agree?" Then her gaiety vanished. "Listen to me run on; I'm as ghoulish as Philip. Mary is still queen of England."

"At this point," Throckmorton said gently, "the queen's death can only be a mercy to us all, including her. She's been suffering so long."

"Be careful, Bess," Cecil warned, frowning. "I can't help worrying that Pole and Bonner and King Philip will come up with another wild scheme to secure the succession. Don't let anyone lure you away from here by telling you the queen is dead. We ought to arrange some sort of a sign, a token."

Laura remembered the betrothal ring the queen had

shown her. "What about the ring King Philip gave Mary? Surely nothing but death could get that away from her."

"Excellent," Cecil declared, gathering up his notes. Then he wagged his head. "Poor, unhappy woman. If you ask me, she is hanging on to her life out of sheer obstinacy."

Elizabeth smiled, almost proudly. "Mind, Sir William, that you never underestimate any Tudor's capacity for that."

Chapter 25

In the face of the wild swirl of speculation and rumor that gripped England during the last months of 1558, Elizabeth Tudor did her best to keep to the regimen Laura remembered from her earlier stay at Hatfield House. In the mornings the princess rode or took long walks about the grounds, undaunted by the onset of winter. After that, she had her lessons in languages, history, religion, and philosophy. Four times each day Father Burton came and said the Mass; four times Elizabeth went straight on with whatever she was doing while he said it. Laura worried what Père Talbot might think of this arrangement, but the Guernsey priest took to Father Burton immediately, and the two men could as often as not be found together in some corner, arguing amiably over theology.

Hannay helped Laura look after the twins, regaled Elizabeth with snippets of life on Guernsey, and astonished everyone by revealing a hitherto unsuspected talent for winning at cards. Alain, after a few days spent tiptoeing about his unfamiliar surroundings, discovered a young scullery maid named Doris who had a penchant for foreigners. If any of the exiles was restless, it was Guy, deprived of his *télen* and his fishing, fretting over how the Weymouth merchant in whose charge he'd left the *Marie-Hélène* was looking after her.

John resumed his courses in astronomy for the princess, and in early November the household spent a frigid night out on the lawn, plotting the radiant point of the Leonid Shower. Cecil—with Laura's help—finally beat out Elizabeth for the prize, but his exuberance was tempered by the arrival of a messenger from London the following day, demanding that he and Nicholas Throckmorton return to court immediately.

Throckmorton had no qualms. "This is it, milady," he told

Elizabeth as she saw them off. "When next we see you, you'll be wearing a crown."

Cecil was far more solemn. "Be wary," he said, kissing the slim young woman to whom his fortunes were hitched. "Don't you dare leave this house until either Nicholas or I show up with that ring of Mary's. The game's not over yet."

"I'll wait," she promised. "Do be careful riding, sweet William. The roads are a sea of mud."

Something was afoot in London, but what that something might be was unclear. Several times each day peculiar messages from the queen arrived at Hatfield House. The Lady Elizabeth—Mary could still not bring herself to style her half sister "Princess," any more than she could stand to name a woman she still suspected of being Protestant her heir—was not to leave the grounds of the manor. The Lady Elizabeth was to fast and pray for the health of the queen. On the seventh of November Elizabeth was instructed to write to the council daily; on the eighth she was told to eschew communication with the council entirely. Mary sent her cloth for a gown, a handsome red velvet; two days later she wrote that Elizabeth was to wear only black. The Lady Elizabeth was to touch no food not tasted by a tester and prepared in the Hatfield House kitchens; the Lady Elizabeth was ordered to accept a gift of game pies. "It is enough to make one dizzy," the object of these conflicting orders declared, staring at the pies the latest messenger had brought.

"Just imagine," said John, "how the queen must feel!"

One by one, the longstanding members of Elizabeth's household were called away from Hatfield on one pretext or another: Kate Ashley's mother supposedly took ill; Roger Ascham was needed at court to write a masque for the holidays. "You might think Mary would make that bloody mathematics teacher leave instead," Elizabeth said crossly, bidding her old friends farewell. "I never could stand him." The next day he went too.

The princess put on a brave front as her circle of companions diminished. "At least Mary can't make you leave," she told John, "seeing as she doesn't know you're here!"

The most sinister directive arrived on the fourteenth of November. With the courier who brought it came a hundred armed men. Elizabeth kept them waiting at the gates while she read the message beneath Mary's wax seal. "What now, do you suppose?" she asked idly of Laura and John, who had joined her for breakfast. She scanned the contents, then looked up with narrowed eyes. "To assure my greater safety and comfort," she said slowly, "the queen bids me replace my household guard with these men that Cardinal Pole has kindly lent her."

"Don't do it," John said immediately.

"I'm afraid it's an order and not a request." She went to her chamber window and looked out on the rows of sturdy archers her sister had sent.

"An order that smells of fish," John told her squared shoulders. "What possible reason could she have for replacing your men?"

"I don't know." Elizabeth Tudor leaned against the glass, then straightened cheerfully. "Here comes a messenger in Cecil's colors. Bless my sweet William; he'll let us know."

The letter from Cecil was brief and to the point. Cardinal Pole had uncovered, or said he had, another conspiracy. Two London merchants had been arrested; under torture they confessed a plot to assassinate Mary by drilling holes in the bottom of her barge and making her drown. They claimed the idea for the plot had come from Elizabeth.

"Oh, honestly." The princess rolled her eyes. "The things people come up with on the rack never fail to astound me. If I intended to murder Mary, I should certainly think of something more clever than that!" She crumpled Cecil's note and threw it onto the fire. "I'd bet you a hundred pounds, if I had it, that Reginald Pole made the whole story up just to force me to admit his guards."

"Which I certainly hope," Laura said worriedly, "you are not intending to do."

"I'll have to. If I don't, Mary or Pole or whoever is in charge will use my refusal to prove I'm part of the conspiracy. Don't you see? I'll wind up in the Tower. And if you think I'm about to let myself get stuck in there, to be poisoned or suffer some 'accident'—" She smiled faintly. "I surely am glad you decided to spend your exile with me. Isn't it grand being royalty?"

That same morning she dismissed her own soldiers, paying each a week's wages from her dwindling household coffers, apologizing that she had no more. "We'll stay on without pay, milady," Captain Guerrin said stoutly, "if thee asks us to."

"I only wish I could. But believe me, Guerrin, you can help me most now by going home. Give a kiss to your wife and the children. If the Lord wills it, I'll be summoning you to serve me in London someday."

"Someday *soon,* God willing," Guerrin muttered. He led his men in a salute and a cheer. Then they tramped out through the gates and Mary's soldiers trooped in. Laura watched this changing of the guard with a troubled frown.

But the next days passed with no incident more momentous than the cutting of a new tooth by Elizabeth's namesake, to the accompaniment of horrendous wailing. Laura, under Talbot's direction, was applying a mustard-seed compress to the offending portion of her daughter's jaw on the afternoon of the sixteenth when Elizabeth rushed into her rooms. "You'll never guess who Mary's sent here!" the princess exclaimed.

"Who?" Laura asked.

Elizabeth puffed up her cheeks, threw out her chest, and boomed in a deep bass voice. "This session of the queen's Court of Wards is now—ah—in session!"

"Oh, Lord." Laura laughed at the deadly accuracy of the impression. "Francis Englefield."

Her friend nodded. "It's a mixed curse, though. He has orders from the Privy Council to look over my accounts to see if my allowance ought to be raised. Poor Mary must be in dire straits if those stingy old ministers of hers are suddenly concerned about my comfort after all these years! The problem is, he is going through the house to take inventory. So I rather thought, under the circumstances, you and John might want to make yourselves scarce."

"Quite so." Laura handed the baby to Talbot. "If you don't mind, Father, I've a sudden urge to go with my husband to market day at Hertford. Didn't you say licorice root helps soothe teething pain?"

It was a splendid day for a ride, if one were warmly dressed. Laura had borrowed a fur-lined cloak from Elizabeth, and John had on Father Burton's black cape. The air was crisp as a pippin apple beneath steel-blue skies; the brisk north wind hinted of hoarfrost that night, but the only clouds to be seen were from the horses' breath as they cantered over fields empty of all but scavenging sparrows and crows.

The Hertford marketplace was oddly empty too; what merchants there were seemed more interested in gossiping with their neighbors than in hawking their wares. "How strange to be Mary," Laura murmured as they passed rows of vacant stalls, "and have a whole nation waiting for you to die." There was a candy seller, though, a fat round-cheeked man, and they bought licorice root and, in keeping with John's policy of equity among his children, almond comfits for Paul. "And what for you?" he asked as Laura surveyed the man's display.

She pursed her lips. "Cinnamon drops. No, lemon. No—wintergreen."

"Some of each," John told the grinning candy man.

"You spoil me," Laura said happily, sucking on cinnamon as they strolled away. "I like that." She reached up on tiptoe to give him a sugary kiss.

"As I live and breathe," said a stunned, familiar voice beside them.

John pulled away from the kiss. "Polly? Is that you?"

"Sure as ye're livin' and breathin'!" The cook bobbed in a curtsy, yellow braids swinging beneath her cap.

John put his hand to his dagger. "Is my brother here?"

"Lord, no, Master John, he's sent me to to do the shoppin'. But tell me, where the devil has the two of ye been?"

Laura laughed and gave the woman a hug. "It's a very long story. But I thought Theo did the shopping for Thomas."

Polly looked about cautiously, lowering her voice. "Theo and Master Thomas had a fallin' out, they did. Theo's up and left him."

"After all these years?" John asked in surprise. "Must have been one hell of an argument. What was it about?"

"Well," said Polly, settling into gossip, "Theo, he accused Master Thomas of keepin' secrets from him. That started them in to shoutin' and hollerin', and Theo started breakin' stuff, just like he always does. And then Master Thomas, he hauled off and smacked him a good one, and then Theo, he just marched out!"

"Keeping secrets about what, I wonder?" Laura mused.

"I'm sure I don't know, missy, lest 'tis somethin' to do with them hoods Master Thomas has got Charlotte makin'."

"Hoods?" she echoed.

"Aye, hoods! Black ones, a dozen of 'em, all the same. Keeps 'em in the chapel of all places—well, Lord knows he don't use that room much. I swear, it gives me the chills just to see the things."

"What in God's name could Thomas want with a dozen black hoods?" John asked, bewildered.

Polly shrugged. "If he wouldn't tell Theo, then he surely ain't about to tell me! All I know is poor old Charlotte's been sewin' her fingers down to the bone, seein' as Master Thomas insisted they be done by tonight. He sure don't want me round, neither, fer he gave me the night to go to my sister's, and he ain't *never* done that before. Oh, my, there's been strange goin's-on these last weeks at Guilford Hall, what with that queer foreign fellow always droppin' by—"

"What foreign fellow?" John interrupted.

"Some ambass'dor or such, how should I know? The Count du Fairy, Master Thomas calls him."

"The Count of Feria," John said thoughtfully. "King Philip's man."

"Oh, and that there Bishop Bonner, he's been back too, though I'd never have believed it after you put the lot of them to sleep with that potion of yours, missy. Ooh-ee, ye never did see such a bee in a bonnet as when they woke up! 'Twere almost worth the beatin' I took."

"Oh, Polly," Laura cried, "I am sorry!"

"Faith, missy, 'tis just Master Thomas's temper, ye knows that." Polly laughed, but her dark eyes glinted with concern. "He'll be worse'n ever, I reckon, now that Theo's gone."

"Polly, *why* do you stay with a master who treats you so badly?" Laura demanded.

Polly rubbed the toe of her boot in the dirt. "I told ye before, missy. I can't lose my post—who else would hire me? I don't cook proper, I don't talk proper—I don't do nothin' proper. I'm lucky Master Thomas keeps such a numbskull as me."

"You only *think* you can't do things because Thomas tells you you can't," Laura cried in exasperation. "If you were to leave him and get yourself another post—" She broke off, seeing the stubborn resistance on the cook's round face.

"Well, missy, I reckon we gets what we deserves out of this life, that's the way I sees it." She brightened, nudging Laura's side. "Speakin' of seein', whatever became of that great big stomach I last seen ye with?"

John laughed, slipping his arm through Laura's. "I'm pleased to tell you, Polly, Laura and I have a son and a daughter."

Polly's eyes boggled. "You're the father, Master John? A son *and* a daughter?" One could almost see her counting up the months. "Why, ye ain't had time to, less'n—missy, was it twins ye had?" Laura nodded, giggling. "Well, won't I be damned! A boy and a girl! What did ye name 'em?"

"Paul and Elizabeth," John told her.

"Oh, fer yer father. My, my, that's fine. And Elizabeth— who's that fer?"

"Elizabeth Tudor," said Laura. "We're staying with her, at Hatfield House—though you mustn't mention that to Thomas."

"Hatfield House?" Polly cocked her head. "Funny. That's the place Master Thomas was talkin' about with that Fairy fellow."

Suddenly Laura felt the same sick, sour sensation in her stomach she'd known when she saw Helier Gosselin on the chapel stairs at Castle Cornet. Secrets from Theo. A dozen black hoods. Visits from Feria and Bonner, and now talk of Hatfield House? That was a strange string of coincidences to involve Thomas, when he'd once plotted to slip a baby into Queen Mary's rooms in a chamber pot.

John must have shared her forebodings, for he asked Polly slowly, "How long did Thomas tell you to stay at your sister's?"

"Oh, just 'til the morrow."

"Then it must be tonight..."

"What's got to be tonight, Master John?"

"Damned if I know." Laura glanced at him; he had that look of the wolf in his eyes. "Laura, how would you like to take Polly back to Hatfield House to see the twins?"

"Oh, I would love to see 'em, missy," Polly said eagerly.

"Then you must go see them," Laura told her warmly. "But I'm sure you can find Hatfield House on your own. It's not far away."

"That," said John, "is out of the question."

"Why? Don't you think she can find it?" Laura asked with sweet innocence.

"That's not the point, and you know it."

The cook was looking dazedly from one to the other. "Polly," said Laura, "would you please excuse us a moment?" She yanked at John's cape, pulling him behind an abandoned stall.

"There is *nothing* you could say," John began, "to con-

vince me to take you with me. So you may as well save
your—"

"John, when you and the Guernseymen set out for Calais,
you took more than one ship, so you'd have more chance of
getting through."

"If I thought I needed help now," he said promptly, "I'd
fetch Guy."

"Guy may know the tides in the Channel, but he doesn't
know Guilford Hall. I do."

"Laura, it's going to be dark in an hour. I don't have time
to debate this with you."

"I agree. We had better set out right away."

"Don't you know what Thomas will do if he ever gets
hold of you again?"

"Kill me," she conceded cheerfully. "But he'd do the
same to you."

"Don't you think Apollo and Elizabeth are a trifle young
to be orphaned?"

"John." Her gold eyes stared at him steadily. "If anything
should happen to Elizabeth, they'll likely end up orphaned
anyway, sooner or later. Anyway, there is more to think
about here than just our children. The whole universe
doesn't revolve around us, you know."

He scowled down at her. "Blast your memory," he said at
last. "The really peculiar thing is, I would rather have you
along than anyone else in the world."

"Well, of course you would, darling." And she kissed
him. "Now we really had better get started, don't you
think?"

They put Polly and the pony cart she had driven on the
road to Hatfield House, after having her memorize an
obliquely worded warning to give to Guy. Then they set out
south to Guilford Hall, galloping beneath the cloudless sky
that twilight had turned to amethyst.

They spoke little on the journey, concentrating on hard
riding, keeping to the shelter of the woods. Once Laura said,
"Do you suppose Englefield's visit—"

"The timing is curious."

"And the soldiers Mary sent?"

"That's curious too."

"But what in the world do you think Thomas is planning?"

"Knowing my brother," John said grimly, "I wouldn't
even venture a guess."

The moon had risen by the time they left the forest and reached the foot of the hill on which Guilford Hall stood in all its jumbled, built-up glory. "I don't see any lights," John grunted, considering the jagged black outlines of the towers and battlements. "Maybe we were wrong. Maybe those hoods are just for some weird masked ball."

"John. Up there." Laura pointed toward the front of the house, where the road wound up to the gates. In the wavery light of the quarter moon they saw a figure on horseback gallop to the crest of the hill, stop to look about, and then vanish inside the yards. "Strange behavior for a social visit, wouldn't you say, without a single candle lit?"

John nodded, pulling his dagger out of his boot. "Let's have a closer look. We had better leave the horses here."

They crept up the hill to the gates, crouched low to the ground. John peered through the iron bars into the courtyard, then turned back to Laura. "Ten horses inside."

"Ten horses and twelve hoods," she mused, then gasped as he pushed her back behind a prickly shrub. Another horseman was pounding toward the house. John tucked himself into the shadows of the gatepost; the rider, his cloak pulled up over his face, peeked back down the hill behind him, dismounted, and led his horse through the gates.

"Stay back," John warned, but Laura crawled from behind the bush to stare as the man hitched his mount to a post by the others and went to the door. He bent to pick something up from the stone threshold, shook it out, and pulled it over his head—a tight-fitting black hood.

Then he rapped at the door. It swung open slowly, and a man in a black cape, already hooded, appeared. "Welcome," said the eerie black figure, and Laura shivered as she recognized Thomas's voice.

"I hope you don't think all this cloak-and-hood business too silly," John's brother went on smoothly. "But it really is best that our identities remain secret from one another. The most stalwart conspirators have been known to sing when confronted with St. Catherine's wheel."

"Everyone here?" the newcomer asked, his voice slightly muffled by the silk hood.

"We are waiting for just one more. Come along inside to the chapel." Thomas ushered the man over the threshold, and the door closed again.

"That does it," John muttered. "He is up to something, and I intend to find out what it is."

"How?" Laura whispered back.

"You heard Thomas. There's still one more conspirator due to arrive. I can take his place."

"John, no! It's too dangerous. Let's just go tell Elizabeth."

"Tell Elizabeth what? We don't know their plan. Here, hold this." He pressed his dagger into her hand. "I'm going to grab that last hood."

"John!" Laura reached for him, but he had already darted out of the bushes and through the gates.

She watched, heart pounding, as he limped over the bricks to the door. Just as he bent to snatch the black silk, the door opened again. "Jesus," Laura breathed, but quick as lightning John had tugged the mask on and straightened up to confront his brother.

"Aren't you the quiet one!" Thomas said, and laughed. "I was just coming to look for you. I didn't even hear your horse."

There was a moment's silence. Then John cleared his throat and said in a thick North Country drawl, "Hmph. Yas. Well, I was told to be careful."

"Quite right, my good man. Well, we're all here now. Come right this way." He beckoned John inside.

John paused on the threshold. "Eh, so I'm the last, am I?" he said in his North Country accent. "Seems I'm always last these days."

"After tonight," Thomas purred, "all of that will change. Come into the chapel." John followed him into the house, and the door clanged shut.

Laura sagged against the gatepost, clutching the cold steel dagger in her hand. Then, to her utter horror, she heard hoofbeats coming up the hill. The last of the real conspirators! Good Lord, what was she to do now? If he got into the house, Thomas would be sure to know something was wrong!

She looked down at the dagger John had given her. She would have to kill the latecomer. There was nothing else she could do! But, oh, God, she didn't have the stomach for killing: she'd learned that when she confronted Valotte in the kitchens of Calais.

She peered down the hill through the bushes and saw the rider, a faint black speck on the ribbon of moonlight that was

the road. She tried to force herself to think calmly. The
horses were tied in the yard. That meant the stableboy, like
Polly, had been sent away. She could hide the conspirator's
body in the stables and leave his horse for John.

But first she would have to kill him. Her insides were
churning just at the thought. One step at a time, Laura, she
told herself firmly. Before you can kill him, you'll have to get
him down from that horse.

The gates. She could close the gates; he would have to
dismount to open them. Bending low, she darted out from
the shrubbery and tugged at the iron bars. Then she snapped
down the latch and crept back into the bushes, waiting for
her prey to arrive.

It seemed to take him forever to climb that hill. Laura
never would have believed a horse could gallop and still go
so slow. Crouching in the darkness, she tried to steel herself
for what was to come. The man on the horse wasn't just a
brute like Valotte. He was a traitor. He was in league with
Thomas. Surely that meant he deserved to die.

The hoofbeats stopped halfway up the road. Laura
pushed aside a leafless branch and saw the rider was just
sitting, bundled head to toe against the bitter weather. He
started the horse forward again, then stopped it, tugging at
the reins. She heard a rustle of clothing, a pause, and then
another sound—the pop of a cork. The stout swaddled figure pulled a bottle from beneath his cloak and drained its
contents. Then he let out a belch. He nodded, seeming to
reach a decision, and rode on.

Laura ducked back into the bushes. He reached the gates;
she heard the whining creak of leather as he slid down from
the horse, pitching the empty bottle into the shrubbery right
at her feet.

God, give me strength, she prayed as, stumbling a little,
he groped for the gate latch. She darted forward from the
bushes, the point of the dagger aimed straight between the
man's shoulder blades. But her foot had hit the bottle he'd
thrown; it made a small clink, and he turned toward her. She
saw his flushed face, and, in the moonlight, his eyes, blood-
shot but still glowing gold. Her indrawn breath escaped in a
rush.

"Laura?" her half brother Humphrey said.

"My God," she whispered, still aiming the dagger. "My
God in heaven, so you've come to this. It wasn't enough for

you to betray my father—now you're betraying your country too!"

He blinked at her and let out a hiccup. "Aw, come on, little shis—little sister. Don't you start on me too. Blench—Blatch—Blanche does enough of that. I don't need—" He stopped, looking vaguely at his horse and then back at her. "Do you know what I do need?" he asked brightly. "Another drink. Wouldn't happen to have a bit of ale on you, would you?"

Laura shook her head. "I ought to put this knife straight through your heart."

"Well, why don't you then?" said Humphrey, and sat down heavily on the road. "Go on. You'll only be doing me a favor. No doubt Blanche would be grateful too."

His hat had fallen off; Laura stared down and saw that the bald spot atop his head had gotten much bigger. "Oh, Humphrey." She picked the hat up for him. "How drunk are you?"

"Don't know," he said morosely. "Been trying to get up my nerve for this kidnapping thing. Chances are I won't even feel the knife. Why not get it over with? Here." He fumbled with the front of his cloak. "I'll make it easy. Go on."

For the second time, Laura's intended murder victim was offering himself to her. And for the second time, she knew she couldn't go through with it. "Oh, Humphrey," she said again. "How in heaven's name did you ever get mixed up in this?"

"Blen— Blanche. She volun—hic!—volunteered me."

"But why did you agree?"

His watery gold eyes were accusing. "Oh, well. That's easy for you to say. You can laugh at the chance to make ten thousand pounds. You're not a—a no-good drunk and a bo-bo-bogus baron. That's what Blanche calls me and that's what I am. But you've had it all easy, haven't you? It's all been easy for you." Still hiccupping softly, he began to cry.

Laura didn't know whether to join him or to laugh. "It hasn't been so easy as all that," she said with a sigh. "Would you mind telling me what Thomas is going to do?"

"Go to Hatfield House. Kidnap the princess. What else?"

"And then what?"

"Take her to the Tower. King Philip is going to keep her there until Mary dies and then m-marry her." He shook his head in wonder. "Can't imagine any man wanting another wife when he's managed to get rid of one."

"Who else is in there?" Laura demanded, nodding toward the house.

"Don't know. Even Guilford doesn't know. That little foreign fellow, Feria—he rounded 'em up. Guilford only took me on as a favor to Blanche."

"Since when does Thomas Guilford do favors for Blanche?"

"Since she—hic!—started doing favors for him. He brings—brings men by. You know. Feria came. And that bishop. Bonner. And God knows who else."

"My Lord." Laura stared at his shamed face. "You mean she—"

"Don't. Don't say it." He clapped his hands to his ears. "Why shouldn't she? I'm no good that way or for anything else."

Laura tugged his cloak closed. "Button up before you catch the ague. What time were you supposed to get to Hatfield House?"

"Midnight."

Midnight—that was just like Thomas. At least it gave her time to get back and warn Elizabeth. But what was she to do with Humphrey? He couldn't ride. He couldn't even stand. She looked at him again, judging the extent of his inebriation with a practiced eye. More drunk than she ever had seen him. If she didn't move him while she could, he'd pass out right there on the cobblestones. And she had to get his horse into the courtyard for John to ride.

She yanked his arm, trying to get him upright. "Come along, Humphrey."

"Where—where are we going?"

"Somewhere there's more ale to be had," she lied.

He looked up with interest, trying to bring her face into focus. "You don't shay. Well, then, lead on!"

Combining cajolery and sheer force, she managed to pull first Humphrey and then his horse into the yards. The horse she tied with the others; Humphrey she dragged to the stable doors. "Here we are!" she said cheerily, pushing him through. He stumbled facedown in a pile of straw, sending a pitchfork teetering. Laura leaped and just barely caught it before it crashed to the ground.

"You'll be all right here, Humphrey, won't you, while I fetch you some ale?" She leaned over his immobile body.

The only answer was a wheezing snore. Once he fell asleep, he'd stay asleep for hours, she knew.

She lifted his booted feet over the threshold, closing the doors, barring them from the outside. There was still no sign of life or movement in the darkened house. She looked up at the sky. There was Polaris, sparkling high and bright in the heavens. "Just once," she muttered as she slipped through the gate to reclaim her horse, brushing straw and briars from her cloak, "just once I should like to arrive at Hatfield House without looking a mess!"

Chapter 26

The soldiers on duty at Hatfield House paid scant attention to Laura's disheveled appearance when she arrived at the gatehouse; they were in great high spirits, laughing and jesting with one another, letting loose a stream of hoots and catcalls as their leader let her pass into the yard. Laura, intent on her mission, ignored their raucous shouts as she hurried into the house, though the thought did cross her mind that since Cardinal Pole had sent them they were likely aware of what was to take place that night.

Hannay and Talbot were pacing back and forth in the front hall, and they did notice the briars and straw that clung to Laura's cloak and hair. "Where on earth have you been?" Hannay cried, running to embrace Laura. "Where is John? Has there been an accident?"

"Didn't Polly get here and give Guy our message?" Laura asked in surprise.

"She got here," Talbot said grimly. "But she's been in tears ever since she arrived. The soldiers out front were teasing her and calling her names. They're in a queer mood this evening, that's sure." He looked again at Laura's worried expression. "Is something wrong?"

"Something's very wrong. Where is Elizabeth?"

"In her room, playing chess with Englefield," Hannay told her.

"Damn." Laura chewed her lip. "Hannay, can you manage to tell her, without alarming Englefield, that I have to talk to her right away? I'd best go see Polly."

Hannay hurried off, and Talbot went with Laura to her chambers, where she found the twins sleeping soundly and Polly in a terrible state. "Oh, missy," she blubbered, wringing her hands, "I ain't never been so scared in all my life! Those soldiers was all over me, pinchin' and pullin' my hair, callin' me names—why, the Lord only knows what would've become of me if this here gentleman hadn't come to my aid!"

She blinked back her tears and nodded tremulously toward Guy, who was hovering solicitously over her.

"Polly, I am sorry you were frightened," Laura told her. "But didn't you give the gentleman the message we asked you to?"

Polly cowered in her chair. "Land sakes, missy, I clean forgot, what with those men mishandlin' me. I'm sorry, missy! Please don't tell Master Thomas or he'll whip my hide!"

"Whip you?" Guy frowned at the yellow-haired cook. "What are you talking about?"

"Polly works for John's brother, Thomas," Laura explained. "He mistreats her terribly."

"Good God, woman," Guy growled, "why do you stay with him?"

"Because," Polly wailed, "I ain't got no place else to go! I'm no good fer nothin', there's the plain truth of it."

"Hush, woman!" said Guy, so fiercely that Polly, astonished, stopped crying. "Don't ever let anyone tell you that. Every one of us had a reason why we were put here on earth."

"I'm sure I don't know what mine might be," Polly said dubiously.

Guy reached down to touch one of the cook's yellow braids. "Perhaps," he said, with an odd tenderness in his French-shaded voice, "to remind the world in the dead of winter of the bright summer sun." Laura just had time to register the shy, surprised look in Polly's dark eyes before Hannay rushed into the room.

"Laura, I did just what you told me. I brought Elizabeth and Englefield wine," she said, "and spilled some on him while I poured. Then when he went to dry himself off, I gave your message to Elizabeth. But she only said she would come by and by."

"Oh, for glory's sake!" Inwardly Laura cursed the princess's Tudor intransigence. "I'll go get her myself. Where is Alain?"

"In the kitchens," said Guy. "Flirting with Doris."

"Would you fetch him, Guy? I don't want to explain all of this more than once."

Guy looked down at still-shaken Polly and then at Talbot. *"Mon ami—"*

"Right," said Talbot. "I'll go."

Laura tiptoed down the hallway to Elizabeth's doorway.

From the room within she heard Francis Englefield boom
out, in the voice Elizabeth mimicked so well, "Your move,
milady."

Elizabeth's reply was cool and serene as a bell. "King's
knight to bishop three—is that the king's bishop's gambit
you're playing, Sir Francis?"

There was a moment of silence. Then, "I'm not familiar
with that sequence," Englefield said.

"Really. I thought you must be from the moves you are
making. 'Tis an exceedingly risky opening, for it leaves the
knights exposed. Your play."

Laura peeked into the room and saw Englefield sitting
with his beefy back to her, while Elizabeth, facing the doorway, refilled their wine cups. As Englefield leaned over to
peer at the board, Laura waved frantically to the princess.
Elizabeth glanced up briefly, black eyes sparkling, and gave a
tiny shake of her head.

Laura shook a fist at her. The princess turned her attention back to the board.

Englefield made his move, nodding in satisfaction. Elizabeth's lovely hand hovered over the pieces like a humming-
bird choosing a flower. Then her slender fingers wrapped
around a pawn and pushed it forward. "I warned you, Sir
Francis," she said softly. "I have your knight *en prise.*"

"Aha!" Englefield boomed, chuckling as he seized his
queen and galloped it across the squares. "But I have your
castle! You left it unguarded!"

Elizabeth's black eyes narrowed very slightly. "As unguarded, Sir Francis, as the king left Calais?" Her own queen
rose in the air and settled down again. "Check," she told
him, and added, as he sputtered in surprise, "actually,
checkmate. Did you know, that word comes from the Persian. *Shah mat.* It means 'The king is dead.' "

Sir Francis Englefield raised his big head and stared at
her. Elizabeth smiled enchantingly. "And now that our little
match is finished, I'll bid you good night."

The knight pushed back his chair with an angry scrape.
"Good night, milady." Laura ducked back into the shadowy
hall. Elizabeth's serene voice floated out to her:

"Sir Francis! Does King Philip play chess?"

"I don't think so, milady."

"Pity," said Elizabeth. "Sometime I should like to match
wits with him." She closed her bedchamber door in the fat
knight's face. Sir Francis contemplated the length of wood in

front of him, muttered something beneath his breath, and waddled off downstairs.

He'd barely reached the landing before Laura darted for Elizabeth's door. It opened before she could knock; the princess motioned her inside. "Sorry to have kept you waiting," she apologized blithely, "but you know I hate to leave a game unfinished."

"That silly game may have cost you your life!" Laura exclaimed. "Thomas Guilford is on his way here with a dozen men to kidnap you and take you to the Tower, so that King Philip can force you to marry him after Queen Mary dies!"

"And I suppose," Elizabeth said calmly, "that Sir Francis is here to open the gates to them."

"Englefield must be here to open the—" Laura paused. "You certainly don't seemed surprised."

"Well, it was obvious my brother-in-law and his bishops were up to something. Though for sheer harebrainedness, this takes the cake. No, on second thought the plot to steal your baby for Mary— Oh, it really is hard to decide, isn't it, which is more—"

"Elizabeth," Laura broke in urgently, "you have to get away from here!"

"Of course I must. But I wasn't about to make Sir Francis suspicious by interrupting our game. By the by, where is John?"

"He's one of the conspirators," Laura said absently, wracking her brain for a ruse to get the princess away.

Elizabeth arched a thin red brow. "Really?"

"Oh, I don't mean—" Hastily Laura explained what had happened that night at Guilford Hall. Elizabeth listened closely, then headed for the corridor.

"Let's go and talk to the others," she said. "We've less than an hour 'til midnight. We need a plan!"

Even in such trying circumstances, Elizabeth displayed the Tudor touch for making friends. She noticed Polly as she entered Laura's rooms, realized that the tearful woman had not been presented to her, and insisted on taking care of that before anything else. "Why are you crying, Mistress Vaughan?" she asked after Laura had made introductions.

"The guards at the gate were bothering her, milady," Guy explained. "Making rude remarks about her hair."

Elizabeth touched her own fiery red curls. "I've been called everything from 'Carrot-Top' to 'Madder-Head' in my time, Mistress Vaughan. For what it's worth, I think your hair is lovely."

"That's what I told her, too," said Guy.

"Th-thank ye kindly, mum," Polly mumbled, fingering her long braids with an uncertain smile. As she straightened from her curtsy, Laura was struck by the fact that the cook and the princess were very nearly of a size.

She looked slowly from one to the other, then said thoughtfully, "Polly, would you be willing to make a very great sacrifice, if I told you it might save the princess's life?"

Polly's dark eyes widened. "I don't know, missy. Would it get me in trouble with Master Thomas?"

Elizabeth, following Laura's gaze, stifled a laugh. "I'm afraid it would."

"What do you need that bully of a master for?" Guy de Carteret demanded gruffly. "I'll give you a post if that's what you need. You can work for me."

Polly looked up at the burly Guernseyman. He smiled at her, and his smile broke the bonds of a lifetime. "Well—all right," she said timidly.

"Hannay," said Laura, "fetch the scissors from the sewing basket, if you please."

Twenty minutes later, a small pony cart rolled out of the stables of Hatfield House and across the yards to the gate. "Halt!" cried one of Cardinal Pole's guards, brandishing his sword beneath the driver's nose. "Where d'ye think ye're goin'?"

"That's one of 'em, missy," said a small, timid voice from the bed of the cart. "That's one of 'em what was talkin' dirty to me."

Laura, clutching Paul in her arms, pushed back her hood and confronted the guard. "Sir," she said frostily, "what have you to say for yourself?"

"About what?" he demanded. Laura's companion in the cart bed began to blubber, hiding her face against blanket-wrapped baby Elizabeth until all one could see were the long butter-yellow braids that hung from her cap.

Laura tucked a protective arm around her, glaring at the soldier. "My maid tells me you and your men were making sport of her earlier this evening. Is this true?"

"I don't know what she's talkin' about."

"Oh, missy, he's lyin'!" the yellow-haired woman sobbed.

"Polly, are you sure this was one of the men? Take a good look at him," Laura urged.

The woman beside her peeked at the menacing guard with wide, frightened dark eyes and then buried her face again. "Aye, aye, missy, that's one," she moaned, nodding so her blond braids wagged.

"What's your name, soldier?" Laura demanded.

"What's that to ye?" he countered belligerently.

"I intend to report your impudent behavior to my good friend, Sir Francis Englefield," Laura said.

"What's the problem here, Mack?" another soldier asked, coming to join them.

"Oh, Lordy, missy," the woman with the braids wailed, "there's another of 'em!"

"'Tis that yellow-headed wench," Mack muttered to his cohort, "that we was jesting at."

"So you admit it!" Laura said triumphantly. "Alain, turn the cart about. I'm reporting these men to Sir Francis immediately."

Alain obediently clucked his tongue at the pony. The second soldier caught the reins. "Hold on just a minute, mum. Let's not be hasty here."

Laura gestured to the blubbering blond. "You and your men frightened my poor Polly out of her wits!"

"Well, now, mum, ye knows how men can be sometimes. We didn't mean no harm by the teasin'—"

The yellow-haired woman raised her face from the blankets long enough to blurt, "Teasin'! Teasin', he calls it!" Then she burst into tears again.

"That settles it," Laura declared. "Turn the cart about, Alain."

"Hold on, hold on," said the soldier, still clutching the reins. "How would it be, mum, if we apologized to her?"

"You will have to ask Polly," Laura told him archly.

The soldier sidled along the cart to make a direct appeal. "What do ye say now, lass? We didn't mean no harm, honestly we didn't." The only answer was another outburst of sobs. "Fer Christ's sake, lass," the soldier said, "don't put us in hot water with that bloody Sir Francis; he'll dock our wages! Ye're a workin' girl yerself; ye know how that goes!"

"Polly," Laura prompted, "will an apology suffice?" The yellow-haired woman nodded hesitantly. "Very well," Laura told the soldier. "Tell her you are sorry."

"Oh, we're sorry all right," the man said hurriedly. "Ain't

we, Mack?" Mack, glowering, said nothing. "Ain't we, Mack?" his mate repeated, elbowing him in the ribs.

"Aye," Mack grunted at last.

Laura beamed at the men. "There, now, Polly, don't you feel better? If you two fine fellows will just open up those gates, we'll be on our way."

"And jest where d'ye think ye're goin'?" the recalcitrant Mack demanded.

"To meet my husband in Hertford," Laura told him.

"Have ye got permission from Sir Francis?"

"I didn't know I needed it."

"Well, ye does. We've got orders not to let nobody out of these gates tonight."

"If you insist," Laura said somewhat peevishly, "I shall go and talk to Sir Francis. And while I'm at it, I think I will mention your treatment of Polly. I know your name is Mack, but I didn't catch your friend's name."

The other soldier had thrown open the gates. "Jest call me accommodatin', mum. Fare ye well!"

"Alain," said Laura, settling back down in the cart, "drive on."

Inside Elizabeth Tudor's chambers at Hatfield House, Hannay turned down the linens on the testered bed. "Do you prefer the bed drapes open or closed?" she asked the tall, slim figure who stood before the looking-glass, adjusting her nightcap.

"Lordy," the woman at the mirror whispered, "I don't know. I ain't never slept in no bed with no hangings before."

"Open, then," said Hannay, and helped her climb up on the mattress. "Sleep well, milady." She fluffed the pillows up around the trembling bait.

"Lordy," the woman muttered, the voluminous bed-clothes billowing around her, "I won't sleep a wink!"

Hannay patted her shoulder, blew out the bedside candles, and left the room, quietly closing the door.

In the hallway she nearly collided with the corpulent chest of Sir Francis Englefield. *"Mon Dieu,"* she gasped, hand at her heart, "you gave me a start!"

"Did I now?" Englefield leered at the lovely Guernsey-woman. "I can think of a few things I'd rather give you!" He reached to pinch her, then remembered his mission. "Drat. I've got to see the Lady Elizabeth."

"She's already retired," Hannay said primly. Englefield

pushed her aside, moving toward the bedchamber door. "Sir, you can't go in there," Hannay insisted, trying to hold him back. "She's asleep! She can't see you now."

Englefield yanked open the door and stared at the night-capped woman who lay curled in the bed with her back to him. "Didn't say she had to see me, did I?" he asked, and grunted in satisfaction as he shut the door again. "I only said I had to see her."

Chapter 27

In the courtyard beneath the dark towers and spires of Guilford Hall, twelve men clad in black silk hoods paced across the bricks to their horses. Two of the men, both very tall, both broad-shouldered, were in the rear of the procession. While the rest claimed their mounts, one of them bent and fumbled with his right boot strap. "You're limping, my good man," Thomas Guilford observed of the kneeling conspirator.

"Hrmph, yas. Old war wound," John said in his North Country drawl. "This cold weather makes it act up a bit."

"I hope you won't slow us down," Thomas said sharply.

"No, no. No need to worry about that." John looked up through the slits in his hood. All of the horses had been taken but two, one of which was his brother's big bay. He straightened from his crouch and strode over to the slightly spavined gray mare that remained. Until he saw the horse, he was not at all sure how Laura had handled the situation he'd been forced to leave her with. Now he knew: she had killed the last conspirator.

He swung up into the saddle and grasped the reins. The gray mare, unaccustomed to the hand that now controlled her, whinnied in protest. John yanked the reins, drawing up the bit as the hooded men turned to him. "Keep that nag quiet, for Christ's sake," someone ordered.

"Hrmph! Sorry. This hood must have spooked her." Whoever had owned the mare had the shortest legs in Christendom, John thought; the stirrups were at his knees. He adjusted them quickly, taking a certain grim comfort in the fact, hoping Laura had had an easier time dealing with so diminutive a foe. He'd meant to dispatch the latecomer himself once he seized the hood from the doorstep, but Thomas's sudden reappearance had ruined his plan. At least she had my dagger, he thought, and hoped desperately she would forgive him for leaving her with such a horrible task.

Thomas spurred his magnificent bay through the open gates. "Gentlemen!" He flourished his sword, relishing the high drama of the moment. "We go to make history!"

From the direction of the stables, John's keen ears detected a rustling of straw and a rumble of snores. He covered the sound in a loud fit of coughing, doubled over in his saddle. The conspirators whipped to face him accusingly. "Hrmph! Touch of ague," he apologized. So Laura hadn't killed the last conspirator after all . . .

"Jesus," one of his companions muttered, "there's always one, isn't there?"

"You don't have to have brains to want to be rich," said Thomas, glaring back at the North Countryman.

In neat double file, except for the North Countryman, who was having trouble with his saddle and lagged behind, the king's men rode north to Hatfield House along the moonlit road.

In a pony cart four miles down the same road, an argument had flared up. "Absolutely not!" Laura said sharply.

"But, Laura," Elizabeth Tudor argued, "it only makes sense!"

"There must be twenty manors within ten miles of here. Pick another one. Any one but Guilford Hall," Laura pleaded.

"And run the risk that manor's master is riding with Thomas? No, thank you!" Elizabeth said vehemently. "Humphrey told you they were going to take me to London. Guilford Hall is just sitting there empty. We'll be perfectly safe."

"Guilford Hall is built on bad rock."

"Oh, for glory's sake." Elizabeth yanked so hard on one of her borrowed braids that she pulled it right out of her cap. "Don't tell me you actually believe those silly Guernsey folktales Guy tells."

"Whether I do or not, that house is evil," Laura insisted.

"Laura, please. It is absolutely freezing out here! Alain, just drive straight on."

"Alain, don't!" Laura cried.

"Laura Darby," Elizabeth said impatiently, "if you trust me to be queen, you might also trust me to decide where to spend the night. Unless you can come up with some better reason not to go to Guilford Hall than that it is made of bad rock, I am going there. I've always wanted to see John's observatory. And his library is there. We can read together to pass the hours. Maybe that will calm your nerves."

Laura nibbled her lip.

"Well?" said the princess.

Baby Elizabeth began to cry.

"Oh, all right," Laura said reluctantly. The house was empty. And it *was* too cold to argue; Paul's teeth were chattering.

Alain clucked his tongue at the pony, and the cart rattled on through silence punctuated only by little Elizabeth's occasional wails of "Bwah-ah!"

They had just reached a bend in the road when Alain yanked the reins, halting the cart so suddenly that both women lurched forward. "What now? Evil spirits?" Elizabeth demanded crossly.

"*Écoutez.*" The winter wind carried the distant thunder of horses' hooves.

"The conspirators!" Laura whispered. "I knew we shouldn't have come this way!"

"Everything will be fine," Elizabeth assured her. "Alain, get the cart off the road and into the woods."

The boy obediently steered the pony over the berm and through a break in the trees, then hopped down and threw his jacket over the animal's muzzle to keep it from shying when the horses went by. The jolting ride through the woods had further enraged baby Elizabeth. "Give her to me," Laura said, reaching for her daughter, "and you take Apollo; he won't fuss." But before they could complete the exchange, the first of the horsemen appeared on the road. Laura froze. Elizabeth the elder held Elizabeth the younger dangling in the air.

Elizabeth the younger did not care for being dangled. "Bwah-ah!" she screamed, then gathered in all her breath and screamed it again.

The horseman hauled his fine bay to a stop, hooded head cocked, and stared into the trees. Laura grabbed her irate daughter and tried to silence her against her breast. A second horseman, this one on a spavined gray mare, rode up beside the first. "Hell's bells," he shouted in rich North Country tones, waving his crop, "did you hear it? Did you hear it?"

"I heard it all right," said the first man, and Laura shivered as she recognized Thomas's voice. "And I intend to find out what it is."

"What it is?" his companion cried excitedly. "I'll tell you

what it is—a yellow-bellied red marsh plover!"

"A what?" Thomas demanded, hooded head swiveling.

"A yellow-bellied red marsh plover," the man on the gray mare repeated. "And jolly well south of its usual range. Sounds just like a baby crying, don't it?" And he raised his head and bawled through his black hood, "Bwah-ah! Bwah-ah!"

"Bwah-ah!" came a slightly muffled wail from the bushes.

The rest of the conspirators galloped up to them. "What in hell's going on here?" someone asked in bewilderment.

"The king's sent a bloody birdwatcher along with us," Thomas said in disgust. "Let's go."

"Go?" The man on the mare started down from his saddle. "What, are you mad, and miss a yellow-bellied red marsh plover? This is a once in a lifetime chance!"

Thomas hauled him back by his collar. "You've a once in a lifetime chance to earn ten thousand pounds this night, you bloody fool. Now come on."

"Oh, very well," the North Countryman said reluctantly. "Bwah-ah! Bwah-ah!" he called one more time, and followed as Thomas cantered away.

The drumming hoofbeats of the twelve horses faded into silence. Laura kissed her indignant daughter. "There, lovey. There, there."

Elizabeth Tudor pulled the hem of the skirt she'd been biting on out of her mouth, and her laughter erupted. "Yellow-bellied red marsh plover— Laura, was that John?"

"I'm afraid so." She let out a giggle, and Alain snorted as he climbed back into the driver's seat.

"Bwah-ah!" said baby Elizabeth.

The rest of the journey to Guilford Hall was blessedly uneventful. The cart reached the yards just as a distant church bell pealed twelve long strokes. Elizabeth turned and stared at the lights that flickered in the valley below them, like far-off stars. "They'll be there by now," she said, almost to herself. "I wonder what is happening."

"We will hear soon enough," Laura told her. "John knows that was Elizabeth crying. He'll come and tell us as soon as he can." That realization helped to ease the qualms she felt about entering Guilford Hall again; she smiled and handed her daughter to Alain. "I've got to check on Humphrey out in the stable; he'll freeze to death in this cold. Why don't you two take the twins inside? There ought to be a lantern on the table to your right, Alain, just inside the doors."

Faint snores were still issuing from the stable. Laura pushed up the bar and peered in, calling Humphrey's name. When there was no response she entered, kneeling beside her sleeping brother. "Humphrey, get up and come into the house," she said, shaking his shoulder.

He stirred slightly and mumbled, "Leave me alone, Blanche."

"Humphrey, it's Laura!" She shook him again, and his heavy arm came up, shoving her backward.

"I said leave me alone!"

Laura picked herself up from the floor, dusting straw from her skirts. "All right for you, then." She pulled off her cloak and laid it over him. "Stay here in the cold if you like."

He rolled onto his side, bundling the cloak to his chest. "Wish I'd never met you, Blanche," he muttered. "Wish I'd never listened to you." He let out a beery sigh and recommenced to snore.

Laura left him there, with the door unbarred in case he did awaken. Then, shivering in only her dress, she ran across the courtyard to the house. The front doors were standing wide open. That's odd, she thought, hurrying to shut them behind her against the winter wind.

The hallway inside was utterly dark. "Alain?" she called, and heard her voice bounce up from the marble floor. "Elizabeth! Where are you?"

The echoes died slowly around her. In the remaining silence she heard only the steady pulse of her heart. "Elizabeth!" she called again, inwardly bemoaning the princess's puckish sense of humor. "This is hardly the time or the place to play games!"

Nothing, not even a giggle. As though the house swallowed them up, she thought, and then wished she hadn't. She groped for the lantern, wondering if Alain had somehow missed it, but the table was empty. Around her, above the sound of her own heart, beating more quickly now, she imagined she heard another deep, low throbbing: the pulse of the house, demonic and malevolent.

Stop it, Laura! she told herself sharply, regretting having admitted to the princess that this place made her afraid. "Dammit, where are you hiding?" she called into the inky darkness. "I don't think this is a bit amusing, I honestly don't!"

From the top of the wide marble staircase at the end of the hall she saw a flicker of light, heard a whisper of laughter. Exasperated, she gathered up her skirts and chased after it, across the smooth floor and up the stairs, only to see the light dance away down a corridor. "Please, Elizabeth," she pleaded. The light disappeared ahead of her, turning a corner. Laura followed it reluctantly, already losing her bearings in the dark, twisting hallways. Like a tiny firefly, the lantern light flew up a staircase and darted down another hall.

The swift pursuit was making Laura breathless. She paused, leaning against a table, feeling its intricate mosaic top beneath her fingertips. The light ahead of her stopped, wavered, and again she heard the high-pitched giggle. "Now look here, Elizabeth Tudor," she cried, starting out again, "you are not queen yet, you know. And if it wasn't for John and me, you'd be getting kidnapped out of your bed tonight. So let's end this nonsense right now and unhood that lantern!"

For answer the little gleam of light bobbed up another flight of stairs. Swearing beneath her breath, Laura hurried after it.

By now she was thoroughly disoriented. At first she'd though Elizabeth was heading toward the west tower; then she imagined they were climbing up to the east one instead. But as the dancing point of light spun off to her right, Laura remembered the princess had never been to the house; she and Alain must be wandering aimlessly.

She stopped where she stood and heard the silence close around her. "Please, Elizabeth," she called breathlessly, "please unhood the lantern. The twins must be starving; you are not being fair to them."

Out of the thick blackness ahead came the groan of a door as it opened, then closed. Then there was silence, and then a small scuffling noise. At long last Elizabeth answered, her voice sounding strange, strangled with laughter. "In here, Laura!" she cried.

"Well, you certainly led me a merry May dance," Laura said angrily, heading down the corridor. There was another sound, of the lantern shades being drawn back, and a thin crack of light appeared ahead. The bottom of a door—but which door? She ran toward it, finding the latch and pushing it open, ready to give the future queen of England a furious scold.

She stopped, blinded for a moment by the lantern that shone like a sun beneath a great expanse of stars. "The ob-

servatory," she exclaimed, looking up, admiring Polaris and
Casseopeia and the Bears. "How did you ever manage to
find it? Lord in heaven, 'tis a beautiful night."

"Beautiful," agreed a voice, high-pitched, reedy—male.
Laura's spine went rigid. Her startled gaze fell from the stars
to the platform in the center of the room.

"Theodore," she breathed, seeing the lantern light glint in
his strange green eyes.

He smiled slowly, waving her toward the two bound and
gagged figures on the floor behind him. "Come and join your
friends."

She whirled for the door instead. Theodore laughed his
thin, high laugh, and she heard another voice, even higher,
cry out, "Bwah-ah!"

She spun back, her heart leaping into her throat. The
glow of the lantern caught the gleaming edge of the knife
Theo held against her daughter's chest.

"It's up to you, of course," Theodore went on, still grinning. "But for old times' sake, I'll give you just one more
chance. Are you absolutely sure you won't join your
friends?"

Thomas Guilford could not have been more pleased at
how smoothly his plan to abduct Elizabeth Tudor was pro-
gressing—except, of course, for the idiotic bird-calling buf-
foon King Philip had stuck him with. Precisely according to
schedule, Francis Englefield was waiting at the gates to Hatfield House at twelve. The one dozen riders were promptly
admitted, while the guards sent by Cardinal Pole saluted
them. Thomas was smiling beneath his hood as he dismounted and handed his bay's reins to one of the soldiers.
"Any trouble?" he barked at Englefield.

The fat Master of the Court of Wards was sweating nervously despite the frigid weather. He shook his head. "She's
fast asleep in her bed. This way."

The bird-calling North Countryman was once more having trouble with his saddle. While he fumbled with cinches
and straps, Englefield led the rest of the party into the entrance hall and up the stairs to the princess's chambers. Having successfully dismounted at last, the North Countryman
limped after them, pausing in the dim-lit hall to shout,
"Hallo! Hallo! Where is everyone?"

Thomas's hooded head appeared at the top of the stairway. "Shut your frigging mouth, you ass," he said softly but distinctly, "and get the hell up here."

"Well, I never!" the North Countryman huffed indignantly, mounting the stairs.

"Neither have I," Thomas muttered. "Neither have I."

Englefield paused at the door to Elizabeth's bedchamber. "You don't need me for this part." He gulped, mopping sweat from his brow. "I'll just go back down and—and see to the horses, shall I?"

"Get out of the way, idiot." Thomas shoved him aside, and the knight scurried for the stairs. Grabbing a torch from a hallway sconce, Thomas tested the latch and pushed the door open silently.

The hooded conspirators crowded in behind him as the torchlight fell across the high carved bed, the snowy linens, and the tall, slim figure in a white nightcap who lay curled quietly with her back to them.

Thomas nodded in satisfaction. The linen hangings stirred gently as he entered the room. One by one the conspirators followed. The tall North Countryman was last; as he entered he shut the door behind him smoothly, silently.

Pale eyes glittering through the slits in his mask, Thomas leaned over the bed.

"Time to wake up, milady," he said.

"Why?" Laura whispered, slowly crossing the richly patterned floor of the observatory.

Theo giggled, the dagger still tickling baby Elizabeth's rib cage. "Why what, Mistress Laura?"

"Why are you doing this? What do you want?"

For an instant the smirk slipped from his thin face, and she saw his awful, naked suffering plain in its place. "As if you didn't know," he told her, voice trembling. "As if you didn't know what you've done!"

"If you mean Thomas, Theo," she said softly, still advancing, "you must know I never wanted to wed him. I tried time and again to get away from him—"

"Then why did you come back here?" he shouted, brandishing the dagger. "What are you doing here?"

Laura stopped. Breathing heavily, Theodore pushed his lank blond hair back from his forehead. "Ever since you came here," he whispered, "nothing has been the same. We used to be . . . so happy together, before you came."

"It can be that way for you again, Theo," Laura promised. "Just let all of us go, and I swear, I'll never come here. You can have Thomas all to yourself—"

He was shaking his head over and over again. "Too late. Too late for that now," he murmured.

"You mustn't say that, Theo. It is never too late."

"I tell you it is!" he screeched. "You came here and you changed him. He doesn't want me anymore. I begged him to tell me what he was planning for tonight." Tears streamed down his face. "I begged him on my knees! Do you know what he said?" His spectral face contorted in a sob. "He said, 'Get up, you bloody old fairy.' He called me—an embarrassment."

"Oh, Theo." Despite her desperate fear, Laura's heart went out to Thomas's spurned lover. "Oh, Theo, I am sorry." She took a step toward him.

Instantly the knife jerked in his hand, and a small blotch of crimson stained baby Elizabeth's blankets. "Are you pitying me?" Theo snarled. "Are *you* pitying *me*?"

The sight of her daughter's blood had driven any such thoughts clear out of Laura's head. "No, you despicable creature," she said in fury. "Put my daughter down."

He complied, setting the child atop the princess's tangled skirts beside Paul, who was watching his mother with a steady blue stare. "Why did you come back here?" Laura demanded, even as she remembered her own dagger, the one John had given her, which was still tucked into her boot. "To beg Thomas again?"

"I'm all through with begging," Theo said proudly. "I came back to tell Thomas that. But now . . . now I've got a better idea."

"And what might that be?" Laura asked, trying not to stare at the knife he held.

"Thomas wanted the Princess Elizabeth." Theodore's snake's eyes were narrowed. "He thought I didn't know what he was up to, but I listened. I know. And now I've got her." His grin was a horrid thing, rigid as a death mask. "I've got her," he repeated, "and I think Thomas will be very pleased with me. So if you'll just come over here, I'll tie you up nice and tight, and we'll wait for him." For an instant he turned the grin on Elizabeth Tudor.

In that space, that heartbeat, Laura yanked out her dagger and sprang, knowing this time she would find the strength of purpose she'd lacked before. Nonetheless, as she closed in, as Theo, starting in surprise, turned back, as the dagger point pierced his doublet and shirt and hit flesh, she could not help clenching her eyes. She pushed the knife harder, feeling it plunge with astonishing ease deep into his body, not stopping until the hilt rammed home. She heard him gasp, staggering back against the platform railing.

"Bitch," he cried, clutching the end of the blade protruding from his ribs. Blood welled up over his fingers. "Filthy bitch, you've killed me!"

"I hope so," said Laura with infinite calm.

He came at her, snarling, spitting, swinging. He was amazingly strong for so thin a man; his first wild blow knocked Laura to her knees. He followed with a vicious kick to her head that landed just below her ear.

High above the glass dome, the stars went spinning in crazy circles, exploding against each other in bursts of white flame as she crumpled to the floor.

"Do you remember how your father died, little Mistress Laura?"

Theodore was looming over her, blocking out the night sky, but still she could see those mad stars careening past her eyes.

"Good night, Mistress Laura," Theodore whispered.

And then the sky went black.

Chapter 28

"Milady Elizabeth," Thomas Guilford said more sharply, leaning over the princess's bed. Remarkably enough, the woman lying there was sound asleep. Thomas called her again, shaking her by the shoulder.

"What the—" Polly Vaughan started, stretched, and turned. The nightcap slipped back from her new-shorn curls as she sat up in bed, facing her master, light from the torch he held playing over her terrified face as she saw the band of hooded men.

There was a moment of silence. Thomas stared at her, uncomprehending. "Polly . . ." He whirled around. "What the devil's going on here? Englefield!" he roared, starting for the door.

His path was blocked by a tall, broad-shouldered man. "Good evening, brother," said John, dropping the bumpkin accent. "The bird has already flown the coop."

"John," said Thomas, a lifetime of loathing seething in the name.

"At your service," said John, and swept off his hood.

Thomas went for his sword.

"What's going on here?" one of the conspirators demanded, looking from John to Thomas, and then to Polly. "That ain't the princess, is it?"

Thomas ignored him, pale milky eyes never leaving his brother's face. "There are eleven of us to one of you," he spat out.

"So there are," John conceded, fist on the hilt of his own blade. "If you all take me on at once, a few might still be alive at the end. But I don't think it likely—not if King Philip needed a dozen of you to abduct one sleeping woman."

He could almost see the workings of his brother's mind behind those colorless eyes, knew what he would do next, but the distance from the doorway was too far to stop him. Thomas whirled to the bed, yanking ashen-faced Polly from

364

under the covers, putting his sword to her throat. "You've played your little trick on us, brother," he growled, holding Polly in front of him as a shield. "But it's over now. We're getting out of here."

"It's not over yet." The deep French-inflected voice came from the shadowy hangings behind the bed. Guy de Carteret reached out and wrenched Thomas's sword from his hand, then pulled Polly to safety behind him. "What do you say now, Guilford, when it is eleven to two?"

"Four," Talbot corrected him, emerging from the window curtains with Father Burton at his side. Their gentle faces were suffused with wrath.

"And the angels," Father Burton added, eyeing the black-hooded men, "are surely on our side."

Thomas gripped the dagger he had stuck in his belt. "Come on," he exhorted the conspirators. "Look at the odds! Better than three to one!"

His companions were singularly silent, sizing up John, burly, bearded Guy, the avenging priests. "I—I don't know," one said at last, rather timidly. "It sure as hell ain't what I bargained for."

"For God's sake," Thomas cried in fury, "there are a hundred crack archers lining the yards! All we've got to do is make it down the stairs!"

Another of the black-hooded men reached to unbuckle his sword belt. "I've already lost ten thousand pounds to-night," he declared, throwing the weapon down. "I don't fancy losing my life as well."

"Same here," said one more, and his sword dropped too.

"Fools!" Thomas screamed at them, shaking with rage. "Incompetent ninnies!" He spun in a circle, hurling angry words. "Cowards! Milksops! Do you call yourselves men?"

From the rear of the group came a sneering taunt. "We're men all right, Guilford, you crazy queer."

Thomas lunged for the man who mocked him, but before he could reach him, the sound of a distant explosion rent the night air. Every head swiveled toward the south-facing windows. Atop a far-off hill the sun seemed to be rising; the night sky was alive with a warm red glow.

"It's—it's Guilford Hall!" Thomas stammered, thunderstruck. "It's my house! My house is on fire!"

"My God," John breathed, staring at the distant inferno. "My God. Laura's in there."

* * *

Theodore was still hitting Laura as slowly, confusedly, she returned to consciousness. But his touch seemed so gentle now, she thought, her mind dazed. The soft pommeling continued; she lay with her arms curled over her head, hiding her face against the platform floor. I've got to make him stop, she thought with weary detachment. I am going to tell him to stop. She summoned the strength to lift her head—

And found herself gazing into the small, haughty face of her son.

"Paul?" She struggled to sit up, holding out her arms to him. But now that he had her attention he lost interest in the game, crawling across the platform, blankets dragging behind him. Laura smiled, watching as he crept over to his sister, ready to torment her. Then she caught her breath as she saw the bloodstain on the cloth her daughter wore.

"Oh, dear Lord," she gasped, remembering Theo and the knife. She scrambled over to the baby and unwound the woolen covering with shaking fingers. Relief coursed through her as she saw the knife had barely nicked her skin. She started to rewind the blanket, then looked up as she heard a muffled thumping noise. Elizabeth Tudor, black eyes flashing above the gag that silenced her, was banging her red head backward against the platform rail.

"Oh!" Laura set her daughter down gently and hurried to tear off the princess's gag. "It's about time!" Elizabeth burst out. Laura reached to untie her hands. "All the crying your daughter does, and now when she has really got something to cry about—a knife wound—she doesn't make a peep!" As the ropes fell from her wrists she shook a fist at the unheeding baby. "Shame on you, Elizabeth Guilford!"

Laura laughed and crossed the platform to untie Alain. *"Merci,"* the boy said, hazel eyes wide with worry. "He must have hurt you very bad, *non?* Even the thunder did not wake you up!"

"Thunder?" Laura echoed.

"A sound—" Alain paused, searching for words. "Like the end of the world!"

Elizabeth yanked the bonds from her ankles and scooped up her namesake. "Some kind of explosion. God only knows what that creepy little man has done. Let's get out of here!"

"Follow me—and keep close together," Laura instructed as she caught Paul up in her arms and headed for the door. "That's odd—"

"What's odd?" asked Elizabeth, close behind her.

"The hallway—it sounds like the sea pounding on the Guernsey cliffs." She laughed at the fanciful thought, then yanked open the door and screamed.

The corridor outside was a solid, roiling tunnel of flame.

"Close the door!" Elizabeth shouted, and when Laura did not move, rushed to do so herself. "That bastard's set the place on fire! Is there another way out of this room?"

Laura was still staring at the door, face tingling with the heat that had swept in from the hallway, lungs filled with the ghastly scent of burning wood and cloth. Elizabeth caught her sleeve, pulling her around, slapping her gently across the cheek. "Laura, listen to me. Is there another way out of here?"

"Another—" Laura choked back the bile that had risen in her throat, trying to forget her fear. Outside the glass dome the night sky shone red as a fiery coal. She shook her head. "No. There is only the one door. If we could reach the—" She swallowed once more, hard. "Reach the servants' stair —but we would have to go through the fire."

Alain looked at the two white-faced women who clutched the twins. "I will try it."

"No, Alain!" Laura cried.

"What other choice do we have?" He shrugged, pulling the cloak tight over his face. "If the stairs are clear, I will shout for you. Listen for me." He threw open the door and ran straight into the swirling inferno outside.

Elizabeth slammed the door shut behind him. Then she and Laura waited, ears straining, hearing only the fire's blistering roar. Seconds passed, each one seeming a hundred hours. Then something thudded back against the door with an agonized groan. The princess rushed to open it again. There was a living, squirming ball of fire on the threshold— Alain.

"Jesus," Elizabeth cried, dragging the boy back into the observatory. "Jesus, Laura, help me!" Shielding her hands in her skirts, she fought to beat down the flames that had engulfed his clothes. Laura wanted to help, knew she *must* help, but found she could not move. Right before her horrified eyes her worst nightmare was coming true. Burned alive ...they would all be burned alive. She could smell the sickening odor of charring flesh, heard the spark and sizzle of searing hair.

Burned alive. Alain. Her beautiful, beloved children. Elizabeth Tudor. Burned alive, just like her father, like the martyrs on Smithfield Plain. It was over. King Philip had won the game, thanks to Thomas Guilford's crazed, spurned lover. King Philip had won . . . and England was lost.

In that moment Laura understood clearly for the first time what had driven John to go to Calais with the Guernsey fishermen, what he meant when he told her, *I love . . . what England could be.* It was only a dream, yes, but a dream that men and women died for, the candle that the martyrs' pyres kept alive through the dark night that had been Mary's reign.

She understood too, in a startling flash of clarity, why it mattered that the earth revolved around the sun. What was at the center, what stood at the foundation—in a family, in the universe, in a kingdom—was the focus that set man's perspective, that decided the dream. A nation learned from its ruler as surely as her babies learned from her and John.

I shall be nursemaid and mother to four million Englishmen, Elizabeth had said. Laura stared at the tall, slim woman fighting desperately to save a crippled French boy whose life, in the scheme of the world, had no more consequence than a shooting star.

What England could be . . .

She rushed to the princess's side.

Together they managed to extinguish Alain's burning clothing, tearing off his cloak, smothering the smoldering sparks on his shirt and breeches. "Laura," the boy whispered.

"I'm right here, my brave Alain."

"Can't—" He coughed, throat scorched by the heat. "Can't get out—that way."

"Then we'll find another way," she promised, brushing seared blond hair from his hazel eyes.

Elizabeth nudged her, pointing toward the door. Tongues of bright flame were creeping underneath it, licking at the paneling, curling the tiles on the floor. "We'd better find one fast."

When John saw the spires of flame in the southern sky, he did not hesitate for an instant. All thoughts of Thomas and the conspirators vanished from his head: all he could think of was Laura, Laura and the fire. He pushed through the ranks of dispirited kidnappers and tore down the stairs; Thomas snatched back his sword from Guy and pounded after him.

Sir Francis Englefield, his forehead still dripping sweat, was pacing nervously in the yard by the waiting horses. He looked up, blinking in confusion, as first John ran past him, black cloak flying, and then Thomas, ripping his hood from his face. "What's going on here?" the fat knight sputtered. "Where's the princess?"

Thomas paused just long enough to shout, "Guilford Hall is on fire! Send every man that's here!"

"B-but what about the princess?"

"To hell with the damned princess!" Thomas snapped, waving toward the distant inferno. "That's my bloody house!"

John had grabbed his brother's fine bay and was already through the gate, galloping southward, ironically blessing his brother's eye for horseflesh: his mount ran swift and true as an arrow sprung from a bow. Still, there was so much distance to cover . . . and already he imagined he could smell harsh smoke on the breeze, and hear the far-off crackle of flames.

Crouching low in the saddle, plunging on into the night, he prayed fervently that he was wrong, that Laura and Elizabeth hadn't gone to the house after all. But in his heart he was sure that was where they'd been headed when he heard his daughter crying from the bushes beside the road. He sensed that the princess's wayward humor would find appeal in seeking refuge from Thomas in his own home.

How in God's name could the place have caught fire? From Hatfield House it appeared both of the towers were ablaze—an unlikely circumstance. Unless . . .

Unless the fire had been deliberately set.

He glanced back over his shoulder. Thomas was a few hundred yards behind him on the darkened road; with his hood torn away, the white hair at his temples glowed in the pale moonlight. He was driving his horse so hard that already a froth of foam showed below its bit. John thought of the treasures his brother had amassed in the house on the hill, bought with the fruits of bribery and informing and scheming, and smiled grimly. If not for his fear for Laura and his children, he would have rejoiced to see Guilford Hall destroyed.

At last the manor walls came into sight on the hilltop above him. Shuddering at the pillars of flame rising up from the towers, John spurred the bay up the drive and through the open gates. When he saw the small pony cart tethered in the brick courtyard his heart jolted into his throat. So they *had* come here . . .

A flat wave of blistering air assaulted him as he leaped

from the horse. Cloak pulled over his face, smoke swirling around him, he ran for the front door and yanked at the latch.

It was locked. Fear coiling tight around his bowels, he threw himself headlong at the sturdy wood, trying to break it down. His first blow didn't budge it; he drew back to try again, then froze as from the courtyard behind him he heard a high, wild giggle. "Theodore," he whispered, and knew who had set the blaze.

"Theo!" That was Thomas, racing into the yard and flinging himself from his saddle. In the light of the flames his face was taut, diamond-hard. "What have you done, you goddamned fool?"

Despite face and clothing seared by flame and a wound in his ribs that had turned his shirtfront black with blood, Theodore was grinning. "I did it, Thomas!" he announced gleefully. "I did what you wanted! I killed them!"

"You what?" the master of Guilford Hall demanded, his voice an animal snarl.

Theodore staggered toward him, clutching his bleeding chest. "I killed them," he repeated with that giddy, pleased grin.

John stared at the crazed, dancing man. "Killed who? Laura?"

Theo nodded happily. "Laura and the princess and the babies and the boy. I killed all of them! I knew you would be proud of me, Thomas. I did it for you."

"You lunatic bastard!" Thomas roared above the blaze. "What have you done to my house?"

Theodore stared up at him, a sudden sickly light igniting his grass-green eyes. "But I thought—I thought it would please you. My love, I only did it for you. Please . . . please don't be angry. I can't bear it when you're angry at me."

A change came over Thomas at these quavering words. He smiled warmly, seductively. "I'm not angry with you, pet," he cooed, and then, as Theo returned the smile uncertainly, he added in the same caressing tone, "There's little point in being angry with a dead man, is there?" He drew his sword and ran Theodore through the heart with it, pinioning him to the ground.

The blade quivered, rippling back and forth with a sound like far-off thunder. Theo's eyes were greener than grass, wider than the night sky. He whispered Thomas's name, a

small, short question punctuated by a trickle of blood from
the side of his mouth, before he died.

Thomas yanked the stained blade from Theo's chest and
wiped it clean on his dead lover's breeches. Then he tilted
back his head, staring contemplatively at the fire.

John lunged at him, appalled by his brother's offhand cruelty. "Give me the keys, damn your soul!"

"There's no point in it," Thomas said calmly, eluding his
grasp. "You heard Theodore. They're dead."

"Damn you, give me the—" John's voice was drowned
out by a thunderous crash as the doorway collapsed in a hail
of sparks. He turned, breath catching, heart breaking, as he
saw the roiling mass of smoke and flame that had been the
front hall.

"Dead," said Thomas from behind his shoulder. His voice
held a certain detached curiosity. "Not exactly the way I
planned it. Still, I ought to be able to get something out of
King Philip for it, don't you think?"

John turned to him slowly, blinded less by the smoke than
by his unspeakable grief. "You inhuman son of a bitch," he
said, and drew his sword.

Thomas's upper lip curled. "A duel with a cripple—how
quaint." Shrugging off his cloak, he pulled out his own blade
and assumed the ready position. "Have at it, then, brother
dear."

"The wisdom of the ages." Elizabeth Tudor shook her
head wryly as she hauled another weighty book from the
shelf. "Cicero and Sophocles, Aristotle and Plutarch, Dante
—God, I hate to see them burned."

"It's either them or us," Laura said grimly, taking the volumes Alain passed on from the princess.

"I wonder what history might have to say about that
choice," Elizabeth mused, and pulled the last book from the
shelves. "That's the lot of them."

Laura eyed the makeshift staircase of books, testing its
sturdiness with her hand, then fetched John's heavy astrolabe
from the platform table. "Here we go," she announced.
"You two take the babies and keep to the far side of the
room. Stay back until I signal you." Clambering up the pile
of books, she held the astrolabe by its chain and swung it
hard as she could at the glass-paned dome. Her first try
failed; she moved back a step atop the books and swung

again. This time the glass shattered, letting in a gust of sulphurous wind.

With the edge of the astrolabe she knocked out the shards of glass from the frame, making a hole large enough to put her head and shoulders through. Then, balancing precariously on the stacked texts, she surveyed the scene.

It was worse than she'd expected. She was looking out at the west tower; great billows of smoke and flame were shooting from its windows, driven by the wind, feeding on the luxe furnishings. Directly below the spot where she stood, perhaps three feet down, was a wooden bridge built to span the space between the dome and stone parapets; beneath that, a sheer hundred-foot drop led to the yards. Across the little bridge the old battlements beckoned, with their maze of turrets and crenels and merlons, and the rocky ledge from which John's father had leaped to his death.

"What do you see?" Elizabeth, with baby Elizabeth in her arms, had climbed up beside her.

"I thought I told you to stay on the other side of the room," Laura said crossly, pulling her head back inside.

"We couldn't," Elizabeth said succinctly. Laura turned and saw that Alain, clinging tight to Paul, had climbed up on the books as well. Then she saw something more. The floor on the far side of the observatory had collapsed inward, so that the platform in the center of the room was tilting crazily into the storey below. Through the hole she could glimpse the raging conflagration that threatened at any moment to swallow the entire upper room. Even as she watched, the tile floor buckled and sagged, and the platform tore away with a wrenching crunch, disappearing into the yawning chasm of smoke and fire. "Lord in heaven," Laura murmured as the staircase of books tilted toward the hole.

Elizabeth pushed her toward the broken glass pane. "Go on! We've got to get out of here!"

Hurriedly Laura smashed the pane beside the one she'd already broken and pushed out the frame. Her heart sank as she saw that the little wooden bridge to the parapets had already caught fire. Elizabeth poked her head out beside her, looked down, and gulped. "We're trapped, aren't we?"

For some reason Laura found herself thinking of Midsummer's Eve on Guernsey, and the bonfire John had carried her through. In the twisting, churning flames curling up from the bridge she imagined she saw again the shadowy dancers who'd surrounded her that night, the spirits of La Roque

Balan. Their dark hands wavered, motioning her onward, into the flames...

"We are not trapped yet," she told the princess.

"But there's no place to go!" Elizabeth said desperately. "The bridge is on fire!"

"Alain," said Laura, "hold tight to Elizabeth's shoulder. Elizabeth, you hold tight to me. And both of you, close your eyes."

"Laura, what are you—"

"Just trust me, Elizabeth, and do as I say."

With the princess's hand gripping her shoulder, Laura climbed through the hole in the dome and stepped down onto the burning bridge. Elizabeth clambered out after her, and then Alain, each of them clutching one of the twins. Laura stared at the flames licking the soles of her boots, the hem of her gown, and very nearly lost her nerve—

Invisible fingers tugged at her hand, coaxing her onward. She took a step through the fire, then another, and another, moving along the bridge toward the stone parapets, and above the raging roar of wind and flame thought she heard the high, wild strains of Guy's *télen*—

Her boot touched stone.

Trembling, she turned and yanked Elizabeth and Alain off the blazing bridge and onto the parapet. The instant they left it, the span caved in, tumbling all the way down to the yards like so much charred skeletal kindling, too frail to support a feather.

"You can open your eyes now," Laura said.

Elizabeth did so. Her wide black gaze took in the stone wall on which she stood, then darted back across the empty space where the bridge to the dome had been. Then she looked at Laura. "I don't think I want to know how you got us here." She surveyed the haphazard architecture of the house from above. "My God, who designed this madhouse?"

"John's father made some additions."

"I'll say he did."

Baby Paul was watching the flaming tower with haughty serenity, but the princess's namesake was screaming at the top of her lungs. "What's that over there?" Elizabeth asked, pointing toward the west tower.

"A water tank," Laura shouted back above her daughter's wails. "It collects rain for the privies in the house."

Alain was shifting from one foot to the other atop the

narrow parapet. "The stones—they grow hot!" he called.

"So they do," Elizabeth agreed, brushing beads of perspiration from her brow. "If only we could cool them off long enough, maybe someone will see the fire and come and rescue us!"

Laura looked once more at the water tank atop the west tower. "Well," she said, starting to climb toward it, "there's one thing we might try. . .

In the courtyard a hundred feet below, John was locked in deadly combat with his brother, fighting for his life. Thomas was a better swordsman than he'd remembered from their adolescent bouts; clearly he hadn't neglected dueling practice in his climb up the social ladder. John's fishing work had tempered the muscles in his shoulders and arms, but his bad leg was a serious liability in this swift, lethal contest. He had all he could manage to fend and parry his brother's thrusts.

Thomas had managed to drive him back across the bricks, past the gates and the pony cart, nearly to the stables. The heat from the fire was building steadily; John was breathing hard as he broke a clench and beat off Thomas's following riposte. The effort cost him two more steps backward toward the stable wall.

Thomas was smiling, his pale eyes turned milky white. "You're beaten, brother," he told John. "I'm only toying with you now."

John shook his head, regaining his balance. "No. You're beaten, Thomas. King Philip will have your head when he learns Elizabeth is dead through your bungling."

"I bungled nothing," Thomas snarled. "It was those idiots he sent to work with me." He attacked viciously, the slashing edge of his broadsword gleaming in the firelight. Again the brothers came together. Thomas lunged in a quick caricado; John met the assault with a two-handed rinverso; Thomas ducked and landed a blow to the flat of John's blade that sent him staggering.

"You're the one who is beaten," said Thomas, teeth showing white in his dark face as he grinned. "You've nothing more to live for. You've lost your wife, your children. And with Elizabeth Tudor dead, you've lost your hopes for England too."

John smiled back. "I can still kill you."

But despite his brave words, he knew he was losing this battle. The old wound in his right leg gave Thomas just enough of an edge in agility that John had to work twice as hard just to stay even. The effort was rapidly sapping his strength.

He managed to counter one more series of driving blows with a pass and answering attack, but as Thomas parried it easily, not even panting, John knew the end was near. The stable wall was at his shoulders; he tried to twist off into a reprise, but Thomas stopped him with a volley of left and right blows. He felt a sudden flash of pain in his wrist as one landed; his fingers flew open, and he watched his sword sail off across the bricks. With blood streaming from the slash, he reeled back against the wall.

"There's a certain poetic justice in this," said Thomas, gripping his hilt, moving in for the kill. John crouched at the wall, chest heaving, disarmed, unable to defend. "The end of Guilford Hall and of your little branch of the family all in one day," his brother went on, relishing the moment. "Tell me, what have your stars to say about that?"

Behind Thomas's back the stable doors flew open. A short, bald, cloak-wrapped figure staggered into the yard. He stared at the blazing manor, the two disheveled duelists, and blinked. "What in hell is going on here?" he demanded. "Where's Laura gone?"

Thomas glanced back over his shoulder. "Well, well, look who's here. I don't believe the two of you have ever met. Humphrey, say hello to your brother-in-law; you've just time before I run him through."

"Where's Laura?" Humphrey repeated in bewilderment.

Thomas jerked his head toward the torched house. "In there."

"In there—" Humphrey took a step toward the manor, straw clinging to his clothes and hair. "We've got to save her!"

"It's too late," Thomas told him. "She's already dead."

"Dead?" Humphrey shook his head to clear it. "Dead—Laura?" He looked down at the cloak he wore. "She gave me this—to keep me warm."

"Christ, don't go maudlin, you drunken fool," Thomas sneered. "I'll inherit her money. Don't worry. Our little bargain will remain intact."

Humphrey stared at him, rubbing his bald pate with a shaking hand. "Our bargain." His dazed gold eyes, so much like Laura's, reflected the roaring flames. "By God, I wish—

I wish I'd never listened to Blanche. And I wish to hell I had never met you."

Thomas laughed, shortly, coldly. "Without me you'd still be a nothing. A nobody."

Humphrey drew a deep breath. "What in hell do you think I am now?" And then he drew his sword clumsily.

"Idiot." Thomas raked the half-drunken man with his milky-white gaze. "I'll kill you before you can get that sword up to your shoulder."

"Between you and Blanche, Guilford, you've taken my heart, my self-respect, even my manhood. There are worse things in this world than to die for—well, to die for something." Humphrey stumbled, lifting the weapon. *"En garde."*

Laughing, disbelieving, Thomas watched him come. "You're right, Humphrey—you are a nobody," he said mockingly. "And you never—" The rest of his words were drowned out as, from a hundred feet over their heads, a torrent of water came pouring down. Thomas glanced up, raised his arm to ward off the flood, and slipped on the slick wet bricks. He caught himself, twisting in the air, but misstepped again. Fighting to keep his balance, he sprawled forward—

And skewered himself through the chest on Humphrey's outstretched blade.

"My God," said Humphrey, goggling. "What have I done?"

"I believe," Thomas gasped, "you've killed me." He laughed, shaking his head, hands clawing at the sword that had pierced him through. "How utterly—humiliating." His milky eyes turned pure white, rolling back in his head. Then he pitched facedown onto the bricks.

Slowly John pushed himself up from the stable wall, his bleeding hand wrapped in his cloak. Humphrey stopped staring at the dead man and peered at the sky. "Where did that water come from?"

"From God," John told him. Then, as Humphrey turned those wide gold eyes on him, he caught his breath in a sob. So much like Laura's eyes . . . He would not think of that now. "One of the water tanks on the roof must have burst," he said, trying hard to hold his composure. "We had better get away before the whole place caves in."

"What about—" Humphrey nodded toward Thomas's body.

"Leave him here—with Theo." John contemplated

Thomas's lover's corpse and thought, I very nearly felt sorry for him at the end. He truly did love Thomas. God rest his tortured soul . . .

With Humphrey, still shaking, trudging beside him, he led the way across the yards to the gate as fire raged through the skeleton that had been Guilford Hall. At the wall they turned for one last look.

"I've never seen a house collapse like that," Humphrey marveled. "Even the stones are falling."

"It's built on bad rock," John said softly, staring at the wreckage of his father's folly.

"There's still water pouring down." Humphrey squinted blearily at the old battlements by the west tower. John's own eyes, sharpened by years of stargazing, found the trickling stream Humphrey meant and then something more—a spot of black against the red-gold backdrop. Debris from the water tank, he thought, and then, as the black shape separated, moving apart, his blood rushed to his heart all at once in a dizzying spin.

"Merciful God in heaven." Disbelieving, he raised his arm and waved.

The small black figures waved back.

"John!" He turned at the French-tinged shout and saw Guy galloping up the drive with Polly in front of him in the saddle. Behind them rode Talbot and Hannay and Father Burton.

"Land sakes!" Polly stared at the inferno that had been her home as Guy drew the horse to a stop. "I've sure lost my place now!"

"Guy." John ran toward the big Guernseyman. "Don't ask me how, but they're still alive. They're up there! Can you see them?"

"*Sacré bleu.*" In horror Guy peered up at the figures far above them. "How will we get them down?"

"I don't know. Where are Englefield and his men?" John demanded.

"We can't expect help from them," Father Burton told him. "They turned tail back to London as soon as they heard the princess was gone."

"Along with all the conspirators," Talbot put in, eyeing the burning building. "Can we climb up to them, John?"

He shook his head. "The whole place is gutted. The foundations never were any good. It's a miracle that ledge they're on hasn't fallen too."

At that moment the east tower collapsed with a deafening crash, showering sparks and stones and burning timbers all over the yards. Polly screamed, covering her eyes; the earth shook beneath John's feet. Jesus in heaven, he thought, if only they could fly. . .

If only they could fly. Suddenly he remembered all the vain attempts his father had made at flying, while he waited below with the yards draped in blankets and straw. "That's it!" he shouted, running to Thomas's bay and yanking off the saddle blanket. "Polly, Hannay, get as much straw as you can from the stables and bring it here." He shook out the blanket, wincing as he saw how small it seemed. It would have to do, though. They hadn't much time. "Talbot, Guy, Father Burton, we'll each take a corner. Now move right in under the wall—"

"Will Laura know what you want her to do, John?" Guy asked worriedly.

John stared at the tiny figures high above on the battlement. "Let's hope to God she does."

"Laura Darby." Elizabeth Tudor, standing ankle-deep in the water that flooded the parapet, peered down at the square of wool the men were holding in the courtyard. From that height it looked the size of a handkerchief. "You don't suppose your husband actually means for us to jump into that thing!"

"I'm afraid he does!" Laura shouted back over the roar of the gusting flames. The water from the tank they'd broken open had cooled the overhanging ledge enough that they could climb onto it, but even the water was getting hot now. "You go first!"

"*Me?*" The princess stepped quickly back from the edge. "I'm not going at all!"

"Elizabeth, the building's going to collapse! You saw the east tower fall."

"But what if they miss me?" Elizabeth wailed.

"We've got to try!"

Alain handed Paul to Laura and moved through the water to the edge of the parapet. "I go first," he announced. "I show you it can be done. You wait here. You see if I end up smashed like an egg."

"Oh, Lord," Elizabeth moaned.

Alain climbed onto the skirt of the battlement, waved to

the men below, and flashed a smile back at Laura and the
princess. Then he jumped.

"I can't look!" Elizabeth buried her face in the blankets
wrapped around her namesake.

"It's all right. They caught him," Laura told her, peering
over the edge. Cautiously Elizabeth crept to the wall and saw
the boy scramble out of the nest of wool and straw John had
assembled below.

"He's hurt! He's limping!" she shouted accusingly.

"He has a clubfoot!" Laura shouted back above the noise
of the fire. "Go ahead and jump!"

"When I said I would sooner do anything than go back to
the Tower of London," Elizabeth cried, "I didn't mean this!"

"Jump!" Laura screamed.

"Oh, Lord." Elizabeth clambered up onto the wall and
stepped off into space, clinging to her hysterical namesake.
Her voice floated back above the baby's ferocious screeches:
"You would give me the one that cries!"

Holding tight to Paul, Laura stared over the battlement
into the yard below and saw the princess land in a flurry of
straw, bouncing back into the air, skirts billowing like a bell.
She looked at her son; his small face was proudly serene.
"Well, if you're not afraid," she whispered, "then neither am
I." He arched a tiny black brow. "Oh, all right, maybe a
little." Hugging him even more tightly, she stepped up onto
the wall. "Here we go . . ."

And then she was flying, flying down from the rooftops of
Guilford Hall just as John's father had so many years ago.
The wind rushed by, making her hair stream out like a flag,
and the moon in the distance seemed to be falling with her in
a trail of white fire. Down she hurtled, past the blazing windows, past smoke and flames and the top of the courtyard
wall—

"Ooph!" She landed with a gasp, the breath knocked out
of her but baby Paul still clutched to her heart. John pulled
them from the blanket, and his arms had never felt so strong
and warm.

"Oh, Laura. Oh, my sweet love." He was laughing and
crying at once, hugging her so tightly she still could not catch
her breath. "My dear heart."

"Elizabeth?" she asked anxiously.

"Which one of us?" the princess demanded, grimacing at
the screaming baby she held.

"Both of you!" Laura declared as John enveloped them in

his arms too. And there was Alain, grinning broadly, and Hannay, and Talbot, Polly and Guy, Father Burton—and Humphrey. All safe, Laura thought joyously as John kissed her. All safe and all loved . . .

John drew away from her as again the ground rumbled beneath them. "Come on," he said. "Let's get away from here."

The caravan of the horses and the pony cart was halfway down the hill when the west tower of Guilford Hall fell with a cataclysmal blast that seemed to rock the sky, pulling every stone left standing right down with it. "'Tis like the judgment day," wide-eyed Polly said as the cinders settled, as sparks streamed toward the heavens like bright shooting stars.

"It *is* the judgment day," John told her, thinking of his brother and Theo.

Laura, sitting beside Humphrey in the cart bed, squeezed her brother's hand, smiling at him. "I believe it is."

"Where to?" Talbot asked from the driver's seat, while Hannay leaned her head on his shoulder.

"Hatfield House?" Elizabeth Tudor suggested. "Since you're sure Englefield and his men have left." Laura began to laugh, and the princess looked at her questioningly.

"It's just that only tonight I was thinking," she explained, biting back another laugh as she pulled bits of ash from her soaked gown and hair, "how I should like sometime to arrive there without looking a wreck!"

"You've never looked more beautiful to me," John said, and bent to kiss her.

She burst out laughing again as he pulled away with his nose smudged black.

Chapter 29

The seventeenth of November, 1558, dawned overcast and gray as slate in Hertfordshire. Gloomy mists rolled over the empty fields, and from a hilltop south of Hatfield House there still rose a pillar of soot-black smoke. While the rest of the household breakfasted hungrily in Elizabeth Tudor's chambers, Laura stood at the window and watched the black plume coil in the wind.

John came up behind her and curled his arm around her waist. "Come and eat," he urged gently, his cheek against her hair. "You must be starving."

She leaned against him, darting a glance at the table to make sure no one else could hear. "I cannot," she whispered. "I keep thinking—King Philip and Pole and Bonner will only come up with some other scheme now." She heard Elizabeth's bright laughter and sighed wearily. "Sometimes I wonder how she keeps on going."

John's mouth brushed her ear. "You can't give up on a dream."

"But what if the dream never does come true?" She shivered, glimpsing movement far ahead in the mists that choked the London Road. "Look there—do you see what I mean? Englefield and his men are coming back again."

"Elizabeth," John called softly, turning back to the table. "You have visitors."

The princess grimaced, setting her napkin aside, coming to the window. "Englefield, I suppose. Well, we've barred the gates."

"Those bars can't keep out that many men." John stared at the long lines of riders coming through the fog. "It looks like he's brought the whole bloody army."

"Drat," said Elizabeth, tugging at her loose red curls. "And I've lost Polly's braids."

"Look at them all!" Laura marveled. "And those banners and flags and heralds—and everyone all dressed in black."

"Black," Elizabeth murmured thoughtfully. "I wonder..."

"Be careful, Bess," Father Burton warned, joining them at the casement. "It could be a trick."

"Aye, I suppose it could." Elizabeth strained to see the horsemen at the front of the long procession. "John, is that my sweet William there on the right?"

"So it is," he said, recognizing Cecil's stiff beard and dark-ringed eyes.

"And there, just behind him." Elizabeth pointed. "Who is that?"

"I'll be damned," John said slowly. "Nick Throckmorton, as big as day."

Elizabeth stood on tiptoe, nose pressed to the glass, while the rest of the breakfasters crowded in behind her. "Can they see us, John?" she asked.

"They're looking up this way."

"What on earth is Sir Nicholas doing?" Laura asked, watching the big knight pat the front of his doublet conspicuously.

"He has the ring," Elizabeth murmured in wonder. "My sister is dead." She crossed herself, then gazed ruefully down at her soot-stained, water-marked clothes. "A fine sisterly revenge she has on me still—no time to bathe or change... Oh, well, I shall put on a cloak and receive them out of doors. Alain?"

"Yes, milady?" asked the boy, springing to attention.

Elizabeth Tudor tucked back a few wayward strands of red hair. "Would you please be so kind as to open the gates?"

When the lords of the Council of England rode into the yard of Hatfield House that morning, they found Elizabeth walking on the lawn beneath a great, bare-limbed oak tree. Clustered close around her was a bizarre assortment of companions. There was a tall, black-haired man with keen blue eyes, his arm circling a small, lovely woman who held two babies. There were a big, bearded fellow, standing beside a maid with cropped yellow hair, and two priests, and a club-footed boy, and a bald man with a red face, and a pretty brunette who looked as if she might be French...

"Milady," said Sir Nicholas Heath, Archbishop of York and Lord High Chancellor of England. He looked down at the slim, black-eyed woman with flame-colored hair. "The queen is dead." She looked back at him steadily. He swallowed, dismounted, and bowed. "Long live the queen."

Elizabeth knelt on the frozen ground, amid the crackling leaves, and Laura heard her whisper a verse from the Psalms: "This is the Lord's doing; it is marvelous in our eyes." In her mind Laura thought of the next verse: "This is the day which the Lord has made; we will rejoice and be glad in it."

One by one the mighty lords of the kingdom came forward to pay the new queen homage, kneeling to kiss her hand. She received them graciously there on the lawn, in the chill morning cold, until Edmund Bonner, Bishop of London, genuflected before her. Then she withdrew her hand.

"Where is your colleague, Cardinal Pole?" she inquired sweetly.

"Sick abed, mila— I mean, Your Grace."

"Is he grievous ill?"

"He's dying," Bonner said bluntly, avoiding her gaze. "He'll not last out the day."

"I trust," said Elizabeth, "he will depart this world to the afterlife he so richly deserves." Bonner looked up then.

Cecil was near the end of the lengthy line. "Bess." He knelt, smiling as he kissed her hand. There was teasing sadness in her voice as she greeted him:

"My sweet William. I fear you must call me 'Your Majesty' now."

He grinned. "A burden I've looked to this many a day."

"Will you wait upon me in my chambers, William, when all this"—Elizabeth waved a shapely hand at the crowded courtyard—"all this rigmarole's through?"

"I've waited this long, haven't I?" Cecil asked. He leaned over her hand again, his keen nose twitching. "Do you know, Your Majesty, you smell rather markedly of smoke."

Twilight had fallen by the time the dignitaries and officials and well-wishers, both sincere and reluctant, left Hatfield House and rode back to London. Elizabeth, having got a bath and changed her clothes at last, summoned Sir William Cecil and Sir Nicholas Throckmorton to her chambers, where John and Laura were already waiting. Then she shut the door and, as briefly as she could, with occasional interjections from Laura and John, recounted to the knights everything that had taken place the evening before.

Cecil took notes frantically as the story unfolded, while Throckmorton listened openmouthed. "And then," Elizabeth concluded, pouring wine with a steady hand, "we all came home."

"My God," said Throckmorton, and Laura saw the big knight was shaking. "My God."

"Little wonder you smelled of smoke," Cecil said angrily, gathering up his notes. "So. Thomas Guilford is dead already. Pole died this evening at seven—did you hear?" Elizabeth nodded; a messenger had brought the news. "I'll have the rest of them arrested at once," Cecil went on, "Bonner, Englefield, and Feria too, and sent to the Tower. I know Feria; he's a snake, a weasel. A few turns of the rack will wring the names of the rest of the conspirators out of him. As for King Philip, well, just wait until I get my—"

"Excuse me. Sir William. Sir William!" Elizabeth was signaling for his attention. "Sir William!" He looked up at last, his heavy eyes smoldering. "What would be the point?"

He blinked at her across the table. "The point of what?"

"Of rounding up all those men and sending them to the Tower and torturing them—"

"The point," Throckmorton burst out, "is that they tried to kidnap you! They very nearly got you killed!"

"But they didn't, did they?" Elizabeth asked reasonably. "I am queen now; there's nothing they can do about that. And as for Philip, he hasn't got a ghost's chance of ever marrying me."

"Dammit, Bess—dammit, Your Majesty." Cecil was fuming. "They have to be punished!"

"I say they do not. I don't intend, Sir William, to begin my reign as my sister launched hers—with a flurry of trials and imprisonments and hangings and beheadings," the new queen said briskly. "I rather thought I would begin it with a banquet instead. And, of course, a ball. If you insist on taking notes, you might as well take some that are useful. Write this down. I should like a great deal of food to be served. And plenty of music. Oh, and you might just arrange for a masque."

"Now look here," said Cecil, beard quivering. "You can jest all you want about this, but those men can't get off scotfree. What in hell will King Philip think if you let him get away with this?"

"I rather imagined," said Elizabeth, "it would give him a very good idea of the sort of queen I intend to be."

"And just what kind is that?" Cecil barked. "Feebleminded?"

"Sir William, if my mind is feeble then yours must be mush, considering our respective records at chess." The queen leaned back in her chair. "No. I will not rule by fear and hate-mongering and retaliation, as Mary did. This is a new age, Sir William. I will rule my people with—with temperance and mercy. And love."

"As a good mother rules her children," Laura said softly.

"Precisely." Elizabeth beamed at her.

"Your Majesty." Throckmorton's round face was pleading, earnest. "You don't understand. The English people— your subjects—they're not intelligent. They're not educated. They're peasants, the most of 'em, slow and dim-witted—" He stopped; the queen's black eyes were blazing.

"Don't you ever, *ever* speak of my people that way!" she cried furiously. The big knight quavered visibly; she relented, reaching out to pat his hand. "Sir Nicholas, it is you who do not understand. That's the way Mary thought of my people. She showed that again and again, with her laws and statutes about what they must think, what they must believe, how they must behave." Her dark gaze slanted to John. "The intellect, whether of a person or of a nation, cannot grow within such restraints. Tell someone he is stupid or hopeless often enough and he will believe you! No! My people must be encouraged to think for themselves. The mind must be free to reach, to explore, to soar all the way up to the stars!"

"And that's what you're going to tell the English," Throckmorton said dubiously.

"That I am, Sir Nicholas," said Elizabeth, black eyes aglow. "And just you watch them soar!"

"You. Guilford." Cecil glowered at John. "For God's sake, talk to her. Make her see what King Philip is going to think of all this."

"If I were King Philip," John said very seriously, "I would be scared out of my bloody wits."

"Thank you, John," said Elizabeth.

"Pah," said Cecil. "Pah. And how long do you think this new age of—of temperance and mercy and love is going to last?"

"Until every chopping block in my kingdom is rotted," Queen Elizabeth said softly, "and the grass grows thick and green out on Smithfield Plain."

Cecil stared at her for a long, long moment. Then, "By God, Bess," he murmured, "you just might be man enough to do it."

She laughed. "Woman enough, Sir William. Now, your notes again, please. Under the heading, 'To be done immediately.' Appoint Guy de Carteret the Seigneur of Guernsey." She glanced at Laura. "Do you think he would like that? He did promise Polly a place, and I hardly think he will need a maid for that cottage you told me about."

Laura laughed, remembering Guy's tenderness toward the yellow-haired cook. "I suspect he would have found a place for her at the cottage. But he will make a splendid seigneur."

"Good. Next, Sir William, we must repeal the heresy statutes, as well as the law against married clergy. You might just drop in tonight on that nice Père Talbot and let him know about that. What else? Let me see. Ah, yes, a knighthood for Alain—what's his last name?" she asked John.

"I don't know. I don't think he's got one."

"Oh. Well, come up with one for him then, Sir William. Something good and dashing. And calling cards for Laura. Ten thousand or so."

"I don't think I will need them, Your Majesty," Laura told her.

"Why not?"

"Everyone on the Isle of Guernsey already knows who I am."

"You don't mean you intend to go back to that awful little island!" the queen cried, dismayed.

John grinned, squeezing Laura's hand. "I'm afraid we have to. It's the only place in the world where we're legally wed."

"And the only place where our children are legitimate," Laura put in, then added slyly, "Surely Your Majesty can appreciate that."

Elizabeth stuck out her tongue at them. "Father Burton could marry you tonight. You are just being stubborn. Don't you want to rebuild Guilford Hall?"

John gave a shudder. "Bad rocks."

"Well, then, what about Howarth Manor?"

"I thought perhaps," Laura said tentatively, "you might let me sign that over to Humphrey. And maybe you could make him the baron? If it wouldn't be too much trouble, that is?"

Elizabeth stared. "After what he did to your father?"

"You said yourself," Laura reminded her, "a new age. Temperance and mercy. And love."

"But that dreadful wife of his!" Elizabeth exclaimed.

John grinned, thinking of the way Humphrey had set off for home that afternoon, square-shouldered, clear-eyed, and resolute. "I suspect a new age is about to begin for Blanche too."

The queen laughed. "Well, let's hope so!" She reached across the table, taking their hands. "I should like to do something big for the two of you, though. Something truly grand. Tell me, what shall it be?"

"Just what you said, Your Majesty," John told her, and smiled at his wife. "Let those chopping blocks rot, and the grass grow on Smithfield Plain."

A long time later that night, Laura was perched in the window seat of her old bedchamber in Hatfield House, knees tucked up, gazing out at the distant hill where Guilford Hall once stood.

John came and crouched beside her, twining his fingers through her long, loose hair that was the color of oak leaves in autumn. "What are you thinking about?" he asked.

She smiled at him, moonlight pouring over her shoulders. "What my father would say if he knew his practical Protestant daughter intends to have a Guernsey fisherman examine the site of her new house for evil-spirited rocks."

He kissed her forehead, drinking in the scent of her, sweeter than bergamot, wild as honeysuckle. "And what do you think he would say?"

She leaned against the pane, her slim white arms circling his neck. "I hope he might quote Plato. 'The beginning is the most important part of the work.' And then, perhaps, St. Matthew. About the wise man who built his house upon a rock."

"'And the rain descended,'" John said softly, "'and the floods came, and the winds blew and beat upon that house, and it fell not.'" He looked into her shining gold eyes. "Do you know what I thought the first time I saw you, Laura Darby?"

"That I was a rock." She grimaced. "I was never so insulted in all my life as when you told me that." She stroked his cheek, his bristle of black beard rough against her fingertips. "Papa said, the last night I saw him, that there was a difference between learning and understanding. I've been a long time learning. But I think now I understand."

His blue eyes, clear and dark as the midnight sky,

searched her small face. "What do you understand?"

"Why Papa died. Why you went to Calais. Why it matters that the earth moves around the sun. It's all the same reason, really."

"And what is that?" he challenged her.

"It is all in the foundation. The center. The base. I can't think why it took so long to realize it. But if what's at the center is wrong, then everything else is wrong too."

He rose, pulling her out of the window seat. "I love you. Come to bed."

"What do you think Humphrey and Blanche are doing tonight?" she asked as he unlaced her bodice.

"Fighting." He bared her breasts and kissed first one rosy nipple and then the other. "Over what will be at the center. Over what the foundation will be."

"And Hannay and Talbot?"

He unbuttoned her skirts, lifting her up as they fell to the floor. "Playing ruff-and-honours."

She looked at him with wide gold eyes. "Really?"

He laughed, tugging off her drawers. "No." His mouth brushed her mouth; he ran his hands over her throat, her shoulders, her hips.

"And we—what shall we do?" she asked as he pulled her down onto the soft feather bed.

"Oh, Laura. Reach," he whispered, and did so, snuffing out the candles. "Explore." He kissed her in the darkness. "Soar."

MALLORY BURGESS

MALLORY BURGESS, a native of Bucks County, Pennsylvania, graduated from Duke University in 1978. She began her literary career writing obituaries for a legal newspaper and eventually became managing editor of the *Pennsylvania Law Journal*. Finding that job singularly unromantic, she resigned in 1981 to concentrate on fiction. She lives in center-city Philadelphia with her husband, Doug, a jazz trombonist, and two cats, Zelda and Mick, who are convinced they're helping when they walk across the keys of the typewriter. Her spare time is devoted to vacuuming the house, reading anything and everything, and fussing over a ridiculously small garden in which she grows flowers and herbs that flourished in Tudor England. She is also the author of three previous Avon romances: *Wild Land, Wild Love; Passion Rose;* and *Passion Fire.*

*If you enjoyed this book, take advantage
of this special offer. Subscribe now and . . .*

GET A *FREE*
HISTORICAL ROMANCE
NO OBLIGATION(a $3.95 value)

Each month the editors of True Value will select the four best historical romance novels from America's leading publishers. Preview them in your home Free for 10 days. And we'll send you a FREE book as our introductory gift. No obligation. If for any reason you decide not to keep them, just return them and owe nothing. But if you like them you'll pay *just* $3.50 each and save at least $.45 each off the cover price. (Your savings are a minimum of $1.80 a month.) There is no shipping and handling or other hidden charges. There are no minimum number of books to buy and you may cancel at any time.

send in the coupon below